CHARLES NODIER

THE MEMOIRS OF MAXIME ODIN

TRANSLATED AND WITH AN INTRODUCTION BY
BRIAN STABLEFORD

THE MEMOIRS OF MAXIME ODIN

CHARLES NODIER (1780-1844) was one of the pioneers of French Romantic prose; his salon at the Bibliothèque de l'Arsenal, begun in 1824 and known as *Le Cénacle*, brought together many of the key figures in the Movement and spun off other *cénacles* in which it was anchored, including Victor Hugo's. His best work consists of short stories and novellas.

BRIAN STABLEFORD's scholarly work includes *New Atlantis: A Narrative History of Scientific Romance* (Wildside Press, 2016), *The Plurality of Imaginary Worlds: The Evolution of French roman scientifique* (Black Coat Press, 2017) and *Tales of Enchantment and Disenchantment: A History of Faerie* (Black Coat Press, 2019). He has translated more than three hundred volumes from the French, mostly in the genres of *roman scientifique*, *contes de fées* and Romantic and Symbolist fiction. His recent fiction includes the visionary science fiction novel *The Revelations of Time and Space* (2020) and its sequel *After the Revelation* (2021); the last in his long series of "Tales of the Genetic Revolution," *The Elusive Shadows* (2020); and the comedy fantasy *Meat on the Bone* (2021), all published by Snuggly Books.

Contents

Introduction

This collection of fiction by Charles Nodier follows three earlier volumes: *Outlaws and Sorrows*, which assembles works published in the first phase of his fiction writing, from 1802-06; *Jean Sbogar and Other Stories*, which contains works published in the second phase, in 1818-21; and *The Story of the King of Bohemia and his Seven Castles)*, which supplements the novella that commenced the third phase of his fiction with three related works. The present volume assembles a series of stories published in the early 1830s, while two other volumes. *Perfectibility and Resurrection* and *The Four Talismans and Other Stories*, sample the remainder of his work published in the period that extended from 1832 to his death in 1844.

The introductions to the earlier volumes in the series include a synoptic account of the author's early life, explaining—so far as is possible—the relevance of its circumstances to the pattern of his literary production and its thematic obsessions. That production was interrupted twice. In 1804 after identifying himself as the author of an "ode" criticizing Napoléon Bonaparte, then the First Consul of France, he was imprisoned and then banished from Paris and placed under official police surveillance, making it difficult for him to place his work with publishers. Although he made a comeback in 1818-22, when the official surveillance ended and he was able to return to Paris, his first publications during that period were issued anonymously, and not long after he began signing his work again there was another long hiatus, perhaps not unconnected with the increasingly hostile political climate of the Restoration, but more likely due to recurrent bouts of illness and his appointment in 1824 as the librarian of the Bibliothèque de l'Arsenal, after which he became the host of the cénacle at which the leading members of the French Romantic Movement met regularly to discuss their work, their cause and their ambitions.

For one reason and another, it was not until 1830 that Nodier began publishing fiction again—but once he had resumed, he quickly became prolific, publishing a flood of works in the early 1830s, including a twelve-volume set of his *Oeuvres* collecting the work from his earlier periods of productivity and adding a good deal of new material. Some of that work had probably been written in the 1820s but had not been able to find publishers then, but most of it was undoubtedly new, representative of a new burst of enthusiasm and productivity. That revivification of his career was doubtless assisted by a partial remission in his poor health, but 1830 was also a year in which the political and economic climate of Paris changed dramatically. The so-called July Revolution got rid of Charles X, and although it disappointed its republican instigators when the government of the day found a substitute king in Louis-Philippe, it instituted a constitutional monarchy to replace the oppressive absolutism of the former regime.

In truth, the change in the circumstances of everyday life brought about by the new monarchy was not so very great, and it did not take long for people to realize that; for a brief period, however, political censorship was considerably relaxed and publishers believed, at least for a while, that they had acquired a new and much greater freedom to publish what they liked—and to experiment in order to discover what the public could be persuaded to want. Nodier, along with all the other members of the Romantic Movement, took rapid advantage of that thaw to test the boundaries of public taste and tolerance, as expressed in the willingness of publishers to deviate from their established ruts.

The presumed license granted to publishers was interpreted by the editors of several periodicals as an opportunity to publish more controversial work, and several of them began to promote the Romantic Movement enthusiastically as a regenerative force in French literature. One of the periodicals that did so most pugnaciously was the *Revue de Paris*, which became Nodier's principal showcase for several years, both for philosophical articles flamboyantly setting out his controversial theses regarding literature and its historical and psychological contexts, and for fiction in which he practiced what he preached. Inevitably, he set about revisiting and refining the ideas that had fuelled his early fiction, in order to recapitulate and re-examine them from a more mature viewpoint.

Nodier's early novelettes and novellas—he never wrote a full-length novel—had been obsessed, as befitted pioneering texts in what was then just beginning to be called *romanticisme*, with the operations of exaggerated sentiment on contemporary human life. They examine the existential plight of young men who find it impossible to accommodate themselves to the norms and conventions of society, who feel alienated from it even when they are not literal *proscrits* [outlaws] cast out by the abrupt upheavals of political revolution. Within that state of psychological desperation, they invariably—sometimes to their surprise—become amorously infatuated, and glimpse a possibility of existential salvation via amour; but the glimpse is always deceptive, offering an impossible illusion even when the sentiment of extreme infatuation is mutual—in fact, especially when the sentiment is reciprocated, because that makes the impossibility more tragic.

Because writers exercise a godlike power over their fictional worlds, being the omnipotent determinants of what happens therein, it is always a writer's prerogative to determine that amour, however difficult and treacherous it might be in reality, can provide his favored characters with the rewards that it seems to promise, securing providential "happy endings" for them. Readers know that, and in large measure, that is what they expect of their reading matter—for many people, that is what "romance" means, in the context of literature and life alike. Many writers, however, do not like to do that, irrespective of the pressure exerted on them by readers, filtered through the concentrating lens of editorial policy, because they feel that it is essentially dishonest, a treason against accurate representation of the world and, more importantly, their own experience of sentimental treason. People who are happy and socially successful generally feel no inclination to be writers, writing as an activity being psychologically useful primarily as a means of escape from social expectations and commitments.

Happy endings contrived in fiction are not, by and large, representations of the actual and potential successes of their writers and readers but imaginary compensations for their lack. There is, however, some truth in the adage that misery loves company, and readers can occasionally find comfort in exaggerated literary accounts of their actual tribulations, because they are able to sympathize with the plights of unlucky heroes and heroines, and to obtain some consolation from the reassurance that their own plight is not as bad as it might be. The appetite of readers for that kind of consolation is slight, and the overwhelming preference, most of the time, is for compensatory wish-fulfillment; the avidity is, however, more widespread and more intense among writers, some of whom become connoisseurs of tragedy, sadistically inflicting suffering on their protagonists in a fashion that seems to many readers to be frankly perverse, irrespective of its artistry.

Writers who specialize in that kind of work—of whom Charles Nodier is a paradigm example—have the first line of defense that their work is more honest and realistic than that of dealers in happy endings, and that defense seems perfectly adequate to most of its employers. Those who take themselves more seriously, however—and few ever took themselves as seriously as Nodier when he was in the mood to do so, although he was too intelligent not to be capable of occasionally taking an imaginative step backwards and finding his own pretensions absurd—take that defense further by believing, and sometimes explicitly arguing, that what they are doing is not only realistic in its representations but useful in analyzing and commentating philosophically on that supposed reality, the exaggeration of which in their fictions becomes a rhetorical strategy of concentration and illumination.

Precisely because Nodier took his writing seriously, as well as his other difficulties, he became very interested in its methodology and its purpose, and his perennial attempts to figure out what he was doing, how and why when he took up his pen, fed back into the practice itself as he experimented with possible ways to do it more effectively. The stories in the present volume represent a particular phase in that evolution of his ideas and their application. While the stories translated on *Outlaws and Sorrows* represent what might be termed the "hysterical phase" of his *romanticisme*, concentrated on exaggerated representation, and those in *Jean Sbogar and Other Stories* modify that hysteria with attempts at more penetrating analysis of their own exaggerations, the novelettes collected here are more conscientiously distanced, observing rather than simply participating in the emotional upheavals of their protagonists, with a measure of scrupulousness. They make a concerted attempt to get to grips with the essential nature and variation of amour, and to evaluate its role in human affairs in a more level-headed and more contemplative fashion.

In 1831 Nodier began to publish a series of "Extraits des mémoires de Maxime Odin" in the *Revue de Paris*, evidently intending to spin out an extensive series sampling the crucial moments of that fictitious individual's amorous career, illustrating thereby a progressive learning process. In fact, he only published two episodes bearing that label in the *Revue*, although he published several other stories in its pages in which the narrators are identified in passing as "Maxime", as well as several in which the narrators are not named at all, and who might or might not be the same person. Although "Odin" is an anagram of the first four letters of Nodier, Maxime's biography is markedly different from Nodier's—unlike Nodier, he remains alone in life after the events detailed in "Amélie," whereas his creator had married in 1809 and remained part of an intimate household until his death in 1844.

The projected series was swiftly complicated when Nodier put together a volume of the 1832 *Oeuvres* entitled *Souvenirs de jeunesse, extraits des mémoires de Maxime Odin* [Souvenirs of Youth; extracts from the Memoirs of Maxime Odin], which does not include the second item in the *Revue de Paris* series, "Mademoiselle de Marsan," but does include three previously-unpublished novelettes connected by internal references, plus one story, "Thérèse," whose protagonist is explicitly identified as "Charles Nodier" and not Maxime Odin (I have held that story over to the final collection in the present series).

The four-part serial version of "Mademoiselle de Marsan" in the *Revue de Paris* in 1832 was rapidly followed by "Comment je me suis donné au diable" (*Revue de Paris*, octobre 1932; tr. herein as "How I Gave Myself to the Devil"[1]), which was not labeled there externally as part of the Maxime Odin series, although its protagonist is named Maxime, nor was it included

---

1 This story was retitled twice in various reprints, as "Amour et le grimoire" and as "Le Nouveau Fausr et la nouvelle Marguerite."

in *Souvenirs de jeunesse*, perhaps because its tone was considered ill-fitting to the development of the sequence, and it is possible that "Thérèse" was a late and arguably ill-judged substitute for it in *Souvenirs de jeunesse*. Of several later stories in the *Revue* whose protagonists are addressed as "Maxime," the one most closely connected with the *Souvenirs* thematically is "La Neuvaine de la Chandeleur" (*Revue de Paris*, juillet-août 1838; tr. as "The Candlemas Novena"), and that is the only one that I have included herein.

All writers are routinely suspected of disguised autobiography, especially when they frame their stories as first-person narratives, so it is not surprising that some commentators have mistaken *Souvenirs de jeunesse* for actual memories of Nodier's youth, and episodes from his stories are occasionally drafted into service by his biographers as straightforward or distorted representations of real incidents in his life. The commentators cannot be blamed overmuch for that, because Nodier apparently did the same himself; Jules Janin, who undoubtedly knew him far better than any of his other biographers (not excluding his daughter Marie) commented in his memoir that Nodier often recounted anecdotes about his supposed past experiences that were actually taken from his fiction, and observed that if such impostures were pointed out to him, the author appeared genuinely confused, as if he truly could not separate his memories of real events from events that he had only imagined—which probably seemed, in some instances, more real to him, and more meaningful, than mere mundane occurrences. The relationship between the author and "Maxime Odin" is far more complicated than a simple transfiguration, and although all the stories in the present collection are entirely fictitious, the intensity of the author's imaginative involvement with them should not be underestimated. There is no point in searching for "real" equivalents of the heroines of the stories within Nodier's actual biography, but the fact that they are imaginary does not devalue the analyses of feeling that the stories are attempting to carry out and to organize coherently.

Although they are more controlled in their construction and depiction than the stories in *Outlaws and Sorrows* and *Jean Sbogar and Other Stories*, the stories adopting the fictitious viewpoint of Maxime Odin are just as extreme in their own fashion. Because they are written as a series, some of them looking back over a long interval of time from a viewpoint assumed to be far older and wiser than that of the actor whose adventures are being remembered, there is no possibility of the stories ending—as many of their predecessors do—with the death of the protagonist. Maxime is obliged by his narrative frame not merely to survive to love again but also to learn from each experience as it comes along. That is difficult to accomplish, in a series built upon the axiomatic assumption that true love ought to be unique, exclusive and eternal—a difficulty particularly pronounced in the uneasy transition between "Clémentine" and "Amélie," in which the duration of Maxime's unique, eternal and unsurpassable amour is reduced to a matter of months before recommencement. It might have been that logical difficulty that dissuaded the editor of the *Revue de Paris* from publishing those two stories, if they were submitted to the publication between "Séraphine" and "Mademoiselle de Marsan."

The difficulty confronted by the series of Maxime Odin's adventures—and, more broadly, but the entire series of Nodier's stories of amour—is implicitly esthetic as well as logical. The stories that employ a sequence of distinct protagonists can end conclusively, as most of them do, with the death of both the protagonist and the heroine; that is logically and esthetically befitting in stories whose fundamental assumption is that true amour is something that can only be experienced once and is all-consuming to such an extent that its mateerial consummation can only be a disaster, because any aftermath, including—and perhaps especially—marriage could only be an anti-climax. As that pattern is repeated, however—and what else is an honest writer to do, if he wants to carry his explorations and explanations forward?—its repetition is bound to have a devaluing effect, as well as disappointing readers in quest of more optimistic consolation. Within the context of a quasi-autobiographical series, there is nowhere that the narrator of the stories can end up except where he ends up in the last of the stories assembled in *Souvenirs de jeunesse*, "Lucrèce et Jeannette," deliberately passing from sublime ambition to bathetic resignation, exemplifying the adage that even those who do learn from history are still condemned to repeat it, eventually as farce instead of tragedy—although Maxime had already been revealed in "Mademoiselle de Marsan" to have moved beyond ridicule to resignation in the context of his own fictitious life-story, and the later additions to the series could only emphasize that non-conclusion.

In reality, Nodier had married long before he wrote any of the stories in the present volume, and we can only wonder as to the extent that he thought of his relationship with his wife as fulfillment, resignation or farce. Jules Janin, who knew whereof he was speaking, insisted in his memoir that Nodier loved his wife very dearly, and was loved in return, and there is no reason to doubt his sincerity or his judgment, but the circumstance does add an extra level of complexity to the question of exactly what Nodier was trying to do when he wrote his two climactic representations of perfect celestial amour in "Célestine" and "Amélie" and then presented them to his audience in paradoxical tandem, immediately followed by a rueful anticlimax.

Although "Amélie" is the longer and more melodramatic of that awkward pair, and arguable the most artistically-satisfying of all Nodier's melodramatic love stories, there is a sense in which it is "Célestine" that is the purest and the most extreme in moral terms, because its image of perfect amour is even further from physicality than the one in "Séraphine," where Maxime's prepuberal youth guarantees his innocence of adult lust. In "Célestine," lust is undoubtedly a component of Maxime's feelings, and Célestine's too, and that makes the conscientious restraint of their behavior more remarkable, putting a much heavier burden on the symbolism of the purely metaphorical consummation of their amour, which is no less effective for its simplicity. The modern reader, accustomed to the notion of the "pathetic fallacy" and the theories of Sigmund Freud as well as having seen fictitious lightning strike with uncanny accuracy hundreds of times in hundreds of texts, is unlikely to read the story with the same naivety as its original readers, but that modern consciousness is not a simple subtraction from its appreciation.

Nodier was by no means the only practitioner of *romanticisme* to conclude that "true" love is impossible of attainment for human beings in this life, and that in that regard, as in so many others, human life is simply not fit for purpose—indeed, it requires such a level of self-delusion to conclude otherwise that few writers can maintain that level of unintelligence for long—but he not only reached that conclusion sooner than most, and expressed it more extravagantly than most, but he was one of the few courageous enough to draw the logically inevitable conclusion that there must be a further life in which love can become literally celestial if we are to resist the conclusion that all humans are doomed to fail ignominiously in that particular quest for fulfillment. He insisted, in his fiction and his "non-fiction" alike, that there had to be some such further existence, but the force and manner of his insistence suggest strongly that he was incapable of convincing himself of it.

Such fantasies are inevitably possessed of a boundary that is very difficult to cross, even for a writer prepared to assume the full responsibility of his godlike power of creation. It is not possible for protagonists, no matter how passionately they believe in eternal celestial amour, actually to experience it; they can only glimpse the remote possibility. In order to describe the paradisal amour of the resurrected, a writer not only has to discover a narrative device that will permit hypothetical communication from beyond the grave but has to invent an entire metaphysics to contain and configure that hypothetical state of being.

Nodier did, in fact, attempt that feat in one late story, "Lydie, ou le Resurrection" (tr. in *Perfectibility and Resurrection*), but it does not appear that he found the result fully satisfying, because his next and final story of perfect amour, "Franciscus Columna" (tr. in *The Four Talismans and Other Stories*) reverted to the strategy of "Célestine," with the additional twist of nesting the story within a fantasy of bibliomania, deliberately placing it in a fictional situation much closer to the actual situation of the author's fantasies within his own existence. In esthetic terms, Nodier's quest for hypothetical personal amour had already ended, in literary terms, with the diptych comprised by "Célestine" and "Amélie," just as it had already ended in real life with his marriage to Desirée and his fatherhood of Marie; there is a wry significance in the fact that when the diptych in question first reached print, it was already attached to a bathetic reaction in "Lucrèce et Jeannette" as well as equipped with an elaborately disillusioned prelude in the first few pages of "Séraphine." After that assemblage, nothing remained but recapitulation, and although the recapitulations could be elegant and elaborate, like "La Neuvaine de la Chandeleur," and thus thoroughly worthwhile as literary exercises, there was nothing else they could do without undergoing a radical philosophical transformation.

Nodier had the courage to attempt that transformation, in "Lydie," but the cost of the move was a complete removal from the imaginative arena in which the stores assembled in the present collection operate. The unnamed narrator of "Lydie" might be Maxime Odin, or a fictitious Charles Nodier, or a third shadowy literary *persona*, but his eventual fate could not be Maxime's or Nodier's. Whether he is imagined to have an afterlife or not, Maxime Odin's career ended with the sour reflections of "Lucrèce and Jeannette," although his memory was still capable of further filling-in exercises, like "La Neuvaine de la Chandeleur."

Readers remain, of course, free to wonder what might have happened to Maxime Odin after the end of his fictitious life, if his convictions were justified. If he were, in fact, resurrected in an existential condition amenable to the perfect amour of which mere humans are incapable, with whom would he be savoring that eternity: Séraphine, Célestine, Amélie, or Cécile . . . or are there harems in Heaven somehow devoid of competition for attention? Or is the question irrelevant, because Maxime, like Charles Nodier, really had given himself to the devil, in spite of letting himself off that hook with a deft stroke of his godlike authorial pen, and thus bound for the loveless Inferno? As a fictitious omniscient Odin, he could command the lightning, and cause his thunderbolts to strike where he wished, while as Charles Nodier he was only human, admittedly not fit for purpose, but in either guise, can he plausibly be imagined as a permanent resident of paradise? Judge as you wish; readers, unlike writers, can only take texts as they find them, but they do retain omnipotence in the matter of their evaluation.

As a writer with an intense interest in the nature and practice of fiction and fantasy, Charles Nodier knew as well as anyone how untrustworthy writers and fiction are, and as a prolific writer of "non-fiction" he was also well aware that the principal difference between "fiction" and "non-fiction" is that the former is more honest in its mendacity. Although his fiction became more studied and more circumspect in its representations of amour over the course of his career, it always retained a frankness and an attempted sincerity that he could never attain in his non-fiction. In consequence, the stories in the present collection represent the true culmination of his thinking—and, more importantly, his feelings—in that regard. That culmination could not be his "final word," and the collection makes that clear too, but the fact remains that amour is exemplified to the best of his evolving ability, in all its heroically bathetic paradoxicality, by the stories in the present volume.

The translations of the stories are all taken from versions of the text contained on the Bibliothèque Nationale website *gallica*.

—Brian Stableford

THE MEMOIRS OF
MAXIME ODIN

Advertisement

I shall not say how these memoirs came into my hand, and what secret sympathy of sentiment or adventures prejudiced me in favor of their author, to the point of making me forget the concern of my own studies in order to stitch together a few shreds of his journal. The mystery of such an intimate impression is not one of those ideas that can be revealed in words, and if I succeeded in making it comprehensible it would not justify me with regard to readers who are not disposed to savor my enterprise. What I owe them, above all, in order not to disappoint their expectation, is the confession of the scant importance of the personal memoirs with which Maxime Odin takes pleasure today in charming the henceforth-incurable ennui of a disillusioned life, and which I have gathered almost randomly from his notebooks.

When young, he was one of those emotional men who only live, in the midst of our artificial society and our conventional mores, by heart and by thought; who arrive in the world out of place, foreign to the language that is spoken there, the law of the necessities to which one is subject there and to the destiny that one has there; and who, after having lavished in vain around them the expansions of a credulous sensibility, end up by cultivating, whether they like it or not, a species of solitude into which they carry their illusions, for want of realities.

The state of mind that results from that voluntary aberration is what is known as the romantic life; I have often heard it said that it is not without rewards. At least it has the advantageous one that it conciliates marvelously with independence, and that it can do without exterior aliments—or, rather, that anything is good that takes their place. The imagination, condemned to search incessantly for the ideal type that it has formed, finds nothing in the end but despair. It only has one means of possessing it in all its ideal perfection, and that means, which would be too comfortable if nature had put it within range of all organizations, consists of imprinting that fantastic ideal on the first object that comes along.

This is a man who shows you his hand, full of sand and says to you: "What is this?" You reply: "It's sand." A gross error! He sees there rubies, sapphires, topazes and emeralds, and what he sees is really there for him, because he is gazing with a prism. If God is solitary—and one cannot dispense with thinking that without mistaking the nature of his eternal and supreme bliss—I suppose that it is thus that he must see and must love the creatures that proceed from him.

The romantic man is, therefore, not the one whose existence is varied by the greatest possible number of extraordinary events. It is almost always otherwise. He is the man in whom the simplest events develop the keenest sensations; the man whose soul, indifferently avid for disturbances and sensualities, never wearies of those extreme alternatives; the man whom everything stirs, and who exercises upon everything that moves him the inexhaustible faculty of enjoying and suffering, without submitting his fears, his hopes, his pains or his pleasures, to the judgment of reason.

If he writes, do not ask of his book scenes of dramatic effect, the skillful combinations of fiction, the marvels of the fantastic; do not search there for a plan, a method, a literary theory, a settled style; he does not understand any of that. He only knows of the world what he has felt. His life has been his affection; his genius is his heart. His sketches will only have one very relative merit, truth: not positive truth, the truth of the indifferent and the wise, the truth of thinkers and pedants, but all the truth that his nature can comprise. He will refrain from adding to it or retrenching from it a single detail. That would be something else, it would not be him. What is charming about his memories is that they are memories. And the most seductive of poetic inventions do not distract him from those utterly simple, utterly vulgar memories, which could not be invented and would not be worth the trouble of being invented.

But is that which is not worth the trouble of being invented worth the trouble of being read? That is what it remains for you to decide, and do not waste time, for he is about to speak for himself.

Séraphine

The kindest privilege that nature has accorded to a man who is growing old is that of recovering with an extreme facility impressions of childhood. At that age of repose, the course of life resembles that of a stream whose slope is approaching, after a thousand detours, the vicinity of its source, and which, finally free of all the obstacles that have embarrassed its futile voyage, having vanquished all the rocks that have broken it in its passage, purified of the torrential foam that has troubled its waters, suddenly evens out in order to repeat once again, before disappearing, the first shade that was mirrored in its borders. To see it thus, calm and transparent, reflecting on its motionless surface the same trees and the same banks, one could easily wonder in which direction it commences and in which it finishes. It requires a willow branch, debris confided to it by yesterday's storm, to float momentarily before your eyes, in order for you to recognize the place toward which its slope is drawing it. Tomorrow, the river that is waiting a short distance away will have carried it away, and that will be forever.

All the intermediaries are effaced thus in the memories of old age, reposed of stormy passions and disappointed hopes, when the long voyages of thought bring a man back, from circuit to circuit, to the verdure and the flowers of his merry cradle. That sensuality, I can testify, is one of the most vibrant of the soul, but it does not last long, and it is the only one that those who have the honor of dying young can envy those who have the misfortune of living for a long time.

At the age of twelve I had finished the superficial studies of children and, in consequence, I knew nothing; but I had learned, fortunately, what one rarely learns at school, which is that I knew nothing, and that even the majority of scholars know very little. I was so avid for instruction that I often spelled out, effortfully, the alphabet of an unknown language, in order to enable me to read books that I did not understand, and in circumstances other than those in which I lived, that vague and sterile curiosity might have become an aptitude; but of all the written or rational alphabets that I tried to decipher, there was none that inspired me with as much fervor as that of nature. It already seemed to me—for I have not changed opinion—that the profound study of the facts of creation was more worthy than any other of exercising a healthy intelligence, and that the rest was only good for occupying the futile or extravagant leisure of degenerate peoples.

A sojourn of a few weeks in the home of a good minister of Vindenheim in Alsace, a great lover of butterflies, had aided me to lift the thickest veil of the beautiful Isis whose delectable secrets were to mingle so many charms, a few years later, with the miseries of my exile. I had returned from my mountains, gauze net in hand, a cork-lined tinplate box in my pocket, magnifying-glass and pin-cushion in my knapsack, rich and proud of a few shreds of a venturesome nomenclature that at least initiated me into the language of another world, where I could walk with a free heart, my head high and my elbows free, with more independence than the artificial world of humans promised me. When one is not organized in a manner to live with them, one receives that revelation early, and whoever has received that revelation without obeying it ought not to blame anyone but himself for his misfortunes; he has been the sole artisan of his evil destiny.

In my natal town at that time there was a man of about forty years named Monsieur de C***, although at that time he was more commonly known as Citizen Justin, the name of his patron saint, because the Revolution had taken away that of his father. He was a former officer of genius, who had spent his life in scientific studies and spent his fortune in good works. Simple and austere in his mores, mild and affectionate in his relations, inflexible in his principles but tolerant by character, benevolent to everyone; capable of everything good, worthy of everything great, and modest to the point of timidity in the midst of the treasures of knowledge that his patience had amassed and his genius had divined; rarely arguing, or making speeches, and never contesting; always ready to enlighten ignorance, to spare error, to respect conviction and to sympathize with folly, he might have put you in mind of Plato, Fénelon or Malesherbes; but I shall not compare him to anyone, because comparisons would do him wrong.

The vulgar suspected him of being well versed in medicine, because he was the first and last person to be seen at the bedside of poor invalids, and was at his ease because he furnished remedies; but he was also thought to be eccentric, because like me, he was the only person in the locale who walked in the countryside armed with a gauze net, and who scythed the summits of tall plants lightly, without damaging them, in order to plunder a few flies with gilded scales, whose usage no one could understand. That analogy of tastes brought our very disparate ages closer together. Hazard had made him a friend of my father and I did not take long to find in him another father, of whom mine was momentarily jealous; but they came to an understanding better for my contentment than the two mothers of the judgment of Solomon. They shared my life in order that they could both embellish it.

That was necessary. A terrible law arrived, on I no longer know which day of Floréal, which exiled the nobles from towns at war, and the sagest of sages had the irreparable misfortune of being noble. When the deadly news had spread, I was no longer alive; I no longer embraced my poor father without drowning him with my tears, because my friend had gone away.

"Console yourself," he said to me one day, "he won't go far; I've obtained a retreat for him three leagues away; I've consented to let you leave with him, and with your legs of a stag, you can come to embrace me without weeping once or twice a week."

I thought I would die of joy, for it seemed like quitting neither of them. We left, therefore, and people murmured as we went by: "There are more nobles going away!"—and that was the only time in my life when I had the pleasure of hearing it said that I was noble.

We went to live in a little village distributed along the banks of a little river called the Biez, in accordance with the custom of the region, which was garnished on either side with a row of young poplars. They must have been very tall! Our house was, in its simplicity, the most magnificent in the commune, and the apartment we occupied on the first and last floor would have been the envy of ten kings that I have encountered since, in the most wretched inns of Europe. It comprised two rooms coated with smooth white plaster, whose neatness charmed the sight.

Citizen Justin's, which was the larger, as was reasonable, did not lack a certain luxury of furniture, although the principal items were reduced to a straw mattress—he had never had any other bed, and I have been very glad since that I acquired that habit in his company—two strong walnut-wood chairs and two tables of the same wood and the same workmanship, waxed like parquets and as shiny as mirrors.

The first, which was at least five feet in diameter, occupied with its vast circumference the middle of the superb drawing room, of which I am commencing the description with a sentiment of locality so vivid and so present that I could recognize all the details by touch if I were transported there at night by the magic wand of a good fay even today, the twelfth of October 1831, thirty-seven years to the day since I left there almost the only part of unalloyed happiness that has ever fallen to me on earth. That one bore all the utensils of our daily work and observation: the presses, forceps, scalpels, scissors, awls, magnifying-glasses, microscopes, cotton wool, glass eyes, iron wire, pins of various dimensions, gray paper, acids and briquettes—the indispensable items of a naturalist's equipment.

It was there that we analyzed, dissected and stuffed animals; it was there that we counted the sections of the legs or the mouth-parts of insects imperceptible to the naked eye, the stamens or divisions of the stigma of a plant, a dwarf of the floral empire; it was there that, after having dried them, we laid out plants with minute precaution on the blank sheets where they would live again for science, their stems and ramifications fixed a by light strip of cloth stuck with gum Arabic, taking care to display their most characteristic parts and not to alter their bearing or their physiognomy; it was there that we tested stones in contact with the most developed nerve-clusters of our organism, along with the impacts of iron, the sympathies of the magnet, the sensible play of affinities and the effervescence of the decomposition produced by reagents; it was the modest laboratory to which all the secrets of nature came, one after another, to reveal themselves.

On the partition wall at the back—for I am determined not to spare you any detail—was the bed I have mentioned, flanked by our two ceremonial armchairs, terminated at the foot by the exiguous equipment of philosophical toilette, and, supported by the arsenal of our great expeditions: butterfly-nets of all dimensions, forms and colors, instruments for digging and rummaging, poles for spanning ravines and beating trees. All that was lacking was a rifle, but that was a weapon forbidden to a suspect naturalist, and ours would have inspired too much mistrust in the hands of a philosopher and a child. Underneath lay the rock-breaking hammer and the pike for dislodging roots. Two light but knotty staffs, to ward off wolves and snakes, completed that formidable apparatus of war. I can assure you that it was terrible to behold.

The only window in the right-hand wall overlooked a murmuring spring, which went to join the Biez, bounding over pebbles, the melodious sound of which I can still hear. In the part of the room preceding that casement we had placed three graceful shelf-units, of which the first, the inferior, supported boxes of caterpillars and chrysalides closed with fine mesh, which were confided to my particular care, and the second bore the polished shelves on which we displayed our butterflies under plates of glass that contained their wings without crumpling them. The last was garnished with bottles stoppered with emery paper, which contained the camphor destined to be sprinkled over our hunting bags every evening, the volatile alkali for treating the stings of wasps and the bites of vipers, and the preservative alcohol for reptiles and little egg-layers. A cupboard fitted nearby, of which Citizen Justin always carried the key, was reserved for the treasures, a hundred times more precious, of the domestic pharmacy.

The other side of the casement was occupied by our second table, about which I have said nothing as yet, although it was worth the trouble, but I thought I ought to sacrifice logical order to descriptive order in this truly special topography, to which no one will refer after me, because I am the only person on earth who remembers it, unless Monsieur de C*** has conserved at eighty years of age some memory of those days of exile, which were days of ineffable delights for me. I do not even know whether he was suffering, and whether his attentive kindness dissimulated from me, under a cheerful good humor, chagrins that might have poisoned my happiness.

The table in question was very long, in the idea that I have of it today. All our academies, destroyed by a brutal but naive vandalism—which at least had the excuse of inexperience, which it will not have in future—were embodied in my eyes there in a single person. A man of genius wrote thereon the admirable pages, of which a few rare friends have received the confidence, printed in ten or a dozen copies of which posterity, which could no longer understand them, will be unaware. Before him, his favorite books were amassed on three shelves, the first of which had difficulty accommodating our usual authors: the *Systema naturae*, the grave Fabricius, the good Geoffroy, the ingenious Bergmann, Lavoisier, Fourcroy, Berthollet, the eclectic Macquer, and Bernardin de Saint-Pierre the poet. Above them were arranged a good edition of Horace, a stout Seneca the philosopher, which I did not read then, Montaigne's *Essais*, which I read twice in succession, and a few tattered volumes of Amyot's Plutarch, which I read perpetually. Higher up there was a large *Gerusalemme liberata*, whose sumptuous margins I never fatigued too much; and Ariosto, which enabled me to love Italian; a Spanish *Don Quixote*, which I divined for want of comprehension; and five or six tragedies by Shakespeare, which transported me with enthusiasm when Citizen Justin translated them as he read them in our moments of recreation. I should not forget that he had taken advantage of an empty space to slip in his album of drawings, and that he had suspended his violin over the exterior.

Facing my friend's bed was our second casement, which overlooked the Biez, and from which one could follow its detours in the distance, between charming buildings and islets of verdure all the way to the point where its course ended in a brilliant dot that trembled for a long time like a meteor and ended up being extinguished under the sun's rays.

It was on the left-hand wall, however, that we had gradually assembled all the marvels of our exhibition: the birds on their perches, in the vivacity of their natural attitudes, which only lacked foliage to depict a living aviary; the butterflies deployed in beautiful golden frames that we had brought from the town, the splendor of which was effaced by the brilliance of their wings; the snake with its mouth agape that defended our door like the dragon of the Hesperides; and the bats that plunged their petrifying gazes, like those of Gorgons, from the height of their pine frame. The museum of that village, now that I think about it, would have been the envy of more than one city, but what is most certain is that its Aristotle merited another Alexander.

Our day of investigations commenced regularly at noon, after the morning meal, and lasted until nightfall, for we were intrepid walkers. We went forth and came back at a run, me questioning everything we encountered, him always replying, and always by means of clear solutions, ingenious and easy to remember. There was no natural event that did not furnish material for a lesson, and no lesson that did not have the effect on me of a new and unexpected pleasure. It was an encyclopedic course of study put into action, and I am sure now that anyone but me would have obtained great profit from it, but my imagination was too fickle not to be forgetful. Having arrived at fields or a forest, we went hunting, and as my collections had scarcely commenced, every step procured me a discovery; I was marching in conquered country.

There is no expression to render the joy of those innocent usurpations of science over rebellious and mysterious nature, and those who have not savored them will probably have some difficulty in conceiving them. Even today I sometimes catch myself quivering with a voluptuous tremor in remembering the sight of the first *Carabus auronitens* that appeared to me in the moist shadow cast by the fallen trunk of an old oak, under which it reposed, as dazzling as a carbuncle fallen from the Mogul's tiara.[1] Be careful of its name, please; it was the *Carabus auronitens* itself! I remember that it fascinated me momentarily with its gleam, and that my hand trembled with such emotion that I had to make several attempts to capture it. How fortunate children are, and how much adults have to lament, when they no longer have enough wisdom to be infantile!

The joys of life are not the same when one has acquired the dolorous experience of their instability. I have sought out many of them since the age of twenty; I have savored many that the most fortunate would envy, but not one that my mouth did not welcome with a bitter smile, and which did not penetrate my heart with anguish and despair. How many burning tears I have shed in the ecstasies of happiness that have been counted as tears of delight because they were misunderstood! Enable, if you can, a soul smitten with amour to understand that it is a moment of your past days whose tenderness cannot fill the eternal void, and that the moment whose imperious and triumphant rivalry eclipses all your pleasures is the one when you found the *Carabus auronitens!* There is, however, nothing truer.

On days of rain or snow—for in 1794 there was snow in the mountains at the end of May—we spent the time arranging the disposition of the furniture that I have just itemized, or we took turns to read; and in our lessons as in our walks, every fact had its instruction. Every hour also had its employment, and nothing is more appropriate to take a severe physiognomy away from work than the variety of studies. Mathematics relaxed us from chemistry, and the fine arts from the sciences. I maintained the recent memory of my Latin studies easily by the assiduous and passionate study of our taxonomists, who had taken so much empire over my thoughts that I could not

---

1 *Carabus auronitens* is a varicolored beetle, usually red and green as well as gold.

conceive of one without his work being suddenly formulated in concise and descriptive phrases, bristling with ablatives, like those of Linnaeus; and if I had recognized in myself since that characteristic gift of the talent that is called style, I would not have been embarrassed to explain its qualities and its faults by means of those first habits of my laborious childhood.

The style in question is full, precise, picturesque, and appropriate to make ideas stand out in their most salient aspects, but overloaded with technical terms and verbal descriptions; it is abundant in accurate epithets, but which often only express nuances; strangled like an arithmetical proposition every time I try to intrude the expression in a forceful form, complex and diffuse as an amplification, when I feel the need to extend and develop it; it is obscure for being curt, or pale for being clear, but always recalling aphorism in its turns of phrase and Latinism in its wordage. In sum, it is a poor style, if it is a style—and there are not ten men per century who have their own style—but a style that emerged, such as it is, from my singular education, and which circumstances have not permitted me to modify since. It is the ultimate instrument of an existence that has had no choice, and I throw it in the waste-bin without regret, as I no longer have the time or the strength to change it.

The mornings were my own. That was the time when Citizen Justin went to stride around the commune, visiting the poor, caring for the sick or lending the surrounding farmers the aid of his agronomic knowledge. Scarcely an hour remained to him before midday to examine the species he had collected the day before, to observe under the lens of a microscope the interior economy of previously-unknown animalcule republics, which he had discovered in conserves or cloth, or to add a few lines to his weekly correspondence with the Societé Philomathique de Paris, the sole depository then of all the brilliant acquisitions of physical science, of which the Institut has since recovered the heritage.

My particular ministry was limited to extending reconnaissance around the village, to all the points where some accident favorable to certain developments promised us an abundant harvest of new genera. I knew with no deception the small grove of elders or birches that balanced on its leaves *cumolpes* as blue as sapphire and *chrysomeles* as green as emerald; the pretty hazel copse of which the elegant red *attelabes* were found, so similar to the American berries with which the savages make necklaces; the plantation of young willows where the large musky *capricorne* came to display the riches of its aventurine armor and spread its perfumes of amber and rose; the pool of water veiled by nenuphar lilies with large corollas, and little ranunculi with silver buds, where the *Dytiscus* floated, flattened like a barge, and from the depths of which the *Hydrophilus* elevated its back, sounded like a keel, while an entire population of *Coccinellidae* caused all sorts of metallic reflections play over their resplendent sheaths or the *Lucanus* lived in tribes, and the beech tree with silky white bark where giant *Prionus* climbed.

There is something marvelously soothing in that study of nature, which attaches a name to all beings, a thought to all names, an affection and memories to all thoughts; and perhaps the man who has not penetrated the grace of those mysteries lacks a sense with which to savor life. The nomenclatures themselves, the work of an entirely poetic genius, which is probably the ultimate poetry of the human species, have an inexpressible charm at the age of imagination in which fable and history have not yet lost their prestige.

Can you see those brilliant families of butterflies, which are only butterflies for the vulgar? It is a wonderland complete with enchantments and metempsychoses for a child with a slightly cultivated mind, who pursues them with his light net. Those are the "Greek and Trojan knights".[1] By its coat

---

1 The reference is to species of exotic Asian butterflies that were named

of mail checkered with yellow and black you will recognize the prudent *Papilio machaon*, the almost-divine daughter of the divine Aesculapius, and, faithful as of old to the cult of the plants that contain precious specifics for maladies and wounds, it will not fail to alight on the fennel.

If you go down to the pastures, do not be astonished by the simplicity of their inhabitants. Those butterflies are "shepherds" and nature has only gone to the expense for them of a rustic garment. That is *Pyronia*; that is *Maniola*; that is *Papilio corydon*. One alone is distinguished among them by the hue of his azure cloak, under which innumerable eyes radiate like nocturnal stars in a clear sky, but he is the king of the pasture-lands, he is *Argus*, who always guards the flocks.

If you have crossed the edge of the wood with a curious tread, defended by *Silenus* and the *satyrs*, here is the band of *sylvans*, which wander in the milieu of the solitudes, and the *nymphs*, even lighter, which play with your pursuit, soon leaving a stream between them and you, and disappear, like the nereid Lycoris, without fear of being seen, behind the bushes of the opposite bank.

If you have attempted the summits of the highest mountains you will have had no difficulty recalling Olympus and Parnassus there, for you will have found the "heliconians" and the "gods" there: *Mars*, distinguished by his armor of burnished steel, struck by the sunlight with transparent and varied glazes; *Vulcan*, flamboyant with ingots of ardent red, like iron in a furnace; or even *Apollo* in his most superb apparel, delivering to the air his snow white robe, heightened with purple stripes.

I enjoyed all those ravishing harmonies with an enthusiasm that I can no longer express, but I enjoyed nothing in the

---

after various Homeric heroes in a volume published in French and Dutch in 1779. The names were retained by Cuvier in the early years of the nineteenth century but then abandoned.

world as much as my own existence. All the intimate sensualities of the soul have been depicted; I regret that no one has described the immense sensuality that grips a twelve-year-old heart formed by a little instruction and a great deal of sensibility to the knowledge of the living world, taking possession of it like a bequest, on a beautiful spring morning. It is thus that Adam must have seen the world that was made for him when he awoke from an infantile slumber at the breath of his Creator.

Oh, how beautiful the earth appeared to me! How I held my breath in order to listen to the wind in the wood and the sounds of the stream! How I loved the chirping of the birds under the leaves and the hum of bees around the flowers! And I was there, like another bee, caressing with my gaze all the flowers that they caress, and I named all those flowers, for I knew them all by their names, whether they rounded out in tremulous umbels or bloomed in cups, dangling like bells, or whether they dotted the grass like little stars fallen from the firmament.

My hair abandoned to the wind, I ran, to convince myself of my life and my liberty; I pierced the bushes, jumped over ditches, scaled banks, bounded, shouted and laughed; I leapt with joy, and then I fell down, in a fatigue full of delights; I rolled over the elastic and embalmed lawns, intoxicating myself with their emanations, and, lying down, I embraced the blue horizon with a gaze devoid of envy, saying to it with a conviction that I never found again: *You are no purer and more peaceful than I am!* It was me who said that!

Omnipotent God, what have I done in order to be unable to recover, at the price of what remains of my life, one of those moments of my childhood? Alas, every man who has expected, as I have, the illusion of primal happiness and primal hope, has been subject, without meriting it, to the punishment of primal guilt. We too have lost a paradise!

Sunday was different. While hunting, herborizing and chatting, we went to visit our neighbors, to talk about history to a gouty old rentier who had sagely taken refuge in a village from the tempests of the city, and who knew all the alliances of all the princely families like the back of his hand, since Robert le Fort and Gontran le Riche; to talk about botany and medical matters with a worthy surgeon who maimed the language of the natural sciences intrepidly—his patients would have been fortunate if that had been all he maimed!—and to talk about political economics with a stout farmer who had made a considerable fortune in business, and who was very proud, in his patriotism of a publican, of plowing from time to time with the patriciat fallen into agriculture. I remember that the last-cited had a twenty-year-old daughter of remarkable beauty, brought up in the fine arts and fine society, nourished on all the beautiful prose and all the beautiful poetry of Year II of the republic, and so romantic, so sentimental and so nervous that I regarded her for a long time as an exception. Five or six years later, I perceived that the exception was not there; it was in natural and simple hearts that no longer felt what they could not express, and which did not make a display of their emotions.

Our visits of predilection, however, were for an old château a league at the most from the village where we lived, and which was, by a fortunate hazard, on the route of our familiar excursions. It is true that at the end of a short time, that hazard had become so infallible and so regular that one might have seen it as the effect of a premeditated plan. The journey was well worth the trouble. Three amiable sisters lived there, exiled, like Monsieur de C***, for the crime of their birth, and who composed, with an aged domestic and an alert little negress, the entire population of the venerable manor.

I shall not speak about the two elder sisters, which whom I was scantly occupied, although they were charming, and who

40

were not occupied with me at all. The youngest was named Séraphine; she was nearly fourteen years old, which was sufficient to give her all the ascendancy over me of a big girl over a small boy; but nature had provided compensation for our ages in the delicacy of her fragile constitution and the premature development of my already almost adolescent organization. The habitude of active and stimulating exercise, which fortified my robust childhood every day; the practice of rude labor and walking, running and climbing, over valleys, hills and rocks; the assiduity of obstinate studies, which imprint on thought a virile character of which the physical faculties feel the influence, had given me even over the children of the country, ordinarily so superior to us, a pronounced advantage of vigor, skill and audacity.

I was not feared—that sad glory would have poisoned all the memories of my life—but people willingly sought the support of my amity, because weakness and timidity are drawn by an instinctive affection toward courage and strength. As I did not lack vanity—and I perceive by virtue the complaisance with which I review these details that I am not entirely cured of that shameful mental infirmity—I took pleasure in multiplying, especially before women, and without knowing why, the adventurous exploits of my gymnastic skill. They like temerity. When one astonishes them, one interests them, and when one interests them, one is very near to pleasing them. I have understood all that since.

The liaisons of that age are soon made; it is without suspicion, because it is without experience. It is necessary to have surprised some evil thought in one's own heart to suspect it in others. After Séraphine and I had seen one another twice, we would have liked no longer to quit one another. Our pleasures were so pure, our conversations so pleasant, we wept together with so much abandon, and it is so good to weep! That was because she had a great deal of chagrin. Her mother was in prison ten leagues away, her father fifty leagues away; of her four brothers, three were outlaws wandering without resources in three different states of Europe, the other was detained in Paris under the knife of the tribunal that had cut the throats of ten of her relatives; and around her a populace armed with pikes and firebrands was roaring every day, which even menaced her, a poor fearful and defenseless creature whose touching grace would have tamed famished panthers.

"Come on," I said to her, "console yourself. The reign of the assassins will not last long. My family is republican, but I shall become an aristocrat in order to defend you. I am not far from the moment of handling a sword or a dagger, like anyone else, and since it requires blood, I shall shed the blood of your enemies pitilessly."

"Don't talk like that," Séraphine replied. "I would be even more unhappy if I feared seeing you become wicked. The wicked are more to be pitied than we are. Continue to acquire knowledge and reputation, and when you are big enough to make those patriotic messieurs listen to you, do what you can to prevent them from killing us, for if I am killed too, who is the woman who will love you as much as me?"

That need to be together had become so intense that it absorbed all our thoughts. It was the object, the goal, the life of our life, and neither of us ever arrived without finding the other looking for us. When I came down from the mountain I was sure of seeing her white veil in the distance, floating in the air, or her straw hat flying away without her stopping to see where it had fallen, while she ran to meet me. But I spared her detours by running toward her, cutting across plowed fields, leaping hedges, parting brushwood and emerging from a thicket while she was still searching for me behind it, and I would not have elongated my course by a single stride to avoid a ditch ten feet wide. The elastic earth obeyed my flight as a racket does a shuttlecock, and I arrived, so brisk and so joyful, my arms around her neck and my lips on her cheek, that she did not have time to be frightened.

The time passed too quickly, alas, on my part, in innocent teasing, on hers in tender and serious conversation. My foolish expansion was constrained then, because I remembered that Séraphine was sad, and that she could only associate herself effortfully with the turbulent sallies of my joy and my insouciant happiness. My ideas, so cheerful and so frivolous, were gradually fashioned, on the contrary, to habitudes of melancholy, and of two elements incompatible in appearance a strange combination of character was formed in me, which darkened my youth by turns with dolorous sympathies and cheered up my mature age with the instincts and tastes of a child. All the developments of my soul dated from those distant days. I have acquired nothing and lost nothing, but if I had died in those days, my life would have been no less complete. Life is complete when one has loved once.

It is necessary, however, that I explain that love, to which the refinement of our language and our mores has not yet given a name. Nothing resembles less amour as people understand it, and yet it is a sentiment quite distinct from the affections of family and the amities of school. That difference I sensed, without being able to explain it. I confess, as if I were writing under the empire of the ideas I had at twelve, that I had formed a singular opinion of the amour of poets and novelists, whom I had read with avidity, in the firm persuasion that the passions they described so well were fictions, like the subjects of their fables. I took them for a fantastic image of the simple emotions of two spouses who had loved one another in childhood, as I loved Séraphine and as I was loved by her, who found themselves happy to spend their life together and to whom marriage accorded the delectable privilege of prolonging the charm of that mild intimacy in the mysteries of the night and the solitude of slumber.

I admired how, from the effusion of tenderness that confounded two well matched beings into one, the existence of a new being resulted, hatched under caresses and kisses, the fruit of harmony and amour; and I saw in that moral phenomenon, which maintained forever the reproduction of a virgin species, the most evident sign of the superiority of humans over animals. I did not have the pretention of having invented at that time a conjugality more solemn than that of God, but that was what I had made, and the joys of youth taught me nothing that could console me for having lost the illusion. What am I saying? The regret of my error has survived the feverish realities of pleasure that intoxicate the senses at the expense of the soul, and which precipitate it from the heights of Heaven into the miseries of lust.

How many times have I feared being as fortunate as others in the accomplishment of my desires, happy as I was in the enchantment of my hopes? Even today, there is not one of my lovers' tears that has not left me with better memories than all the delights of a joy without a tomorrow, over which the sad convictions of life fall like the curtain at the end of a play, like the obscurity of night over an extinct firework. It is probably in that sense that one says that the first inclination was the best. Its charm is in its ignorance.

I loved Séraphine, therefore, with the naivety of an entirely ideal, entirely poetic impression, the innocence of which must have something in common with the amour of angels. As pure as me, I suppose that Séraphine was a little more knowledgeable, and it is easy to see that that would not have been difficult. She was my elder by almost two years, she was a woman, she had lived since the cradle in a society that I had only glimpsed. Her ingenuous conversation often left me vague doubts through which I had difficulty finding the stray thread of my doctrine. I meditated alone on what I had not understood, but I did not meditate for long, because I was not curious, because I believed firmly in my ideas and, above all, because I preferred thinking about her to wasting time building futile theories.

She was with me everywhere; I knew how to make her enter into all my conversations, to link her in memory or in project with all my actions, and to bring her into all my dreams. Always to dream and only to dream about her was a benefit of my slumber, a faculty that I had, which I have conserved for a long time, and which has compensated me for many dolors. I had succeeded in fixing in my mind one of the most common scenes of our jolly mornings; it is as present to me as if I were still there.

After having fatigued myself for two hours searching for her where she was not, I usually fell wearily on to the sofa in the drawing room, and I feigned sleep in order to provoke my indifference or not to contradict her in her malice. She arrived then, lightly raised on tiptoe, stretching out her suspended footsteps with precaution, shivering at the noise of the parquet, which had creaked, a basket over her arm, her hair escaping everywhere in golden waves from the poorly-attached straw hat that could no longer contain it, her head slightly tilted over her shoulder, her eyes fixed and fearful, her lips parted, her arm extended to gain space. She passed gently over my lips a cluster of cherries less red than her own.

I saw her turn thus, white but animated, charming in her grace and her childish emotion, pausing on me her round blue irises as transparent as crystal, plunging a fiery gaze through my half-closed eyelids in order to catch the moment of my awakening and caressing me at close range with her flowery breath, as if challenging me to kiss her; that was what I was waiting for, and when she tried to flee she was captured. Then there were cries, moans and never-ending sulks. Her sisters arrived to help; Lila, her little African, pulled my hair and menaced my eyes. One kiss more paid her ransom, but she detested me for at least an hour; I went away, came back, wept, begged for forgiveness, did not obtain it, went away again at a run toward the canal in order to precipitate myself into an abyss ten inches deep, until the moment when a little voice, vibrating like a silver bell, deigned to enchain my despair. I had been sick with a frightful woe, a woe worse than death, a woe that one would like to savor, today, at the price of the conflagration of a kingdom!

I was far from imagining the aspect under which those anguishes of first love would appear to me before long. I was not twenty when I resolved to put a nail in my wheel, as Montaigne says, and no longer to grow older by a moment; I found myself well enough, but I would have done better to stop at twelve.

I have said that my little friend's health was delicate. I scarcely suspected that all young girls were more or less ill at the age of fourteen or thereabouts; that mystery surpassed the range of my knowledge. Séraphine was subject to headaches, dazzlings, sudden hallucinations and bouts of fever. One evening I had left her suffering; I was suffering from her illness, which my fears exaggerated.

I went to bed fully dressed; I did not sleep; I turned over on my bed of straw as if on the steel spikes of Regulus or the hot coals of Guatemozin. I got up to walk around my room; I found it too narrow; I opened my window; the sky also seemed to me to be too narrow. The château was invisible. I measured the height of my window: fifteen feet at the most, if I remember correctly. I was far away; I do not know whether I ran or whether the earth fled beneath me, but I did not take more than a quarter of an hour to reach the gate of the park.

That was not all. The only place where the enclosure was accessible was defended by a basin lined with large slabs of stone, where the waters of the canal ended, after having irrigated the garden. There they lay dormant at ground level in the pond,

46

and were then lost momentarily under the road, emerging a few paces away, but free and capricious, between the willows of the meadow. We called that the salamander pond because a great many were seen there, striking the motionless water with their tails, like an oar, or dragging themselves over the pavement, delivering their bright yellow marbling to the caprices of the light at intervals; but they could not be seen at the time of which I am speaking; one could not see anything at all.

The night was calm and warm, but dark, and I could only measure from memory the width of the reservoir that it was necessary to cross. I was only sure that there was no more than a foot of border on the side where I was about to fall, and that I ran the risk, depending on the range of my leap, of breaking my head against the wall if I abandoned myself recklessly, or, if I moderated my leap too much, of frightening the population of sleeping newts with the fall of a new Phaeton.

With the aid of God, amour or skill, I descended on the target as if I had been borne by the wings of a bird. With one leap I reached the top of the wall and jumped down to the level of the garden. There still remained a privet hedge, as tall and dense as a palisade, but on which I could easily place my hand, and I did not touch it with any other part of my body in leaving it behind me. I was in the broad avenue of chestnut-trees, with terminated at the foot of the tower in which Séraphine slept; but her window, elevated one floor above the terrace, was hidden from me by thick foliage, and the time that I put into searching for the light that finally sprang forth in scattered rays between the last branches appeared to me to be longer than the rest of the journey.

I stopped then, leaning on a chestnut-tree in order to get my breath back, for I was already tranquil. The light was that of a candle, the pale flame of which trembled against the panes alongside the place where Séraphine hung the little mirror that served for her nocturnal toilette. She was standing there, lightly dressed, smiling at her loveliness, rolling up her hair with a coquettish grace, and then taking pleasure in unrolling it, in order to see it undulate again. I remained there for as long as the candle was not extinct, and I don't know whether it was a minute or an hour, but I know that it was worth a whole lifetime, and that it was only the hope of recovering a few similar instants that could determine me to recommence it.

I took longer to return. The day was ready to break when I perceived that access to my room was far more difficult than the descent. The exterior of the house resembled the interior; it was so neat, so smooth, so carefully plastered that flies had difficulty fixing their hooks thereon. Not one projecting stone, not one fissure in the plaster, not one crack into which to slide the fingers that might serve me in order to hoist myself up as far as the sill—and add that the Biez was running too close behind my heels for me to take a run. A discarded plow-wheel, which it was necessary to bring from a distance, finally served me as a ladder. I arrived; I slept as one sleeps at twelve when one has no chagrin, and I was still asleep when Monsieur de C*** informed me for the third time that it was time to go and enquire after Séraphine's health, about which I had been so anxious the day before.

"Good, good!" I said, rubbing my eyes and extending my arms. "It's not dangerous."

Monsieur de C*** looked at me, astonished. I flatter myself that it was the first time that he had found me so insouciant with regard to my amities; and my tenderness of a troubadour or a paladin, which lent itself to jokes every day, rendered that indifference inexplicable. His misapprehension cheered me up, and as I would not have dared to make the reasons for my security known to my friend, I found it piquant to accompany him, while diverting myself with all the trivia of the route, and without mentioning Séraphine to him, all the way to the corner of a dense thicket where she usually waited for us, in order to surprise us mischievously or frighten us with a cry. She was there, and I had, as you know, reasons for not doubting it. She fell into my arms, withdrew, returned to me, knocked off my hat, ran away in order to be chased, and ended up allowing herself to be caught, crying with chagrin and joy.

"You were right just now when I extracted you from such a good sleep," Monsieur de C*** said to me. "It wasn't dangerous."

I ask you whether that was a great subject for anger: bleak, silent and scornful anger. Séraphine took the lead with dignity, giving herself the disdainful manners that noble young women learn, I believe, at birth. When we had reached the avenue of chestnuts, she sat down in front of us, at the end of a long stone bench on which we chatted almost every day. I went to join her there, and she ran to the other extremity; I followed her; she resumed her first place, and so did I; but I fixed her there with an arm that I had raised over her a hundred times, the force of which she knew.

"Halt there, sulky!" I said to her, pretending to be seriously annoyed. "Why are you sullen, Mademoiselle?"

"Me, sullen, Monsieur? For what reason, if you please? One is only sullen with those one loves and by whom one is loved. I'm not sullen with you because you don't love me and I don't love you. That's natural. One isn't obliged to love someone."

"Ah! I don't love you and you don't love me, Séraphine? That's nice!"

"No, I certainly don't love you, since I detest you, since I hold you in execration, Monsieur, and I'd like to know, in fact, why you are taking the liberty of addressing me as *tu!* I forbid you to do so! But consider," she added, striving to laugh, "whether it isn't necessary to be sullen with a Monsieur who sleeps so well when one is mortally ill, and who excuses himself by saying that *it isn't dangerous?* If you had been ill I wouldn't have been so tranquil. But let me go, I beg you! Let me go immediately, or I'll make a noise. I'll summon Lila . . . I'm going to weep."

"No, truly, you won't weep, ugly and wicked as you are— and I'd like to see someone decide to weep!"

"Someone decide to weep! As you said, that's nice! That's very polite! And besides, I'm ugly now. And this is what you do to make an ugly girl weep when she wants to weep? Would you prevent me from weeping and crying if it gave me pleasure? Perhaps you won't permit me to weep when you stifle me? You're very advantageous!"

Advantageous was one of those drawing-room words that always disconcerted me. I put my other arm around her and hastened to explain myself . . .

"Are you able to believe, Séraphine, that I would have slept without making sure that it wasn't dangerous, and that you're quite well? Listen to me for a moment, and don't try to run away; it won't succeed. Do you believe that the condition of my sweet and beautiful Séraphine was dangerous when she came at midnight, behind the window of her turret, to wind around her pretty fingers, which I shall kiss momentarily, the long tresses of the blonde hair that I am kissing now in spite of you—*vous*, that is—when she opened her window and leaned out silently, in order to listen for the nightingale, which had stopped singing because I had frightened it, and when she challenged it with the tender cadences of her favorite ballad: *Amour, one must bless your chains, when two lovers have to suffer . . .*"

"What horror!" Séraphine cried. "You were spying on me, Monsieur?"

"You can call it what you wish, but when you are ill, I'm afraid, and when I'm afraid for you, I no longer know what I'm doing."

She reflected for a moment. I sensed that I no longer had any need to retain her. How can one divine that?? My arms had relaxed. She disengaged hers, stretched them a little in order to relieve their numbness, and threw them around my neck.

"Poor friend that I accuse and I render anxious," she said, leaning her forehead on my shoulder. "Perhaps he won't forgive me! Because you're quite capable of that, silly as I know you are, for having passed through the *owl-hole?*"

"The route isn't easy, but it's the shortest, and I was in too much of a hurry to take the other."

"It makes one tremble, what you're saying! A path carved in the rock over a frightful precipice!"

"A path as wide as that of a kitchen garden, over a drop as profound as the terrace from the mansard of your pavilion."

"Well, that's not reassuring. Accidents happen every year in broad daylight. What if you had encountered the owl?"

"I'd have carried it away in my net like a nocturnal moth, even if it were only a short-eared owl. Three months ago I would have stuffed it, but a nasty owl of that species is only good for nailing to the door of the château as a scarecrow."

"Wait, wait," she said, suddenly composing her pretty face in order to assume a solemn expression, and drawing away an inch or two with an admirable dignity. "That isn't all, Monsieur; that's nothing! What is inexcusable in your conduct is that you didn't think of the danger of compromising me."

Compromising was even worse than *advantageous.* I was thunderstruck.

"Compromise you, Séraphine! I would be in despair if I compromised you . . . but I don't know, exactly, what that is."

She let a smile of indulgent superiority fall upon me.

"It's sufficient, Monsieur," Séraphine continued, "that I absolutely do not want anyone to permit himself to be in the park at night. Today I'll forgive you," she added, holding out her hand for me to kiss, "because I know that your heart is pure; but it must never happen again. Society is so perverse!"

It is necessary to note that *perverse* had a foot and a half in Séraphine's mouth; it was the *verbum sesquipedale* of my Horace.

"Eh! What does perverse society matter? What has it to say to my tenderness and my anxiety? It would ill befit perverse society to think badly of my being in pain for Séraphine when Séraphine is ill! To fear for your life and not to do anything, not to brave anything in order to see you! Certainly, I won't promise that!"

"Good, good," she said, taking my hand again, "if I were truly in danger. Do you think that I would want to die without seeing you again? That would be worse than death!"

At the same instant, her sisters and my friend rejoined us, and that day we embraced before them for the first time.

The moments of which I speak were so sweet that it is not surprising that I have abandoned myself to the pleasure of recounting them at length.

That lasted for four or five months, and then it finished forever.

At the beginning of October—I no longer know which day of Brumaire it was—we saw Chapuis arrive, a former domestic of Monsieur de C***, an honest, faithful and even affectionate old man, but whose severe and forbidding face had always seemed to me to be appropriate to bearing bad news. The news concerning me on that occasion was devastating. My parents, delighted with the progress they believed they remarked in my studies, had agreed to testify their satisfaction by allowing me to spend the winter in Paris under the supervision of an amiable and sage man whose attachment they had experienced.

The ninth of Thermidor[1] had just put an end to the bloody

---

1 The ninth of Thermidor of Year II (27 July 1794) was the day when Maximilien Robespierre was denounced by Jean-Lambert Tallien and stripped of the power he enjoyed as the dominant figure of the Committee of Public Safety, thus marking the end of the "Reign of Terror."

sacrifices of the druids of the Revolution. France, intoxicated by its liberation, was beginning to repose from the convulsions of the Terror in a purer atmosphere. It was reborn to the sciences, the fine arts, and the leisures of civilized people. It was almost reborn to happiness, for everything was able to seem fortunate the day after the anarchy. Of the entire world, I only knew the rural and simple nature of our solitudes. It was a matter of enabling me to see the collections, the libraries, the monuments, the people—the world, in sum—in which the imagination of the best of fathers assigned me in hope an agreeable, and perhaps distinguished, position.

All of that would have made me smile at him in circumstances in which the journey would not have cost anything to my heart, but the exile of the nobles still subsisted, and I felt faint at the idea of quitting my friend for such a long time, for the length of a winter was something measurable to children. I don't know whether you remember that. I did not say anything, but the thought of waking up twenty-five times on a Sunday morning without being able to promise myself that I would see Séraphine and end the day in her company broke my heart so cruelly, that I could only accustom myself to supporting it on condition of dying of it. Twenty-five Sundays, alas, extended far beyond my count!

It was, however, necessary to submit to it. Monsieur de C***, who measured time better and knew better what it was worth, talked to me about the long months of absence as a day that I would pass in pleasures. We merely owed visits to all our neighbors before the time fixed for my departure, of which I was not informed, because I trembled to know it.

The project of visits consoled me slightly; it would take me back to the château, and I demonstrated to myself silently that five hours of amity, regrets and Séraphine's caresses would compensate my life adequately for five months of dolor. I perceived from the following day onwards that our slow walks were taking me further and further away from the unique object of my thoughts, but I was not afflicted by that. I was, on the contrary, infinitely grateful to Monsieur de C*** for having given that direction to our ceremonious itinerary.

So much the better, I said to myself, *it's with her that we'll finish; her farewell kiss will be the last that I take away on my lips, and I shall conserve it there with so much care that it will be during that voyage as if I had not quit her.*

For six days we roamed the country like that, almost without speaking. Monsieur de C*** seemed bitterly sad, and if I brought Séraphine's name, as was my custom, into our conversations, he hastened to change the subject, as if from a disquieting and troublesome idea. I lost myself trying to fathom the reason for that new reticence between us, for he loved Séraphine almost as much as he loved me, and I would have found it quite natural if he had loved her more.

As we occupied the only lodgments that were disposable in the house we had established Chapuis in my room, where he set up a folding bed every evening in front of my window.

On the day in question Chapuis found me, as usual, occupied in taking note of the species that I had collected during the excursion, and he was obliged to interrupt me in order to engage me to go to sleep. That unaccustomed precaution surprised me.

"You see," he said, "We're leaving tomorrow at six o'clock precisely, in order to be at the relay of the Paris diligence, and although I've already packed all your clothes in the carriage, it's possible that you'll still have something to do before mounting it. You only have a short time to rest before I wake you up."

"Tomorrow at six o'clock!" I cried. "That isn't possible! I certainly can't leave without having seen Séraphine!"

"It's necessary, however," Chapius retorted, "for the diligence won't wait, and if you stayed, do you think that Monsieur de C**** would permit you to see Mademoiselle

Séraphine in the state the poor child is in? He'd be too fearful of the effects of contagion, as they call it. He hasn't had any other reason to keep you away from here all week."

"Séraphine is ill and I didn't know! Explain yourself, my friend, I beg you!"

"Ill, ill," replied Chapuis, shaking his head. "I've been forbidden to tell you, but it's necessary that you know one day or another; today's news isn't good. Fortunately, the providence of God is great, especially for young people, and if it permits, you'll find Mademoiselle Séraphine in the spring livelier and lovelier than ever. And then, they won't fail to write to inform you of her cure in Paris, and you'll have the consolation of it without having had the chagrin of quitting her while she's ill."

While he was saying that, Chapuis turned the key, took it out of the lock, put it in his pocket, closed the window and slipped into his bed without undressing, in order to be ready sooner in the morning.

"What are you doing, Chapuis? You've closed the window, and you know that I can't do without air! I've often told you that."

"Good, good," he said, plunging under his blanket, "don't travelers have to accustom themselves to everything? You'll be much more cramped in the carriage, believe me! Do you imagine, my dear young man, that you'll always be at your ease? You won't get open windows in October in your lodgings. In any case, Monsieur is too good not to have any regard for my rheumatism, in this cold! It's a true winter evening!"

I had no objections to raise against that last argument. My situation was horrible. I snuffed out my light but I did not go to bed. I waited until he was asleep in order to turn the window-catch and leap with a single bound into the street over the accursed folding-bed, at the risk of breaking my neck. The desired moment did not take long to arrive, but Chapuis' slumber was as light as it was sudden, and at the slightest movement I was warned by a brutal "Who goes there!" of the vigilance of my inexorable sentinel. I came back ten times, and ten times I was repelled. In the meantime, Séraphine might be calling for me! It was a frightful night.

Finally, the clock struck four—that was more than I believed myself to be still capable of counting, and the alarm bell informed me that Chapuis had chosen that hour to go and make the preparations for departure. I rolled over as if startled on my noisy straw, in order to give him notice of my presence while he struck the tinder-box methodically and lit a hooded lantern. I thought that he would never end. How long his operations appeared to me, and how I cursed the clumsiness and slowness of old age!

He went out, however, and I heard the key turn on me from outside. I scarcely cared about that. Its last creak covered very conveniently the sound of the casement opening. Before the prudent Chapuis had reached the stable, I was on the other side of the village.

It required nothing less than my habitude of the locale for me to steer through the darkness of that rigorous morning. There was not an atom of light in all of nature. The most opaque and the most obscure objects were only outlined by the faintest contour on the horizon, as obscure as them. No rain was falling, but the atmosphere was inundated by a black, thick, almost palpable mist that penetrated my garments and enveloped my limbs like an icy bath. I had seen nothing, divined nothing, and imagined nothing before then that gave me such a frightening idea of Erebus and chaos. I stumbled over all obstacles; I fell; I got up again; I sounded the route with my foot and the darkness with my gaze. I only orientated myself by means of my memory or my heart. I said: *it must be that way*, and I went on.

When I arrived at the "owl's hole" I only recognized it by the projections of the rock, which overhung in certain places in such a way as to oblige me to lower my head, and which I followed with my hand in order not to risk stepping off the path, for it would have cost my life. The path was, in fact, wide enough, as I had said to Séraphine, to leave room, in the narrowest passages, for two pairs of feet like mine, but it was cut into the living rock, and the oozing water that wet it incessantly had sensibly inclined its slope and degraded its exterior edge, the inequalities of which I encountered incessantly when I tried to gain a little terrain in order to relax my constraint. The congealed mist also hid its cold and polished surface, carpeting it with a slippery frost where I only assured my step with incredible efforts, intruding my fingers into all the cracks in the rock and clinging from time to time to those that were deep enough to sustain me while I recovered, at the thought of Séraphine, some strength and some courage.

Suddenly, I heard a singular noise, and my cheeks were beaten by a heavy flutter of wings: two circumstances that, in the disposition of my mind, were not apt to diminish my terror; but I thought instantly that it must be the owl, whose solitude had been troubled by my nocturnal disturbance, and I soon had no doubt of it. It came to alight a few paces away from me, fixing its round and luminous eyes on the usurper of its perilous domain

"Thank you," I said, "for coming to lend two torches to my journey; but I don't trust them as much as is necessary not to give you the pitiless joy of dragging me into the ditches of your pleasure-house. I know that you're in insidious host, and I know, thank Heaven, for having measured them with my eyes more than once, the depths that separate us."

It preceded me thus for a long time, fluttering, hopping, mewling like a cat, hissing like a snake, and alighting at measured intervals with a lamentable groan that would have frozen the blood in a woman's veins. I no longer feared anything. The route was broadening out.

I ran, I jumped, I hopped, I was content; I was going to see her again. Nevertheless, I promised myself to return by a surer route.

I arrived at the avenue of chestnut trees.

The foliage had been depleted since my last journey, and I saw the faint pale light coming from a casement in the tower vacillating from further away.

A fire in Séraphine's room! I thought. *She's still ill, then!*

I did not stop; I crossed the terrace; I sought and found the door that opened on that side. It yielded under my hand; it was ajar. That astonished me. I went into the corridor and reached the entrance to the spiral stairway that led to Séraphine's room. The staircase was illuminated, unusually.

After two or three turns of the spiral I saw that the light was coming from a candle placed on a step above my head, on which poor Lila was sitting to one side, her elbows on her knees and her head in her hands, and who appeared to be asleep, doubtless became she had been keeping vigil and fatigue had overtaken her on the way down. I went past her quietly, in order not to disturb her slumber.

A light was still paling the landing; it was emerging from Séraphine's bedroom. The two battens of the door were applied to the walls. The lamp was on the floor; behind it I discerned two old women whom I had often seen asking for alms at the château; they were crouching, mute and occupied, and by the movement of their arms it seemed to me that they were sewing something.

I went forward; they did not raise their heads. I ran to the alcove; Séraphine's bed was unmade, the pillows overturned, the covers dangling. It was empty.

Assailed by vague, confused, impenetrable ideas, I returned to the place where I had seen the old women, in order to obtain information from them regarding Séraphine and the motive that had caused her to change her bed; but I no longer had the strength to hear their response. That response, I already knew.

What they were sewing was a white sheet, and what they were sewing in that white sheet was Séraphine.

I have often been asked since then why I was sad.

Clémentine

I was twenty-three years old, and I only knew of the turbulent fever that is called amour in that woeful generation whose destiny is to misunderstand all its sentiments: a bitter, sharp, devouring malady without compensation and without hope, whose emotions are crises and impulses convulsions; a frenzy full of tragic visions, among which appears an image of a woman, like Psyche in Hell, an inaccessible, ungraspable phantom surrounded by all the demons of the imagination and all the furies of the heart.

If a circumstance that I was no longer seeking, because I knew that the consequences were always similar, if the caprice of chance delivered me, real and alive, the illusion with which I was madly smitten, if I succeeded in making a conquest—or a prey—when I had snatched away her final veil, nothing remained beneath but an insensible marble statue. My hand froze upon a cold hand unable to squeeze; my kisses were extinguished on icy lips that had never exhaled a heartfelt sigh. That divinity was, at the most, only a woman; I said to myself: "It's not her," and I plunged back impatiently into the vagueness of my dreams, in order to demand of them another amour and other dolors.

That delirium, in which my life was consumed, was not an individual accident, the unfortunate exception of an unfortunate organization. It was the horrible symptom of an unknown passion, unnamed and yet common to the majority of souls that nature had imprinted, in those days, with a certain character of energy and exaltation; it was a profound and dolorous need for ordeals, for agitations, for suffering and, above all, for change, the revelation of an invincible instinct of destruction, of social annihilation, repressed in the bosom of a people tamed by iron institutions or distracted in camps by bloody ambitions, but which roared in the depths of idle souls like the subterranean fires that announce by a long rumbling, before opening a passage, the disasters with which they will terrify the world.

All that frightful power of confused, discordant, irritated elements, colliding and conflicting, catching fire and ending up rolling over the earth, bursting forth in a tempest of revolutions, all those furies mistaken in their object, of which we, the orphan children of liberty disinherited by Napoléon, no longer know what to make, follow us into the narrow career left to us, into the midst of the most natural affections, the mildest sentiments of the human heart.

One more poetic comparison to rid my pen of a few luxurious phrases that prevent the ink from flowing, and I shall make no more. When a stream of molten lava finds itself interrupted in its course by an insurmountable wall of rock, you will see it revolt, rise up seething like a tide against the barrier that imprisons it, bound, rebound and fall back, howling, and finally turn away, expanding in the distance, rolling, spreading its inflamed waves through peaceful valleys and orchards laden with flowers.

Beneath these metaphors there is a story. It is thus that we have savored the felicities of the beautiful age . . .

I sense that I have difficulty today in taking account of those impressions, which I felt so distinctly then. Words, words, and nothing more. The thought is no longer here to vivify the speech. The hearth of the blaze still subsists, but it is no longer anything but ashes.

The change that was operated within my ideas was sudden; it was strange; for a long time it was an incomprehensible mystery for me. The disorder of my metaphysical passions distanced me in Paris from the methodical and circumspect world in which the wild impetuosity that my comrades mistook for enthusiasm had given me the reputation of a peevish child with a deranged brain.

The principles of hostile and violent opposition into which I had precipitated myself blindly, probably in order to throw a few dangers more into my adventurous route, would easily have opened to me two or three salons of the aristocracy of the old order, infatuated with their nobility but quite accustomed to descending from its sublime heights when it was a matter of linking the devotions of a young courage to the to the interests to the good cause; but I only frequented one of them, because I bore more intimate affections there, the penchant that draws us toward compatriots whose name has often resounded around our cradle; the habitude of respect inspired in a province more than elsewhere by the illustriousness of a historic family of which college and tradition have signaled the monuments; the memory, above all, of a particular benevolence, of which my family had felt the effects for several generations, and which had latterly extended as far as me. Soon, I no longer went anywhere else. I did more; I took condescension to the point of ridding myself, apparently at first, but eventually quite genuinely, of the umbrageous melancholy of my sentimental profligacy. What has remained to me is truly nothing. What would one not do to give more pleasure to those by whom we believe ourselves to be loved?

There are people who will think that the sacrifice in question might have had another, secret motive that I have forgotten, and I have thought that too; but I doubt it. At any rate, I gradually became almost well-behaved, and I perceived that I had become well-behaved because I had become happy.

My noble patrons had no children, but amity had given them a charming ward in a young woman of our common homeland, who had emerged some time before from one of the brilliant boarding-schools of the capital, and her mother had judged it appropriate to let her spend an entire year in the milieu of a perfectly chosen society, in order to contract there the elegant habitudes that education does not teach, and which embellish, so it is said, the most fortune natures. (Embellishing the natural—do you hear?)

She too was very noble, of one of those chivalric and feudal nobilities with banners and crenellations, which were accompanied by great fanfares five or six hundred years ago in tourneys, and filled chronicles and romances with their prowess. That was, however, the first thing one forgot in her presence, so simple, modest and gracious was she in her welcome; for even fantasy cannot compose, in the marvelous reveries that surpass the work of art, and sometimes that of God, a more complete assemblage of charms and virtues, naivety and wit, innocence and sensibility. Another might have dared to depict her, but if I knew that Lawrence[1] had conceived that insolent presumption, and if someone had succeeded in convincing me that the sacrilegious painting were suspended behind me, in the empty panel, sad to behold, that faces my alcove, which some less precious ornament might suit well enough, I certainly would not turn around, unless a friend had veiled it for the sake of pity. No, I would not turn around, for fear of damaging the idea, so vivid and still so pure, that I have conserved of the model. I hold portraits in horror!

Clémentine was eighteen years old.

It was easy for me to misinterpret the attraction, new for me, that bore us toward one another. The calm conversations that filled the heart without upsetting it, the tender effusions in which two friendly thoughts were confounded, the ingen-

---

1 The portrait painter Thomas Lawrence (1769-1830).

uous pleasure of seeing one another and being together, were unfamiliar to me. I had only experienced the relationships of souls that were in friction, which tortured one another, which pushed one another to despair. I had never imagined amour without hallucinations and without fever; and what I felt in Clémentine's company was a universal wellbeing that tended toward ecstasy; a perpetual fête of the heart, which reflected on all my sensations; the preoccupation of a mind fascinated by delectable illusions, which plunged into them with delight without questioning their reality, and which is not even troubled in their possession by the fear of losing them.

There was an atmosphere around Clémentine, a glow, a nature, a sky that was not elsewhere. Her voice had a melody other than music; her gaze had an element other than fire. I could have distinguished among a thousand women the light tread of her feet and the rustle of her dress; and if I arrived before her at the place where I was sure of encountering her every day, there was a moment when my swollen arteries, or my suspended respiration, or my eyes, dazzled by a fantastic light, alerted me to her approach. Like a priestess receiving communications from her divinity, I said: *She is coming!* And she came; for there were currents in the air, insensible for others, in which I found a source of life and happiness when Chementine's breath was mingled with them. I will not take responsibility for the explanation of that phenomenon.

With what a blow a man would have struck me then who had said to me, with the egotistical apathy that is called reflection and sang-froid: "What that young women inspires in you, insensate that you are, is amour!"

Amour for Clémentine! By what entitlement? And for what future? Under the auspices of what religion, and on the steps of what altar, could I receive her oaths? Damnation! The scepters of the twenty hereditary tyrants whose names she bore would have been raised from their marble tombs, making the air whistle, brandishing their swords so long immobile; the wyverns and dragons of armories, suddenly animated by the protective fay of her ancestors, would have descended from the ruined keeps where they still embraced the remains of a shield hidden under the moss, in order to come and place themselves between her and me on the road to the sanctuary.

What am I saying? Would not her mother, whom she loved so much, and by whom she was so loved, have appeared, dying of dolor, and perhaps cursing her? I would have broken my heart a hundred times over if I had thought it capable of opening itself to such a frenzy.

That is not all. Clémentine was rich, much richer than I had any hope of ever being; and on that matter my resolution was irrevocably made. With regard to that kind of incompatibility I did not know of any possible transaction. Amour counted in gold coins on the threshold of the nuptial chamber! What ignominy! Molten lead poured drop by drop into my veins in order to spare her a tear—fine!

I had no idea of those dangers; they never cost me any sleep. It was not amour, in my opinion, it was something very different; I did not know what, however, and I did not seek to define it. Who before me could have taken it into his head to name such a sentiment? Do the people who make words know the secret of all the thoughts that will awaken between now and the end of time in the depths of a human soul? The worthy pedants, with their names and their definitions! I enclose there, nothing is surer, an entire language for which the human voice has no speech; and I know that language even though I cannot write it. And if I write it some day, will anyone understand it?

I perceived at the end of a few months that my visits, increasingly frequent, were received a little more coldly. Clémentine testified in my regard an almost-ceremonious reserve, which appeared more imposed than natural to her expansive character. A frankly tender impulse, an insignificant word that I was able to understand, a gaze without apparent object that I was able to seize, one of those nothings that are everything, sufficed to console me. That equivocal position did not last long enough, in any case, to give me time to conceive any serious anxieties. My sojourn in Paris had a term already exceeded; in spite of the insistences of my father, I do not know how I would have resolved to leave if Clémentine had not been disposed to return soon to live in our province. The day of adieux finally arrived, with all its sadness, but still embellished in hope by a minute of happiness. I was disappointed; Clémentine was not there.

At the moment when I was traversing a small room that preceded the apartment, in order to leave, I encountered her. I have forgotten what I said to her, what I tried to say to her, but I remember that she did not respond. We were distant enough from one another because, from the moment when we had seen one another, we had each remained motionless in our place. I dared to look at her intently, because she was not looking at me, and yet her attention did not appear to be occupied with any other object.

Her physiognomy had a vague, mysterious, extraordinary expression, which I had not yet remarked in her features. She was pale, she gave the impression of suffering, or of having suffered. I did not persist in futile speech; my imagination would not have furnished any; my mouth would have attempted in vain to articulate it. Either because my head had gone astray or because I had judged poorly the rights that amity gave me— the passionate amity of which I spoke just now—I launched myself toward her with an extravagant impetuosity; I seized her hand; I was about to bear it to my lips when she snatched it away abruptly, in a manner that announced anger and fear.

"Clémentine!" I exclaimed, suddenly raising my eyes to hers. I found the same mixture of indignation and terror there, but I scarcely had time to see it, and I persuaded myself quite easily thereafter that I might have been mistaken about the nature and the cause of her emotion. She had disappeared, uttering an indefinable plaint, a dull and profound groan, the tone of which tore my heart. It seemed to me that it was not thus that we ought to separate.

However, I departed.

All that had only filled a minute. That minute filled six months of my life. For six months I saw her in that attitude, with that gaze, and I did not see anything else. For six months I felt her hand being snatched away from mine, which tried convulsively to retain it. The dolorous cry that could have translated as many various sentiments, the ever-new interpretation of which caused me to pass in the same instant from the purest sensuality to the delirium of dolor, I heard for six months. A grave study, a pressing peril, a fête, a duel, nothing could distract me from it, and I would not have wanted to be distracted at any price.

When the world drew me in spite of myself into the torrent of its affairs and dissipations, I never ceased to repeat Clémentine's name in a whisper, in order to isolate myself from the multitude; I made it resound like a perpetual echo of the soul through all my thoughts. I knew how long it took to pronounce it, to write it a thousand times, and that was the sole employment of my hours, the sole joy of my solitude. I had succeeded in imagining that distance and time only kept us apart in appearance; that I had never really quit her; that another self, more constant and more assiduous, with whom I communicated effortlessly, lived alongside her life and her presence, and that I witnessed through him the scantly varied scenes of her days, like an invisible spectator.

That dress suits her, I said; *she has put it on today because she has divined that I can see her, and she has remembered appropriately that no color is more agreeable to me. What concern is making a slight shadow pass over her brow? I can't be mistaken, for it's her habit then to roll her fingers like that in the curls of her hair. Someone has spoken to her about an idea that irritates her and constrains her; I'm sure of that because of the imperceptible crease that has just been designed over her slightly-raised eyebrow. Perhaps she's threatened by some delay in her journey! Thank Heaven, the obstacle has been removed; the crease is fading away; she's smiling. She's happy then, to come back . . . ! And I too am happy!*

One day, it was said that she was arriving, and a few days later, that she had arrived. I doubt that the change in my situation caused me more disturbance than pleasure. I had little understanding of the new order of relations that was about to be established between us. I could not foresee clearly its range and consequences. It seemed to me that I had not had time to prepare myself for it, and that it was too soon to see her; Sometimes, I would have preferred to stay as I was, under a pleasant illusion, which only depended on me, the enchantment of which no will other than mine could break.

When I was told that she was about to pass by, my breast heaved as if it were about to burst; my legs felt weak, my eyes were veiled; I did not see her. It was during an excursion. On the return journey I decided to master myself and affirm my soul, to submit to the overwhelming wellbeing that frightened me because it lacked very little in order to be mortal.

We greeted her. She responded gracefully, but without giving us reason to believe that she had noticed anyone in particular among us. I tried to renew that proof. She looked this time, but her distracted eyes turned away when they were about to encounter mine. The young people who were accompanying me soon swelled one by one the group where she was seated. Then she no longer looked. When she departed, the movement of the crowd had pushed me so close to her that she was almost obliged to brush pass me; she only afforded me as much attention as is necessary to avoid an embarrassment that one finds in one's path.

It was her, however; I had seen her at close enough range to recognize her. I had even heard her; she was laughing.

There were frightful nights.

The next day, the day after, often, I encountered her on her own. She saluted me again, as if regretfully, without looking at me, or, at the most, while letting a leaden gaze fall upon me. I thought I understood.

Nothing is more natural, I said to myself. *It is, indeed, Clémentine, but no longer the one that I have seen; it is no longer the society in which we were both placed, and society is the element in which she lives, the source from which she draws her thought. In the immense chaos of Paris, all inequalities disappear, all conditions are confounded. Thus far, the art of blazoning human faces has not been invented; a man who frequents the nobility receives a reflection of it in the eyes of the vulgar. Have I not heard ten times over imbecile domestics awarding me in announcing me their stupid particule. It was the passport, the letter of credit, of the presumptuous commoner, the insolent explanation of the masters' welcome, a borrowed seal that falsified my social value in the interests of their pride. Here, I am only me, the obscure bourgeois of whom these walls will attest if necessary the honorable but simple origin, the despicable worm that spins a coarse cocoon in the branches of bushes, and whose radiant flight the swarm of stupid butterflies cannot foresee. That humiliation is, fundamentally, the necessary consequence of my error, I have been dreaming!*

No, I went on, immediately; *no, that's not possible. Such a vulgar weakness is easily understandable in that populace of nobles, who are only capable of distinguishing things by their appearance, but it is incompatible with the generous sentiments of a tender, elevated, powerful soul, the masterpiece and honor of creation. A few months suffice to overturn empires, to level moun-*

tains and to displace rivers from their bed, but eternity would not be enough to produce such a metamorphosis in that elite organization where God has deposited the seed of so much goodness and virtue, where a sublime nature has protected that precious seed against the influence of education and prejudice; where I have seen it develop, fortify itself, grow to a height inaccessible to the flight of enthusiasm. It's necessary to search elsewhere for the reasons for my misfortune.

Who knows in what colors I might have been painted before her? Who knows, alas, what pretext has not been furnished to the evil offices of hatred by the agitation, the violence and the excess of the two or three years of epilepsy and dementia that preceded the day when I saw her for the first time? It's in that context that she knows me today, so different from what she imagined, and my veritable character, the one that I owe to nature or to Clémentine, is nothing in her eyes but the odious mask of a hypocrite. She thinks she has seen through me. She despises and abhors me. That's all!

I settled on that idea, frightful as it was. Perhaps I settled on it because it was frightful. Hazard soon procured me the opportunity to clarify the matter.

I no longer know what obligation had delivered me to the ennui of one of those soirées of ostentation and celebration that are insupportable everywhere, but nowhere as much as in "good company." Clémentine arrived late, giving the excuse of a headache that had tormented her, and which left very evident traces on her dejected visage, I had been unable to avoid her sight and the humiliating expression of her disdainful politeness, but when everyone was seated I remained standing and affected to head for the door of the drawing room in order to make her understand that it was not the hope of encountering her that brought me into that crowd.

My intention was, in fact, to leave, but I lacked the strength. I fell into an armchair fortunately distant from the circle of conversations and games, in order that I could believe myself to be alone and abandon myself without constraint to the painful ideas that oppressed me. The species of annihilation into which I was plunged scarcely permitted me to notice that the noise gradually diminished around me, and that the society, attracted by symphonies that were being played in a marquee in the garden, had displaced it entirely into the middle of an illuminated avenue.

Clémentine had doubtless alleged her illness in order to dispense her from taking part in those pleasures, and, her head supported in her hand, from which the waves of her blonde hair streamed, she was still there, leaning over the arm of a sofa.

I shivered and stood up. She uttered a small cry on receiving me and got up to leave. I was in her passage.

"Forgive me, Mademoiselle," I said, opposing my extended arm to her, "but do not go any further without responding to me. The repose, the well being and the honor of my life demand that I obtain an explanation from you."

"An explanation!" cried Clémentine, astonished.

"My impatience and my disturbance don't permit the choice of words. There are interests graver for me than a vain observation of politeness. Forgive me, I repeat, and soon forget, if possible, what is irregular, inconvenient and reckless in my action, but listen to me first. You owe that to yourself. What infamous reports, what cunning lies, have caused to fall on me the anger and the scorn of the only person in the world whose esteem is dear to me?"

"I would have judged singularly," she replied, with some hauteur, "the impression that the sight of you caused me to experience, if it were manifest in my physiognomy in an offensive manner. I have no reason to be scornful of you. Anger, even coldness, suppose a habitude of intimate relations that has never been able to bring us together. No one has permitted themselves to employ on your account a language to which I would not have taken the trouble to listen, and which I would certainly have forgotten. Your repose, wellbeing and honor have, therefore, only been seriously compromised in your imagination, the movements of which I have neither the right nor the desire to repress, but which will oblige me forcefully, in future, to spare myself the disobliging role that it makes me play in its . . . whims. My impatience and my disturbance no longer permit me the choice of words."

She took a step toward the avenue.

"I accept without difficulty that rigorous clarification," I said stopping her, "and I hold it to be a complete satisfaction; but it is important to me to tell you again that you have wronged my character in taxing it with an overly bold presumption for the faith I had put in your amity. An imagination less subject to the whims for which you reproach mine might perhaps have been mistaken about that, like me; the memory of sentiments is not effaced so rapidly in all hearts, and if my heart could open to your eyes, Clémentine, you would be able to judge the depth of its wound . . ."

"I hope that in that case, Monsieur," she said, raising her head in an imperious and decided manner, "you would have enough sense and delicacy to dispense me from receiving your confidences!"

She left, for I did not retain her any longer. Not one idea, not one determination, remained to me. She had killed my soul.

That's as well, I thought, when I was free. *That one too is only a woman, and a woman still noble—which is to say, all that is poorest and pettiest in a sketch of an aborted being, multiplied by all the pettinesses and poverties of a stupid prejudice. Proud little girl! Does it not seem that she holds my existence in her hands, like a toy that is only good for throwing away or breaking? And on what does hers depend, to justify so much arrogance and inso-*

lence? Are the torches that burned her father's château so utterly extinct that vengeance and despair cannot reignite them? Does not my voice have a sufficiently proven power over those men of carnage and desolation, who drink blood but whose thirst is not appeased by blood, to summon them one day to a cannibal feast?

The revolutions are not all in the past, and thus far, I have not marked definitively therein either my flag or my place. Commoners! We will be, in order to return, since you wish it, to working the land. We will dig there with our fingers, like hyenas, and we will open a ditch there that will devour you all. Oh, how beautiful it would be to see her escape semi-naked through the pack of my famished dogs, to seek a refuge in these arms that she has rejected, to press her breast, palpitating with horror, to the breast that she has torn, and, head tilted back, cry for mercy and pity while blinking her frightened eyes in the flashes of the dagger!

Pity for you, viper! And what can you fear? Are you not noble, Clémentine, and has fear troubled your infantile heart to the point of making you forget that the blade of the people breaks or is deflected against the loins of a noble maiden? Where, otherwise, would be the privilege of your race? Your heart? Have you spared mine? Nothing can bring us together, according to you! Who told you that? You did not think of the embrace of the victim and the murderer. Look! It is as complete, as passionate and a thousand times more voluptuous than that of amour!

How pale you are! How you fear death! How you implore me, in a cowardly fashion! Why, there is not a single drop of noble blood in your veins! You are no more courageous than you were good and beautiful when I thought I loved you. What are you saying about sensibility, humanity and forgiveness? Oh, I have a confused idea of the sentiment you are asking of me, but I un-learned it once and for all, I no longer know where, one spring evening, in a ballroom, to the sound of a symphony that went to the soul. Perhaps I would remember it for a child, for an old man, for any human being who might say me: 'Don't kill me!' and who would squeeze my hand. But for a noble young woman, never!

"It's necessary that she die!"

I said that aloud as I ran along the promenade, already abandoned by everyone, to which hazard had brought me by a route I do not know. Those last words struck my ear as if they had been articulated next to me by a demon.

"Oh, my God, my God," I said, fearfully, "efface from the eternal book those execrable blasphemies! It isn't me who proffered them! It can't be me. I have no weapons; I don't want weapons; I have no blood on my hands; I haven't killed anyone!"

And I threw myself down at the foot of a tree near to which she had the custom of sitting down. The sand that struck my head she had trodden the previous day. I ran my fingers over it; I pressed my ardent lips to it and I crushed it between my teeth.

I had understood all my misfortunes at once. I knew, with no more doubt about it, that the fever that she had ignited in my blood was frantic amour, sick and furious amour, an absurd passion, without hope and without excuse, the extravagance of which could only be measured by my misery. I wept with rage and indignation against myself. I feared going mad, and then desired it.

A madman loves whomever he pleases, he sees no obstacle to his desires; he suffers a woe to which he does not expect an end, and he does not suffer alone, for he is sure of being loved. He will marry that sensible and faithful woman separated from him by the hatred of a rival she detests, or the malice of an enchanter who also persecutes her. He must marry her soon, when the galleons from India have brought back his treasures, and when the rebel vassals come to beg him on their knees to resume his rights and his crown. He believes in the future; and I did not know any happiness possible for me that was worth as much as his illusion—for me, whose destiny no event could change; for me, who would not have accepted Clémentine's hand if she had offered it to me.

Frightful tyranny of society, which throws a man into a paradise of delights, and says to him like the jealous God: "You shall not touch this elite fruit of predilection, because I have reserved it for myself!"

Think about it! Even when you no longer exist, except by virtue of the sentiment that is forbidden to you, you are permitted—what am I saying? you are prescribed—life. The chain of your soul is riveted to the odious prison of the flesh, of which everyone carries the key under the handle of his penknife or in the sheath of his sword. Truly, the imagination richest in malevolence, most ingenious in tortures, would not advise such a refinement of cruelty! Misunderstand what a work of divine vengeance might be! The happiness of a maniac or the repose of a cadaver, a padded cell at Bicêtre or a stone slab in the Morgue, that is everything. If you cannot choose, resign yourself with a good grace to all the refinements of a torture that will only expire with your last breath, that will only die when you die, and perhaps will recommence! To recommence, revive, remember, and know that it will be forever! There is nothing comparable to that idea in all the terrors of agony.

I did not appear any longer. I had broken all the fragile bonds that one mistakes for attachments, the bird-catcher's net over a wounded tiger. Nothing smiled at me. Nothing was capable of removing my attention from that chaos of dolorous dreams in which nothing fixed it. I would not have turned round to see the sun collapse.

That was remarked, because everything is remarked in the narrow circle of a small town. Two or three vaporous women, two or three young men harassed by ennui, who came to exhaust the ordinary text of conversation—rain and fine weather, the debut of a singer, the attire of an absent friend, the diaphanous intrigue of a scatterbrain and a fool—deigned to communicate complaisantly their conjectures on the origin and symptoms of the moral malady that had distanced me from society since the solemnly memorable epoch when I had figured for the last time among the actors in a political scandal, the dupes of a coquette or the victims of a card game. The unknown misfortune that had caused my alienation was deplored. That was necessary in order to observe it.

Those rumors reached my school-friends, of whom I had lost sight ten years before between the *Selectae è profanis* and the *Fables* of Phaedrus, when the old colleges were closed.

Ferdinand was numbered among those honest gentlemen of the fields whose dovecot represented well enough a Medieval keep when one looked at it from a distance, with the disposition required to adopt that illusion; who had a large drawing-room garnished with dilapidated tapestry and old furniture, once very elegant; and who strolled after dinner in a gallery clad or masked to the frieze with family portraits unequal in dimensions and frames, but venerable in armor, ermine, tapering beards or ample wigs, heraldic inscriptions and Gothic dust; and who spent the rest of their time hunting with dogs or playing billiards, out of respect for the traditions of noble exercises. He was, moreover, a worthy and virtuous young man devoid of legal encumbrances, because his father had left him a clear and solid fortune that he was not concerned to augment; devoid of public employments because he knew neither pride nor ambition; and devoid of enemies because he was helpful to everyone and did not bear umbrage to anyone.

Nature had heaped him with wellbeing as it had provided him with goodness, and it had done well. He would have loved his retreat instinctively, he cherished it by habitude and by philosophy. An excellent young wife of the same rank and the same character had arrived four years ago to embellish it by sharing it. Two children, a pretty as angels and as healthy as peasants, had doubled the happy family since, to which it is necessary to add a few servants that were treated like other children. Four leagues from the town, on a delightful hillside, close to an immense forest that poured the freshness of its shade and the grace of its murmurs over the château, under a spacious and comfortable roof, between good, thick, well-plastered walls of cheerful aspect, which embraced a superb enclosure of seventeen arpents, of which the river bathed the white fence and maintained the fish-ponds, there was a tableau to make one weep with joy.

Ferdinand came to see me. He sat down beside me, shook my hand cordially and, after a moment of expressive silence during which each of us recalled more good memories of childhood than we would have had time to recount in two days, he said: "You're suffering, and I won't ask you the cause; there are chagrins that are relieved by expansion but there are others that are aggravated by showing them to others, like the wounds that the air envenoms, and of which the slightest contact irritates the pain. So we'll pass over that in order not to annoy you, although there might be more remedy than you think for your affliction."

I signified to him that he was mistaken.

"So be it," he said. "I won't return to it. Don't cure yourself, if such is your destiny or your desire; but don't reject even so the reliefs that might render the pain more tolerable, by giving you the strength to support it. You don't know any? I suspected as much. That's the way one reasons when one is unhappy, or believes oneself to be, which comes to much the same thing. There are, however, three whose effect never fails: amity, study and time. If they don't have any result this time, it's because you're placed in an exception of unhappiness of which no example has presented itself before, and I'm prepared to oblige you in that idea; but you'd render yourself culpable of injustice and ingratitude to my affection by refusing the trial that I propose.

"Listen to me: you probably won't renounce solitude, and I understand that. Solitude is a sad and severe friend for a mournful heart, but in sum, it is one, and anyone can find it. What I ask of you is to change it. Depart with me now. You have no need to be announced. Gabrielle knows you and likes you. Didn't she take part in our childhood games? Wasn't it her, if you recall, who played Clorinde at the château in the beautiful pantomime of *Jerusalem delivreée*, in which you were already so dreamy and melancholy under the armet of the grim Argent? You'll recognize your cardboard shield, magnificent covered in golden paper. It's still hanging from the nail to which you confided its precious weight when the end of the vacation forced us to quit Solyme and the armor of paladins to return to college and pick up the dictionary. You'll recognize the little room in the pavilion to the left of the façade, and in the preceding room, which is only inhabited on extraordinary occasions when we receive visitors, a library that was rather numerous in its time, which I have further augmented."

"I remember all that as if I could see it," I interrupted, taking Ferdinand's hand again. "Have you cut down that pretty section of woodland that made such a lovely curtain of verdure in front of my window?"

"Time has changed some things there, but I haven't. It has grown; it is now an admirable forest, and I think it might be necessary to lodge you elsewhere if you fear too dense a shade during the day and the song of the nightingale by night."

"Shade and a nightingale!" I exclaimed. "Oh, it's certainly there that I'll lodge!"

"You'll come, then?" said Ferdinand, in a tender voice.

An embrace was my response, and we departed.

The temporary pleasure of that short journey mingled with the bitterness of my life must have had a more potent charm, to judge by the place that it still holds in my memories. If I were writing a short story, a history or a book I would efface these details, which would have nothing to do with it, but I am writing what I remember, what I experienced, what I am experiencing, and these details are there.

A few weeks passed. My mind felt the calm of that peaceful abode, where there was not one thought that did not have for its object suspending my ennuis or effacing them entirely from my memory.

"We'll succeed in it, have no doubt," Ferdinand said to me one day. "You'll be reconciled with society, which I seek out very little, but which is not so hateful when one knows how to take from it only what is good, and to lend it the collaboration of a benevolence that is natural to all honest hearts, without engaging one's liberty to it. The commerce of women, especially, is an inexhaustible source of consolations, but until now you have loved them with the vehemence of your character, and I cannot imagine that that manner of feeling can have procured you a single moment of complete and pure felicity in their regard. Romantic sensibilities are always dupes, and it is the fault of their exigency. In order to obtain advantage from the frequentation of society it is necessary to take it as it is. By accommodating yourself to its currency, you will find that it has its price; I want to see you undertake that study, save for renouncing it when it importunes you. We're going to receive a charming society."

"Don't go any further. I believe everything you're said to me, but I'm not at that point in my cure. There is nothing more natural than enjoying a benefit that you understand. Let me avoid a torture that horrifies me; our agreement gives me the right. I'll come back when there's no charming society here except that of your wife and children. Don't talk to me about the other!"

"Under that condition," said Ferdinand, "I won't hinder your liberty; I promised you that. However, I still hope that you won't be obstinate in your excessively sudden resolution. There is one name that might inspire more indulgence for the visits I expect, that of Estelle de B***, of whom you made a rather vivid eulogy the other day, and who would be delighted, I'm sure, to encounter you here."

"I'll come back when she has gone."

"As you wish. Have I forgotten to tell you that her fortune and that of her cousin are much changed?"

"Her cousin? Is that possible? Is Clémentine poor?"

"That's strange! You said that as if you were capable of desiring it!"

"What folly. No one has wishes more ardent than me for Estelle's good fortune . . . and Clémentine's."

"They were only rich. They are much more so. A distant relative has left them a considerable heritage by testament, and, as the most beautiful domain in the region is part of it, I'm surprised not to have received them yet, since they've taken possession of it. It's only two leagues from my land."

"Clémentine as well," I murmured, mechanically, without paying any heed to the expression that the name might have in my mouth.

"Clémentine as well," Ferdinand replied, looking at me with a pensive attention. "Undoubtedly, Clémentine as well. Don't worry, I'm not trying to penetrate this mystery, although it excites my curiosity keenly. What faith is it necessary that I add to the rumor that has run around regarding your antipathy or your hatred, the memory of which escapes me? I only saw in it, in truth, an extravagant fable."

"And you were right! A thousand times extravagant! God preserve from falling under my hand the wretch who has compromised Clementine's name in his impertinent conjectures! Antipathy is a sentiment, and does Clémentine owe me a sentiment, I ask you? Where has she seen me? Where has she spoken to me? Does she even know me? And you do not permit someone to flee into a desert in order to curse men freely there!"

"Calm down. You're forgetting that it was your emotion that just reminded me of that conjecture, and that on another occasion it might have given birth to it."

"I've thought about it," I continued, in the more reflective tone that the momentary interruption had given me time to affect. "It's true that that fatal name awakens a dolorous thought, which my visage must betray when I hear it pronounced, but it relates to another woman, a Clémentine that I once knew, who was dear to me then, whom the earth no longer possesses. That circumstance explains everything. Make what usage of it you wish, and let me leave."

The sun had already set when we returned to the drawing room via the staircase of the terrace, at the moment when the opposite door opened to let in three women: the mistress of the house and two others, whose carriage had just stopped at the gate. The first passed before me, smiling; that was Estelle. The second was Clémentine. She recoiled, as if she had stepped on a snake.

In the disturbance that I was trying to contain, I only caught a few snatches of the conversation at intervals. Clémentine's voice reached me most distinctly.

"We were hoping, in fact, to spend a few days with you," she said, "but a distraction of Estelle's forces us to return to town, and it's not without regret that we've perceived that it was too late to arrive there today. She has been stupid enough to forget in our notary's office the most essential title-deeds to our property."

That phrase, pronounced in an emotional and vibrant tone, had a very different significance than the one that remains under the pen. For Ferdinand and his wife, it was a defeat; for Estelle, it was a caprice; for me it was an insult.

"I don't understand you," Estelle retorted, sharply. "Have

we not thought that we would easily find among the people of the village an exact and reliable man who would spare us that step? It's only, in fact, a matter of taking this note to this address and carefully bringing back the signature of the lawyer."

"I'll take charge of it!" cried Ferdinand, reaching out to take possession of the letter.

"And I," I added, making the same movement, "if Madame will accord me confidence enough not to see another emissary, will take charge of executing her intentions early tomorrow and sending her the response she expects by a domestic, so rapidly that she will not have had time to desire it on awakening."

"You're quitting us?" Estelle said to me, with a tone of voice and a gaze that gave the words the expression of an amiable and sad reproach.

"Before daybreak, as I was informing my friend when you arrived. Only a painful malaise, which the night will dissipate, prevented me from leaving today."

I received the letter from her hands and was able to retire, thanks to the pretext that hazard had furnished me. I went out without looking at Clémentine, but I supposed that she was content.

Darkness had fallen completely when I entered my room, without a candle. I opened the window that overlooked the little wood; I inhaled the exterior air as if it were capable of relieving the oppression that was stifling me; Stupidly, I calculated how many hours still remained before I could set forth in such a manner as to find myself at the opening of the doors. There are emotions that suspend the exercise of thought, just as there are physical pains whose violence, reaching an intolerable degree, interrupts the action of sensibility for some time. One no longer feels, one no longer suffers, one is not ill.

That respite does not last long; the heart resumes its elasticity in order to rise up, to weigh once again the burden that overwhelms it, to exhaust itself in new efforts and always to succumb—always, until it breaks completely.

"It's too much!" I said, finally, while marching precipitately in that obscurity, the darkness of which my shame would have liked to thicken. "It's too much to count thus on the patience of an energetic and proud soul, which knows the worth in despair of an insensate passion but cannot come to terms with the shame. Kill me, if necessary; you have the right, since I have delivered my life to you in a cowardly fashion, but I forbid you to besmirch my character; and be careful, believe me! I would rather tear out your heart with my hand than let a sentiment live there that outrages me! A bloodstain is nothing; a stain on honor is frightful. Her hatred I can understand without being able to explain it—but who can explain the miserable movements of the imperfect organ that palpitates in a woman's bosom? I shall not suffer this offensive disdain! I might perhaps merit it if I had spoken to her about my fatal amour, if I had had the infamy of soliciting hers, the amour of a noble heiress . . . but the inexorable frenzy that consumes me I have hidden with more care than a shameful treasure conquered by murder and rapine. It's my sickness and my secret. And her love, who wants it? Has she debased me sufficiently? Has she taken the refinement of insult far enough? Has she envenomed sufficiently the last blow she reserved for me? To come here, into the sanctuary of my only amities, to force me to blush at an affront that promises me neither reparation nor vengeance; to identify me to this family, where I receive the welcome of a brother, as a man to make the air she breathes repulsive! Oh, I'm very unfortunate!"

The passionate excitement of my mind had used up my strength. A dolorous spasm twisted my nerves; a burning cloud floated over my eyes and devoured my eyelids; my ears were whistling; I was breathing effortfully; I could scarcely stand up. I went to throw myself on my bed, fully dressed, and I was immediately surprised by that confused, stormy, turbulent sleep that, far from anesthetizing the faculty of thought, torments it with countless fatigues, tossing it back and forth with a kind of bitter malice between dreams and reality.

I don't know how many hours that state lasted, when I imagined that I could see Estelle and Clémentine, and hear them talking about me. I could not discern the play of their physiognomy, and I could only follow in part their conversation, but my name fell into it at regular intervals, like a refrain that recaptured my attention from time to time, at the moment when it was about to allow itself to be distracted by another dream.

Contrary to the usual course of nocturnal illusions, that one became increasingly lucid, and suddenly became distinct enough to wake me with a start. I looked around my room in search of the object of my strange vision. I was alone, but a ray of light that divided it in its narrow length, and the conversation that continued in the same tone on the same subject as before, informed me suddenly that it had only been one of my senses that had been mistaken. If I had only seen them by virtue of the caprices of slumber, I could certainly still hear them.

My ideas cleared promptly. The next room was destined for visitors, I knew that from Ferdinand. One of the cousins who was to inhabit it, had been led there by the other, and the inattention of a maladroit domestic, who had left the communicating door open, had made me the involuntary confidant of their conversation.

I sat up abruptly and put my feet forcefully on the floor, with the design of interrupting it, but it was engaged so ardently that they did not hear me. What should I do? To appear or to speak was a scene of terror and phantasmagoria worthy of an English novel, so fashionable then in drawing rooms; it was probably even worse: a pitfall of stupidity that the extravagances of my past life scarcely permitted me to justify by leaving it entirely to chance; and it would be necessary, in order for me to be believed, that they would take the trouble, against all appearance, to listen to me; finally, although it was doubtless an honest action, it might doom me and would not profit anyone.

In any case, there had been mention of me, I was sure, and if I could trust the vague notions of my last dream, there had only been question of me. How could I explain, how could I render sensible to an irritated mind, the prejudice and inimity of which I could not hide for myself, the idea that I had heard everything without understanding anything? Might those words not have been of a nature to disquiet two weak souls regarding their consequences? Was it not a hundred times better to retain the sad mystery within my bosom than to aggravate its consequences by a dangerous, or at least futile, scandal of which my indiscreet generosity would only collect the fruit of a suspicion of cowardice or deception? They were about to separate, and while their footsteps drew away far enough, it might be possible for me, with a little precaution, to shield them from the sound of mine, to reach the open window, which was no more than five feet above the terrace, and I would then be able to descend easily in order to reach the little wood, and even the road. I knew enough exits for that.

That sequence of reasonings seems rather long to follow, but I believe that I would have had time to embrace them all in the duration of a lightning-flash. I remained motionless; and as they had not ceased talking, I heard them involuntarily, waiting impatiently for an opportunity to escape from that insupportable constraint and execute my plan.

"I repeat to you," Estelle went on, "that these excuses, unworthy of your intelligence, as this unjust and mortifying procedure is unworthy of your character, cannot make me change my opinion as to its veritable motive. No one is deceived by it. Because of that bizarre and sudden change of resolution, the gaucherie of your pretext, the interior bitterness announced in spite of you by your manner and your speech, that young man, who is said to be afflicted by profound pains, is in haste to renounce the consolations that he found among his friends. I've seen Ferdinand near to shedding a tear. And you, Clémentine, if your mirror could have shown you the insulting and cruel joy that was in your eyes then, I'm convinced that you would have blushed."

"Enough, enough!" Clémentine interrupted. "Believe what you want. It's possible that you've divined correctly."

"Finish making yourself understood, then. My heart needs to forgive you for this pitiless whim, and you know whether he must desire to see you again quite perfect, as he saw you until now. What obliges you to afflict a stranger almost unknown to us, but of honest condition and estimable life, whose society is sought by people whom we value, with humiliations to which you would not want to subject the least of wretches? A few aberrations of youth, much amplified by the stupid chronicle of provincial drawing rooms, and which only prove, carefully considered, the exaltation of an overly sensitive soul whose movements had not yet been regulated by time and experiences? Have they not been repaired by a conduct without reproach, which has conciliated the indulgence and even the interest, of the coldest, most demanding and most severe judges after a proof of a century? That's not saying too much, since it has lasted nearly a year."

"Since his return from Paris?" sad Clémentine, letting the words fall in the tone of an inconsequential question.

"I don't know . . . but I think it's since his return from Paris. Is it the difference in our conditions? I agree that he isn't of our rank, but nor is anyone else; and society, which forbids us certain alliances, nevertheless tolerates relations of politeness, benevolence and sometimes amity between us and our inferiors. It often renders them necessary."

"Don't persist, to my shame, in that odious supposition; you're not fortunate today in your conjectures. Nobility! What does that matter to me? What have I done to be noble, and do I owe it to nobility to submit to its laws when they revolt nature and reason? Those laws, however, dominate us, unfortunates that we are. They are the rule of our destiny, they are the torture of our life. Nobility! Do you want me to curse it?"

"I don't demand as much of you—but how to conceive, after that . . ."

"Poor Estelle. You interrupted me too quickly, for my soul was about to open. Listen! What if that young man, *almost unknown to us*, whom you mentioned just now, loved the noble young woman to whom society forbids *certain alliances?*"

"I'd feel sorry for him; but that's impossible. His unconsidered expansion, his extreme character, would have let such a secret escape long ago."

"Wait! And what if he loved her more than he had ever loved before? What if he had made her understand it without telling her so? What then? But you're no longer interrupting me."

"I'd feel sorry for him, I tell you, and wouldn't criticize you any less. His passion would be a misfortune, not an insult. It might prescribe reserve, perhaps coldness, and you ought to avoid him for his own sake. But to repel him with indignity . . . no, Clémentine, that inhumanity would add to his misery, and I would be in despair to find that frightful courage in you."

"Alas," cried Clémentine, "does one know what one is doing when one is struggling against one's heart?"

"What are you saying? But you're pale, you're weeping, you're not finishing . . . do you love him?"

"Oh, how I love him . . . !"

"Clémentine!"

That last cry was uttered by two voices, but Estelle's covered mine, which died on my lips. I was upright, for there had been a moment when I commenced to dread not being awake and when I had sought to assure myself of the exactitude of my sense by the liberty of my actions. At that moment I yielded to the inexpressible sentiment that overwhelmed me, a mixture of delight and terror, ecstasy and despair, in which my annihilated thought sought in vain to recover itself.

Nothing reached me any longer but the sound of sobs; nothing appeared to me any longer but the features of Clémentine in tears, unfortunate in loving me. That confession, which had not been made for me, that edict of mercy, impotent to save me, that amour of Heaven, which only delivered me into Hell, the profound tone of which was propagated in all my organs, did not leave me the free usage of them for a long time. My fingers, uselessly clinging to my bedpost, stiffened further, and then slipped. I finally flexed and fell, devoid of strength and almost of consciousness. I believed that I might savor the joy of dying thus, but the resonance of my fall reanimated me and rendered me the dread of being surprised. There was an interval of silence

"Did you hear that?" said Clémentine. "There, in that cabinet?"

"Nothing," Estelle replied. "Perhaps the wind, blowing through these open casements."

She closed the door, and I could no longer hear anything but a vague murmur, soon followed by the sound of another door, which also closed, and the grating of a key that turned in the lock. I breathed out. I launched myself forward; I ran; I had reached my window when my door opened again.

"Ah!" cried Clémentine, throwing herself into an armchair, her head tilted back, covering her eyes with her hands in order not to see me. "You heard me! You know everything! Woe is me! I would never have thought you capable of such a base perfidy!"

I was lying at her feet; I palpitated; I babbled; I dissolved in tears; I justified myself in confused terms, in protestations, in oaths; and without seeing her, without interrogating her, without hearing her, I understood that she no longer suspected me. I don't know how that came about, but a joy so vivid and so complete filled my bosom, a life so new replaced mine, that it seemed to me that another soul had been given to me; I raised my tremulous hands toward her; I found one of her hands, which she had allowed to fall. I seized it; she did not withdraw it. The fire that descended therefrom ran in torrents through my veins; I felt it envelop my heart; I changed my nature completely. I became a god.

"Don't speak! Don't speak!" I said, transported. "What could you say to me? What need have I to know? That phrase, *I love you*, you pronounced it just now; it's the last I want to collect from your mouth. The last! It's enough, it's too much for a single existence, for a single eternity. What you might try to tell me about my impossible good fortune, about my hopeless future, I know. I don't hope for anything, I have no hope. My happiness I possess; my future, I am taking away. My days lack nothing; they are full. Society, misfortune, death, can no longer do anything. My entire being is in one memory, in one thought, in one phrase that no power is capable of stealing from me. The rest I shall dream!

"Have no fear, don't tremble! Be tranquil and happy! You will never see me again, you will no longer hear me named, you will no longer have to fear encountering me, and if hazard should bring me before your eyes . . . your indifference, our scorn, your indignation, I shall submit to everything, I shall love everything, I shall adore you all the more as you reject me more, because I shall measure your tenderness by the effort that you make to hide it. Do you not love me? What more do I need? And opinion, what does it matter? Don't tremble, have no fear, do not regret your secret! If it has fallen into my heart, it is to die there, with me, now, tonight, whenever you wish! Here, anywhere, at the end of the world, my will is yours!

Must I go away, come back, depart forever? I do not ask for a word, a sign, or a glance. Think and I shall divine; desire, and I shall obey."

"Depart, depart, I beg you," said Clémentine, "and whatever happens, forgive me!"

I abandoned her hand, moist with my kisses and my tears, and without turning round to see her again I leapt through the window. I heard an exclamation of fright, but I did not stop. I traversed the wood, I crossed the ditches, I scaled the wall, I marched straight ahead, through the brushwood, through the ravines, through the rocks, without searching for a path, without avoiding any obstacle, without reflection, almost without thinking.

I arrived thus at the glacis of the town, which was still closed. I found that good; I needed to walk for a long time, to respire at my ease, to feel alive. The sky was so beautiful, the dawn so fresh and so pure, nature so cheerful!

It was a festival morning. There were marvels and delights in everything I saw, everything that I heard, everything that I touched. I enjoyed everything, as if I had learned to exist. I noticed everything, as if I had found senses and a soul for the first time: the aspects, the sounds, the perfumes, the eternal miracle of creation that recommences every day . . . and me, happier in myself alone than creation entire, if it had been able to admire itself in its pomp and beauty; reborn likewise to sensualities ha no voice could express; that day, cherished, predestined, heaped with wealth among all the children of God: me, loved by Clémentine!

Happiness passes quickly from the human heart. It was prolonged in mine like an obsession, like the madness that I had desired at one time. It differed little from it in its everyday reality. The madman and I would encounter one another at almost the same end-point. The only advantage that tipped the balance in my favor consisted of a single word from

Clémentine, a single syllable, in a cry that hazard had delivered to me; but that imperceptible difference—it is necessary to have loved to know it—was happiness, and something more. A happiness that exceeded in intoxication, as in purity, all the joys that had ever slaked the most avid hope, all the illusions that had ever fascinated the most fecund imagination in magical dreams!

Our amour had nothing to expect of time, but it had nothing to fear from it. It had no fortunate conclusion to find in the future, but it had no conclusion. It left far behind all the earthly amours that know their destiny. It knew that it was devoid of a destiny, and thus devoid of vicissitudes, changeless and endless.

My sadness was dissipated, my expansion returned. My studies pleased me; I brought back to it familiar affections all the superabundance of glad sentiments that overflowed from my soul. I loved solitude more than ever, because it was there that I lived with her, that I dared to love her and talk to her as if she were present, but I emerged from it more content, more transported, than from a mysterious rendezvous in which everything had been accorded to me or promised.

I knew how to prolong its delights in nights of enchantment that I succeeded in stealing from slumber. There we conversed as lovers, as spouses, with a reciprocal abandon that deceived me, for what she said to me, she would have said. By virtue of summoning her soul toward mine, I believed that I had taken possession of it.

I made her repeat: "Oh, how I love him!" and I seemed to hear it again. I convinced myself, and I could not be mistaken, that she was occupied by the same idea; that she was sustaining the same conversation; that her expressions accorded with mine as well as if she had replied to them. I grasped even their customary harmony, even the agitated and nervous inflexion, even the long and slightly breathless sigh that followed them, when she had spoken with emotion.

How many times I extended an arm over an empty pillow in order to support her fatigued head! How many times I felt it go numb beneath her neck, beneath her shoulders, to the point of confirming me in my error, and not allowing me to doubt that she was really reposing there. "She's asleep," I said, "it's necessary not to wake her." And my mouth lost without savoring it the kiss that it tried to attach to her hair.

When daylight came, I conceived that she was not there. Would her mother and society have consented to give her to me, and did she not have to obey her mother? I had obtained her from her and from God; that was enough.

I had other pleasures too, treasures of which I alone knew the price: a piece of blue ribbon that had fallen in Paris under her scissors; a string from her harp, which had broken under her fingers; a small feather that had been detached from her hair; a ballad that she had written and scored, all the character of which I kissed so often, one by one. A columbine, above all, that she had worn on her breast, which had felt her heart beat and palpitate with it, and of which I took possession under her eyes and with her consent, one day when she replaced it with a fresher columbine. We both loved that sad flower, which only grows in isolated spots, under melancholy shade, and whose somber and bruised brow seems to incline toward a tomb. It has never quit me since. There it is!

And when she was in town, how much care I took to avoid encountering her, how many glances I darted in the distance in order to turn me away from her passage in time, how much attention I paid to obscuring, to hiding my life, in order to spare her even the care of hearing me named. No, never had any lover put more artifice and solicitude into spying on the steps of an adored mistress, in order not to lose any opportunity to see her, than I did in order not to be seen. I dreamed about her, however.

Ferdinand only came to town for business affairs that absolutely required his presence, of which I could not take charge in his stead, but he had taken one of those lodgments that country landowners call their *pied-à-terre*, to which I only went by night when his interests required it, because it was directly opposite the room that Clémentine occupied in her mother's apartment. When Ferdinand returned to the country, I kept the key to it.

One day, at sunset, a storm that was beginning to rumble, and which was racing across the sky with a frightening impetuosity, obliged me, in order to abridge my route, to go along that street, which was severely prohibited to me. Large, heavy, lukewarm raindrops were already marbling the pavements. The storm was roaring in a horrible manner. All the doors were closed and all the passers-by had disappeared. It was necessary to seek the first refuge that came to hand. I went into Ferdinand's room.

The tempest suddenly burst with a din to disturb the most resolute hearts, but which transported mine. I did not suspect that anyone in the world shared my enthusiasm for that kind of spectacle, which made one dream of the annihilation of the universe and the imminent advent of an eternity of repose.

I opened the window. What a scene! Nothing was animated there any longer but the elements.

Night fell. Light no longer came from the occident; it was everywhere in the burning atmosphere. The long straight street resembled the bed of one of those infernal rivers that roll flaming waves.

The summits of roofs, the tips of lightning-conductors and the steeples of bell-towers were illuminated by sparks, aureoles and meteors. Windows, red and ardent, shone like the mouths of furnaces.

Clémentine's were not shining. Her casement had just opened too. She was standing there, motionless, her eyes fixed on me. It was not an illusion. I saw her distinctly; but the cloud swelled, descending toward her, extending as black and impenetrable as a wall of iron.

A flash of lightning traversed it; she reappeared.

The obscurity recommenced, more profound, and was illuminated again momentarily in order to render her to me. Fortunately, the lightning flashes became so frequent that I scarcely had time to lose sight of her, and I was no longer disquieted. I counted them like the pulsations of an artery, like the beats of my heart, and every time that their light brought her back to me, the fantastic effect of that alternation of light and dark brought her so close to me that one might have thought that it was only necessary to extend an arm to seize her and bear her away, and to deliver me with her to the confused whirlwind of darkness and fire.

Then, nothing escaped me. It was her hands that were seeking me, her breast that was heaving as if to come to touch mine, her eyes that were moist and passionate, more resplendent with her tears, and her mouth that was articulating impotent sounds drowned by the rumbling of the thunder. I was speaking too; I exchanged my cries, my wishes, my oaths with hers. I thanked, I blessed, I invoked the lightning. I wanted it to strike us both together, so that the same knell would sing over our neighboring graves, so that the history of that benevolent phenomenon would at least marry our names in human memory.

The lightning did not grant my wish. It fell nearby at the moment when, our bodies leaning forward, we aspired to be united in a mortal embrace—for she had certainly had the same thought. That was our nuptial torch.

Soon afterwards, the interior of Clémentine's room was illuminated. Someone had come into it. She was no longer alone. The casements closed. The enchantment was finished.

I remained in the same place all night, and I would have liked the night to last forever. The weather was so good! The air was purified, the most perfect calm reigned over the earth and in the sky; the moon swam without any obstacle in its blue ocean, scarcely furrowed by a few narrow banks of cloud, dazzling with whiteness like snow and rolled into fleecy tufts. It inundated with light the sill on which Clémentine had leaned for a few moments, and which no one had seen or touched since. It was a gift for me.

Toward midnight I saw a candle reappear; I saw a white dress flutter, an arm that enlaced a white curtain and let it fall again. Then the candle was suddenly extinguished and I no longer perceived anything. I hoped that she might come back, and the rest of the time went by thus, waiting.

When daylight appeared a shadow rose up before the curtain, which opened and closed on its movement; it was Clémentine, who had spent the same hours sitting with me, whose vague form and slight movement I thought I had seen several times . . . Clémentine or a shadow, indeed!

That was forever . . .

A week later she had gone, but I knew better than ever that her soul was with me. I had our initials engraved on a wedding ring, with the date of the storm, and I imagined madly that my wife was traveling. I continued, therefore, to savor the ineffable charm of my solitary walks, when one evening, at the place least frequented, and hence most familiar to me, I was surprised at a bend in the path by the amiable and tender Estelle, whose obliging curiosity had given me the joy of reading Clémentine's heart. It was, according to all appearance, the first time she had appeared there.

"I was impatient to see you and talk to you," she said, taking my arm, "and, to tell the truth, I was looking for you in order to ask you a question—but a singular question. Do you intend to stay in Paris this time in the same house as in previous years?"

"Undoubtedly," I replied, smiling, "since my lodgment there remains at my disposal; but I protest that I do not feel the slightest desire to return there for long."

"You have not yet reflected sufficiently," she said, with an expression that was simultaneously lively and serious. "One more question before giving you time to think about it. Do you know this handwriting?"

It was impossible for me to mistake for a moment the lines that she passed before my eyes.

"I don't think so," I said, trembling. My emotion must have contradicted me.

"I suspect that you might have seen it . . . in a ballad. Divine, then, for this note isn't signed, but read it without scruple; it only concerns you."

I read, and I have not forgotten:

> *There is not a moment to lose; it is necessary to see him, to tell him to leave, to go to Paris; it is necessary to tell him that* I want it, *and that I hope he will remember my last words.*

"You understand," Estelle went on, "and it surpasses explanation. *Him* is you; she is . . . What's the matter, then? As for her last words, perhaps they have left more traces in your memory than her ballad.

I remembered them, her last words: *Whatever happens, forgive me . . .* but for what? I didn't understand.

The week had not ended when I arrived in Paris. I was astonished to find my apartment prepared.

"Oh, Monsieur was expected," the domestic of the house said to me. "A letter preceded you by two days."

It was from Estelle, and I lost no time before breaking the seal. The first lines froze my blood. It was evident that they had been written to prepare me for a misfortune. I skipped to the last words and my eyes closed, searching them through a cloud.

Clementine was married.

I do not know what followed what was said to me. I fell; I wounded my head dangerously on an item of furniture; physicians were called; I was bled. When I gave signs of life, I was delirious.

I remember that all that remained to me of the past was a confused and dubious sentiment like a dream, but which dominated me with a fixed resolution that occupied me for six months. I had heard mention of a Charterhouse established in Switzerland in accordance with the rigorous observance of Abbé de Rancé.[1] I exercised that genre of life, that habitude of privations. I found therein I know not what bitter satisfaction, which resembled happiness, my own happiness, that which I was still able to conceive. The pious practices, the meditations and the prayers, gradually calmed my blood, and I passed for having been cured.

At any rate, my project was affirmed from day to day, and a second letter from Estelle finished determining me to execute it without delay. I departed for the Alps.

That second letter also contained terrible news, but less terrible than the first. Clémentine was dead.

---

1 Armand-Jean Le Bouthilier de Rancé (1626-1700) revived the Cistercian abbey at La Trappe, which lent its name to the austere order he founded, whose members thus became known as Trappists.

Amélie

When I arrived in Geneva I was already disillusioned regarding the possibility of carrying out the project that had brought me to Switzerland. The obscure and modest establishment of the Charterhouse had excited, not without reason, the suspicion of the French police, who thought it very liable to give shelter to the disappointed enemies of Napoléon's government, and who could not tolerate anywhere the inoffensive existence of an outlaw heartbroken by despair and misery. Europe had no more shelter then against the tyranny incarnate in one man than it had previously had against the diffuse tyranny of the masses. It had been Python; it would be the Hydra.

The monks came to close their doors to misfortune for the first time, and to enclose themselves with more severity than the rule of their founder imposed on them in their rigorous manor of Val-Saint.

In Geneva I had one of those friends that the sympathies of study provide, and also one of those friends that one only owes to sympathies of the soul: Doctor Jurine and Madame P***. I spoke to them about my irreparable chagrins, about everything that one believes one can have in the heart of profound disillusionment and incurable bitterness when one has lived for a long time, of the vocation of eternal solitude that an unexpected contretemps has betrayed.

The philosopher sympathized with me and advised me to seek forgetfulness of woes in the assiduous practice of a few mild sciences that he loved and had taught me to love. The woman wept, allowed me to weep, and occupied herself secretly with trying to provide me with a fixed and laborious employment that might distract my mind from its troubles by the habitude of duty. The relations of her husband's library had enabled her to know that there was an old English scholar in Berne called Sir Robert Grove[1] who had devoted much of his life to petty philological research on good Greek and Latin authors, and whom the loss of a learned collaborator forced him to require the aid of a young man endowed with some aptitude for that work, or at least capable of lightening the burden for him. She made me party to those details and gave me a letter to Sir Robert, who took me on as his secretary at a salary of two hundred francs per month, and also took responsibility for defraying all essential expenses.

Deflected by the religious principles that dominated me at that time, which have never abandoned me entirely, of an extreme resolution, the thought of which had often occurred to me, and perhaps also retained by the vague instinct that my active and romantic imagination still populated with emotions and mysteries, I had no other course to take in the state of my fortune. In any case, could I wish for anything except what she had wished for me? Good, charming and worthy woman! Her name alone would be an eulogy, and if I do not allow it to escape here in its entirety, it is because I dread damaging its purity by mingling it with the deplorable history of my passions. Fortunately, enough hearts remain on earth that will have no difficulty divining it.

---

1 Commentators have recognized in this character a portrait of Sir Herbert Croft, for whom Nodier worked for several months as a secretary in 1809-10 before going to Illyria to work there as a journalist, but Nodier only appropriated a few items from Sir Herbert's biography in making up an entirely fictitious character.

Sir Robert was a singular man. Emerged from a family already chivalric and illustrious in the time of Camden, he had made excellent studies at Oxford. His literary debuts announced an ardent and passionate soul that amour and enthusiasm might have taken a long way, and who was obsessed without knowing it with the impulse of renewal of which society did not yet know the name. No one was able to tell me what had happened to him, but toward the age of twenty-five he appeared to have devoted himself to a piety that was initially mystical and contemplative, but had not taken long to become scholastic and militant, because the impetuosity of his temperament and his mind did not permit him to accommodate himself to moderate parties. The third and last of his irresistible penchants devoted him permanently to the clarification and illustration of classical letters, with which he was more familiar than any other man of his epoch; but the latter fused so naturally with the other two that one could have sworn that the three were only one, and that there was in that phenomenon, for a theologian of his strength, a peremptory argument against the ergotism of Servet;[1] with the result that if one succeeded in representing him distinctly as a composite of an impetuous Luther, a punctilious Saumaise[2] and a sentimental and sophistical Werther, like his model, one would be very close to knowing Sir Robert Grove in his triple unity.

His new passion had drawn him to the continent to research the manuscripts of Germany, France and Italy. One day he had stopped in Switzerland, where he had been living for nearly twenty years when I arrived, and he had realized as an annuity an honest fortune, although mediocre for an Englishman. He liked to say that it was the dread of seasickness, of which he had nearly died during his first crossing, that caused him to make the decision never to cross the

---

1 The Spanish humanist Miguel Serveto (c1510-1553), who played a significant role in the Protestant Reformation.
2 The Classical scholar Claude Saumaise (1588-1653), also a Protestant.

Channel again, but it was generally supposed that hidden chagrins might have influenced that resolution, and that an encounter with one of those complete amities with which nature does not gratify all those who have need of them had completed his determination.

He had found it in Berne in Jacobus Th***, younger than him by a few years, animated like him with a melancholy and dreamy sensibility, penetrated like him with vast and exercised education, but superior even to Sir Robert, in the latter's judgment, in the imperturbable tact of his criticism. It was that friend whom death had taken away from him two years before; the baronet was then confined to bed by a stubborn gout that had not quit him since, but he had had himself transported to the bedside of the dying man in order to receive his last sighs. From that moment on, he seemed to have abandoned his cherished labors, and only the need to occupy his ennui with some distraction useful to science had determined him to resume their course. It was to second him in that laudable design that he had appealed to the first person to come along, which was me.

That story interested me; I do not know what power foreign to my will drew me toward that old man, so cruelly deprived of his adoptive brother, but I imagined, in my young man's pride that those serious, meditative and solitary destinies were not without a rapport with those that the future had in preparation for me, and I thought I had discovered in the apparent hazard that opened a career for me too austere for my age, one of those providential premeditations that one never ceases imagining when one has awakened to everything. That intimate superstition has played a great role in all my enterprises, and I feel that it would deliver me again if I were unfortunate enough to have to recommence.

My conjectures were not mistaken with regard to Sir Robert. In that unique complication of bizarrely contracted characteristics, I only found a man whom I did not think any more than that—a good, easy-going, expansive man abundant in his ideas, with the naivety of a child content with himself—happy to believe in himself and to inspire confidence in others, but tolerant, and even docile for opinions opposed to his own, when they were not presented in quarrelsome and hostile fashion; demanding for those forms of mind as he was in amity; sulkier at the slightest cloud than a little girl whose doll has been broken; recovered at the slightest sign of deference or affection, always making the effort of a reconciliation and according more than was demanded of him; hyperbolic in words and sentiments, eulogies and reproaches, in his affections and his hatreds, his scorn and his admiration, and knowing nuances of expression between extreme superlatives, because he was a superlative himself, a moral hyperbole, the most excellent man that divine bounty had ever produced.

I can see him again from here in his little room, which I entered an hour after my arrival in Berne. I see him half-lying in a large and profound armchair, which he had invented, and which moved on four castors by means of an ingenious and convenient mechanism, which he had invented; his feet extended on a flexible stool that could be raised, lowered, distanced and brought nearer, which he had invented; his elbow. Leaning on a large pivoting table with five compartments, which he had also invented—for the baronet did not make use of anything that he had not invented. He had invented his tea-caddy and his snuff-box. He had invented his bed and his *somno*. He had invented his writing-desk and notepads. He had invented the boat in which he ran aground on the Escaut as he emerged from Valenciennes. He had invented the safety-carriage that tipped him out in the middle of the best road in France, in the Avenue de Nevers.

As I say, I can see him, clapping his hands at my entry and welcoming me with a gaze as benevolent and a smile as soft as my father's. I can see his noble face, more than sexagenarian but youthful, blooming, red, adolescent with imagination and thought, and his vast bald forehead, as white and polished as ivory, around which rolled curls of golden blond hair that would have done honor to a bachelor; for nature had taken pleasure in leaving him vestiges of youth in his old age as it had left them in his soul.

I have said that his room was very small, and I have no need to say that it had all the elegance, all the neatness and all the appearance of comfortable ease that renders life so pleasant in England and Holland, and which the fortunate Bernese have perhaps outbid. What I have not said is that it opened on to a beautiful gallery that contained the baronet's precious library, precious in its choice of authors, the antiquity of its editions and the exquisite perfection of its copies. I believe I can testify that all the ancient classics were there, with all their commentators, in the most magnificent bindings that ever gladdened a bibliomaniac's eyes.

The mechanical armchair often moved amid those rare marvels, but the baronet had not invented a means of lifting himself up and sustaining him at the level of the topmost shelves. For a long time, in fact, he had no longer been thinking about that perfection, worthy of the genius of Stevinus,[1] because Providence had fortunately provided it, in giving him a Welsh domestic, a massive and perpendicular giant six feet four inches tall, as bleak, dense and unpolished as the dolmens of his ancestors, who scarcely combined his knowledge of the Celtic language with a dozen bad locutions of vulgar English, but who was endowed with a memory for names and places that was truly prodigious. There was no volume indicated by its title and date that did not come to place itself of its own accord under the hand of the obedient colossus. To the right and the left, up and down, day and night, his instinct was nev-

____
1 The Flemish military engineer Simon Stevin (1548-1620).

er mistaken. In the time of Cardan and Agrippa, Jonathas, or "Master Long-Ladder" as the baronet called him gaily, would have been considered a gnome subjugated by magic, and if Walter Scott had known him, he would not have omitted him from his fantastic gallery.

My room was situated on the opposite side of the library, and it was through Jonathan's scholarly domain that I came at ten o'clock in the morning in search of my daily work. Sir Robert had already been working for four or five hours, and his notes scribbled on loose sheets of which, fortunately, they never usurped the verso, had usually reached the hundredth figure of pagination before I got up. It was that enormous labor that it was necessary to reduce to its simplest expression during the rest of the day while the baronet was employed, for his part, in swelling by a few hundred lines his ingenious and interminable poem on a violet flower found in the Swiss Alps or dreaming of some useful invention that he had not yet completed. It would be in spite of me, alas, if a slight shadow of ridicule obscured these details of interior philosophy. There is no mental superiority that is not betrayed in a man by some weakness, and if the man were perfect, it would no longer be a question of depicting him; it would be sufficient to name him. What made intelligence smile in the innocent manias of the baronet also made the soul weep. One said to oneself: *But that's what we are, when we are everything that we are permitted to be outside our species.*

The aspect of the alarming manuscript overwhelmed me at first, but then I felt lightened of an enormous weight on leafing through it. Our first two critical editions were to be Horace and Tacitus, because Sir Robert had understood in two or three words of conversation that I was not strong enough in Greek to assist him for a few months in the publication of Pindar, his favorite classic. That discovery cost him a sigh. It was to cost me more profound and heart-rending ones, and if some young woman with soft eyes and a tender heart were to attempt after my death to decipher those pages muddied by pedantry, she would scarcely suspect the intimate liaison that Pindar might have in the heart of an old schoolboy with a memory of amour. With the aid of a little patience, she would arrive at the solution of that problem, if I had the cruelty to encourager her in it; but I shall refrain from doing so. I am writing for myself a thousand trivia that charm me, because they enable me to relive days full of mildness and illusions. Geometers say: *What does that prove?* Women also say it. I shall therefore return momentarily to my stacks of paper.

It was, I repeat, an alarming thing to see, but which only frightened me momentarily. When Sir Robert had a phrase of Tacitus or a line of Horace under his hand, he despoiled all its editors, all its annotators, all its commentators and all its glossarists. All the explanations, all the interpretations and all the variants were good for him; he would not have omitted a single hypothesis; he would not have disdained a printing error. The text was thus drowned in an encyclopedia of words and ideas, from which it only remained for me to disengage the most probable lesson and the most sensate gloss. The baronet's first collaborator had had the fortunate instinct of election, which is more common than one thinks, or as common as it is said, for it is simply common sense. The essential merit of that immense labor belonged nonetheless to the indefatigable searcher who had prepared and put in order that chaos of materials, and the majority of our stout classical volumes are only inflated by countless pages at the expense of late nights of patient erudition, which has taken the time necessary to know everything and which has not taken that of choosing.

The exiguity of my results appeared to torment Sir Robert at first, although I proceeded in a manner far more prolix than his memorable friend Jacobus. As I expected that impression I reminded him of the Latin adage that says that a reader ought not to be jealous of a sieve, and he offered me his hand as a pledge of consent.

I continued to work conscientiously, but in accordance with my whim, and if I surprised in him a poorly disguised regret at some piquant but ill-judged anecdote, some beautiful philological observation taken from too remote a distance, which he had succeeded in entering into his commentary by virtue of an elastic property of imagination that would not have disconcerted the subtlest transitions or the most lyrical deviations, I consoled him by showing him in a carefully-maintained album all the episodic curiosities drafted in advance for a more opportune occasion. Then his mutinous discontentment changed into expansions of joy and gratitude; I was his other Jacobus, the Aristarchus of his Homeric slumber, the Phocion of his eloquence, the hatchet of his discourse, the adoptive suzerain of his books and manuscripts, the *Paulo-post-futurum* of his renown.[1] That was the *nec plus ultra* of his demonstrative affection. Maxime only had the rights of a passive secretary, but *Paulo-post* could have belabored with impunity a volume of erudition made to dethrone Scaliger.[2]

That concurrence of zeal and good will had accelerated the task. We were able to conclude in four months all the Odes of Horace from *Maecenas atavis* to *Dicere laudes*. Tacitus was scarcely less advanced, and we had already received proofs from Leipzig, where our first two volumes were in press, when I thought I remarked one evening, toward the end of dinner, that Sir Robert was labored by some interior worry. That did not require a great effort of discernment, for that disposition of mind was revealed in him by the invariable symptoms: a sad vertical gaze attached pensively to the ceiling; a scarcely audible sigh that rose slowly, following the same ascending scale, and a slight whistle—or, rather, an almost ungraspable

---

1 *Paulo post futurum* means "after the future," usually referring to a distant future or used as a way of implying "never."
2 The Classical historian Joseph Justus Scaliger (1540-1609).

modulation of breath that would have been drowned out a hundred times over by Uncle Toby's *Lila Burello*.[1] I made the baronet party to my observation.

"It only concerns you indirectly," Sir Robert replied, mildly, looking at me paternally, "but I'm thinking about my end, which might be near; and if posterity only knows me via these two incomparable editions of Horace and Tacitus, *mirum opus et integrum*, the myrmidons of science might contest my Hellenistic studies in a few centuries. Why is it necessary to occupy oneself so little with Greek in your eccentric France, and why have I also to overburden you with work instead of taking you right away, by flowery paths, dear *Paulo-post*, to read Pindar more fluently under my direction than the *Carmen saeculaire?* What an event for your Institut and for the scholarly world would be the simultaneous appearance of Sir Robert's Pindar and Horace, model editions, prototype editions, monumental editions, the ever-increasing success of which would impose silence on the envious future and save me the affront of having been a man of one language and one book!"

"I warned you, Sir Robert, about my unfortunate insufficiency."

"It's not a matter of your insufficiency," replied Sir Robert brusquely, "and I have abundant means of remedying it." He rapped the table forcefully. "But I hesitate to take such a big risk. Hola, Jonathas, my pipe, a bottle of port and Calliergi's Pindar."

"*Such a big risk*, my noble friend? What have you to protect?"

"Your happiness, child, your happiness. Listen to me with attention and don't interrupt. I've often talked to you about Jacobus, who was my sieve, my Aristarchus,[2] my Phocion be-

---

1 This is the form in which Laurence Sterne renders the name of the tune more commonly known as "Lilliburlero," which became a Protestant anthem at the time of the "Glorious Revolution" of 1688 and is still loaded with political significance in Northern Ireland.
2 The grammarian Aristarchus of Samothrace, librarian of the famous Library of Alexandria in the second century B.C.

fore you; perhaps I haven't told you that he possessed imperturbably all the good lessons of Pindar; but that devil of a man didn't write, and my old memory has lost even the slightest memory of those rich oral traditions that I saw no necessity to fix then, since he was younger than me."

"How would it be possible to recover them now?" I murmured, in a low voice,

"That's the question, but I've told you not to do anything about it. The worthy Jacobus had only committed one fault in his life; he had married! Before my establishment in Berne, Jacobus had married a damned French pagan, a beautiful and good creature, if you wish, but infatuated with all the superstitions of papism. And I beg your pardon, my son, if I talk to you thus about your religion. You know that I never contradicted it, and that my entrails do not revolt against the innocent infidel who has had the misfortune to be born outside the way of the Lord. I shall say more; if my heart lacked pity, it would rather be with regard to the apostate who denied the faith of his parents, to whom I would be incapable of granting mercy.

"He had two children, a boy and a girl, piously raised in the profession of the holy Gospel, which is the eternal alliance of true Christians; and he had named the former Mithridate, because he had dreamed over the new-born's cradle, my poor brother Jacobus, of the ideal of a polyglot man who would learn effortlessly in his company all the languages of Babel. The girl was named Amélie, her mother's name, and you can imagine that, as they grew up, all the cares of education were distributed in accordance with their presumed destiny: to the daughter the masters of the frivolous arts, and to the son the lessons of scholars. But Providence, which mocks our projects, had ordered otherwise.

"At sixteen Mithridate was an agreeable musician and a fine dancer; as for Greek, he had never been able to get the first lines of Aesop into his head. He would have paled in vain for a week over a monostich by Theognis. Either because the labor had broken that young organism or because he had borne within him since birth the seed of the deadly malady that had taken away his mother, he died at seventeen. Jacobus' despair was inexpressible, but that strong soul only abandoned himself to it in spasms, when the poignant dart of the dolor came to reopen the wound unexpectedly.

"One day, when one might have thought that it had run its iron fingers over all the keys of the keyboard on which the memory of the dead child resounded, to breaking point, it found one that had not yet vibrated. I was there, and we had opened before us this Pindar you can see.

"'Brother,' Jacobus said to me, shaking my hand, 'I believe that I no longer know Greek; my memory has melted like the wax of tablets in the fire of this lamp, which guarded his coffin one night. If he had lived, with the fortunate nature that had not yet responded to all my hopes, but which would have fulfilled them one day, he would remind me today of all the scholia of Pindar that I have so often repeated to him.'

"'I know them. Father,' Amélie cried, suddenly, throwing her arms around Jacobus, and covering his eyes, which were ready to weep, with kisses, half-hiding them from me beneath her long hair. 'Those lessons pleased me,' she continued. 'I listened to them; I've remembered them; I haven't lost a word of them.' She did, in fact, know them. Greek was a game for her, like all the sciences to which genius can be raised. Another Olympia Morata,[1] another Maria Schurman![2] An angel, a muse, a divinity descended from Heaven, with a lyre that politeness and modesty kept mute. A few months later, Jacobus no longer existed."

---

1 The Latin scholar Olympia Fulvia Morata (1526-1555), something of a child prodigy, who converted to Protestantism following the example of her father.

2 Another child prodigy, Anna Maria van Schurman (1607-1678) was an exceptional scholar, artist and champion of the education of women, who became one of the leaders of the Protestant sect of Labadists.

108

"But Amélie still exists?" I said, with vivacity.

"Amélie exists," the baronet replied, gravely, "and she knows all of Pindar's lessons. Immediately after the death of her father she collected the meager debris of that scholarly fortune, which were insufficient for an idle life, and retired to a house in the country some distance from the city, among a few respectable ladies who occupied themselves with the education of young Bernese girls. Promptly distinguished among them by the purity of her character and the perfection of her knowledge, she is now at the head of the establishment."

"It appears to me, in that case," I said, smiling, "that Pindar's lessons are not lost. I understand that your temporary infirmity prevents you today from going to fetch her; I understand that it might appear unseemly that she violate the voluntary engagements of her solitude to bring them to you; but if it is indispensable to hear them from her mouth, do you not believe me savant enough at least to serve as an intermediary, and to render you Amélie's words with an intelligence as limited, but as faithful, as the one of which Jonathas has just given proof in depositing Calliergi's Pindar before you?"

"I believe everything you say there, but I believe that the furious brute who would roll powder-kegs toward the hearth of a fire and the ill-advised old fogy who would send his beloved *Paulo-post* to receive a few crumbs of Greek from the lips of an eighteen-year-old girl capable of turning the head of Zeno would merit being deemed equally extravagant."

"Wait, my friend, and do not let that stop you. My heart is pre-armed against all amours, and your Amélie could be provided with the fantastic attractions of that princess in the Thousand-and-One Nights whose gaze was mortal, and I would be able to read with impunity in her womanly eyes. However, what could result from it, at the worst, but a natural emotion for which you still experience tender and eloquent sympathies, and which, between two beings that you deign to love, because they both inspire an esteem and confidence in you, would always remain without danger?"

"Without danger, unfortunate child! Without danger, the love of a Protestant and a Roman Catholic, united by their frenzies for months of delirium, and separated by their faith for eternity! Without danger, the reputation and happiness of the only daughter of Jacobus, which are dearer to old Robert Grove than the pupils of his eyes! Without danger, the malediction of rich and avaricious relatives from whom she expects her daily bread! Without danger, great God, without danger!"

"You've just enabled me to understand, but not to dread. It's in works of fiction, at the most, that one sees the destiny of life depend on a sudden impression that three days would efface if the soul did not take pleasure in maintaining it. What man would be insensate enough to nurture a momentary illusion that an act of will could destroy, if he is sure of dying if he lets it live? Once again, I don't believe in their miracles of fascination worthy of Arabian tales, but if an unexpected movement of my heart forced me believe in one in spite of myself, I would refrain carefully from yielding to it. I tell you this very evening, Sir Robert, renounce your negotiation or your ambassador; my reason blurs as Pindar clarifies it, and you will no sooner have gained two or three variants than I shall have lost my head. Let us leave it there, if you please."

"And that's what you're telling me?" said the baronet, looking at me fixedly.

"I swear it on my honor."

"Halt there, worthy young man. This demands more solemnity between us. To me, Master Long-ladder! Come here, faithful Jonathas. In what unknown crypt of our library have you hidden your fine folio stature and your Atlantic figure? Where are you, Jonathas?"

Jonathas never replied; he only advanced at a methodical pace and placed himself, motionless and perpendicular, precisely facing his master.

"That's good," Sir Robert continued. "Replace on its shelf, dear Jonathas, this noble Calliergi Pindar, and bring me the brave Froben's Greek New Testament, *edition princeps in membranis.* It's a fine book," he added, with an expression of exalted admiration in which one could not easily discern whether the greater part of his enthusiasm was for the beauty of the Gospel or that of the edition.

The volume appeared, with its splendid morocco and its rich clasps; it opened in the middle, deploying its sumptuous pages to the right and the left, and the baronet continued: "You swear then, on this sacred book, my child, on this book that contains the faith of our fathers and our own, on this book of a God who holds lies and perfidy in horror, that if you feel yourself drawn by a passion whose consequences would be mortal for your old comrade, you will come to deposit in his heart that weakness of flesh and blood, and will not hesitate to submit to all that he demands of you! Wait, Maxime, wait! Don't deliver yourself blindly to the presumption of your youth! Don't take the Lord's name in vain."

"I swear, Sir Robert! And never has any engagement appeared to me to be easier to fulfill."

"In that case," said the baronet, after having returned the Gospel to Jonathas, "go and see this diamond tomorrow, this flower of the world, and try to obtain from her these damned lessons of Pindar, which are the pure flowers of all past, present and future scholia; we shall introduce them into mine at the expense of mine, and we shall publish the Pindar this year, under the twin names of Jacobus and Robert. That work will complete, may it please God, your initiation in good Greek letters, and we shall be in a position to launch, next year, Hesiod with Tacitus. *Monumentum exegi.*"

Although I do not like portraits, it is necessary that I give an idea of Amélie. She was sitting in her garden under a flowering cherry tree, which the sun penetrated in all parts with a rain of mobile sunbeams that trembled around her at the slightest breath of air. She stood up on perceiving me. I exercised myself in seeing her. I had already remarked her svelte, slim, harmoniously supple figure, like that with which my poets gratified their nymphs, her floating white dress, and her beautiful black hair gathered negligently over her head, but I had not yet seen her.

She spoke; I was emboldened. The incomparable charm of her features struck me less at first than their dazzling whiteness. Their ensemble, however, had one fault, if it is one. Her eyes were too large, and above all too long, but they had an expression that no words can make comprehensible, which would not pass entirely, and might perhaps vanish, under the brush of an angel. They were a blue deeper than that of the profound and vapor-free sky that I have contemplated so often from the height of the Alps, and the reflection that descended therefrom over her visage had something of the velvet clarity that the moon pours over the surface of lakes and meadows. They were like two sources of divine light, the subtle waves of which spread out around her and enveloped her in a sort of garment. Oh, I do not criticize the materialist disgraced by Providence who has searched for the secret of the soul without finding it, but I could not understand him if he had plunged his gaze once into Amélie's gaze.

I have said that she was pale. She often was. It seemed that the blood only circulated regretfully under that delicate tissue, which a slight effort might break; but the faintest emotion recalled it. I tried to explain by stammering the rather bizarre message that Sir Robert had imposed on me the day before. She blushed then, and I had not imagined until then how beautiful she was.

"I suppose," she said, "that the baronet has not left you unaware of the dolorous combination of circumstances that reminded me that I knew Greek and Pindar, and that he has spared me in your ideas from the ridicule of a pretention so out of place in women. I do, in fact, take pleasure in those studies because they procured my father a little consolation. Since our separation I have forgotten what I have retained and what I have learned; but the desire to do something for his memory and for his friend might inspire me more fortunately than I dare to think; it is necessary that I reopen the books so neglected for two years, and that I demand again memories that flee me . . .”

While speaking thus she had raised her hand to her forehead.

“Listen,” she said, suddenly, posing her hand gently on my arm—but that touch set me ablaze as if lightning had struck me and I do not know by means of what sense I heard the rest—“listen; I will be surer of what I can do tomorrow . . . or the day after . . . no matter; and between now and then, the work in which Sir Robert takes such a keen interest can be commenced.”

It is probable that I promised mechanically to return. I glimpsed Amélie then like a flash of lighting in the night; her voice reached me like a fleeting melody in the silence. I returned to myself like the awakening of a somnambulist who wonders for a long time whether he has been dreaming.

I had gone out into the road, I no longer knew which way Berne was. My legs were weak; my eyes were obfuscated by vague, capricious, formless lights, violet, crimson and orange, dazzling patches extracted from the celestial prism by a gaze too long fixed on the sun. I sat down on a rock. I laid my head in my hands. I wept. I did not know why I was weeping.

Unfortunate, I cried, finally, *your heart is not extinct! You have not used up all the misery and dolor that God has apportioned you! Behold your blood, which is still alive, in ferment, seething! Here you are, rejected, like a soul in pain, into the limbo of a paradise forever closed to you. Here you are, condemned once again to the devouring humiliation of loving without hope. Worse than that—to the horrible misfortune of being unable to love without crime.*

To love! I repeated, getting up violently and resuming at an assured pace the route that I had lost. *Perhaps to love Amélie!*

Amélie! Amélie! That name vibrated throughout my soul, and my thought no longer understood anything but that.

To love Protestant Amélie, I continued, still walking, *and renounce the religion of my father, the esteem of my childhood friends and my brethren in baptism and the eucharist . . . and that of Sir Robert himself, who cherishes me as a Catholic and would curse me as an apostate, to doom him in his fortune, to kill with a murderous hand the old man whose benevolence has saved me from distress and despair, the other adoptive father to whom gratitude and my oath enchain me! And the oath! My God, I forgot it! Come on, come on—the oath I shall keep, and I shall suffer its consequences!*

When I had arrived in the baronet's room I collapsed in my customary place.

"Help!" shouted Sir Robert. "Help, Jonathas! Water! liquor! Port wine! My son is exceeded by fatigue, my son who can no longer sustain himself, my son who is dying! Soul of bronze, ingrate Robert! Do you want to make your *Paulo-post* die?"

"No, my friend," I said seizing his hand, "I'm not fatigued, and I'm not ill; but I was in a hurry to see you and speak to you . . ."

"What news, then?" he said, resuming the thought in which my abrupt entrance had doubtless surprised him. "Are we not going to print our Pindar?"

"We shall print it, Sir," I replied, smiling bitterly at his error. "Amélie merely needs a few hours to collect her ideas. She has, I believe, promised a commencement for the day after tomorrow . . . or for tomorrow."

"Tomorrow," he said, after reflecting for a moment, "would be indiscreet. And what if you have not recovered from your fatigue the day after? You're as pale as a corpse now, and you were burning up a moment ago."

"In truth, I'm neither ill nor fatigued. I'll go the day after tomorrow, I swear to you!"

"You swear to me! By the way, what effect was produced on you by the sight of my Calliope, my Urania, my Mnemosyne—my goddess?"

"The effect that a goddess produces: surprise, admiration, respect . . ."

"Good, good, my child! I expected no less. A Calliope, a Urania, dear Maxime! A young woman who knows the lessons of Pindar better than Baronet Grove! What frightened me yesterday was thinking about so many goddesses who are humanized, like simple mortals, by blue and expressive eyes, or by blonde or curly hair. I could cite you a dozen examples in the mythographies, which we would read with pleasure if they were in a better style, and if Munckerus or Staveren had understood them better.[1] Bring us the mythographies, Jonathan, all the collections of mythographies! They will amuse us while we dine."

I respired. I knew that there would be no more question of Amélie, and that her memory would disappear in the midst of the learned or humorous digressions in which the baronet's imagination loved to stray. What necessity was there, in any case, to reveal pointlessly the insignificant secret of a first impression of which I could scarcely take account myself, about which I might be mistaken, and which I still had time to vanquish? And then, to disabuse my old friend so quickly of the possession of the Pindar on which a part of his glory reposed would be too cruel.

---

1 Thomas Muncherus (?-1652) was the compiler of the oft-reprinted *Mythographi latini* (1581); Augustino Van Staveren was the author of *Auctores mythographi Latini* (1742).

One would not believe how many means the most upright conscience has of deluding itself relative to its duties.

The day after tomorrow seemed to me to be a long time coming.

Amélie had, in fact, already reassembled all that her memory recalled of those precious lessons on the first Olympics. She had written them down carefully, and, in order to render them more intelligible for me she deigned to reread them or sing them to me; for to all the charm of that Greek chant, of which we only have confused ideas, her sonorous, emotional, penetrating voice added the charm of a musicality that was only hers. The power of that enchanting voice also held one of those mysteries that discourage speech. In order to express it today in a comparison worthy of the reality it would be necessary to make comprehensible the empire over the soul that a thought of Lamartine might have proffered by an Aeolian harp or a harmonica.[1]

When she had finished her reading and she was assured that I would let nothing escape of the fugitive nuances of the poetic thought whose secret she possessed better than Pindar, she abandoned the volume. We were in the garden, like the first time; the sun's rays sprang forth like the first time between the white bouquets of the cherry-tree, breaking over her head in light and quivering shafts, or surrounding her with aureoles. A few of the flowers that were beginning to fall were strewn in her hair; the mythological sky would not have fêted the muse herself more gloriously if it had seen her, meditative and pensive, in the dearest of her solitudes. And I remained silent in order not to trouble that solemnity. I am not sure, in any case, that I would have been able to speak if I had wanted to.

"No," she said, "they aren't poets. That magnificence of images, that overwhelming pomp of harmony, and that

______

1 The "harmonica" of the early nineteenth century was not that of today but an instrument more akin to the modern xylophone.

dazzling sumptuousness of words, isn't poetry. What do the vain glories of people, the pride of their triumphs and the intoxication of their games matter? Poetry only exists in faith and in sentiment, in a submissive belief or a vivid emotion of the heart. It does not lend its veritable inspirations to the extravagant vanity of those ancient nations; it will not lend them to the false reason of modern nations, which is only another species of vanity. The poetry of the soul had been made by Christianity; it is reform and philosophy that have killed it. It is necessary to believe in order to hear the poetry and to feel it. What might our Miltons and Klopstocks have produced—oh, they were sublime geniuses—if they had not gone back to the cradle of religion in order to redemand its mysteries? I'm astonished that the ancients, who were so fortunate and so rich in material emblems, have not represented poetry with a blindfold like amour."

I looked at her; her cheeks were vividly colored, her lips tremulous, her eyes fiery.

"However," I said, trembling . . .

She shivered

"Forgive me, Monsieur," Amélie interrupted. "I'm subject to yielding thus to an impression that has gripped me, and I don't observe then that someone is listening. It's a strange infirmity, but I live ordinarily so far from society. Forgive me, I beg you, if I have let a single word escape that offends you in your opinions. You're doubtless protestant . . ."

"I'm a Roman Catholic."

"Roman Catholic!" she cried, suddenly drawing nearer to me. She withdrew again slightly, adding: "That's also the religion in which I've been brought up, although I was born in another."

"That confounds me," I said, before being able to disentangle the ideas that were assailing me confusedly. "It's not what I was told by the baronet."

"Your astonishment is quite natural," said Amélie, "but nothing obliges young students of Greek to confine their confidence to the narrow circle of one version. My mother was Catholic."

"Sir Robert told me that."

"My father was not; he believed his religion to be better, but he was convinced that all the ways of worshiping the true God were agreeable to him if they were naïve."

"I agree with your worthy father, Amélie; I'm sure of it. Could the sovereignly good God, who might find indulgence for crime, be inexorable for a pious and sincere error? I don't believe so; and God cannot have permitted the thought of his creature to be more benevolent than his."

"I was instructed under the eyes of my mother's religion. It was his Catholic daughter that he blessed in me at the moment of quitting me for the long absence of death, and while embracing me tenderly he said this: 'Only listen to your conscience; avoid, if you can, the futile and often scandalous rumor of abjuration. The Lord knows his own. But whatever happens, always remember that the actuary of verity is a pure soul. If you remember that, we shall find one another again with the one we loved so much, in the bosom of the same God; for there is only one, may his name be glorified on earth and in Heaven!' After that he smiled, and I had heard his voice for the last time. That's all."

"Are the relatives that remain to you informed of your dispositions?"

"The fear of afflicting them obliged me to hide them. The dread of deceiving their confidence obliged me to reveal them. I preferred to give them a chagrin rather than steal their affection. None of those from whom I have some fortune to expect is unaware of my sentiments. In that confession I did not even have the honor of a sacrifice. The little that I possess is sufficient for my ambition; the law grants me a few advantages that my economies already render superfluous, and experience has that me, in any case, that there is no independence sweeter and more assured than that which comes from labor."

Our conversation probably lasted for a long time, but it would be as difficult for me to measure its duration as to recall its object, That momentary abandon had led us to an intimacy of the soul; then, all speech, all words, all inflexions of the voice have a significance that words cannot translate, but which is delightful in the memory. It is necessary to have experienced it; it is unnecessary either to recount it or to read it.

There were two existences in Amélie; there were two souls: a soul of genius that floated above all the ideas of humanity, and a soul of a young woman compatible with all the weakness and all the ignorance of inferior creatures. Her exaltation was sublime, and her simplicity charming; she had solemn sorrows, like a queen exiled from her empire; she had childlike joys. I surprised her amusing herself with a butterfly, ornamenting herself with a feather or a ribbon, chatting and laughing like a simple woman, and yet she was not a woman.

What she was, I don't know: an apparition, no doubt; one of those communications of the imaginary world that one believes that one has had, that one represents under an ideal form, that one remembers having lost in a brief time, and which leaves an eternal trace in thought. If I did not have her letters, her hair, her tortoiseshell ring and her portrait I would be certain of having dreamed.

I have read a great deal since; I have read *Julie*, the creation of a sentimental man who knew something about love via hearsay. I have read *Corinne*, the inspiration of a poet who had a great deal of tenderness in the imagination.[1] In truth, those marvels of style and talent were only cold marvels, because

---

1 *Julie* was the original title of the epistolary novel by Jean-Jacques Rousseau better known as *La Nouvelle Héloïse* (1761); *Corinne* (1807) is a story of doomed love by Madame de Staël.

they exceeded the habitual range of our imperfect nature. Amélie was far beyond them, for God is more powerful than genius, and it was God that had made her.

I should not be reproached for having invented her; who could have invented Amélie? How could I make her comprehensible, not having the magical secret of those writers? How could I dare to say: this is what Amélie was, I, whose soul is astonished and still succumbs, after so many years, merely to the resonance of her memory? These inexpressible, nameless, formless, colorless reminiscences are mine, and for me; they cannot speak for anyone but me, like a sign that a voyager has left on the road traveled, like a white stone that a miser has cemented in the earth above his buried treasure.

One day, perhaps, it will be necessary for me to be condemned to write romances and short stories, since I have not been found good for anything useful in the best of possible societies, but I shall refrain from giving them Amélie for a heroine. I know the rules of art too well.

I quit her more tranquil. The capitulations of my conscience cost me less. The danger that Sir Robert feared for his ward was an accomplished event that had not depended on me. The oath that I had sworn to him was an engagement whose object was purely imaginary. I could not keep it without violating a new mystery more important for Amélie's happiness and that of the baronet himself. His two most cherished illusions dependent on the constancy of Amélie in his faith, and the accomplishment of an edition of Pindar as immortal as Pindar.

I did not doubt that I would have been released from my word by a priest and above all by an advocate. The confidences that I had just obtained without wishing it rendered me as free as I had been before contracting a reckless obligation. If I had been able to respond to him when he expressed his anxieties to me: *Amélie is Catholic, and her relatives know it,* what would have remained for him to ask of me? The oath to love her with purity, with an unalterable fidelity, with a resignation submissive to the will of Amélie and Providence? To love Amélie, great God! To hope to be loved by her? Oh, I did not have so much pride.

In any case, the baronet did not ask me. He did not interrogate my gaze, which would have betrayed me, once with his own gaze. He was too absorbed in the contemplation of the scholia that Pindar appeared to have inspired with his genius, and the gloss more poetic, more elegant and more harmonious than the text. How many books consulted! How many authors summoned in testimony! How many scholarly illustrations confronted with Amélie's simple notes! How many journeys for Jonathas! But Jonathas was impassive, and, his arms laden with folios he arranged everything before his master with a mechanical obedience, the precision of which would have disconcerted the most experienced librarian.

"Phenomenon of the century!" cried Sir Robert. "Incomparable child, who has seen in Pindar so many beauties hidden from Schmidius, Benedictus, Suderius, my friend Heyne and, I think, from my brother Jacobus, for I find here discoveries more precious than gold or diamonds, of which I never heard him speak! O Jacobus, where are you, to moisten with paternal tears this generous offspring, this predestined flower of your glorious stem, this virgin animated by a divine spirit to which I shall elevate a temple in my preface. Where are you, Jacobus, for my dear *Paulo-post* is preoccupied with too many serious thoughts to share my enthusiasm?"

I shivered. I had to pull myself together a little in order to conceive that the baronet was reproaching me for not sensing the value of Amélie and for speaking of her coldly. Alas . . . !

Fortunately, that edition of Pindar was not the work of a day. After the *Olympics* came the *Pythics*; after the *Pythics*, the *Nemeans*; after the *Nemeans*, the *Isthmians*. Everyone knows that; but the slightest difficulty required a visit to the oracle, and I would sometimes have wept like Chapelle,[1] because the Theban singer had not lived long enough to fill a volume the size of Jonathas.

Sir Robert, who enjoyed my progress almost as much as his acquisitions, was the first to urge me to multiply my steps. He never complained that I departed too early or came back too late. He thought that the alternation of exercise and study was beneficial to my health, my instruction and my happiness. He made enquires in that regard of Jonathas, while accumulating nicknames with which his mythological erudition furnished him in droves, and caressant epithets that he only found in his heart: *my gentle Typhon, my amiable Enceladus, my gracious Prometheus.* Jonathan, who did not speak, as I believe I have said, unless constrained by an irresistible necessity, contented himself with expressing his approval by a slight inclination of the head and a strange smile. As for me, I have no need to say that I shared Jonathas' opinion.

The baronet's book still occupied Amélie and me, but it did not occupy us for long. I do not know why I found more aptitude in understanding the work from day to day, and less impatience to conclude it. It required so little, moreover, to furnish Sir Robert with countless researches and endless amplifications. So, at the end of a few minutes, the Greek poet was abandoned and delightful hours went by in Amélie's garden, during which we no longer spoke about him. It was not that we were distracted, like the first time, by a sudden and gripping digression that absorbed all thought; we no longer spoke about him because we had ceased to speak.

The more the soul is filled, if I remember correctly, the more insignificant conversation becomes, and when hazard

---

1 "Chapelle" was the pseudonym of Claude-Emmanuel Luillier (c1626-1685), a friend of Cyrano de Bergerac and Molière who studied medicine, and reportedly regretted the death of Pindar in the hands of ignorant physicians—a remark more widely cited in English sources than French ones.

leads to the exchange of a few words, one blushes at finding so little to say. One is ashamed, takes pity on oneself, and shuts up. It is a great deal when one dares to risk encountering a gaze that one seeks—and one avoids it. Oh, when she is close to you, mildly pensive, colored by a slight emotion, her lips parted by a barely audible breath, her eyes fixed on an object that is not you, but which is not distracted, because she is looking at it without seeing it, what a turbulent agitation comes to upset the heart at the moment when she returns them to yours without expecting to find them.

What existence has not felt close to annihilation in that sensuality so disproportionate to our strength? One collects oneself, taking refuge in oneself, and needs to struggle against joy in order not to be overwhelmed by it. How pure and how complete the sentiment of life is! How the breast swells in containing, in possessing the present! And yet, how the time flies, how it disappears! You have imagined in vain that summer evenings are long; the chimes of the hour have hardly expired in the bell-tower than the bell is summoning another. The shadow of the trees increases while one measures it. It is necessary to depart when it plunges into the lawn bordering the pathway, and while you are rejoicing that it is still so far away, it is already there.

Hazard, or a moment of expansion, had brought her hand close to mine one day. I cannot explain by what fortunate skill I linked my fingers with it in such a manner as not to quit it. That communication, more intimate and more tender than all those that amour has invented, became in the days that followed a right or a habit; that, of course, rendered all conversation unnecessary. What can words say that is worth the mute correspondence of two souls united via the surface of an intelligent and sensitive epidermis by the sympathetic vibration of interlaced nerves, by the seething of the arteries, by the transfusion of a warm and penetrating moisture that circulates, so to speak, from one heart to another?

I know full well what the possession of a beloved woman is, but does everyone know it? Is there not for a few tender and passionate organizations a sense unknown to the vulgar, an organ more delicate, purer, more exquisite in perceptions, which transforms, elevates and spiritualizes our essence, and enables it to participate at moments in divine nature? I had it at a young age, the faculty of living differently, of loving better than everyone loves. I conserve it fully alive in the midst of the ruins of my life, and I feel sincerely sorry for men who have only been happy as other men are.

When one separates, that is something else. There commences a new species of wellbeing. The profound felicity that was not understood suddenly remains in confrontation with itself. It contemplates itself with surprise, savors itself with delight. Those sensual calms and silences give way to exaltation, to delirium; all the sensations are resuscitated, and with what vivacity! All the ideas are developed, and with what eloquence! One is no longer constrained; one speaks, one cries out, one sheds tears and sobs of joy. One takes the sky and the universe as witnesses to one's ecstasy, and there is not an atom in creation that is not animated in order to sense it and respond to it.

How could it not respond to it? When one has an immense amour in the heart, one remakes a world. One can tell the light to be, and the light will be! I recomposed everything. I put everything in its place: her, me, and nature; I saw Amélie again; I saw her again more distinctly, as I could see her, as I had seen her. The ensemble of her features escaped me, but what need had I of that? Who has ever seen in their ensemble the features of the woman he loves? Who has ever remembered it? But how I heard her voice, her frank, abrupt, sonorous, slightly metallic speech, which vibrated for a long time, like an emotional metal shaft, like an empty crystal struck by iron, which resounded more and more harmoniously in my ear! It vibrated there, and it still echoes there.

And then, my own thought suddenly took on a naïve self-love, with a childish enthusiasm. It was me, me alone, who had just spent four hours with Amélie in the air that she had breathed, in the perfume of her breath, in the radiance of her eyes. I knew the side of my body that had been able to touch hers. I always sat to her right, because there was a small pedestal at the other end of the bench on which she was accustomed to lean. I had avoided on that side the sacrilegious touch of a golden butterfly or a clump of roses with more urgency than shame puts into avoiding that of a pariah. I looked at my hand, which had touched her hand, I loved it, I deemed it fortunate, I caressed it with my lips, I hid it over my heart; It seemed to me that I was Amélie's Bologna stone,[1] that I reflected something of her, that people who received me in the distance were whispering to one another; "Look!"

The day after the fateful day when I had brought Amélie's last note back to our classical laboratory, the baronet demanded that I spend a few days visiting the marvel of the Oberland, in order to recover from the fatigues of such a long assiduity in toil. He did not know that they were only sensible to me since they had ended. I accepted with gratitude, however, because Amélie was on the way. *I shall be able to see her*, I said to myself, *and even if I do not see her, I shall pass so close to her!*

I found her on her grassy bank. She had taken my place there. She quit it as if she were ashamed of having taken it; I sat down. I did not look at her, because I had to speak to her. I spoke to her, in fact, about my brief excursion in the Oberland, and the desire I had experienced to see her for the last time.

"For the last time!" she replied, drawing closer to me and abandoning her hand to me, which I would not have dared

---

1 The so-called Bologna stones were excavated in 1603 from the volcanic rock of Mount Palermo near Bologna by a would-be alchemist named Vincenzo Cascariolo, who discovered that after being exposed to the sun during the day they became luminous after dark; they were subsequently identified as phosphorescent baryte.

to take so quickly. "For the last time!" she continued, smiling. "Are voyages to the Oberland so dangerous?"

"You're not unaware that I no longer have a pretext with regard to society to come to see you."

"With regard to society!" she cried, with astonishment.

"Even less does any remain in the eyes of the baronet."

"Of Sir Robert!" she said. "Oh, that's true; I hadn't thought of that. For the last time!"

We did not say any more. She was not far away. She was there, beside my breast; she was touching me. She had not withdrawn her hand. Her hand was trembling.

She must have been suffering, for she allowed her head to fall upon my shoulder. This time, I felt and inhaled her breath. Her hair was undone; it mingled with mine; it floated over my face. One of its ringlets came as far as my mouth, and I retained it with my lips.

Some time after that, I felt her body buckle. I put my arm around her in order to sustain her. It is difficult to explain how one does not die in such circumstances, and it would have been so good!

She was the one who perceived that the sun had set.

"Here comes the night," she said, leaping to her feet a few paces in front of me. "Why haven't you departed?"

"I'm going to the Oberland, Amélie. What does it matter to me what my shelter will be tonight? A hut, heather, a rock, anything is good." Nevertheless, I followed her.

We took so long reaching the old somber gallery that led to the door that the darkness became denser. Amélie picked up a lamp in order to accompany me along the passage, which was long, ruinous and difficult, having belonged to ancient monastic constructions. Parts of the vault, which had been detached here and here, were strewn on the damp and mobile ground, in which time had incorporated them like natural rocks. In all the places that the sunlight had reached, handfuls of weeds could be seen springing from the gaps in their joints, including large clumps of yellow flowers.

Amélie preceded me, turning toward me at almost every step, especially when the path offered some dangerous obstacle. The livid clarity which projected shadows upwards over her face, which I had never seen illuminated other than by the sky, gave her something of the aspect of a phantom. She seemed to me to be sadder, taller and paler. An idea of death settled on my heart. I tottered. The key had turned in the lock; the hinges creaked. The air became less cold, the obscurity less somber. It was the exterior already, the world of those who believed themselves to be alive. Already!

I found Amélie's hand again. I no longer knew that it was a woman's hand. I seized it as if to crush it. I bore it to my forehead, to my eyes to my mouth. I covered it and impregnated it with kisses in which I would have liked to leave my soul. What need had I of a soul of my own, a soul that was only good for suffering?

The door closed again. I did not understand that Amélie had not come out too, that she had left me alone—all alone! It seemed to me that there were two of us.

Suddenly, I heard a cry. I launched myself toward the door, as if it were incapable of stopping me. There was one of those little iron trellises there, like the ones in houses of reclusion, through which one can look, speak and interrogate. Amélie was motionless on the spot where I had left her, absorbed by a fixed thought, her eyes nailed to the ground. Her lamp fell.

I attacked the door. I drove my fingers between its moldings. I tried to cry out too; doubtless I did cry out. The extremity of the gallery was illuminated, and I saw Amélie's dress float, hide and reappear by turns amid the debris.

I could no longer sustain myself. I fainted on the threshold; I struck it with my head. I would not have quit it if an ineffable idea, like the one that the resurrection must awaken in an elect soul, had not rendered me strength and life.

I got up; I held myself upright; I walked without effort. I had said to myself: *Perhaps she loves me.*

I spent a week traveling in the Oberland, wandering, climbing, meditating, enjoying the wellbeing of being free and living with my thought. Amélie was not beside me, but I thought I could sense her heart following me. Since I had loved her I had never been as far away from her, but never had I been less really separated from her. What separated us was the ground that one can travel in half a day's march, a little air, a little sky, but no sentiment and no distraction. Her voice was the last one that vibrated in my heart, her hand the last one I had touched, her gaze the last one that had encountered mine. I still spoke to her, saw her and touched her. A happy eternity, a true paradise for the soul, would be a similar emotion, thus prolonged, thus maintained, without alterations, without vicissitudes, without suspicion of the future, and always, always alive!

On the day of my return to Berne it was bright morning when I passed under the house I had not slept. I had got up six times to see whether dawn was appearing. Ought I not to be able to see the house, and could I see it too soon? Finally, it appeared, white and struck by the rising sun, in the midst of its clumps of shade, where it inclined as far as the road over the old wing of dilapidated buildings that probably no longer exist. Many others have disappeared since!

There was only one open casement; it was Amélie's. I supposed that she had wanted to enjoy that delectable hour when nature awakens with so much grace. I flattered myself that her first gaze would have been turned toward the Oberland. I hoped that she would return to it.

She did not appear. Nothing was less extraordinary, and yet I could not help feeling a strange sadness.

That astonished me. What did the charm of the morning lack? The horizon was so pure, the air so mild, the autumn so beautiful with its magnificent foliage, which had scarcely begun to be dappled with resplendent colors, as if each tree bore clusters of gold and crimson.

It lacked Amélie. Amélie was not there.

I was welcomed by the baronet as if I were a cherished child that he had not seen for years and who was arriving from far away. After some time, however, his face darkened and his head slowly tipped backwards until it became horizontal to the ceiling, striking it with one of those vertical gazes, the significance of which I could no longer mistake.

I realized that some misfortune had occurred. My heart was constricted.

"Did you go into Amélie's house as you returned?" Sir Robert asked me.

"Amélie's house?" I replied. "How? On what occasion? A what hour? Why? Pindar is finished."

"She's ill," he said, bringing his head back to his hand as slowly as he had taken it away.

"Ill!" I cried. "In danger, perhaps! Explain yourself, Sir Robert!"

He was too emotional himself to take note of my emotion. He continued: "In danger—that depends. The physicians don't think so. They talk about an indisposition, a species of nervous infirmity that does not threaten her life; but they also said that of . . . someone, another woman, another child, who died following an illness that had the same symptoms. Oh, this one, *Paulo-post*, is dearer to my heart than the lessons of Pindar, dearer to my heart than my own existence. Amélie is all that remains to me of my Jacobus!"

I scarcely heard him; I reassembled my ideas. I reflected. I had heard mention of that extraordinary malady from Amélie herself; I knew its characteristics; her heart suddenly palpitated violently; her ears buzzed as if deafened by the noise of a cataract; her eyes were obscured, extinguished, and then her blood no longer circulated, her pulse no longer beat. She ceased to be, momentarily, for the crisis, having arrived at that point, only ever lasted for a moment; she brought back no other memory than that of a confused dream, a temporary excursion into the darkness of death; but it caused her such scant anxiety that she had almost succeeded in causing me to share her insouciance.

"Unfortunately," added the baronet, "you're too fatigued to go and seek information about her condition, which you could judge better than Jonathas."

I had already departed.

"Mademoiselle has expressly demanded to be left alone," one of the servant girls told me, who came to open the door to me, "but she excepted persons who presented themselves on Sir Robert's behalf."

I flew to Amélie's room. I was astonished, when I went in, that the door was closed on me, but I remembered that she had expressly demanded to be left alone.

She was, in fact, alone: sitting in an armchair, her head supported on the back, her eyes closed, her complexion paler than usual. I launched myself toward her; she did not budge. I seized her hand; it was cold. I uttered a cry; I fell to my knees, I pressed her hand in both of mind; I pressed it to my face. I cried out again; I prayed; I wept. I did not know whether it was one of the fits she had described to me or whether it was death itself.

That lasted for a time impossible to calculate: a minute . . . an eternity. I was no longer crying, no longer weeping; I was dying.

Her hand had warmed up under my breath, under my tears and under my kisses. My fingers thought they discovered there, in rising as far as the artery, the play of life and blood. Finally, it palpitated; it drew away from my lips, and I dared to raise my gaze to Amélie, whose open and staring eyes were attached to me with an anxious astonishment.

"Maxime!" she cried, throwing her arms over my shoulders. "Maxime! It's him! It's you! It's really you! You love me, then!"

"Love you, Amélie, oh, to love you, to adore you, to live or die loving you, to sense my soul annihilated in that thought . . . to die here . . . now . . . now . . ."

"Good, good," she said, passing her fingers over my head and my neck, wiping the sweat from my brow and the tears from my eyes. "So you've returned from the Oberland! It's you! It's Maxime, and I know that he loves me! Fortunate Amélie! I might have died a moment too soon!"

"Die! Oh, you shan't die! I forbid you to die! I have life, I have a future for both of us."

And while I was speaking to her I gazed at her more intently than I had ever done. I was astonished to see her cheeks animated by colors so vivid, and her pupils with a fiery radiance. I dreaded being mistaken regarding her resurrection, and that what remained to me of Amélie was no more than a soul that had completed its transfiguration for Heaven.

"Wait, wait!" I said. "Calm down! Calm your heart in order to conserve it for me! Remember that too strong an emotion might put your life and mine in peril, since they are only one. Think that I could no longer resist the dolor of seeing you as I saw you just now; that you have, from now on, all my destiny to save as well! Calm down, Amélie! Rest! Draw away from me, distance the thought of me. I shall keep vigil close by! At a sign departed from your window, at the slightest cry, the faintest appeal. I will be at your knees, and you will wake up again!"

"Die, die! What an insensate frenzy!" she said. "Amélie, die! What a childish fear! Dying is good for weakness and for misfortune, but I shan't die! Look, are you not here? Are you not touching me? Do I still have an icy hand and pale cheeks? Is my blood still frozen in my veins? Is my heart still shriveled, as if under a serpent's tooth? It is so joyful, my heart! It is dancing, bounding in my breast! Oh, it isn't thus that I shall die, unless death is worth more than life!"

Her exaltation intoxicated me and frightened me at the same time. She perceived that. She leaned her head on my arm, for I had sat down next to her, and, smiling, her eyes full of a mild and reposed joy, with her hands nonchalantly knotted around me, she said to me in a low voice: "Don't be afraid . . . ! Don't be anxious . . . ! I'm tranquil! I'm cured! I'm happy! You've found me happy. You see! Again I'm the first to perceive that the sun is setting, and this evening, you aren't going to the Oberland!"

The sun was indeed setting, and the baronet had been waiting for a long time, impatiently, for explicit information regarding Amélie's condition. That was because on that day, the minutes had passed a thousand times more quickly than ordinarily; it was because that conversation, which is written in so few lines, was, as those who have loved will know, inexhaustible in details always similar and always new.

Who can ever say what nuances of thought there are in the expression of a gaze, in the accentuation of a syllable, in the modulation of a breath, in the very silence that succeeds, more eloquent still, the words and the sighs? Who can say how many different things a word repeated infinitely can signify, if it is exchanged eternally between two passionate souls that send it back and forth like a fantastic challenge in seizing its ultimate thought? Who can comprehend the incomprehensible moment when two lovers who have just confessed that they love one another perceive that they have said it sufficiently?

I left, however. It was necessary. I was tranquil, in any case, Amélie was no longer suffering. She had sworn it to me. When I was outside the old part of the buildings and the circuit of the road brought me back under her window, she was there to give me a sign of adieu, and to follow me with her eyes all the way to the first bend in the road. She was still there then, and the sign as renewed between us, with an abandon that the distance that separated us rendered as innocent as her heart and mine. Perhaps it was a kiss.

Sir Robert had not covered a single sheet of paper—what am I saying? he had not opened a book—since my departure. Jonathas, motionless, upright and perpendicular, in accordance with his custom, had been watching for three hours over the anxious forehead of his master for the whim of the first edition or the copy *in membranis*, which ordinarily amused his solitude with such pleasant distractions. I sensed that it was the anxiety in which I had left him for too long regarding Amélie's health that had absorbed all the faculties of that tender soul, accustomed to live via others much more than itself, and I regretted having been happy for such a long time.

"Amélie's condition is better," I said, leaning on the baronet's armchair, "and I hope that in a few days it will no longer give us cause for alarm."

Sir Robert's features were disengaged from the cloud that covered them. His mouth resumed the smile that was habitual to it, and he squeezed my hand.

"In that case," he said, "you'll return tomorrow at the same hour, and I'll be reassured sooner."

I did not know for sure whether that was a reproach, but I promised myself not to take the risk again.

When I arrived, Amélie was not alone, as she had been the previous day. Her recovery had made sufficient progress for her to receive her friends, before whom she would have feared to appear in the state of annihilation in which I had surprised her. My visits did not excite any suspicion in the house, and no one guessed that I was attracted there by an amour other than that of Greek. It did not take long for us to be left alone.

It is a strange situation, that of lovers who are meeting

again for the first time, a few hours after the first expansion of a sentiment that has been betrayed on either part, and which has confounded their souls into one for the first time. Something extraordinary happens then in the mind. The happiness that had preoccupied it with a conviction so profound and so delectable becomes almost an object of doubt. One wonders with anxiety whether one has not been dreaming, or whether a temporary gleam of felicity that would suffice for an entire lifetime can be reflected without deterioration on a single morrow. It seems that the entire future has been devoured in a minute of delirium. One does not dare to gaze or to speak, because one knows everything that one might lose in exchanging against a present notion, chilled by reflection or caprice, the burning emotion of the past. Once I was assured that she was better, I would have liked not to have come. I would have liked, at least, to have left before the strangers, before the indifferent individuals. I would have had less fear of being confounded with them . . .

"I shall announce to Sir Robert, then, that Amélie is no longer suffering," I said, rising to my feet in order to extract myself from the inexplicable embarrassment of my thoughts and my heart.

"Yes, Maxime, you can announce that to him, thanking him for his interest and his kindness."

"*You can announce that to him!*"[1] I cried, at her knees. "Oh, speak to me as you did yesterday, once, only once . . . or do not hope that I will live long enough to see him again and name you to him!"

She put her arms around my neck again, and drew me toward her; she let her head fall next to mine, and covered my head with her hair, as she had the day before.

"Poor friend!" said Amélie. "What have I done to make you doubt me? Yesterday is forever!"

---

1 Maxime is upset because Amélie has addressed him formally as *vous*.

"I was sure of it," I said, weeping with joy, "but I needed to hear it said again."

From that day on we were no longer in pain, and we did not forget again to address one another as *tu*. Those conversations were renewed often; they lasted for a few weeks, either because Amélie's full recovery left me a few anxieties, or because the interest of my of my passion and my happiness had reduced me to the vile necessity of prolonging the baronet's. One goes so far, without realizing it, once one has capitulated with one's conscience, once one has lied!

The falsity of that moral position ended up disquieting me, however, to the point of troubling my sleep, poisoning my solitary reveries, until then so sweet and so pure. I surprised myself from time to time in those walks, so full of the thought of Amélie, striking my forehead angrily and saying to myself aloud: "It isn't good, though!"

I had made no mystery of that for Amélie. I had decided to devote an entire day to her. I recounted Sir Robert's initial fears, and the oath I had sworn, and the excellent reasons I had had for not keeping it.

She did not respond to me for some time.

"My friend," she said to me, finally. "We are both free, and nothing can prevent us from loving one another forever, for I shall never doubt your heart; but we are placing our happiness under the auspices of perjury. Keep the engagements you have made. Tell him everything; say that you love me; say, above all, that I love you and that my life depends on you. A duty accomplished is the first of all goods. The event that might prevent us from present happiness is nothing at the price of the future that God can give us."

I argued like a child, but I departed resigned to obeying her. I repeated to myself once again as I went into Sir Robert's room: *She wishes it!* That was an authority more powerful for my feeble reason than an oath made on the Gospel to which I had taken God as a witness.

The baronet was waiting for me, and to my great astonishment the sacred book was open before him, as it had been the first time. I had not seen it again since, but I recognized it immediately.

I trembled in all my limbs. A cold sweat ran over my brow, I wondered whether I was awake.

"Do you remember this?" Sir Robert said to me. "Something similar has already been found between us."

"Forgive me," I said, sitting down, because I could scarcely sustain myself. "One moment, in the name of Heaven, in order that I do not expire before you; but beforehand, do you not think it necessary to send Jonathas away?"

"Jonathas cannot understand you, Maxime. He only knows what his mechanical intelligence has informed him, not more, and the affairs of your soul are in bad order, my poor friend, for you to fear a conversation in French before a Welshman who does not even know English."

"I have recovered, Sir Robert. I'm no longer afraid. In reminding me of my soul, you have rendered my security. You are informed. But I can say everything. The confession that you are about to demand of me, I swear that I had come to make!"

"And on what will you swear this time?" replied the baronet, letting his head fall against the back of his armchair.

"Stop, Sir Robert! You're abusing your advantages. You've condemned me to death without having heard me."

"I'm listening to you, Maxime."

"I promised you my secret, but the day when I learned that deadly secret it was already another's, the secret of Amélie's life. She has just disengaged me of it."

"She has just permitted you to be faithful to your oath, no doubt."

"She has just prescribed it to me. Since our second meeting, I have known that she was a Roman Catholic in her heart."

"Roman Catholic!" cried Sir Robert, bewildered. "Where have you got that blasphemy, impious calumniator?"

"From her words, from her confessions, Sir Robert, on a day when she believed me to be a protestant."

"Roman Catholic! Apostate! Perjury! Sacrilege! Profanation of profanations! Jacobus' daughter Catholic! And he has not risen from his tomb to curse her!"

"He descended into it blessing her. Amélie's father knew that she was Roman Catholic."

Here Sir Robert's consternation reached its peak. His mind appeared to go astray in a chaos of confused ideas and contradictory resolutions. His fixed eyes expressed the terror of a man struck by a horrible apparition. Stammering, he repeated: "Roman Catholic, and her father knew it! And even if that were as true as it is false," he went on, after a few minutes of agitation, but in a strong and assured voice, "if she had betrayed her God, ought you to betray him too? Is that the education that you receive from your Church? Or, if you do not believe in the religion you attest, did not the simple rules of human probity not engage you toward me? What permitted you to deceive the credulity of a friend, dupe his foolish confidence in your promises, the confidence of an old man who had delivered himself to you, is it necessary to remind you, with the blind tenderness of a father?"

"I have had the misfortune of believing that I understood better than you the interests of your happiness, in sparing you an irreparable pain. My error is doubtless grave, but that motive would excuse it, if it could be excused."

"Perjury has no excuse. It always bears its punishment, even if Heaven wishes to spare you. Irreparable, you say! There is nothing irreparable here except, perhaps, your fatal passion! You have told me that she is Roman Catholic in her heart.

That is only too possible, alas. Are you not Roman Catholic? I have also known the heart of young women, and their faith is the faith of the man they love; their religion is their amour. But she has not abjured. If she had abjured, her resources would no longer exist; opinion would have rejected her, would have scourged her. She would be obliged to go to hide elsewhere the opprobrium that attaches to the renegade. The insensate penchant that draws her to papism would vanish as soon as the illusion that has devoted her soul to you for a few months. You are in revolt against that idea, I can tell, but the future will confirm my words, for the affection of women in even more temporary than their belief, and a woman who has let go of God can soon forget a lover. It is, however, to that brief enjoyment of vanity, to a fit of the delirium of the fever of a young man, that you have sacrificed the peace of my old age and the honor of your engagements. Justify yourself, if you can!"

"I believe that I could, but I have no need to do so. Amélie's purity is above reproach. Our mutual amour has only been divined by you. It will leave no blush on her forehead, nor any remorse in her heart, nor any stain on her reputation. As for my obligations, they are intact and sacred, as on the day when I linked myself to them voluntarily. I have only my happiness still to immolate to my duty; but that consideration will not stop me. My life belongs to you, Sir Robert, and you can be sure that I will not dispute it with you."

"Who is demanding your life from you, which I hold dearer than my own?" the baronet responded, holding out his hand. "Am I strong enough to retain you on the brink of the abyss to which I have pushed you both—me, the most culpable of the three of us? Oh, may the lightning obliterate what remains of Pindar, without excepting my beautiful copy of the Calliergi edition! A curse upon Pindar, Calliergi and me!"

"Calliergi's Pindar?" said Jonathas, leaning toward his master's ear.

"I have no need of it, tender and obedient Goliath," the baronet replied, turning his affectionate gaze toward the attentive Welshman. "I have no need of Calliergi's Pindar. I never want to see it again. And yet, it would still make the happiness of my eyes if I had found in the soul of a son of my choice, the unique object of my hopes, the resigned submission of your savage soul."

Then Jonathas understood that it was no longer a matter of Calliergi's Pindar; that was all that he had understood.

The baronet looked at both of us, and he started to weep. He was weeping over me; I was at his knees.

"My master, my friend, my father," I said, sobbing, "dispose of the obedience of Maxime like that of Jonathas. Order! The day is not far advanced. I have time to depart for Berne."

"And to take the road to the Oberland," said Sir Robert, pressing my head in his hands.

"The road that you wish! The one that will take me further away from Amélie, the one at the end of which I will never be able to find either her or you! I will take it if I must, provided that she and you conserve of me a memory of esteem and amity."

"Have you are least reflected on the range of that promise?"

"It will be accomplished within the hour. I only ask of you the time to write, to explain to her in a few words the resolution that you demand of me, to tell her one more time that my heart will only ever live for her. I will not tell her my plans, I will not indicate to her the refuge I shall seek. I have no plans, no refuge. I do not know where I shall go. All that I know is that I shall go where she is not, and that I shall go because you have wished it. After that, it is finished, and Maxime will be for both of you as if he had never been."

"As if he had never been!" the baronet interrupted, excitedly. "My son, my dear son, my beloved *Paulo-post!* As if he had never been! Is Maxime's old friend, then, a soul insensible to the most generous devotion, without compassion for the errors of sensibility, without admiration for courage and virtue; is he a man with entrails of iron? Oh, condescend yourself to the mortal anxieties of poor baronet Grove; take pity on his rigor, and try, if it is possible, not to accuse him.

"Yes, my friend, I hope, I still hope, that this criminal abjuration will not happen when its first, its unique, motive has disappeared. I hope that this frightful scandal, in a person of such rare elevation of character and talents, will not afflict the people who follow the law of verity. I hope that the impression of this deplorable amour, which would doom you both, will be effaced at the same time when you are separated. I am not counting on the impossible to cure you; I am counting on what is most essential in our nature, most inevitable in our destiny, on the instability of two childish hearts that have believed that they loved one another because hazard and the foolishness of an old man have had the misfortune of bringing them together. I am counting on the insatiable need for amour of which you believed yourself to be freed forever when you wanted to make yourself a monk, and which will perhaps still torment you under your white hair. There is no lack of beautiful papist women who will love my Maxime, and who will be proud of being loved by him.

"And if it happens otherwise . . . if the fatality of my life has caused me to fall on one of the irresistible passions of romance that resist the proof of absence and time, then we shall see! And you know, if you have not judged me badly, that you will find in my bosom an assured port against despair. Go away, then, if you have the courage; but do not go as the forgetful friend who wants to be forgotten. Write to me . . . every day . . . and don't go far!"

While the baronet repeated all that in ten different forms, each more benevolent and more expansive than the last, I let my sad adieux to Amélie fall on to the paper.

"Here is the letter," I said, presenting it to him, open. "Now, I'm ready."

He sealed it without reading it.

A few necessary dispositions summoned me momentarily to my bedroom. When I returned I found Sir Robert plunged into the most profound dejection. I took his hand in order to bear it to my lips, but he drew me into his arms.

"And I too," he said, "I whose heart is always softened by the sufferings of others, will give proof of courage—a courage, alas, without compensation and without hope. All of my future, my own, was to be the days—the few days—that I still had to love you, present and happy, and to believe myself loved by you. Who will love me tomorrow?"

I had been calm until then, like a firm man who hears his sentence pronounced, but I began to give way under the weight of his own dolor. I embraced him and I fled.

I passed through Berne without seeing anything. I emerged from it with the confused and horrible impression of an unfortunate precipitating himself into an obscure abyss, who had not even reconnoitered with his gaze the place where he is about to be smashed.

After three hours of aimless marching I arrived I know not where, in a village of which I was never able to remember the name. I was only sure that I had not followed the road to the Oberland.

I walked for several days, stopping everywhere but settling nowhere, from the canton of Berne to the Val d'Orbe. Those romantic and solitary sites suited the state of my soul. I would have liked not to quit them.

I was thinking that, lying on a rock, on a beautiful afternoon at the end of autumn, when the explosion of firearms a short distance away extracted me from my reverie. I supposed that there were hunters. A moment later, bullets ricocheted at my sides. I got up and looked around. I had lain down under a target. That is what society has made of the magnificences of nature.

If I had been killed thus, however, I would have died so pure and so happy, I would have died in the contemplation of God and his works, in the thought of Amélie that was mingled with all my thoughts, which was the source of all that was noble, touching and passionate therein. My life was so complete! The good fortune of choosing, of marking the instant and the genre of death would be too complete for our miserable destiny on earth. Only the suicide is fortunate; he alone can dispose of his days at a fixed hour, and I no longer thought about that, about suicide. Suicides do not enter Amélie's paradise.

It was late when I arrived at Yverdon, in the inn that is the first on the right coming from the region of Vaud.

Yverdon is a pleasant and peaceful town, the position of which, the aspects, the picturesque harmonies, the calm and serious beauties, are struck with I know not what fatality of melancholy that grips the heart. The next day, I was on the shore of its lake before sunrise, still dark, motionless and soundless, because the damp atmosphere, as settled as the water, was not agitated by the slightest wind. I sat down, I waited, I watched; I followed with my gaze, across the gradually broadening horizon, the progress of the nascent day.

There was a moment when the mists, swayed by a movement of their own, commenced to whiten, to relax their web penetrated by pale rays, to scatter in crazy fleeces, to roll, vaguer and lighter, to the tips of promontories, to settle over the waters in the distance like banks of foam, and to come apart in the crowns of semi-defoliated trees like threads of soil floating like stray breath in the sir. The light increased everywhere; the lake turned blue. I distinguished the interlacement of quivering ripples on its surface, not sufficiently excited for them to be audible. One could have heard at a distance of a league the leap of a fish awakened by the warmth of the matinal air or the periodic beat of an oar.

Then, Granson outlined on the opposite shore the white silhouettes of its houses, disposed in an amphitheater, and the unequal enclosures of its orchards. That spectacle, sad and pacific at the same time, suited the state of my heart; it soothed its perplexities by penetrating it with a languor full of charm. I already loved Yverdon as one loves a long impression of regret and dolor that is identified with life, but I did not yet know why.

The inexplicable sentiment that I had just experienced was fortified by every step I took in a walk unique in the world, which brought me back to town through avenues of immense trees, the magnificent and solitary pomp of which would impose a sublime meditation upon the most vulgar hearts. I thought there about Dante's Elysium, about the grave and dream-filled immortality of infants that had died without baptism and ages that had died without revelation. A bitter and profound doubt had warned me a long time ago that eternity did not reserve other joys and other recompenses for me. There are souls long destined to suffer, for whom the mere memory of life will poison forever the felicity of the elect.

I wept, but I did not weep without mildness, and I understood that the endless future in question was good enough for me.

I stopped, with an anguish of sorrow and sensuality that cannot be defined, in the most isolated and wildest place, on thick, deep grass that did not appear to have been trodden. I sounded it with a calculating gaze altered by repose; I asked it for a refuge, and one of the lucid convictions that take possession of thought without one knowing how suddenly told me that I would find it there.

I am, however, very far from it today.

I spent the rest of the morning rolling a large block of white stone around the place and gazing at it with the ecstasy of a mariner whose ship has been demasted by the tempest, who finally sees that he is about to run aground on a pretty shore, garnished with shade, flowers and fruits.

"Praise God," I said. "This is good."

And I did not leave Yverdon.

I arranged my whole life there, between a few sedentary studies of which my sojourn with Sir Robert had caused me to contract the habit, and pensive walks that nightfall always terminated too soon. The sound of the dry leaves that the still-lukewarm wind of a beautiful autumn chases through the air in flocks, or which roll and creak under foot, is so agreeable to a man who is suffering.

"For me too," I said, "autumn has come to wither all the flowers of life, which ought only to appear in a brief morning of spring; I too am going to fall on the earth like those dry leaves that a chilly wind causes to rain from their stems. Adieu, my dreams of happiness; adieu, my hopes of amour; adieu, the broken hiccups of the imagination; adieu Amélie, and the future! To fall wherever the first storm pushes me, to fall and finish . . . that is the destiny of all things.

And I embraced with resignation that necessity of existence, because everything announced to me that nature entire was submissive to it. What could have distracted me from that thought, in the abandonment already similar to death into which my soul had descended?

Once, only once, I heard a living creature by my side, if that wretched state of being can still be called life. I stopped. It was an old woman, horribly decrepit, who was crouching on the ground in order to search among the wild plants for a few fragments of dried wood that the last storm had broken from the branches, who was amassing them preciously in front of her in the flap of an old ragged apron pieced together from fragments of all colors. With what care she rummaged through the dead leaves in order to extract that dead debris with almost-dead fingers, which clutched them mechanically. With what sensuality she seemed to hear them clicking in her tattered garment, and what a strange gaze of satisfaction she plunged into her treasure from time to time, when she had gathered a meager handful.

"What are you looking for, my good mother?" I said, striving to lean toward her.

"Oh, Monsieur," she replied, standing up to the extent permitted by her curved spring in order to look at me at closer range, "I'm not doing anyone any harm. It's my little provision of wood for the winter."

"There, worthy woman," I said, "this might be useful to you."

And I slipped a gold coin into her hand.

She looked at it with an expression of astonishment, and let it fall into her apron with the wood that it held. She had not dropped a single morsel.

The affection that retained her in life is a singular mystery. She was still counting on a winter!

I had written to the baronet. Our correspondence was pursued with a regularity so active that it almost took the place of the pleasure of our conversations. Only a few weeks had gone by. Amélie had gone to see him, he told me. She wanted to write to me once, and he permitted it. I responded, and he transmitted my response to her. I have no need to say what we promised one another; you will not doubt it.

Finally, a letter arrived from Sir Robert that told me that Amélie was ill, more seriously ill than she had ever been before. He forbade me to depart, in Amélie's name and his own; he begged me to remain. Those were his expressions. He had reflected on both our situations, on the nature of Amélie's convictions, on the impossibility of triumphing over them, whatever happened in our relationship and our sentiments. He said that he only had our happiness in view, and I did not doubt it. He added that the sole obstacle that could be opposed to it did not come from him.

I believed him. Sir Robert was such an excellent man! And yet, never had a letter from a friend penetrated a friend's soul with a crueler despair. The obstacle that he feared, I dreaded that I had divined it. I repeated to myself relentlessly that the malady was trivial, that science had only seen it as a slight accident without consequence; that even love, so credulous in its anxieties, was accustomed to not seeing it as anything else, that the obstacle of which he spoke more probably came from Amélie's relatives. That reticence confounded me mortally. I was about to ring and ask for horses when a little note, fallen from the letter already read three times, changed my resolution. It was in Amélie's own hand, and only contained four words:

Don't come; I'll go.

Three days passed in that anxiety without my being able to settle upon a plan, without me being able to disentangle an idea. I had had two, however, two obstinate ideas that had taken possession of me with an equal power, and which subjugated in turn all the forces of my heart.

One obstacle that did not come from him: an obstacle foreign to Amélie's will, but which separated us forever! Oh, who would tell me what that obstacle was? Unfortunate man, you ask that! Woe betide you!

Soon, my agitation calmed. *Amélie,* I thought, *has said that she'll come. I shall see her, we'll be together, and then we'll have nothing more to fear.*

In the meantime, I dared to criticize Providence.

One evening, however—it was the twenty-fifth of November 1808[1]—I was sitting on the expectant stone that marked my grave. A little snow had fallen. There was a chill in

---

1 This precise date does not appear to have had any particular significance in history or in Nodier's life; he married Désirée Charve in August of that year and his father died in October.

the air and my veins were carrying fire. A thousand confused thought flowed in my mind like the chimeras of dreams; a thousand contradictory voices, the tumultuous and discordant echo of my terrors and hopes, howled ungraspable words around me; my eyes could not see, my ears were buzzing.

Suddenly, I felt a piece of paper thrust into my hand; I received it; I crumpled it; I opened it without looking to see who had given it to me. I had recognized the baronet's handwriting. Enough daylight remained to permit me to read it. I shall not try to express in their order the emotions that assailed me while I read. I am copying:

> *Amélie has just departed, and I have consented to it. A man whose devotion is known to me is accompanying her to you. The irregularity of this step has its excuse in the opinion that I have formed of Amélie and you. I impose the responsibility on you before your conscience and before Heaven.*
>
> *I have thought that the scandal and danger will be less than Amélie's public abjuration in a city where she was born and under the eyes of her family. I could not have been the witness to it myself, and I hope of your tenderness that she will spare me that dolor, by advancing the ceremony before the moment that will reunite us. Marry without me, since you are authorized to do so by her relatives. Amélie's papers are in order and I have taken charge of regulating all her interests here.*
>
> *I have not seen her again. I still dare to believe that amour and happiness might cure her, if there is something real in amour and happiness. The God that has permitted her to abjure might permit a great deal.*
>
> *Those are the last rigorous words that you will hear from me. Do not think about them any more.*

I got up. I looked for the emissary but he was no longer
there; I only saw a large figure disappearing in the distance
through the tall trees of the nearby avenues.

My situation had changed greatly. Five minutes before my
heart had been breaking between two extreme impressions
that were mutually exclusive: the hope of soon seeing Amélie

as I had been promised and the dread of being separated from her forever by the unknown obstacle of which I shuddered to fathom the mystery. Such a state of perplexity is not absolute misfortune, but it comes immediately after. It does not crush the soul but it undermines it dully, using up its resources slowly, weakening it in order to kill it. It is the captious web of the spider, the poisoned saliva that the viper distils over its living prey. Lying on the deck of a vessel driven from the port toward the reef and from the reef toward the port at the mercy of the wind that is pushing it and the wave that is sending it back, closer every time to the place where it will perish, wagering one's life against destiny on a throw of the dice without thinking of defending oneself: I was there.

Now everything took on another aspect. He had not seen her, but he did not say a word about the temporary malady, and that was to enable me to foresee a cure. He was counting on amour, he was counting on happiness; the obstacle no longer existed, therefore, since amour and happiness could triumph over it. Of amour and happiness we had enough for our life. And that future was no longer an illusion of my imagination, since it was founded in the calm and repose of reason, in such imminent hopes. What am I saying? It was already the present.

Was it beautiful enough, complete enough in pure joys and inexhaustible sensualities? One would never have dared to hope for a similar outcome for oneself; at the most one might have invented it for a brother. Assured independence, the favorite labor that pays well in the enjoyment of its pleasures, the amity without which there is no full felicity, and the amour that completes everything, the amour of Amélie, which surpassed all amours.

I was no longer in possession of myself; I did not sense myself, with enthusiasm and delight. I did not walk, I flew. I appealed to Amélie aloud, as if she could come to meet me, and I had won the prize of a tender competition in enabling myself to recognize her before she had perceived me.

I went like that into the town, moving gently with my arms two or three astonished passers-by, in order not to waste time by lengthening my walk with an unnecessary step; and everything that I saw appeared to me to be her: a woman's hat, a floating veil, a dress paling in the first reflection of the stars; and when I could no longer see anything, I stopped, out of breath, in order to assure myself that I had not heard her.

It was thus that I arrived. I nearly knocked Henriette down—Henriette, a good, intelligent, zealous, affectionate girl who took charge of the petty cares of the house, and who was lighting the gas on the stairway at that moment.

"Has anyone asked for me, Henriette?"

"Someone has asked for Monsieur twice."

"Who is it?"

"A very sad and distressed young man who went out to look for you, and who is sleeping in number nine."

"Whether he searches, whether he sleeps, or whether he goes away, what does it matter?"

"And then a young lady, very ill . . ."

"Very ill, Henriette, that isn't true! Where have you got what you're saying? And what are you waiting for to go up?"

". . . A young lady who appears to be ill and who has a mute domestic taller than Monsieur by a head. The young lady asked for a room next to Monsieur's, and as she could no longer sustain herself I believe that she is asleep, fully dressed, in the large folding armchair with springs, in which Monsieur sometimes says that it would be comfortable to die. When I repeated that to her, she said: 'Very good, very good,' with a charming smile, 'I want no other bed.'"

"What are you thinking, stopping me with all that ver-biage about the sad and distressed young man, with whom you're preoccupied like a little girl? Are you finally going to open up for me?"

"Oh, Monsieur," she replied, climbing the stairs and lighting the way for me with her lamp, "I commenced with him because he told me that you would never have a greater need to see him, and the manner in which he said it frightened me."

"You're afraid of everything, extravagant as you are. You said just now that the lady was very ill, but if she was ill to that extent she wouldn't have been able to undertake the journey from Berne to Yverdon. Will you hesitate any longer to open that door? I've never seen you as awkward."

"It's because, if the young lady really wasn't well, a moment of sleep would be necessary to repair her fatigue," said Henriette, inserting the key into the lock and looking at me anxiously.

"Stop, Henriette, stop. Forgive me, it's me who is wrong. Refrain from opening it. Wait until she rings, dear Henriette, and when she has rung, tell her that I've returned."

At the same moment, Amélie rang.

She was half-lying in the folding armchair. She held out her arms to me and I ran to her. I kissed her forehead, her eyes and her hands. I didn't speak. I had been surprised by a sudden seizure that almost took away from me the strength to feel.

Amélie had changed in an incomprehensible manner. She was no longer anything but her soul. Henriette's lamp showed her to me as I had seen her once before, when she guided me under the broken arches of the old gallery, to the door that opened to the road to the Oberland. I remembered that cruel vision, shuddering. I remained mute and motionless for some time.

"Candles, Henriette, candles!" I exclaimed. "Illuminate this lugubrious room, the darkness of which is saddening the brow of my Amélie. She's my sister, Henriette, she's my beloved, she's everything to me! It's Amélie, my Amélie, who will be my wife tomorrow, whom you will have for a mistress, a protector and a mother if you don't want to quit us."

The candles finally arrived. Amélie had not taken her eyes off me. They were still full of amour and life, but her pallor had not dissipated.

"That's good," said Amélie. "I've seen you again. The hand that I'm touching is your hand. The voice that I can hear is your voice. Now I exist, and I'm awake. All the objects are distinct around me, and if I can only distinguish them poorly, it's because you are here, and all the power of my soul is occupied in hearing you, touching you, and seeing you. I can no longer doubt," she continued, with expansion. "I'm close to you; I feared so much not getting this far, and never saying: *I'm close to you*. It's good, it's finished. I'm well. What more do I need? Where is your heart? Give . . . closer . . . stay . . . oh, I can feel it beating! You won't leave me? You won't go away again? Stay here! It's like this that I want to die."

"No, my Amélie, I'll never leave you. Today is forever, as you said. Be tranquil now. Don't feel any chagrins, no more are possible between us. Leave ideas of death behind. It's a matter of marriage and happiness. Believe me, one peaceful night that ought to be followed by a cloudless day will render you strength and health."

"A peaceful night that ought to be followed by a cloudless day! It's you who have said that. You're right. Perhaps a long night, but what does its duration matter? To have seen you, to see you again, to sleep or die on that thought, it's all the same. One peaceful night, Maxime, a happy night! I shall dream."

"Yes, dream," I said, affecting to misunderstand, "dream about the mild future that is promised to us. Do you know the baronet's intentions?"

"Very nearly. I know the baronet, and what I have not yet learned about the kindness of his heart, I divine. "Do you know," she continued, in a mysterious tone, "that I did not see him at my departure, and do you know why? It's because it seems to me that if he'd seen me as I am, he would no longer have permitted me to come . . ."

152

She was tearing me apart. I looked away continually in order to hide my disturbance from her, to stifle a sigh, to devour a tear.

"You're distracted," she said. "You're looking where I'm not. That's not good. What have you to look at that isn't me? I'm afraid that you find me less beautiful; for I was beautiful, since you said so. Henriette asked me just now, after having helped me to lie down, whether I wanted to see to my toilette a little. 'It's because Madame has something singular in her face,' she said, 'something earthen.' I laughed. Earthen, you understand? I thought it scarcely worth the trouble of removing it."

"Alas, it's because I suffer from seeing you suffer, and hearing you talk like that. I flatter myself that I find you better than you believe yourself to be."

"Oh, I'm a thousand times better than you can believe yourself! Since I began to respire, there has not been an instant when the sentiment of existence has appeared to me more agreeable to savor. Child, who fears that I might be ill, when I would not exchange one of these minutes for centuries of delights! Your first confession, Maxime—or mine, for I no longer recall which of us commenced—was doubtless an intoxicating ecstasy, a supreme sensuality, but it was far from being worth as much as this! Between the happiness of that day and what I feel now, there is a difference for which one would not be paying too dearly with one's life. Who would have thought it, though? The poverty of our hearts is so great that only one thing, but only one thing, is lacking to my contentment, and you can still supply it."

"Speak, Amélie, speak, in the name of Heaven!"

"Listen," she continued, in a low voice, because Henriette was not far away. "Listen—I have not abjured . . . not abjured, you hear! And the Heaven that you are going to take as a witness, the Heaven, Maxime, is still entire between Amélie

and you. It will never reunite us, if tomorrow . . . I can't say
that. Go and fetch me a priest this evening."

"Heaven is in your heart, angel of faith, innocence and
virtue! If Heaven repudiated you, it would be necessary to
repudiate Heaven! In any case, that care can be postponed,
and an emotion as grave, as imposing, might perhaps be dangerous in the state of exhaustion to which fatigue has reduced
you . . ."

"Don't blaspheme again," she replied, imposing her finger
over my lips, "and go fetch a priest, in order that I can obtain the right to ask our judge for mercy. And then, must the
abjuration not precede our marriage, and can that concern
be postponed? Why not attribute to amour the impatience
that you attribute to a presentiment that disquiets you? Have
you not said yourself that tomorrow I will be your wife, or
have you forgotten so quickly . . . ? Oh, I'm wrong! Go fetch
a priest, go! I promise you after this not to afflict you again
throughout my life . . . except once."

I left Henriette with Amélie and I went out almost at hazard. I had given orders for a physician to be summoned, but
a Roman priest appeared to me to be more difficult to find in
Yverdon.

The first person that appeared in my passage was the young
man who had asked for me during the day. I uttered a cry and
fell into his arms.

It was Ferdinand.

I have spoken before about Ferdinand, my childhood
friend, my comrade at college, my brother in affection—
Ferdinand, whose house became my house, whose family became my family, in an epoch when I was tormented by other
dolors. I sought then to describe his mild retreat, his interior
full of charms, his happiness, so perfect in calm and security.
It was no longer thus. All that no longer existed. His wife was
dead. A contagious disease had taken away his two children in

the same month. He alone was left of all that had comprised his happy life.

He had had the strength to survive everything; he was a Christian. Since then he had parted from his fortune, half in favor of his less opulent relatives and half to the profit of the poor of his village. What he had conserved, he destined for work of beneficence and piety. He had embraced holy orders. He had consecrated himself to the holy ministry of foreign missions.

That vocation demanded varied knowledge that he had hastened to acquire. He had just come back from a voyage to Germany and Italy, where he had spent nearly a year perfecting himself in the study of medicine, so useful to an apostle of the faith who bears to people without enlightenment the benefit of the truth. He was on the point of heading for the port from which he was to quit Europe when the desire to bid me a last adieu had taken him to Berne.

I knew all those details; his letters had informed me of them. I had expected that last meeting, mingled with so much bitterness. I had desired it . . . and then I had forgotten it; I was no longer thinking about it.

In Berne, Ferdinand had asked about me. He had seen Sir Robert. He had conversed with Amélie's physicians. He had been informed of her departure with enough time to arrive a few hours ahead of her. That was why he had been searching for me.

We had few words to exchange. Nothing remained for him to learn, not even my trouble, my anguish and my despair. He expected that.

"A priest and a physician!" I cried, embracing him. "It's Providence that has sent you!"

"It's my duty that has brought me," he replied. "But before seeing Amélie I need to assure myself entirely of the state of your heart. Are you quite certain of having finally fixed its perpetual mobility? Your decision is made? Do you believe firmly in your amour?"

"Oh, if you had seen her, if you knew her, you wouldn't ask me that!"

"I'm interrogating your conscience. I'm not disputing, I'm not contradicting anything. Your conviction will be mine. So you still persist in believing that the determinations to which you made Sir Robert party . . ."

"Are inviolable."

"I subscribe to that. One more question. Do you know that there is nothing inalterable and eternal in the affections of man except that which is placed beyond this temporary life? Do you know that the joys of the earth are only temporary, and that the felicity firmest in appearance is often the least durable? Do you know that the most essential of the virtues of our nature is resignation to the will of God?"

"If I had not known it in advance, unfortunate friend, your example would not have permitted me to doubt it."

"Enough, enough," he said, in an austere tone. "The Church has given me the powers of which you have need; take me to your young woman."

Amélie had not expected me to return so soon. I had often spoken to her about Ferdinand. She was not unaware of any of his virtues, his misfortunes and his resolutions, or of the dual ministry to which he had consecrated himself. His name, the sight of him and his words recalled a gleam of hope to her brow. I too thought that Heaven was commencing a miracle. What tender soul has not expected one for the person he loves?

I left them alone; half an hour later the door opened again.

Ferdinand looked at me with a calm sadness that did not frighten me. It had to be the habitual expression of his physiognomy. Amélie's was radiant with a pure and reposed satisfaction that had something celestial about it.

"Kiss your fiancée's hand," Ferdinand said to me, "and leave her to the rest that she needs. Henriette will watch over her. I'll give you the necessary instructions. Tomorrow, we'll see one another together. I'll have you called early."

Amélie's hand seemed less cold to me, her respiration more even, her complexion more animated; she smiled as she said to me: "Until tomorrow."

Ferdinand quit me on the threshold of my room. "Be a man," he murmured in my ear as he pressed me to his heart. "Life is short, but eternity is infinite."

And he disappeared.

What a night that was! I was only separated from Amélie by a light partition, and the slightest noise made in her room could not escape my anxious attention. Then I stopped in my precipitate but mysterious march. I was barefoot; I held my breath, I listened, I trembled to hear a plaint or a cry. I trembled above all not to hear anything. When the silence had lasted for a long time, it seemed to me that Henriette was asleep, and that Amélie, suffering without being helped, had lost the strength to call out. I would have liked, at such moments, to be assured again of her life, at the price of a groan.

Sometimes, I heard a voice and I remained in suspense. Sometimes, I distinguished two, and then nothing any longer, and I was more tranquil for a while. Often, I opened my door quietly. At Amélie's, I could listen better. The holes in the lock and the poorly-united joints of the panels allowed me to perceive a little light. When the light moved, I felt a mortal frisson run through all my limbs. When it resumed its place, I breathed out.

Henriette is watching with care, I said, *and Amélie is asleep. There's no danger.*

I went back to my room, I sat down, and, with my head in my hands, I remained plunged in a vague reverie similar enough to sleep, until a further sound came to return my terror or my anxiety. How happy I would have been had I been able to spend those interminable hours with my hand applied to her heart or my ear attached to her breath! How long the day seemed to take to arrive! With what impatience I searched for the first light in the sky! I had not paced the length of my room three times in succession when I came back to stick myself to my window in order to see whether the orient was not paling.

The sun finally rose. I thought that the danger was past. I was calmer, happier than I had been since her arrival. I perceived that I was cold.

A moment later I recognized Ferdinand's footsteps. He knocked faintly. He went into Amélie's room. Henriette did not take long to withdraw. She told me that Amélie had had a few choking fits, a few fainting spells of short duration, but that she seemed no worse than the day before. I came to kneel down at her door. More than an hour and a half passed thus, but I prayed with confidence; I was almost tranquil.

Ferdinand found me in that position. He lifted me up and embraced me. I noticed that he was a little more emotional, but that impression was so rapid that I thought I might be mistaken.

"Amélie has entered into the life of salvation," he told me. "Her duties are fulfilled. It remains for you to fulfill yours."

I was about to respond when he stopped me with a sign. He went on: "Don't allege sentiments to me with which I can't sympathize, as long as the sacraments of the Lord are not legitimate. It isn't the faith of the lover that I'm requesting, it's that of the Christian. The tenderness that you bear to that angelic soul would become in my eyes a motive of condemnation against her if you are not resolved to sanctify it by marriage. The step that has led her into your arms is a crime weighing upon her head, which would fall back on yours if you hesitated to repair it; it is in the title of a duty that I impose an obligation on you of accomplishing what you only see as happiness. Maxime, will you take Amélie for your wife?"

"Yes!" I cried, in a stifled voice. "Yes, Father!"

He introduced me into Amélie's room. The shutters were still closed; four candles were burning beside her on a table placed alongside the folding armchair that she had not quit, because Ferdinand had judged, as a physician, that she would be better there than anywhere else. All the preparations for the ceremony were made.

My first movement was to precipitate myself toward Amélie, but Ferdinand retained me.

I stopped then in order to look at her. She had turned toward me and she was smiling at me as she had done in saying; "Until tomorrow!" Her complexion presented something extraordinary that I had never remarked. It passed with a strange rapidity from the most frightful pallor to the most vivid red, and then it became paler than before; and that alternation, which made I know not what expression of effort and dolor run over her face, almost responded to the beating of my heart. I took it for an illusion of my own organs, fatigued by the long vigil and tears. Her eyes also had something vague and indecisive that I attributed to the same cause. I thought, in addition, that she might be dazzled by the light of the candles that separated us, through which her gaze was seeking to peer.

"Turn your eyes away from the candles," I said to her. "They must be doing you harm, for they're troubling mine and preventing me from seeing you."

"Me too," she replied. But she did not change her position.

At that moment Ferdinand came to fetch me from my place and take me next to her. He took my hand and placed it in Amélie's.

The prayers continued.

He interrupted himself to ask me if I had a ring. You will understand that the idea had not occurred to me.

"Take this one," he said, "and pass it over her finger." He had just taken off his own. "Take it, take it," he continued. "It's Adèle's."[1]

I shivered.

Then he gave us his benediction, knelt beside me, got up and helped me to my feet. I leaned on him in order to sustain myself.

"Am I his wife? Is he mine? Does his name belong to me?" said Amélie.

"The formalities that your union lacks depend on men," Ferdinand replied. "It is holy and indissoluble before God."

Amélie uttered a cry of joy.

I launched myself toward her, Ferdinand dragged me to the door; he enveloped me with his cloak and, pressing my head against his breast in such a manner as to stifle my response, he applied his mouth to my ear and said to me in a low voice: "Now, remember your promise. Raise your soul toward God, who has given you what you love, and who has only given it to you for a moment in his life of misery. The aneurism is reaching its final phase. Go receive your wife's last sigh, as a man worthy to recover it."

After that, he left.

I drew nearer to Amélie, tottering. I sat down; I seized her hands; I approached her as closely as I could without forcing her to move. I slid one of my arms under her bare shoulders; she palpitated as if she were afraid.

"Have no fear, Amélie. You are my sister, you are my wife."

"I know," she replied, rolling my hair around her fingers. "It's just that I can't see you; I don't know why I can't see you. Why are the candles no longer there? But you're there, you,

---

1 It appears that Nodier has forgotten that Ferdinand's wife was named Gabrielle, and that his effort to remember might have confused her with the eponymous heroine of another of his novelettes of doomed amour, "Adèle" (1820). "Clémentine" and "Amélie" were published simultaneously in 1832, but might have been written earlier at dates quite far apart.

nothing but you! Oh, I'm happy! Wait, lay your head here, close beside me. I'm your wife! There is no evil, is there? Come even closer, so I can feel your breath on my cheek. Happy! Happy! I didn't imagine that one could be so happy!"

She raised her neck slightly on the arm on which it was lying and leaned her head toward mine, and our lips united for the first time.

"Oh, my God!" she cried.

My reason was annihilated in that kiss. All that I recall is that she ceased to return it . . . and it took me some time to comprehend the reason. My senses abandoned me; I fell; I only conserved of my existence the sensation of a confused tumult of footfalls and voices, and the vigorous grip of two arms of iron folding over my breast in order to bear me away.

When I came round, I was in Ferdinand's room.

I darted my eyes in all directions. I saw Jonathas. Ferdinand, facing me, was staring at me without speaking.

"And Amélie! Amélie! Where is she?"

"In Heaven," Ferdinand replied.

Lucrèce and Jeannette

Baronne Eugénie de M*** is no longer young, as you shall see more pertinently in the continuation of this story; but those who have the good fortune of knowing her know that she has conserved all the youthfulness of mind and all the vivacity of imagination that once distinguished her among the pretty and made her preferred to the beautiful. It is still a pleasure for her to hear tender adventures narrated, and it is with her intention alone, it is necessary to say, that I have collected these sad memories of my youth, better to forget than to write. I cannot refuse her anything. It is a habit that I have conserved with women, old though I am, and even when they are old.

One evening in autumn when we were together by the fireside—for in Paris, it is necessary to warm oneself in autumn—the conversation flagged because my portfolio was exhausted, and because at our age, conversation necessarily languishes occasionally. She writhed impatiently in her armchair, she poked the fire with irritation, she coughed, with the nervous cough that signifies intelligibly that one is bored, and I gazed at her with a consternated eye, as if to say to her that I had nothing to tell her.

"Do you know, Maxime," she said, suddenly, "that your amours are the most lamentable that I have ever heard in my life, I am no longer astonished, given what I now know, by the morose and chagrined humor in which I have seen you inclined for many years? Those passions have something akin to a fatality, and it is enough to attach to the slumber of the healthiest man all the demons of the nightmare. The first of your mistresses only loves in you an amiable child; she marries and dies. The second loves you a little, I suppose, but not enough to sacrifice her prejudices for you; she marries and dies. The third loves you recklessly and marries you, but in marrying you she dies. Abbé Prévost, who was read so much in my youth, and who did not have, it's true, a light-hearted imagination, never invented a fictitious hero more unfortunate."

"What do you expect, Baronne? You asked me for the story of my life, and I don't invent."

"I believe you and I feel sorry for you, but if I remember rightly, and if I can believe your reputation and your own words, for you were passably advantageous, amour has not always been so rigorous for you. Sentiment is a lottery that you have played too often not to have encountered a few lucky draws, but you've only shown me losing tickets."

"It's true, Baronne," I said, seizing her hand with the most passionate expression of which I was capable. "It's true that once, amour . . ."

"Let's leave it there," she said, with a sort of anger. "It's probable that you have nothing to teach me on that subject. But why do you never cheer me up with one of those anecdotes that awaken gracious ideas and, at least, do not cause spasms or bad dreams?"

"I can admit it to you," I replied, laughing. "It's because amour has never forgotten to render me very unhappy, except to render me sovereignly ridiculous."

"Well, out with the great evil! I'll amuse myself at your expense."

"I can do that. It ought not to go any further, and no one is listening."

"Add that you ought to begin to put your pretentions in order, if you don't want to be sovereignly ridiculous again."

"The first time . . ." I said, after a moment's reflection.

"The first time you were amorous or the first time you were ridiculous?"

"Both, if you wish. The first time was a certain Alexandrine. Blonde, a trifle languorous, but slim, sleek, made to be ravished, and charming, believe me, who had a fury for abductions."

"I can see you from here abducting the blonde Alexandrine."

"And the most fortunate of mortals, all the way to the first relay. We got down in order to pick flowers while the horses were being changed. It was not only flowers; a ribbon was required to attach them. When I returned, no more Alexandrine. She had mistaken the carriage and was running across country with an Englishman who had been waiting for her for two days."

"That was the year of the peace. I remember the story as if it were yesterday."

"A pretty brunette deigned to console me, and I confess that it required courage to do it, for there is nothing so mortal to amour as a well-averred ridicule. I loved Justine as much as a procedure so generous merited. I would have got myself killed for her, and it nearly came to that. A young captain of hussars, as handsome as Adonis, built like Hercules, with whom I lived in the most perfect amity, having permitted himself to ogle her one day at a play in a familiar manner that displeased me, I provoked him brutally to a duel.

"His regiment was leaving at daybreak the following day for another garrison, so the matter could not be postponed. He gave me a rendezvous at midnight in a little avenue under my queen's windows. Such a stimulant was unnecessary for my courage, but I acceded to my adversary's proposition without demanding an explanation of his caprice. We were punctual, and we were drawing our swords when a frightful downpour forced us to throw ourselves under a coaching entrance that happened to be open. We continued to cross swords regardless, but blindly, and after a few passes that had given him the advantage of the terrain, the point of the captain's sword cut my upper lip and staved in a tooth."

"I remember that, to my taste, that scar suited you perfectly."

"I'm glad to have received it at that price, but that was not what occupied me for the moment. I hastened to bandage my wound with my cravat and to run to the domicile of the nearest surgeon in order to submit myself to a more expert dressing. Imagine my surprise, as I passed under Justine's casement, to hear myself addressed by a voice that wished me goodnight and a prompt recovery!"

"You must have been grateful to your mistress for such a delicate attention."

"It wasn't her voice, Madame, it was the hussar's!"

"Poor Maxime. That brunette was worth as much as the blonde, truly."

"When I reflect on it, my dear Eugénie, I think they were all worth as much as one another. Finally, in 1803 . . ."

"Oh, you're going to bring that up! Let's pass over 1803, for Heaven's sake!"

"I'd like to, with all my heart, Eugénie, since you desire it; but the most frivolous compositions have imperious rules that force the will of a poor author, and I don't want to leave a lacuna in my memoirs."

"I'll fill it, then. I deceived you, my friend, I deceived you for a fool; it was wicked—but remember that we were both in our twenty-first year: you, tender, exalted, vehement, fanatical in all your illusions; me, widowed for a year, indiscreet, flighty, inexperienced, joyful in being free, with a perfectly empty head and a heart emptier than my head. I can do the honors of that age; I was a different person. When you told me that you loved me, I said the same, because it was absolutely necessary to love you, if one didn't decide to hate you mortally, and I couldn't find so much resolution.

"A quarter of a hour later I would have given an empire to have begun again. I only wanted independence and repose, and you were only at ease in the region of tempests. Your oaths were blasphemies, your joys frenzies, your jealousies convulsions. Remember, however, that romantic passions had not yet been invented, and there was no more question of it in the *Contes moraux* than at the Opéra-Comique.[1] Imagine my condition when I contemplated coldly the terrible destiny that you had made for me! I woke up trembling with fright under Maxime's dagger like Damocles under the tyrant's sword.

"I did not know how to save my wellbeing, when the fool in question presented himself, so ugly, so stupid, so surly, so indolently conceited, so profoundly absurd that one could not have chosen otherwise in a hundred thousand in order to avenge you in betraying you, and I would have done a hundred times worse then, if it had been possible, to extract myself from the terrors of your amour. A fool, at least, apparently lives like another man, he talks, acts and exists in the manner of everyone else, or very nearly. He is often boring, but never perceives it. He is not preoccupied with the soul or the mind. He is neither inconvenient nor imposing. He's a fool, and that's all. You wouldn't believe, Maxime, how marvelously imagined fools are to provide lovers for coquettes!

"Well, have I filled in that lacuna in a satisfactory fashion? What's stopping you now?"

"Nothing, Madame. I'm breathless with admiration, and I'll return to my story at the point where you've left it. I was not of a character to desist easily from my rights, and I must, on that account, have inspired cruel anxieties in you, since you only found a means of removing yourself entirely from what

____

1 Jean-François Marmontel's *Contes moraux* were published between 1755 and 1759; he went on to write *opéras comiques* in some profusion, abandoning his early penchant for tragedy. His work is witty, delicate, mannered and thoroughly reasonable, the epitome of the kind of controlled literary endeavor to which the Romantic Movement was opposed.

166

you deign to call the terrors of my amour by putting all of France between yourself and me. You made the decision to return to your lands in Touraine. All my happiness disappeared with you. Your absence made a land that I cherished into the saddest of solitudes, and I decided all the more willingly to quit it too, after three misadventures so glaring that there was not a son of a good family for twenty leagues around who did not make fun of me."

"If you were not more amiable and gallant than sincere, you could have stuck to that last reason; it would have dispensed you of the other."

"I agree that it had a great deal to do with my resolution. Having arrived in Paris, I made the decision for the first time to put a certain order in my conduct. And in order not to be equivocal regarding the order of which I was capable, I'll explain to you briefly what I meant by that: it was quite simply a methodical disorder, a systematic misconduct, a regulated plan of irregularity, a good manner of living badly. As amour was my principal, not to say my only, affair it was on to its terrain that I transported all my philosophy.

"*If misfortunes form youth*, I said to myself, *you are, my dear Maxime, adequately formed for your age. Since your brilliant advent in society you have loved three women and you have been duped three times. It's a kind of providential warning that has been given to you to renounce sentiment. Since the destiny of tender and confident hearts is always to be deceived, the science of being happy consists of not allowing oneself to be taken by surprise. Sincere engagements and eternal passions belong to the world of Astrée and Celadon; only children do not know that, and you now have good reasons for not doubting it. What remains to be feared in the perfidy of a mistress when one knows in advance what her good faith is worth? The most inconstant is the best for whoever has verified that the most constant is hardly at all. Henceforth, therefore, treat affairs of the heart with the insouciance they merit and accept amour as it is, if you cannot do without it. Another will not be made just for you."*

"I admire in my turn, my friend, how you have perfected yourself since our rupture. Here you are, entirely recovered from your romantic extravagances. You're talking principles!"

"Perhaps those ideas would not have come to me of their own accord, and gratitude makes it a duty for me to confess that my education owes a great deal to you. Fully convinced, as I have had the honor of telling you, that the surest means of not being deceived anywhere was to expect it everywhere, I only occupied myself with finding a worthy theater for my gallant expeditions, and it was on the theater itself that I settled. It is not usual to go there in search of exemplary fidelities and to contract indissoluble bonds of the genre of Amadis. Intrigue there is light, knots fragile, peripeties multiple, and there is not a scene in the amours of that country that does not run to its denouement in accordance with the rules of art. That was precisely what I needed. I gladly made arrangements with a view to a commerce in which I would be betrayed almost as soon as I was loved. It is as amusing as any other, when it is amusing, and it wastes less time.

"I had, in any case, a sort of predestined vocation for that genre of sentiment, and I owed that to nature or to my father. My heart had beaten since childhood in my schoolboy breast with the trills of a virtuoso or the pirouettes of a bayadere. There is an incomparable charm in the possession of a beauty with a thousand names, which takes on all faces, which dons and embellishes all costumes, which speaks all languages and interprets all passions, which changes its language and genius with every evening of passion, as it changes its attire.

"In the provinces, above all, where the attributions of an actor are ordinarily more extensive, there is something divine about it. In the same encounter, at the end of a jolly supper, you can be tender to the point of tears with Aménaïde, sulky with Hermione, flirt with Célimène or melt your heart

in pastoral languors with one of the musky shepherdesses of
Favart and Marmontel. If the perfidious Eulalie has given you
yesterday one of those motives for misanthropy that vex ill-
made minds, you will have difficulty tomorrow resisting the
proofs of the innocence of Zaïre. Add to that the triumphs of
vanity, so flattering and intoxicating for the man who is loved,
or believes himself to be, which is exactly the same thing, and
you will agree without difficulty that the lover of a fashionable
actress is one of the privileged individuals for whom life is a
concatenation of beatitudes and apotheoses!"

"This time, thank Heaven, you are on the way to perfect
happiness, and if some demon had not interfered, we would
not have anything else to talk about except your triumphs.
I dread like you, that they were not durable, but they were
numerous, and you can savor their quantity."

"I flatter myself on that. To tell the truth, the economy
of my plan of campaign left almost nothing to be desired;
I had planned all my maneuvers, chosen all my positions,
marked out my encampments retrenchments and fortresses
with a prudent gaze. I had drawn up in advance the map of
my conquests and I already saw myself progressing from one
ovation to another by a long cortege of captives."

"Caesar, I salute you. I await with impatience the publication of your Commentaries."

"There, unfortunately, is where the conqueror becomes
embarrassed. I had no sooner set one foot on enemy terrain
when I perceived that it was impossible to put the other forward without knowing the language, and that was a study that
would have disconcerted Pico della Mirandola. I thought I
possessed well enough my Marivaux, my Crébillon *fils* and my
Bijoux indiscrets,[1] but that sacred idiom had fallen into neglect

---

1 The classics of the "libertine fiction" that first became fashionable during
the rein of Louis XV included *La Vie de Marianne* (1731-45) by Pierre
de Marivaux, *Le Sopha* (1742) by Crébillon *fils*, and *Les Bijoux indicrets*
(1748) by Denis Diderot.

neither more nor less than hieroglyphics. I made the decision to return to sentiment, which I still regarded as the universal go-between of amorous negotiations, but at the first word that escaped me in that style, they laughed in my face in chorus, and all my Sylphides flew away.

"I was on the brink of renouncing my magnificent ambitions and descending to grisettes, a naïve people, happy and faithful to ancient traditions, among whom that delicate language has remained vulgar, under the favorable auspices of fiction, when and unforeseen event came to render chances to my fortune. You have probably never known, Madame, that there once existed at number forty-eight Rue Saint-Martin an avatar of Thalia, placed under the auspices of Molière?"

"I am at least certain of never having had a box in that quarter."

"People did not go there, Baronne, to gaze at the boxes, which would indubitably have happened if you had frequented the theater. People went there to see an enchanting actress with dainty and gracious features, an ideal physiognomy, a supple and aerial bearing, a fresh and pure voice, delicate intentions, witty and mordant. When she smiled, all hearts flew to her smile; when she allowed a gaze—or, rather, a fiery radiance—to escape between golden lashes, the conflagration took hold everywhere. When she finally spoke, the sagest lost their heads. When I tell you that I suffered the fate of the sagest, you will easily take my word for it. She was the diamond of the petty theater, the pearl of the merchant country, the Mars[1] of the arrondissement and its faubourgs. She was the Jenny Vertpré of the Consulate![2]

---

1 The reference is to "Mademoiselle Mars" (Anne Salvelat, 1779-1847), who quickly became the star of the Comedie-Française after its restitution in 1799 and was still there more than thirty years later when the present story was published.

2 "Jenny Vertpré" (Françoise Vausguen, 1797-1865) became a leading actress at the Théâtre des Variétés in 1821 and then moved to the Gymnase

"One saw that every year, the divinity of the vogue, and nothing is lacking now but her name."

"I will tell you that, Madame, in a better style than mine, for I could not employ one of Monsieur de Chateaubriand's pompous and grandiose turns on a more solemn occasion. That prodigious sovereign of minds and souls was named Lucrèce."

"Mercy! Who has ever heard mention of an actress named Lucrèce?"

"That is not the most extraordinary thing. The most extraordinary thing—and Madame de Sévigné would not have omitted a page of synonyms in such a case—was that she sustained the responsibility of her terrible name with a philosophical resignation of which there had never been an example at the theater in the Rue Saint-Martin, and perhaps in few others She was known to have a thousand worshipers, and not a single fortunate one was cited."

"I'll stop you there is a flagrant lie. You promised real stories, and at the first leap you fall into the fantastic. One would think, to hear you, that nature has kept some phenomenon in reserve everywhere in order to furnish a text to your hyperboles. What would the ingenious and malign critic say who suspends over all your full stops a defiant and mocking question mark? Do you believe that this terrible doubter, who hesitates to believe that you were ever twelve years old, that hazard had given you a Capuchin from Cologne as a schoolmaster and that the crowd pushed you, one day when you had nothing better to do, into a square in Strasbourg where there were only twelve or fifteen thousand people, will lightly pass over a Lucrèce of the wings? We suffer the implausibilities of historians, but we are intractable with storytellers."

"The critic can think what he wishes, my dear Baronne, but I am, with your permission, much better informed about my

---

in 1826, where she was still the star when the present story was published.

adventures than him, although he knows almost everything. I flatter myself, moreover, that he will relax something of his Judaic rigor, and, since I have permitted him to have Abbé d'Olivet dine at the home of Marion Delorme fifty years to the day before the birth of that worthy academician,[1] it would be ill grace for him to contest an almost anonymous virtue at the theater in the Rue Saint-Martin. Also note, if you please, that I have not said that I put an end to the enchantment at the first step merely by raising my visor, like one of King Arthur's knights. It happened quite differently, and Lucrèce did not receive me any more kindly than the Roman Lucréce received Tarquin, although mine had no Collatinus.

"As you know, difficulties, especially difficulties of that sort, inflame a generous courage. My amour had many reasons for going to the expense of urgency and obstinacy. Molière's theater had just closed by superior order, for lack of receipts, in spite of the attraction that Lucrèce lent to its repertoire. Lucrèce was about to disappear, and my parents were recalling me by every post in order to make me conclude a stupid affair in the province. They had decided to marry me off, and, after the glaring disgrace of my first three intrigues, I ask you, what figure of a husband would I have made? It was exactly like a man who embraces the party of war before having obtained vengeance for a public insult. I needed a reparation."

"Why do families have to get mixed up in it? Your parents chose their moment well."

"They never do otherwise. I went to bed toward dawn, as was my habit. Less fortunate than the poet Villon, who only had one care, I was carrying two in tandem, blacker than one can imagine: a wife whom I did not want and a mistress who did not want me."

---

1 A memoir published after Nodier's death repeats this remark as one made verbally, alleging that he attributed the sin in question to "J. J***" (presumably Jules Janin), but the "critic" to whom Maxime is referring is surely Charles Nodier.

"Tell me, in passing, what was the poet Villon's care?"

"That of knowing, Madame, what becomes of old moons; and he was so preoccupied by it that he only forgot it in the day when he was due to be hanged. I had just woken up in the paroxysm of amour, which is, as Fontenelle has observed, the most matinal of our sentiments, when my domestic brought me a letter, the postmark of which made me dread a further paternal summons. Imagine my surprise and my pleasure when I perceived that it came from the director of a theater company that was exploiting my province, and in which there was no mention of anyone but Lucrèce. The closure of the Paris theater furnished him with the opportunity to recruit a precious subject capable of causing fury in a small town, and my known liking for theater had enabled him to suppose that I might serve as an intermediary with regard to a magicienne who had turned so many excellent heads. It was Lucrèce who was being summoned to all the desires of a population idolatrous of talent and beauty; it was me to whom the care of that fortunate embassy was being entrusted. O foolish joys of youth! My first prize for rhetoric had enthused me less. The return of Tasso's crown to the Capitol, in the amaranth of the floral games, could have been announced to me without distracting me from my delight. Meanwhile, I had concurred.

"I shall not leave you to divine the first thought that occupied me; you would never guess it. 'In truth,' I said to myself, while getting dressed in haste, 'I don't know why I shouldn't marry. A good dowry in ready money is not to be disdained in the state of dilapidation in which the turmoil has put my affairs, and the majority of moralists say, moreover, that there is nothing as sweet as the union of two well-matched souls. I would have to renounce, as reason demands, the tumultuous pleasures of a dissipated life; but the glamour that the latter cannot fail to produce should be sufficient for the ambition of a young man favorably treated by women, who has not employed his best years badly. Lucrèce will doubtless be chagrined, but it's necessary. She'll have a great deal; I'll even arrange for her to miss the spectacle twice by reason of indisposition; but she'll be consoled, I'm sure of it, for she's not one of those who can't be consoled. The main thing is that she isn't consoled before the ceremony—that would ruin the effect. I shall marry as soon as I arrive.'"

"Be careful, Maxime. I understand marvelously that the success of that plan would have saved the interests of your vanity, but you haven't said yet that your affairs were so advanced with regard to Lucrèce."

"You're counting as nothing the progress that they had just made. Have you read Ballanche's *Oedipus?* Have you never seen Ingrès'? It's all the same thing. Well, Madame, the enigma was divined. I had penetrated the Sphinx. The talismanic phrase was known to me; the magic words that would dissolve the charm were known to me. A superb engagement and a seat in my post-chaise! There is no Lucrèce who could resist that!"

"O fatality of our weak virtues! That rigorous heroine, so skillful at playing all roles, could not sustain until the end that of the chaste Roman whose name she bore!"

"She did her best to sustain it, Baronne, save for two slight circumstances, the resistance and the suicide."

"I understand, as I witness in imagination the pomp of your triumphal arrival."

"You're going too quickly. We traveled very slowly. Lucrèce had all the qualities that you could desire in the fantastic figure of a fictional heroine. She was idolatrous of the beauties of nature, and never fund the time passed in contemplating them too long. We stopped at Brie-Comte-Robert."[1]

"The beauties of nature at Brie-Comte-Robert! Where is your enthusiasm going to settle?"

We had only just departed, and it's necessary to have experienced it to know how many charms nature has in

---

1 Brie-Comte-Robert is thirty-two kilometers from Paris.

174

twenty-four hours, when one is traveling with one's mistress. At Nangis, another halt.[1] The solitary avenue of old trees that circles around its ditches would have been the envy of the gardens of Armide. And then, he moonlight has something so suave and velvety at Nangis! If, one day, someone paints that moonlight as I sensed it, as I savored it, when its pale azure radiance rained down through the nascent foliage over the creases of her veil, enveloping her with their limpid light, revealing to me a thousand beauties that I had not yet perceived, I protest to you that none would want Claude Lorrain any longer. It would be necessary to feel sorry for the insensible heart that did not palpitate with a tender emotion at the sight of the delightful plains of Nogent, which the Seine embraces with a silver girdle, over which all the stars in the sky sow sparkling fires. All that is never so ravishing as when there are two people to see it. As for the poetic promenades of the modern Troyes, they are almost as classical in the memory of travelers as the boscage of the banks of the Simoïs, where it is not sufficiently demonstrated that there was any boscage!"

"Suspend your flight, Muse! I didn't believe, at the rate we're going, that we would have had the good fortune of reaching the département of the Aube so soon. Your pegasus must have needed to alight there!"

"Your presentiments have informed you only too well. We were in Troyes on the fourteenth day as time was beginning to press us as much as you, but there was no means of departing therefrom. Lucrèce was tormented by an ardent fever, and the physician, whom I was obliged to summon, recognized at a glance that she was in no condition to continue the journey. The poor girl had smallpox.

---

1 Nangis is seventy-six kilometres from Paris. As the distance from Paris to Besançon is more than four hundred kilometres, Maxime's journey would have taken nearly a fortnight at that rate, and the baronne's momentary surprise to find him in Troyes (178 kilometers from Paris) before the end of his speech is ironic.

"You're making me tremble, Maxime. Your demon is carrying you away and we're heading straight for a tragic denouement!"

"Reassure yourself, Madame; we're heading straight for a rather comical denouement. I have no need to tell you that I did not want to abandon her during the danger, but my affairs were summoning me, my parents were dying of anxiety and Lucrèce's own interests required that I go to explain her delay. The physician had not left me any anxiety as to the outcome of the accident, and I had paid for her care in expectation of the success for which she caused me to hope.

"I arrived at the terminus of the voyage alone, therefore, but the rumor of my expedition had preceded me, and I regarded the welcome that it was about to procure for me as an embarrassing ordeal for my modesty. I got out of it more cheaply than I thought; the provincial mind is suspicious when it is not denigrating. Accessible to all unfortunate prejudices, it armors itself against admiration; it fortifies itself with superstitions, restrictions and reticences against the invasion of new glories. Renown had not run its course when letters patent had been sent to the good cities under the banner of an accredited newspaper, and the newspapers of the year of grace 1804 did not say a word about the actresses of petty theaters. The civil list of the dramatic princesses of that time was much too restricted to permit them to maintain a pack of historiographers. The epoch had not arrived when their deeds and gestures would be registered every evening in officious chronicles, like those of the Emperor of China. I was only welcomed, in consequence, with a certain very dry *we shall see*, accompanied by a very dubious shake of the head. *We shall see*, Madame, do you hear? They saw all too soon, alas, what you are about to see!"

"Permit me to spare you the dolor of reopening with your hands a wound that is still bleeding. Is it not true that Lucrèce had changed slightly?"

"Changed slightly, Madame! Oh, I recognize the tender precautions of compassion of a woman's heart. Changed slightly! Great God, she had changed fearfully!"

"Deplorable evidence of the instability of human things! That is, however, the property of smallpox."

"There was only one cry on her account, and it was a cry of fright. No, never has nature humiliated with a more perfidious trick the vanity of a young woman!"

"And the conceit of a young fop . . ."

"I was going to spare you, Madame, the trouble of the marginal note, for in the circumstance in which I found myself, there could not remain to me any other pride than that of a humble and repentant resignation. Nevertheless, my hopes secretly remained attached to the infallible effect of her talent. *It will be necessary for them to admire her*, I protested proudly, *and their intoxication will avenge me on them and contrary destiny.* I only sighed after the day of the debut. The posters had finally announced her; the affluence was emotion, and in order not to hide anything, the public appeared well enough disposed. I came and went, feeling no impatience. I was counting one by one the measures of the never-ending overture when the curtain went up. The play commenced with a song by Lucrèce. O dolor! The rigors that the smallpox had exercised on her epidermis were no less than those they had afflicted on her larynx. The unfortunate woman had lost two notes, and what she conserved of her siren voice would have nailed the alms of charity to the hand of the most benevolent auditor of a street singer."

"Nothing like it had ever been heard!"

"That was what everyone said. After two sufficiently troublesome disappointments, I scarcely dared to glimpse one last means of salvation in the incomparable resources of her acting, like a man who, seeing himself drowning, clutches with a desperate hand the frail reeds of the bank, and God knows that I was well advised not to count on them. Either because the impertinence of the public had paralyzed her means—a theatrical style if ever there was one—or because smallpox also has psychological influences previously unknown to scientists, Lucrèce spoke her lines as if she were singing. All the delightful nuances of which her celestial visage had made the most so many times had become common and surly in an ugly physiognomy. The subtle finesse of detail, the exquisite features of nature and sentiment, which had caused the orchestra stalls and the gallery to swoon in Paris, appeared gauche in their naivety, and mannered in their delicacy. Finally, the discontentment of the spectators was manifest in an explosion so noisy that the auditorium threatened to collapse to the sound of whistles when the director came, all a-tremble, to promise a new debutante to his turbulent audience. Lucrèce fainted and I ran away, for if I had been beside her when she recovered consciousness, she would certainly have scratched my eyes out."

"You have made me feel sorry for the fate of that poor creature. I'd like to know that she's established in a good place."

"You have only to speak, Madame, and I shall make her, if necessary, like Hippolyte Clairon,[1] the president of the council of a margrave; but, fiction aside, I will grant your wish in a few words. Her misadventure was an inexhaustible source of prosperity for her. She returned to Paris, where one of her most oft-rejected lovers, a man of scant intelligence, so history reports, but seemingly endowed with an incredible power of memory, thought himself very fortunate to recover her as she was—which is to say, with the changes that had been operated in her between Brie-Comte-Robert and Troyes inclusively.

---

1 "La Clairon" (Clair Joséphe Hippolyte Leris, 1723-1803) was one of the stars of the Comédie-Française, who achieved a scandalous notoriety by virtue of her conduct, greatly exaggerated in a vicious pamphlet published in 1746 and a scabrous volume of memoirs supposedly authored by herself, published in 1796. Her lover, the Marquis of Brandenburg, renovated his country house for her as the White Castle.

He offered her his heart and his hand, which she carefully refrained from refusing; travel had formed her too well for that. And as the bridegroom was one of those fine characters who do not do things by halves, ten months later he left her a widow and dowager with an income of fifty thousand livres. She keeps a grand house today with numerous servants and horses, an open table and a notable salon."

"I can respire—and I have need of it, after such rude catastrophes."

"You see that I alone require the sympathies of your sensibility now, and you have others to provide. Lucrèce had departed without allowing me to see her again, and I was all the more grateful because my letters to her did not testify any regret for that. She left me, however, to bear all the weight of derision and malign gibes, and I can assure you that two of us would not have been too many to share them. The country resounded with them; the columns spoke them, as the ancients expressed it, and if my modest Athens had had a Ceramic, you can guess what name little children would have scribbled on its walls.

"My arrival in drawing rooms never failed to excite a murmur that had nothing sad about it—entirely to the contrary—but which appeared to me to be infinitely disobliging. In truth, I attracted when out walking the gaze of pretty women to a greater degree than in the past, but even if I gave their curiosity the most favorable interpretation, I was not unduly flattered by it. I rarely went to the theater, and only when a spectacle that attracted a crowd gave me the hope of avoiding the frightful popularity of the boxes and the forestage.

"Somewhat hardened, however, against the inconveniences of great reputations, I went with dignity one day to the front bench in the gallery during the fifth act of a new tragedy whose author had just dethroned Racine in two or three feuilletons. I was ingenuously proud of that new genre of scandal, forgetting myself entirely, when I suddenly remarked that the confidante was taking advantage of an unnecessary and mortal tirade that the juvenile lead was delivering in order to whisper a malicious aside in the ear of the princess, which probably had no direct connection with the play and was not intended for the public.

"My heart constricted and a cold sweat inundated my brow, for I believed that I read distinctly on the accursed duenna's lips Lucrèce's story and mine. In fact, the gaze of the princess described a long parabola that embraced almost the entire hemicycle of the hall and finished by arresting intrepidly on me, like the gaze of the basilisk. At the same instant, the two Megaeras were seized by a fit of hilarity so expansive and so deafening that the drama, which had reached the most pathetic point, could only any longer limp as far as the denouement amid bursts of laughter.

"Fortunately, I took advantage of the universal confusion produced by that unexpected twist to reach the corridor, the staircase, the vestibule and the street. When I was outside, my breast dilated like that of a man escaping a bad dream. 'I vow,' I cried, with all the strength of my lungs, 'never to set foot again in that *tripudium* of street performers, even if I'm reduced to spending all my evenings henceforth in the marionette theater.'

"'You're really not too disgusted,' said one of my friends, abruptly taking possession of my arm. 'It's nine o'clock precisely, and I'm going there.'

"'Where?'

"'What are you talking about? I'm going to see the celebrated marionettes of Master Siméon Balland of Wintertour, the most skillful and the most ingenious of the numerous heirs of Brioché. Whoever hasn't seen Master Siméon's marionettes hasn't seen anything, and above all, hasn't seen Jeannette. Only the Swiss are as adroit in mechanics, and only the daughters of the thirteen cantons are as pretty. It's the rendezvous of the best company of brats, appetizing nursemaids and sprightly chambermaids—an excellent society!'

"'Why not?' I replied, laughing. 'In any case, the theater is detestable and the actresses . . .'

"'Would make a company of mercenaries recoil,' said my scatterbrain. 'Uglier ones haven't been seen since . . .' He interrupted himself out of commiseration. I understood, sighed, and went to see the marionettes.

"It isn't to you, Madame, that I would try to justify my puerile penchant for Polichinelle.[1] I remember that you once shared it, and that one of the sweetest and cruelest moments of my life, the one when I saw you and fell in love with you, was accorded to me by bizarre destiny at Fantoccini's theater. I scarcely suspected them that in your hands I was myself only a slightly more ingeniously-engineered puppet whose string . . ."

"Resume, for God's sake, the thread of your adventures, without making me play an untimely role in your intrigues of marionettes, with which I have nothing to do, and permit me to enjoy peacefully the good fortune of having escaped in time the deadly ascendancy of your star."

"I'm doing that, Madame. But Master Siméon's marionettes were not vulgar marionettes. His Polichinelle was the Talma of all Polichinelles past, present and future. What imperturbable aplomb! What a marvelous stagecraft! What naïve verity, and yet what academic perfection of pauses and declamation! What energy of delivery! What magic of diction! What surprising play of physiognomy! And in all that, what profound intelligence of the human heart! Take note, Madame, that I

---

1 Nodier's fascination with Polchinelle and puppetry had been abundantly displayed in *Histoire du roi de Bohême et ses sept châteaux* (1830; tr. as *The Story of the King of Bohemia and his Seven Castles*) and was further expanded in the eulogistic essay "Polichinelle" (1832; tr. in the same volume as "Polichinelle").

am only speaking here about Master Siméon's Polichinelle, for all the Polichinelles I have seen since were wooden. Only that one had a soul.

"However—would you believe it?—after a few days, for I never missed a performance, I became less exact at my customary place. Scarcely had Jeannette lent the hero's wife or mistress the charm of her slightly monotonous but natural, expressive and melodious speech, than I came to join her in the booth where the director had placed her, like the cunning traffickers who put the riches of the store on display. Motionless against one of the portable pillars of the architecture of painted canvas, I admired her without ever wearying of it, welcoming the patrons with an irresistible smile, distributing tickets or receiving coupons with a hand whiter, more agile and more gracious than that of the pretty Israelite money-changer in the Galerie de Foy. I spent hours there that went by too quickly, and above all nights. It would have been easy for me to mistake her, in that posture, for a tax inspector, and I would not have been astonished if good people, who had heard favorable mention of my dramatic talents, had imagined in passing that I was only so assiduous in that place to regulate my authorial rights."

"I tremble to tell you what I imagine myself; you remind me, Maxime, of the prince in Oriental tales who disdained the good graces of the Queen of the Peris, who avenged herself on him by rendering him passionately amorous of a goose in the poultry-yards, who sought fortune in a pink domino, like the flighty goose she was, in the ponds of the palace. I was kind enough to forgive you for the theater in the Rue Saint-Martin, but I warn you that, with the best will in the world, I'm incapable of pardoning you an extravagance for the commère of Polichinelle."

"That's because you've never seen her, Baronne! I believe that I've spared no effort to elevate her modest condition by means of the illustriousness of the great actor or miraculous automaton whose fortune she followed. In that arrangement there was a certain art of composition on which I counted in order to justify myself; but you are inexorable because you know that I am not a painter of portraits and you are challenging me secretly, in your profound malice, to interest you in Jeannette's attractions.

"Oh, if I could show her to you, as straight, slender and supple as a reed; her skin sometimes wintry but clouded with fresh colors; the nose as fine as an awl, straight, classic, almost divine, like that of a Green statue, and terminated by a cheerful and capricious little plane surface . . . like yours; the mouth redder than a pomegranate; the teeth resplendent with an enamel more diaphanous and more polished than alabaster.

"If only I knew words to represent her long almond-shaped eyes, with indigo blue irises, their long lashes as soft as silk and as brilliant as burnished steel, her long black eyebrows traced in an arc on a smooth and harmonious forehead with the precision of a brush, and yet so voluptuously mobile when they deigned to express pleasure and amour . . . ! If only it were permissible to reveal to you her dainty legs, the precious contour of which David's magic chisel would have respected, to which two feet were attached that would have made a Chinese princess die of jealous chagrin, with their elegant shoes and pretty white stockings with pink spots. And when I think about it, that would not have been difficult, for her green skirt with a nacarat fringe was extraordinarily short.

"In sum, if you had seen her, as I desired her just now, is the simple and seductive apparel of her delightful Swiss costume, you would not have had the courage to criticize me, and my extravagance would change its name."

"I want to believe in all these marvels. But I've made up my mind, Maxime, not to budge. Your Jeannette, even if she was Venus and better, was still Polichinelle's commère, and you make me feel pity."

"She was, alas, as you say, Polichinelle's commère. The vulgar, at least, did not know then of any alliances more elevated. I shall spare you, therefore, the ennui of my stormy tribulations; I shall not tell you about my passionate gazes fixed upon her by an invisible power that tended to fascination, nor my sighs of flame incessantly exhaled toward the banquette where she received the money and the tributes of the curious, nor my frenetic letters in which I outbid the hyperboles, still imperfectly naturalized here, of the German Romantics."

"You wrote to Jeannette!"

"In prose and in verse, and I affirm to you that she read as fluently. However, for a week I paid the expenses of sentiment at a pure loss, and my intrigue was so painfully stitched, my action dragged on so nonchalantly, that it would have been justly whistled in Polichinelle's theater.

"Suddenly, the poster indicated the final performance, the last and veritable closure, the closure without appeal and without remission. It was now or never to think about the denouement; I resolved to cut it short. Far from the paternal house I had a clandestine small apartment, very elegantly decorated, which I had obtained for myself in a spirit of prudence, in order to give free rein to the melancholy and solitary meditations that have always been my delight, in order to return from time to time at leisure to my excessively neglected studies, and perhaps also for a few unexpected opportunities that sometimes presented themselves by chance in the life of a busy young man. I was convinced that that auxiliary domicile was only known to me, and to five or six people at the most who were particularly interested in keeping my secret. I had carefully designated it to Jeannette in the postscripts of all my love letters. The postscript is the positive part of amorous correspondence; it is there that one treats the material interests of grand passion. I have encountered women who do not read anything else.

"As I had not received profound marks of indifference from Jeannette, and I believed that I discerned, on the contrary, some evidence of tender condescension to my desires in the indigo irises that I have had the honor of mentioning to you, every time she deigned to turn their dazzling disks toward me, I usually spent all the time that I did not spend begging her to come waiting and hoping in my philosophical retreat. The day after the closure—I knew that she was due to leave in the evening—I reviewed the means of bring her there the same day, before the diligence stole her from me forever, and I began to glimpse that it would doubtless be necessary, in order to succeed, to have recourse to more or less imperious procedures that would leave her the entire honors of resistance, since she was decidedly a formalist.

"I had, in consequence, formed ten projects, each more idiotic than the next, without settling on any, when I heard the key of my door turning quietly in the lock. The door opened and Jeannette appeared, more beautiful than ever, beautiful with emotion, dread and amour, but so troubled that her legs buckled at the moment when I launched myself forward to receive her; I supposed so at least, for she fell into my arms. We remained mute for some time—how long I cannot tell you exactly; those moments are very difficult to measure.

"Eventually, she came round gradually, repaired a slight disorder in her clothing, which my urgency had not permitted me to preserve perfectly while assisting her unexpectedly in a crisis so new to her innocence and timidity, and sat down in an armchair next to mine. Since she had been in my room the poor girl had not yet sat down.

"I took pleasure in gazing at her, as one gazes at the woman one loves the first time one has good reason to believe that one is loved. There was no time to lose. Imagine my astonishment when her face, on which I hoped to find the same expression, gradually came to settle in I know not what mysterious meditation, to the extent of attaining the most imposing character of solemnity. I thought at first that she was meditating a role for a stage more eminent than the one on which she had been taught to exercise her talents, and it was something like that. I tried to take her hand with the familiar liberty permitted to me by an encounter so favorable to the development of the most perfect intimacy, but she maintained me in my place with a gesture that was grave and gentle at the same time, and finally began to speak in terms that I would willingly report if I did not fear that you have already found this story too long."

"I would not be sorry to form an idea of the degree of dignity to which the oratorical means of Polichinelle's commère might rise in such a circumstance."

"'I shall not try to excuse, Monsieur,' Jeanette said, 'the step that puts me, in a sense at the discretion of your delicacy and your virtue. Only the esteem inspired in me for you by your language, your letters and the reputation of your noble sentiments can justify it in my own eyes, For a long time I have needed to pour out the sadness of my heart into a generous heart, and I have not been able to resist the confidence that I have placed in yours, since the first day that I saw you. If I am mistaken in my hopes, the blood from which I emerge will fortunately give me enough strength no longer to hesitate to submit to the rigors of the misfortune that pursues me.'

"I shuddered with surprise and impatience, but I did not interrupt Jeannette."

"And you did marvelously, Maxime. This promises, if I'm not mistaken, revelations of an entirely new genre."

"She went on: 'I am not, Monsieur, the obscure and miserable creature that my present condition seems to announce. You might have heard mention of the worthy Comte de C***, a superior officer of the Cent-Suisses, murdered defending the dwelling of your kings on the fatal day on the tenth of August 1792. I am the unique daughter and last offspring of his illustrious family. My father, attained by ten mortal wounds, succeeded in reaching our house in the Rue Saint-Florentin, which is not far from the château. I was only six years old then, and only a very vague idea of that horrible event remains to me. He scarcely had the time and the strength to ask to see me and to confide me, bathed with his tears and his blood, to the care of a valet de chambre whose fidelity he believed to be proof against anything, for I no longer had a mother.

"'My parents' fortune, which was entirely realized in France, could not escape confiscation. The feeble resources produced by my father's ready money and jewels were soon exhausted. It was then that Siméon Balland—that was the valet de chambre's name—found himself reduced to taking up again, in order to live, the ignoble profession that he had practiced in his early youth, and to giving me an employment in his theater, in order to pay the expenses of my keep. A child, I was subject to that necessity without judging its baseness and without appreciating its consequences. Having arrived at the age of thought, I submitted to it without complaint, because I could not see any remedy to it. However, I knew my birth, the titles of which had not been destroyed. I knew at they were deposited at Langres in hands that I believe to be secure, and from which I hope to recover them without difficulty, but I have had the good fortune to make a resolution in conformity with the cruel extremity to which I was reduced, and from which I might never have departed if my unworthy tyrant, widowed two years ago, were not pushing my courage today to the utmost excess of despair by imposing on me the frightful obligation of accepting his hand and his name.

"'You are shuddering, Monsieur, and I sense that I am understood. You will not be astonished to hear me swear that nothing can determine me to resume a chain that I detest, and if you love me, as you have pretexted so many times in such eloquent terms, the moment has come to keep the promises that you have made me. Wife, slave or ward, I am putting the fate of my life in your hands and I am abandoning my destiny to you as well as my heart.'

"As she finished speaking she made a movement to fall at my knees, but I was already at hers."

"Bravo, Maxime! I can see you in the position of Don Quixote, when he attempted to steal the child Melisandre from the pursuits of the grim Marsille. Woe betide the marionettes!"

"'Mademoiselle,' I cried, in the respectful position that befit henceforth my relationship with her, 'know that you will not be mistaken in the flattering hope that you have founded on my character and my principles. The rights that I have over this modest apartment are, thank Heaven, a mystery for the entire town, and I believe I can be assured that it will easily preserve you from the research of your persecutors. From this day forward you can regard it as your own; I shall only present myself here with your consent, and if I do not succeed in rendering it worthy of you, I can at last guarantee that you will lack nothing of what can aid a young and sensible woman to support solitude patiently, while I occupy myself with an indefatigable zeal in rendering your rights and your liberty.'"

"I would be curious, my friend, to know whether you give that to women."

"I fulfill in every regard, Madame, the duties that a conscientious hospitality prescribes. I confess to you, on reflection, that I was passably embarrassed by that affair, which I had not expected to take a serious turn. I had not thought for a moment of marrying Jeannette, and that was perhaps the only means of untangling the intrigue, since she had complicated it, in spite of me, with an appearance of seduction and abduction.

"*I must be very ill-favored by Providence*, I said to myself at first, having always had bad luck with nobility, *to be en-*

gaged body and soul in an aristocratic relationship by choosing a mistress of marionettes. Who the devil would have thought that the patriciate could have passed that way? Since Jeannette is a comtesse, I ask you who would dare now to be so proud?

"On the other hand, I had just recognized in Jeanette qualities that rendered me more amorous than ever. Her beautiful sentiments, which were marvelously redolent of her birth, had also penetrated me with a profound admiration, and I was also engaged by honor, the supreme rule of the conduct of a well-born man. I had little dread that the secret of her retreat would be penetrated, where she might at the most, as I have said, chance to receive the visit of a few women of good enough company, naturally very sympathetic to amorous difficulties. They were proven hearts. I therefore delivered myself without reserve, as usual, to the intoxication of the present happiness, without worrying overmuch about the future, and on the morning of the fifth day I came without suspicion to inform myself regarding Jeannette's slumber, when I found the door open and a chambermaid moaning, weeping for her beautiful mistress, brutally taken away by agents of the police."

"I expected that. The Moors were on campaign and Marsille had unearthed Melisandre."

"Add, if you please, Baronne, that he had just unearthed Galiferos. A local commissaire who was tracking the abductor, and who flattered himself, with sufficient plausibility, that he had caught him in his lair, asked me politely to render to Monsieur le Maire, the sovereign judge of all the affairs of the secret police that interest the honor of families, the inviolability of provincial actresses and the good moral order of marionettes.

"The Maire of my good town was then an excellent and respectable old man whom you might remember, Monsieur le Baron D***, who loved me in a very paternal fashion, even in the aberration into which the impetuosity of an irreflective youth had drawn me. He scolded me loudly on occasion, pardoned me in a low voice while scolding, and turned away from time to time in his greatest wrath against my follies in order to laugh surreptitiously at my follies and his anger, for he combined a perfectly tolerant soul with an amiable and slightly facetious turn of mind.

"Next to him was seated the Vaucanson of Wintertour, the honorable Master Siméon Balland, who had retrogressed in his itinerary by twenty leagues in order to come and demand justice when he had perceived that his female lead, who should have rejoined him by diligence, had missed the roll-call of the comic troupe. I was emotional, but untroubled, because the purity of my intentions reassured me, and apart from a few details of scant importance in the matter, which essentially escaped the scope of the municipal investigations, I could take Heaven as my witness of my innocence and envelop myself in virtue. I felt affirmed in any case by the justice of the case that I had come to defend. Oh, Madame, it is very pleasant to plead on behalf of beauty, innocence and misfortune!

"'*Quo usque tandem, Catilina*,'[1] Monsieur le Maire said to me at first; but, probably fearing that that magnificent model of abrupt exordium might be too pompous for the circumstance he immediately began again. 'So it's you,' he continued, in a less emphatic but similarly gravely burlesque tone, 'who, to the scorn of the excellent principles of the education you have received, have borne insubordination, disorder and perhaps dishonor among the nomad subjects of this gallant man, whose memory your fellow citizens have conserved with delectation and gratitude. There is, then, no shelter inviolable against your recklessness, since modesty cannot even escape it in Polichinelle's box.

"'It is difficult to foresee after this to what excess you are capable of going, and if you had not, let it be said between

____

1 "When will you cease abusing our patience, Catilina?" From a speech by Lucius Sergius Catilina's adversary in the Roman Senate, Cicero.

us, lived for some time without soiling with such college profanations the vestals and festivals of the good goddess, you would not have got away with it so cheaply. Nevertheless, in the impossibility in which I find myself of rebuking you otherwise, which I ought to do, in despair of the cause time and experience, the honest Siméon here, wanting to recover the litigious object without submitting it to an expertise that I would not have been able to refuse him in order to determine the deterioration, damage and deficiency, it remains to us to regulate the indemnity to which you are liable, by reason of the expenses of the journey and forced idleness, since you are in possession of the necessary actress who represents in herself the entire feminine personnel of the troupe. That amounts to nearly a hundred francs by his count, and it is to that demand that I await a response from you, warning you that it does not appear to me to be possible to give a better outcome to your escapade.'

"I was not disconcerted for a single moment, and while I might have been thought to be occupied in formulating, privately, some act of repentance, I was meditating the most audacious incursion into enemy territory.

"'No, Monsieur,' I cried, as soon as the respectable magistrate's allocution had concluded, 'I will not subscribe to the unworthy concession that is proposed to me! My duty is to enlighten your justice regarding the maneuvers of a great villlain, and I sense the strength to fulfill it. It is me, Monsieur, who comes to demand in my turn, in the name of the public mores of which your tutelary authority is the primary safeguard, that the unfortunate Jeannette be returned to my hands, because it is for me alone, as her counsel and the holder of her power of attorney, to answer for her before the law.'"

"'Oho!' said Monsieur le Maire. 'That's something else! Of such procurations and such cautions we have no lack, if they are held to be valid in law!'

"Master Siméon said nothing. He put his hands on his knees, like a man who needs to ensure his equilibrium, and fixed bewildered eyes upon me.

"'There are here, in fact, Monsieur,' I went on, untroubled, 'misdeeds that imply the highest degree of criminality, to wit, the iniquitous and arbitrary detention of a person and he supposition of estate; and the great culpable that promised to designate to you is Master Siméon Balland of Wintertour, so-called mechanician.'"

"At those words, Siméon drew himself up to his full height, folded his hands over his belt and gazed sadly at the ceiling. Never had I seen a physiognomy that bore so naively the characteristic imprint of an honest man.

"'Continue,' said the Maire.

"I had obtained sufficient advantage from my futile studies to possess a least some of the secrets of the bar, the invective and the exclamation, the repetitive padding, the verbal redundancy, the disorderly gestures and spasmodic shrugs of accredited advocates. I therefore recounted everything that Jeannette had told me, with such effluvia of eloquence that I thought I was assured of winning my case, and felt myself moved by a residue of pity as I darted a triumphant glance at the mechanician. He had fallen back on his chair before my speech and, with his hands over his eyes in a sign of confusion, seemed to be sobbing as he waited for me to finish crushing him."

"Pitiless vengeance! He was weeping bitterly!"

"He was weeping, Madame, nothing is more certain than that. Bitterly, that's another question. Perhaps you have learned in your excellent reading that the lachrymal glands and the zygomatic muscles belong equally to laughter and tears. Montaigne has observed it somewhere."

"I tremble now that such a beautiful harangue did not respond to your hopes."

"Precisely, like the first speech of Cicero for Milo. Siméon spoke in his turn, without deploying in my example, the resources of rhetoric, of which I presume he had made a superficial study.

"'All that would be well and good,' he said, cheerfully, to the Maire, 'if there were a word of truth in the story that you have just reeled off, but it is nonsense that would make my marionettes die laughing. I don't say that Monsieur is capable of lying—far from it—but our Jeannette is a player who has put one over on people more refined than he appears to be, saving the respect that I owe him. God, what mischief! Oh, she's a charming child, who would have made her way if I hadn't kept her in order. Probity before all, The fact is that she's the legitimate daughter of my poor brother Jude Balland, who died ten years ago in my homeland without leaving me any heritage but that she-cat. That was two years after the unfortunate death of Monsieur le Comte de C***, of whom we were both domestics, along with my sister-in-law Marion, the mother of my niece Jeannette; for he loved our family, but not to the point of taking the trouble to make us children, all the more so as the good Marion, God rest her soul, was as ugly as sin, although a very worthy woman. You can see the entire genealogy of Jeannette's story in these famous papers from Langres, which I recovered the day before yesterday as a precaution.'

"The Maire laid them out on his desk.

"'How did these papers come to be in Langres and by what hazard did they fall into your hands?' I asked, more modestly, for my conviction had been shaken increasingly as he spoke.

"'It's quite simple,' said Balland. 'I had expedited them for Jeannette's imminent marriage, and her future husband returned them to me when he saw that she wasn't coming. I suspected that they might be useful to me.'

"'It isn't you that she was going to marry, then?'

"'Marry my niece, Monsieur! Heaven preserve me from that. She has too much wit for me, but she was about to make a superb establishment.'

"'A superb establishment!'

"'Undoubtedly. She was about to pass through a second wedding, because, in order that you know, she's the widow of my trumpet, who was a fine fellow. She was on the point, as I said, of marrying an artiste of the top flight, who was combining his troupe with mine. It's a golden affair; no one like him has ever been seen for jumping the hoop, dancing on baskets and vaulting, a fellow who could come down the Jungfrau on an iron wire. It's impossible that you haven't heard of the Incomparable Peruvian. We were born next door to one another.'

"'Malediction! May lightning strike the marionettes of the incomparable Peruvian!'

"'There's no need for Monsieur to be afflicted,' said Siméon, craftily. 'The affair isn't far advanced, and it's my opinion, between us, that the Incomparable Peruvian hardly cares. If Monsieur persisted in his good intentions toward Jeannette, it would be a great satisfaction for the family. It's true that she isn't a comtesse, but the Ballands are honest folk.'

"'Do you think, Master Balland, that we're playing a scene of Polichinelle here?'

"'No, my friend,' replied the Maire, leaning toward my ear with an ironic smile that was also amiable and tender. 'It isn't a scene from Polichinelle,' he went on holding out the papers that he had just perused, and which I pushed away gently with my hand. 'God forgive me, it's a scene . . .'

"'From Gilles, no?'[1]

"He only added one word. I took a hundred francs from my purse, deposited them before him, pulled my hat down over my eyes and escaped without looking back."

There, naturally, is where my story ended.

"Do you think that anecdote became known to the public?" the baronne asked me, after a moment of silence.

---

1 "Gillles" or Gilles Bon Ami, was the protagonist of a number of farces produced in the French derivative of the *commedia dell'arte*, often paired with Arlequin.

"What, Madame! Become known? It was made into a comedy for marionettes, and as the play wasn't bad of its genre, I believe it became a classic, with the result that I've never dared to set foot in Séraphin's theater for fear that I might see it performed there."

"Deplorable friend! To be subjected to so many tribulations in order to please a Parisian nymph who became a crone in Champagne and to make a Menelaus out of the Incomparable Peruvian!"

"The first project that passed through my mind was to go and throw myself in the river with a stone around my neck."

"That would have been an extreme resolution. Haven't you told me that there was a proposal to marry you off? And by the way, why haven't you told me anything of your intended wife?"

"In truth, Baronne, I was no longer thinking about it."

"Too bad! You were in the best disposition in the world for the matter in question. It would have gained a great deal for the future. There are people without foresight who would have thought of nothing else the next day."

"When my father perceived that my dolor was beginning to calm down and I showed myself in the streets with my head held high, it was necessary to make me resolve to visit Henriette's family. That was the young woman's name. As I was reputed to have expectations of a very acceptable fortune, and the grandparents had not taken account of the worthy Salomon, the sage steward of my meager pleasures and my secret expenditures, I was given a very good welcome. After a few moments of idle chat, Henriette came in. She was pretty. I won't talk about her attire. You've seen more than one young woman just out of a pension. She resembled all of them. For some time her mother made futile efforts to constrain her gracious and modest head to rise vertically over the inflexible perpendicularity of her body, which it overhung in an alarming manner. However, curiosity was mingled with it, and when Henriette was sufficiently exercised to extend an adventurous reconnaissance over the parquet as far as my shoes—people were not yet making visits in boots—it gradually gained terrain in height, and ended up looking at me almost horizontally. I dare not dissimulate that I counted a great deal on that impression, which had always been so singularly favorable to me, but I was not vain enough to dread that the results would be fatal to a woman who was seeing me for the first time. However, the indefinable and convulsive constraint that her physiognomy expressed gave me a serious anxiety when I saw that she was obliged to flee to her room in order to hide the disorder into which that glimpse had thrown her mind."

"One has never heard talk of such a sudden effect of sympathy."

"Make no mistake, Eugénie; sympathy had nothing to do with it. The innocent Henriette had heard my adventures recounted, and all the memories of my lamentable amours had just appeared to her at once. Scarcely had the door closed behind her than she felt at ease and burst out laughing uproariously."

"Poor girl! It was just in time! She might have died holding it in."

"Her mother affirmed to me that the crises of mad joy to which she was subject did not possess her for long, but I did not feel the slightest desire to know positively what their duration implied for me, and I escaped, as I had the habit of doing in such circumstances. I beg your pardon if I have repeated the circumstance often in my story; it's one of the inconveniences of the subject."

"You've never married, then?"

"No, truly."

"Not so ridiculous! Suppose that we've just acted out a proverb."

"Which one?"

"Every cloud has a silver lining."

MADEMOISELLE DE MARSAN

Episode One
The Carbonari

Among the former émigrés who had welcomed me to Venice with benevolence, in consideration of my quality as a Frenchman, my opinions and my misfortunes, there was one who inspired the most profound sentiment of respect and affection. That was Monsieur de Marsan.

Monsieur de Marsan, whom a few old courtiers might remember, had been one of the most brilliant officers of the military household of Louis XVI. His handsome face, his fine manners, his intelligence and his courage had enabled him to be remarked in a time and in court where those fortunate personal recommendations were not very rare. He owed to them a rapid advancement that did not excite any protest, and a considerable establishment of which everyone approved. His daughter, born in 1788, was held over the baptismal font, in the name of the Queen of France, by one of the friends of that august and unfortunate sovereign who enjoyed the firmest credit at Versailles. Monsieur de Marsan's daughter was named Diana.

Monsieur de Marsan, broken by the fatigues of war, was old in 1808;[1] he had married at thirty-five and had lost three

____

1 This date makes the present story chronologically incompatible with

children before Heaven accorded him the unique daughter in whom all his affections were finally concentrated. Madame de Marsan, attached to the service of the king's sisters, had not long survived their establishment in Trieste. She preceded them to the tomb.

At least the old émigré drew some advantage from his long misfortunes; he had become a philosopher. Rich enough to live in a modest ease, sagely preserved by precautions taken with regard to the universal catastrophe, he spent the rest of his life peacefully between agreeable studies and sedentary distractions. A liking for natural history had suddenly brought us together and I was faithful in playing piquet with him every evening. Thus his predilection for me, among all the young men whose conversation he enjoyed, had gradually taken on something paternal, of which Diana would have had the right to be jealous. I never perceived that he attached much importance to the vanity, really rather puerile, that is called the prejudice of nobility, and yet I was quite convinced that he sometimes regretted that I was not noble, to the extent of making a certain effort to forget it.

"Your deal, Monsieur le Chevalier," he said to me one day, handing me the cards.

I do not know in what crypt of my memory, closed for twenty years, I have found that frivolous anecdote.

"I'm not a chevalier," I exclaimed, laughing, before dealing them.

"On my faith as a Christian," said Monsieur de Marsan, "the gentlemen of my household have armed more than one of them less worthy of that honor."

"I suppose," I replied, getting up in order to go to him, "that it was not without giving them the accolade."

"Amélie," which must precede the events in "Mademoiselle de Marsan" in Maxime's memoirs. The several affinities between the present story and *Jean Sbogar* suggest that it might have been planned and perhaps written much earlier than its publication.

And I embraced him wholeheartedly, for I have always put a high price on the affection of old men.

It was necessary, however, to forgive him a violent and passionate stubbornness on one question that often came up in the conversations of those days. The mere name of revolution caused him a veritable revolution, and although he regarded the imminent reestablishment of the Bourbons on the throne of their forefathers as an infallible event, he had promised never to return to Paris, all the stones of which still seemed to him to be bathed in the blood of proscriptions. That antipathy against all political movements of the same genre did not spare the conspirators of his own party, and, in his resignation to the equitable and assured decrees of Providence, he criticized bitterly the insensates who sought to precipitate the accomplishment without regard to the sage temporizations of the prudence of God.

The idea of which I speak was manifest so quickly and so frequently in his speech that it had soon deterred me from communicating to him all the secrets of my turbulent youth, and even more so the relationships that I had formed on my arrival in Venice with the Carbonari and the emissaries of the Tugendbund,[1] the name of which inspired no less horror in him than that of the Jacobins. It is necessary to agree, moreover, that I was beginning to feel some tendency for his opinion, even before knowing him, and that I was only retained any longer in the perilous net of secret societies by the impossibility of breaking it without violence. I was twenty-six years old, proven by adversities almost without example at my age, and the taste for mild occupations and studious leisure recalled me incessantly to another kind of life, which I ought never to have quit; but it also happened from time to time

---

1 The Tugendbund [League of Virtue] was a quasi-masonic society founded in Königsberg in reaction to the defeat of the Prussians by Napoléon in 1808. Ostensibly devoted to educational reform, it soon became a focal point of subversive resistance to French occupation.

that my stormy passions got the upper hand and plunged me back into a new chaos of agitations and miseries from which my heart could only deliver itself by attaching itself firmly to the hope of some durable happiness.

It was that happiness that my insensate imagination was obstinate in seeking in amour.

Diana de Marsan was twenty years old and did not appear less, for her bright and brilliant but slightly tanned complexion, as that of Venetians usually is, lacked the freshness that is in a woman's skin what the fugitive down that still covers them is to fruits collected from the tree. Her figure, tall and quite robust, gave something imposing to her aspect, which further heightened the ordinary expression of her physiognomy. One did not know whether what carried her away in her sad and proud gaze, in the anxious and haughty quiver of her eyebrows and the scornful and bitter movement of her mouth was the habitude of a hidden chagrin or a disdainful disillusionment. It is thus that antique sculpture has represented the truly divine Diana, whom the chisel made the worthy sister of Apollo, as mythology had. That impression was not personal to me with regard to Diana, for the most accredited poets of the era reproached her, at the end of their sonnets, for being formed of a marble as cold as that of Veletri. Diana was, however, as everyone admitted, the most beautiful of the young women of Venice.

The human heart, especially that of lovers, is irritated by difficulties. I loved Diana with all the more ardor, perhaps, because everything about her told me that she did not want to love me. As for the consequences of that sentiment, they had nothing that was capable of frightening me. Diana's fortune was too mediocre to tempt redoubtable suits, and the condition of an aged French gentleman exiled to the edge of the lagoons did not promise more chance to the ambition of a son-in-law than his cupidity. My position would, on the contrary, be magnified, according to all appearance, by the triumph of my party, of which Monsieur de Marsan had no suspicion. I had risked so much, I had suffered so much, and fortunate kings are so grateful.

Diana was not scornful of the passion that she inspired in me; woman are never scornful of that. I did not perceive, however, anything of its discovery except a sinister darkening of her gaze and the more severe measure she retained toward me in her speech. I would have construed that ever-increasing rigor as proceeding from the difference in our conditions, for I knew already what the pride of nobility was and how it could affect the forms of hatred, if Diana had been informed of that circumstance, but I have already said that Monsieur de Marsan stubbornly persisted in ennobling me, and from the memorable day when I had received the order of chivalry from him from one side of a card table to the other, the title of chevalier had been so identified with the honorable but obscure name that I had received from my ancestors that the Chérins and the Hoziers would not have dared to contest it with me.

It is sufficient to know the hyperbolic genius of the Venetians, especially in the class of the people, to be sure in advance that the politeness of domestics would not be stopped by so little. I was at least a comte in the antechamber, and an illustrious comte, if I was only exactly as good a gentleman as was requisite in the drawing room. I had ended up no longer taking any account of it and submitting casually to a meta-morphosis that humiliated my modesty slightly, in order not to wound the capricious but innocent vanity of a great lord in whom I had found a friend.

I had promised to commence with Diana by means of that explanation if she gave me the slightest sign of condescension to my sentiments, but she spared me the embarrassment. Her coldness progressed rapidly to rudeness, her indifference to disdain. After a few days there was no means of being mistaken about it, and a man more convinced than I ever was of his ascendancy over women's hearts would not have hesitated to renounce, as I did, pretentions devoid of hope. A few young men of Venice, better founded in their steps, had already shown the example of that sacrifice.

I did not sulk. That is all that would have been needed to make me completely ridiculous. Nor did I weep. One only weeps when it necessary to lose the hope of being united with a woman by whom one is loved. I was indignant; I revolted against myself; I gnawed my fists in anger; I pretexted indispositions, occupations and voyages to explain the rarity of my visits; I gambled for high stakes. I fought duels, and then I threw myself back with frenzy into the reckless conspiracies from which I had thought myself separated forever a month before. I rejoiced in the idea of dying in a tragic and glorious manner, in order that she would be ashamed of having scorned me. I lulled myself in the furious fantasy of conspiracies, proscriptions and tortures, as in a dream of amour and sensuality.

In a word, I went mad again.

Our assemblies were held in the vicinity of the Rialto, in the most dilapidated apartment of an old palace that had been abandoned a long time ago, the owner of which I shall not indicate, whose present high position in the court of Germany had probably disabused him of our foolish popular theories. He no longer appeared there, but he had left it at the disposition of our leaders while retiring to the Venetian countryside and perhaps a little further from the danger.

It is almost needless to say what species of men make up those clandestine meetings. One can divine it without having a great habitude of political machinations, and even without having delivered oneself to a profound study of history. Five or six young men, sensitive and generous, but embittered by the woes of humankind and the excesses of tyrants, hold a more or less imperceptible place therein, and, gradually disillusioned, like me, they occupy themselves with it more rarely from day to day; the rest are what the host of enemies of any established order are everywhere: an ambitious mob devoid of talents whose pretentions are increased and irritated by reason of their nullity; men doomed by debts, mores and reputation, the vile refuse of gambling and debauchery; and a few wretches a hundred times viler who are only waiting for the first opportunity to sell to any power that comes along the list of their accomplices or their victims, for an infamous price of gold and an ignominious impunity. That judgment is the one that I had commenced to bear even then, but it was less general, and above all less firm, in my mind. It is necessary to have seen all that everywhere during the course of an overly long life in order to arrive at believing it.

You will agree that my ambition for death was not as vainly presumptuous in such an assembly as my projects of amour with regard to Diana. There were risks, and few men, in truth, would have consented to run them in my place; for success, almost foreign to the destiny of my country and my own, would not even have procured me the feeble satisfaction that winning a pot gives us in a card game in which we are only interested by chance. In the contrary case it would be different; the executioner would take away my stake. That insensate prodigality of life is the effect of a nameless passion that is only comprehensible to those who have experienced it, and that is no bad thing.

Associations like ours operated openly in all the countries where Napoléon had not deigned to leave his administration and his soldiers in passing. They agitated there freely, not publicly admitted by the governments, which did not have that courage, but flattered, emboldened and covertly protected, with more cunning than skill, and with a certain mental reserve, the secret of which ought to be known to all the sincere and devoted men who engage their lives in the defense of crowns—which is to say, save for the cowardly premeditated intention of sacrificing them, if necessary to a plan of peace.

That organization, however, would have been incomplete if it had not penetrated all the way to the heart of the States already submissive to the great Emperor by virtue of victories and treaties, and there was no city in which the elements necessary to its development could not be found. Such was the goal of the audacious propaganda of European liberty that raised human barriers here and there against the oppressor of the world: adventurous outposts of scouts thrown before the holy coalition of people is the enemy camp, which would have been so powerful if they had been purer.

I am abusing the privileges of the storyteller somewhat by introducing that page of history into a petty script whose form only announces a work of fiction, but it will only be counted as a page of fiction by anyone who has not seen history at close range, and of all the judgments that might be made of it, that is the one the worries me the least.

The original goal of the carbonarism of those days, which has nothing in common with the formless work we see manifest today, like the gigantic and hideous monsters that sprang forth from chaos in the first days of creation, was certainly the noblest that a conspiracy can propose. Its only objective was the pious federation of patriots of all lands against the progress of an insatiable despotism that aspired, without disguise, to universal monarchy and the division of Europe into prefectures to give to its captains. That magnanimous idea had stirred minds profoundly everywhere that the independence and wellbeing of the natal soil still countered for something, but most particularly Italy and Germany.

The movement imprinted on the thought of peoples by those grave questions had brought up others. By virtue of occupation with guarantees of universal equilibrium, debris was exhumed every day of ancient liberties, which progressive usurpations of power had slowly destroyed, and which are an imprescriptible property for nations. The opportunity was good to reclaim them; and it was then that something happened that had never happened in the world before and might never arrive again: an amiable stipulation, solemnly promised between peoples and kings, sworn in palaces and guarded in cottages, the synallagmatic terms of which were, on the one hand, unanimous resistance to the armies of Napoléon, and on the other, frank and entire recognition of political rights written of old in all the States of the alliance.

It is possible that the contract in question is not found in the official documents of diplomacy, and I do not see that history has had much to say about it thus far, but history knows nothing in France, and does not say, moreover, what it ought to say if it were permitted to speak. That accidental combination of interests, so cruelly betrayed by events, was, in any case, too transient to be grasped in all its details by the most sudden and most advantageously placed observers.

It is understandable that it had given a great importance to the position of secret societies, which became a legitimate authority for the first time in the old European system, and which did not aspire as yet to replace all the legitimate authorities in order to attempt tyranny in their turn.

They did not profit from it then. The diffusion of egotisms, ambitions and vanities made itself felt too quickly for that in those sad conventicles, imprinted with all the vices of the mother society from which they separated. Two months had not gone by when the initial unity was broken into four or five fractions in the supreme *vendita* and all those that depended in it. One had taken the terms of the treaty in so broad a sense that it only intended to make victory serve for the absolute emancipation of the people and the reestablishment of the deadly democracy of which Venice conserved a bloody memory. The other, which could not fail to unite the majority in recruiting, at the decisive moment, by virtue of the ascendancy of interest, the indecisive and the corrupt, had sold to Austria, by means of a secret pact, the liberties of the countries so vainly reserved. A few were thought to be maintaining mysterious intelligence with Napoléon's government and thus maintaining a gilded transaction in case of defeat.

The least numerous party, but certainly the most energetic and the purest, had only engaged its intrepid and sincere cooperation under the express condition of the independence of the Venetian States and the restoration of their ancient republic. They were supported externally by the imposing coalition of montagnards, and had for their leader one of those resolute men of far sight and powerful execution, whose name alone was worth a party. That leader was Mario Cinci, nicknamed the Doge; and it was to that party that my particular sympathies had attached me.

Mario Cinci descended from the unfortunate Roman family whose execrable crime had not cried up forever all the sources of pity, and which furnished the unique example of a condemnation of parricides washed by the tears of religion, justice and the people.[1] The younger brother of Beatrice, banished in perpetuity from the Estates of the Church, had taken refuge in an old castle on the banks of the Tagliamente, where tradition reports that he died after being struck by lightning, at a rather advanced age. A vengeful fatality had weighed

---

1 The reference is to a story recorded in Ludovico Muratori's *Annali d'Italia* (1749), perhaps more accurately reckoned legend than history, about the execution in 1599 of a young woman, Beatrice Cenci, for the murder of her tyrannical father. It was employed as the basis of a notorious play by Percy Shelley, *The Cenci*, composed in Italy in 1819 and printed there before an edition appeared in London. It was considered unstageable at the time, and generated controversy for many years before eventually being hailed as the great English tragedy of its era; not unnaturally, it attracted the support and enthusiasm of the French Romantics, who would have discussed it in the *cénacle*, although it is unlikely that many of them, apart from Victor Hugo and Nodier, actually read it. Nodier's embellishments of the story, and the character of Mario Cinci, are entirely fictitious.

thereafter, from generation to generation on each of his descendants, whose chronological history composes a tragedy in several acts, like that of Pelapides. The last had died on the scaffold of the Italian revolution, and of that blood proscribed by the law and by Heaven, nothing remained on earth except Mario Cinci.

Mario's youth, commenced under such funereal auspices and deprived of all support in human society, had been violent and fearful; it even seemed that no mild sentiment could ever have tempered its transports, for the mere thought of being loved by him was a subject of terror for Venetians, who only mentioned his name with a shudder. He never appeared in public places, but when he passed along one of the narrow streets of the city, either alone or accompanied, at the most, by a few friends as mysterious as himself, the most hardened men withdrew from his passage as if to hide from his gaze. However, and this was typical of that strange character or to the somber impression of alarm that he produced without being aware of it, he was feared without being hated, as lions are feared, and it is not far from that sentiment to the exalted admirations that sometimes become a cult. No one could reproach him for an unjust action or a reflected cruelty; on the contrary, a multitude of generous actions were reported, but executed without tenderness and without sympathy. He had often saved children from death by pulling them out of the waves, but he had never embraced one.

From the age of twenty—he was then twenty-eight—his fortune, exhausted in blind prodigalities and bizarre and solitary dissipations, had reduced him to retiring to his sad manor on the mainland with a single Albanian domestic who had not wanted to quit him. Since then he had only returned at intervals to Venice, which was then under a new aspect, at least hopefully, in the affairs of Italy. It was noticed that he spent as much as two successive months there, but no one knew where he resided.

Although Mario Cinci was the real leader of the *vendita*, where his empire increased even in his absence, I had never seen him, either at the vendita or elsewhere, but I knew these details via the voice of the people, which is more communicative in Venice than in any other country.

In fact, Mario Cinci had no sooner disembarked in the environs of the Piazetta than the people were informed of it in all directions—a people infatuated with the extraordinary, willingly prejudiced in favor of dominant characters who frightened them—and conversations then rose up, in groups in the port and the Piazza San Marco, almost as strange as the man who was their object.

"What has he come to do here," said one, "that demon of misfortune who brings calamity after him wherever he appears, and who only lands in Venice under a storm wind? Is it an announcement of a plague breaking out in the Orient or a new war at sea? I believe that his tower was struck by lightning in the last storm; so rumor has it, for no Cinci has escaped in three hundred years the scourges of Heaven, the dagger or the scaffold."

"In truth," replied another, "I wouldn't be sorry, although he's done me more good than harm when he had the means, but because I'd no longer have the worry, and it's inevitable sooner of later, since it's his unfortunate destiny. May God have mercy on him in the other world!"

"What!" cried a third, who appeared better informed, and around whom the groups tightened in order to hear more clearly. "Don't you know yet what has brought him. While still a child Mario only thought of resuscitating our old republic, with its independence and its commerce, and its ships, king of the seas and the world, and its faith, abandoned by miscreants, and the beneficent assistance of San Marco! And as he has more courage and genius in his little finger than all the people of Italy, it's him who'll deliver us from the Germans and the French, and who will be our doge. You know that I don't like him, and I've never heard it said that Mario was liked by anyone, but I call God as a witness that Mario Cinci will be doge of Venice and will reestablish its prosperity."

Those words were repeated every day, and the populace, which carefully kept its distance from Mario for fear of exciting his wrath, cried on his return: "Long live Mario Cinci! Long live the Doge of Venice!"

That is why he was nicknamed the Doge, without the government worrying about it unduly, for Mario was reputed to be an atrabiliary misanthrope who was too scornful of popular opinion to attribute the slightest importance to it—and it is possible that that judgment was accurate.

On the day of my reentry to the vendita the assembly was not very numerous, although the convocation, executed by a very ingenious means completely impenetrable to the investigations of the police, had been expressed in that circumstance by the most rigorous formulae. I was astonished that so many people were missing, but that all of Mario's party was united, in the presence of its most implacable adversaries. I did not take long to understand, however, that the indifferent had been left out by design, because it was doubtless a matter of a decisive struggle, the necessity of which had been foreseen for a long time.

There was, in fact, no question in our ordinary discussions except the grievances imputed to Mario by the members of the association of whom we had the most reason to be scornful, whom I characterized sufficiently just now. Nothing was forgotten that might make us regard him as an ambitious individual animated by personal interests, who only aspired to a new form of government in order the reestablish the splendor of his family and avenge the death of his father, and who covered his instruments and his enemies with an equal disdain.

We only responded habitually to such odious declamations with the cry of the people: "Long live Mario Cinci!" and did not take the argument any further. What seemed inexplicable to me in this most recent occasion was the confidence that the contrary party was able to found in its forces against the determined group of young enthusiasts whose fanatical heroism alone had sustained my faith in its enterprises. It is probable that the same idea struck us all at the same time, for at the same instant, all our daggers emerged by a third from their scabbards, but we let then fall back, crying "Long live Mario Cinci!" because we were almost equal in number to our accusers, although our youth, our strength and our courage gave us two certain advantages over them, and our opposition, pronounced with that menacing energy, was sufficient to render deliberation impossible.

"It's Mario Cinci you want!" responded the leader of the accusers furiously. "Well, you'll have his head!"

"Come and take it," said a voice that rose up at the same instant at the entrance door, while the man who pronounced those words hastened to close it again carefully, and to take away the key in order to slip it into his belt.

"Long live Mario Cinci!" repeated my comrades, and we gathered at his sides in order to form a rampant if anyone dared to attack us. I saw him then for the first time, but I could only describe him imperfectly for those who did not know him, and especially for those who did. The writer who represents him as an angel of light incarnate, with all his beauty in the body of a Titan, has made an ambitious phrase and nothing more. There was within him another type that I cannot express, that of a tamer of monsters of fabulous times, or a giant paladin of the Middle Ages. For a moment I thought that he was coiffed like Hercules with the mane of a black lion; that was his hair.

He crossed the room slowly, swinging his hips with a savage nonchalance, leaned on the table of the dignitaries, uttering a grim laugh, and repeated: "Come and take it!" The vault echoed it.

Then he returned to us, shook his head and folded his arms.

"The victimizers have brought everything," he said. "Where are the prepared garlands? It would certainly be a sacrifice agreeable to Hell, if the purveyors of demons were where they think. Give me your hand, dear Paolo. Bonjour Annibal, my Patroclus and my Cassius! Hail to you, Félice, to you, Lucio, worthy and intrepid children! Courage, my little Petrovich; your martial moustache is thickening; powder will blacken it. Who's this?" he continued, pausing in front of me. "I ought to recognize his stature, almost as tall as mine, as I've been told. It's the French voyager that our friend Chasteler[1] has recommended to us so warmly. What design do you propose, young man, in the events that are in preparation?"

"To serve you against all tyrannies and to die with you if you are surprised before the accomplishment of your virtuous enterprise; but I will break my sword on the battlefield on the day when the French are there."

"Good, good," said Mario, looking at me intently. "The bond that unites us would not be of long duration if you had responded in any other way. We shall strive to render you useful to the salvation of nations without committing you with the men of your homeland, who have, in any case, the same interest as us in the general liberation, since we want for everyone the independence of everyone, and for ourselves the old liberties of Venice. But it will be necessary to quit Venice, the burning paving stones of which cover a volcano under your feet, and Frenchmen of your age cannot spend a few days within the walls of a voluptuous city without delivering themselves to a few foolish amours—for that distraction of young women is your greatest affair, after the glory of conquests."

---

1 The reference is to Johann Gabriel Chasteler de Courcelles (1763-1825), a Belgian-born military leader in the service of the Austrian Empire who was in command of the Austrian troops in the Tyrol in 1808-9 and the effective leader of resistance against the Napoleonic invasion.

"You judge me poorly, Signor Mario. I only aspire to leave Venice forever, and I would leave tomorrow if I could do so without cowardice in the midst of the dangers that threaten you."

"Is that true?" he replied, with a movement of joy. "We'll talk about it again shortly, but it's necessary first for me to re-assure you, by imposing silence on the buzzing of these wasps, who importune me without frightening me, paltry insects whose venom does no harm when one crushes them over the wound."

The tempest that Mario's arrival had interrupted momentarily, had in fact resumed its course, and he appeared until then to be the only one who had not perceived it.

"Enough!" he cried. "Everyone shut up. I've rendered to your appeal, because it suited me, but it's not today that I'll be judged. A few challenges remain for me to exercise, and it's a right of which I'll only make use before the Venetians, in the middle of the Piazza San Marco."

"On the day," replied the most determined of his enemies, "when you board the *Bucentaur* and throw your ring into the sea?"

"Why not?" said Mario, "if I am the most worthy, and if it is the wish of Venice? But you're abusing my ambition, Tadeo, as well as my foresight. I fear the rigors of my justice too much to expose it to the proof of power in a republic inhabited by men like you. As for espousing the sea, it's a destiny too illustrious for a Cinci. The prophet of Ravenna predicted that the last of us would die crossing a torrent."

The rumor had increased at the extremities of the hall and we were putting ourselves on the defensive against one of the sudden attacks that terminate all violent altercations in Venice when Mario raised his voice again.

"Peace, by San Marco and his lion, if you don't want us to force a silence upon you that will only be troubled by the trumpet of the last judgment. I haven't finished speaking! In my quality as grand master of all the vendita of Italy, I dissolve the vendita of Venice; I break the alliance of its members as I break the beveled hazel twig that serves to rally us, and I forbid you the community of roof and bread, water and salt of my brothers, as apostates and perjurers. Who will murmur against my rights? I am using those that regulations have conferred upon me by the accursed occasion in which a vendita is caught *in flagrante delicto* in treason, and the proof of your treason is in my hands. Will you contest it?"

At the same moment Mario deployed before them a paper charged with the seal of the vendita and he continued:

"Look, Tadeo, look at that clock, where the hand is about to mark the twenty-fourth hour. It is when it sounds that we are to be delivered here to the soldiers you have summoned, and which are bringing you, in exchange for our blood, the vile deniers at which you tariffed your perfidious cowardice. They are the written conventions of your Judas bargain. Of that bargain, here is the original. The pacha of the great Emperor only has the copy, and the names you have signaled to our tyrants have been replaced by those of the two cowards that I see by your sides, and who have had the baseness to subscribe to it. I take pity on the rest of your ordinary sinners, who are already drawing away from you, blushing, and whose blind complicity does not merit any other sentiment.

"Don't be alarmed, Tadeo! You have not lost the infamous honors of that negotiation; it bears your signature, and your accusation can conserve a certain credit if you succeed in snatching from me, with life, an equally important document by which you engaged, three months ago, to have all the Frenchmen in Venice massacred the moment when war breaks out. Here is the original of that other assassin's document, like the other. You were astonished, were you not, that such an advantageous proposal remained without response, but that's because you didn't know that it had passed into my hands immediately and that I had hidden it from all eyes, by respect for the title of Venetian, of which I would still be proud if I did not have the misfortune of sharing it with you. There only remains to you for a witness, therefore, your honest emissary, the faithful secretary of your commandments, a good man who only became a courtier of denunciations and an intermediary of calumnies to compensate himself for no longer being an executioner, one of the iniquitous bandits who disguised themselves as judges in order to murder old Andrea Cinci! That one, you can summon as a witness from the valley of death, if the abysms of the gulf deign to render him to you."

Tadeo had made a movement of rage, but he contained himself on seeing that he was abandoned.

"The vengeance that I intend to extract from you," Mario continued, "will not be proportionate to your crime. Tadeo will doubtless be believed on the justification of his accomplices, since they have been able to believe Tadeo in anything, and no one here is tempted to take away from you the ennui of an unworthy and shameful life. If my arms plunge again into blood on a day of battle, it is because it will be as noble and pure as mine, and will not soil them. Go in peace, then, live, enjoy tomorrow, as today, the air and the sunlight, and may Heaven show a large measure of its mercy to those who become better."

And he spoke thus, Mario introduced the key into the lock again and opened the door, through which they went, precipitating themselves upon one another; and, doubtless to their great astonishment, he closed it upon them. Midnight sounded; we had not taken a step.

"What do you think, friends," Mario went on, "of that band of brainless adventurers who imagined foolishly that I had introduced then into this old palace without providing myself with an unknown exit? It belonged to my forefathers; I was born here, and only occupied myself in studying its coverts in my hours of recreation at the age when other schoolboys were ecstasizing over Girolamo's marionettes or arguing over a slice of zucca in the piazza.[1] I lost it in a throw of dice, as I recall, but I had not wagered my secret."

He applied his hand to a hidden spring in the Gothic wood paneling and an invisible door opened.

The impression that scene had produced on me enchained my movements like one of those fantastic dreams by which sleep is sometimes fascinated, and I sought in my mind whether it was not the opportunity to die that I had desired so many times. Either by virtue of resignation or stupor, the sound of the rifle-butts that hammered the door a moment later had not caused me to emerge from the meditation by which I was absorbed when Mario suddenly retraced his steps, seized me with an iron hand, and drew me after him into the passage, which he closed again with precaution. I followed him without resistance scarcely lit in front of us by the lamp carried by his Albanian domestic.

We went down the steps of tortuous stairways and climbed others; we traversed larger and better ventilated spaces, but always covered; we followed several once-sumptuous galleries still charge with blackened decorations but long deserted, and we arrived after marching for several minutes at a low postern, like a wicket-gate, which opened on to a canal. I could still hear in the distance, in either direction, the oars of our friends and the warning cries of gondoliers.

I climbed into Mario's gondola, and to his question I replied: "The Queen of England inn." That was where I was lodging. When we were about to separate, he stood up beside me in the prow of the boat and took my hands with an affectionate emotion that astonished me in a man of that character,

____

1 The Teatro Gerolamo was a famous puppet theater in Milan, but it is not known to have had a Venetian equivalent.

at least according to the idea I had formed of it on the faith of the multitude.

"If you don't change your sentiments," he said, "And nothing, in fact, retains you in Venice, where your liberty and our life are no longer secure, we'll see one another again soon. You can find me within two months, on the day of Saint Honorine, at the chapel consecrated to her in the parish church of Codroipo, when the priest gives the benediction of the first mass."

"I only require twenty-four hours to prepare my departure, which cannot be too soon for my liking," I replied, "and as the employment of those two months depends entirely on my will, I swear to find myself faithfully, at the day, the hour and the place you designate, in order to receive your supreme orders, if death does not prevent the execution of my promise."

"I might die also," said Mario, with a sort of gaiety, "but that accident won't annul our engagements. Take this piece of the hazel twig that I broke at the vendita and follow wherever they wish, whoever they might be, the person who presents the other half to you."

Then he embraced me. I descended on to the perron of the hotel, and the gondola flew away over the canal like a bat.

The light descending from my windows informed me that I was awaited in my room. I went upstairs precipitately and I experienced a surprise that did not cede to any of those of my day when I found Monsieur de Marsan there—not that the advanced hour of the night was undue in Venice, but because there was no reason for a man of that age and quality to make me such a visit.

"Sit down," he said to me as I stammered a few words, "and take the time to answer me in a calm and serene manner. The step that I am making toward you, Maxime, ought to inform you that I need your attention, and if you render justice to my amity, I think I also have some right to your sincerity.

I believed you to be occupied or absent, because I have the habitude of believing you, and yet I know that you have not quit Venice. Will you tell me without hesitation what motives have distanced you from my house?"

I felt troubled; I leaned my head on my hands and I did not reply.

"Do you not fear," he continued, "that I might interpret your silence badly? One only hides shameful secrets from amity."

I shuddered.

"No, no," I exclaimed. "Nothing shameful has scourged my heart, but there is another modesty than that of virtue, and the confession of an absurd temerity that I have hidden from all eyes, and would have liked to hide from myself, might cost my vanity a painful effort. You demand it, however," I continued, without raising my eyes. "At least take pity on the illusions of an insensate. I love Diana!"

"Diana is beautiful enough to be loved, and there is no woman whose amour is forbidden to you. Your only fault is to have attempted to interest her in your passion without informing me of your views. My paternal relationship with you perhaps required more confidence; I thought I had done enough to render me worthy of it. Do you think that I would have spared anything to efface the distance that separates us in the judgment of society?"

As soon as the commencement of that statement my courage had returned. I dared to look at Monsieur de Marsan.

"Interest her heart without informing you of my views! Oh, that could have happened to me with regard to a young woman whom society would have regarded as my equal, with a woman born for me, whose hand might have fallen into mine to the joy of her parents! But far be it from me to think of moving a heart which reasons of the propriety or the pride of rank might refuse me! My mouth has never disquieted

Diana with a declaration, an admission or a sigh; if she has complained of the annoyance that my amour has caused her, it is because she has divined it. To tell the truth, perhaps that was not very difficult."

"You have not told her that you love her? You do not know whether she is in love, and whether it is you that she loves? Oh, if she loved you . . . listen to me, though, for it is up to me to return frankness for frankness, and I shall tell you everything as you have told me. Don't insist, I'm sure of it! Diana is my only child; I love her as my only child, with all the affection that a human heart can contain, although her noble and benevolent, but somber and austere character has procured me few of those tender joys of which the happiness of fathers is composed. My whole life has been spent, since her birth, in dreaming of an honorable establishment for her, and in spite of the mediocrity of my fortune and the temporary lowering of my condition, a considerable number of suitors have been presented that would have been the envy of the most illustrious families in Italy. Diana has rejected them all. The most brilliant qualities, the most signal virtues and the most tender assiduities have all foundered against the stubbornness of that grim caprice, which I cannot explain, and which condemns me to see the hopes of my old age dying in her. There is, I confess, a mystery in it that frightens me and confounds me."

"Permit me, my father," I said, "and pardon me for interrogating you in my turn, for it's absolutely necessary for me to clarify your doubts and dissipate your anxieties. Are you quite sure that her tenderness does not belong secretly to a man who has had reasons for not making himself known, or whose pretentions you have rejected yourself?"

"The idea that has occurred to you is not entirely new to my mind," replied Monsieur de Marsan, with a worried expression, "but the circumstance you suppose has only presented itself once, and if I thought I ought to dissimulate it from Diana it was to spare her a movement of indignation and horror that might have been fatal to her repose. You can judge that merely by the name of the individual who dared to pretend . . ."

"I have no need to know his name, and I sense from the seething of my blood that I would not learn it without danger to one or other of us. What would you say, however, my noble friend—for the hearts of women are full of impenetrable enigmas—if the unworthy lover you have rejected with so much disdain were precisely the one that she had chosen?"

"What would I say?" cried Monsieur de Marsan, rising from his chair angrily. "I would say: 'Daughter unworthy of me, be accursed forever, and may the wrath and vengeance of God be attached to you like a vulture to its prey! May the rest of your days go by in solitude and remorse! May the daily bread of all men change into gravel under your teeth . . . !'"

He was about to continue. I placed my hand over his mouth and pressed him against me with my other arm.

"May Heaven, my friend, intercept that horrible malediction between you and Diana, and rather make it fall upon my head, which has been devoted since youth to all proofs and all miseries. But it appears that my suppositions were completely devoid of plausibility, and I regret having hazarded it, since it was able to develop such a sharp irritation in you. It only remains for me to know," I continued, smiling in order to distract him further from his emotion, "what part you have given me to support in your domestic chagrins, which has been able to resolve you to demand of a feeble heart, but beyond reproach, the humiliating confession that I have made you?"

Monsieur de Marsan sat down again.

"I believed that I had remarked that you loved Diana, and you agree that I was not mistaken. I thought that she might love you; I still think so, perhaps because I desire it and because my own happiness is interested in yours. I attributed her silence to the sentiment that you had inspired in her; your silence I attributed to a delicate and suspicious timidity, and it was that vain obstacle that I flattered myself that I could break by speaking. 'Be my son by blood,' I would have said, 'as you are, or very nearly, by virtue of the amity I have for you.' That is all I wanted.

"Our affairs do not appear to me to be any further advanced, but I have not yet despaired of them. You mentioned in your last letter a firm plan to leave the day after tomorrow. That would not have been bad if I am mistaken in regarding Diana's dispositions, for your difficulties would have aggravated the disappointment of our hopes; and, on the other hand, the society in which you habitually live, at least since you have distanced yourself from me, is not good at the present time for a young man already suspect to the government. Come to dinner tomorrow, then, with me and Diana. You can make her the confession, which I authorize, and one which the future of all three of us depends. Who knows whether we might not wake up the day after under a more favorable sunlight that the one that has illuminated me for several months?"

"Alas," I replied, while he took my arm in order to return to his gondola, "I cannot augur anything as favorable as you in that step, but if it only serves to convince me of my misfortune, I hope at least that it might inspire enough esteem and confidence in Mademoiselle de Marsan to obtain from her the secret that affects you, and to see reestablished in you the tranquility that you have lost. As for my own destiny, it is a long time since I founded such pleasant hopes therein, and other proofs have accustomed me to resignation. But whatever my fate might be, it will not change my gratitude toward you, and the title of son that you have given me I shall treasure forever."

I have no need to say that the night passed in strange agitations; but hope had such a small part in my dreams that at daybreak I completed all the arrangements for my departure the following day, and I employed the morning in regulating them with the impassive calm of a man whose resolutions are no longer subject to any further vicissitudes.

Finally, I arrived at Monsieur de Marsan's house, where everything had a festival air, for the excellent old man only saw in that solemnity of adieux the approach of a happy event that would fix me in Venice, and the assurance of his credulous contentment burst forth in his gaze, in such a manner as to embolden me and simultaneously cause me to despair. I sought Diana's eyes; they had not changed expression, and I knew the symptoms of amour, for I had been loved. It is not necessary to have been unhappy many times to be able to read the heart of a woman, and the most artful could not have deceived me as to her secret impressions; but the ingenuous antipathy of Diana had something crueler, something crushing and cold that weighed upon my breast like lead.

I was, however, placed next to her at table. I shivered with an emotion mingled with dread, and did not look at her again.

The guests were numerous. The conversation was, for a long time, what it is in Venice and what it is everywhere: a frivolous exchange of unimportant news. The Cyprus wine animated it.

"What, then," said one of the signori, "was this new attempt that almost troubled the tranquility of the city yesterday? It's said that the garrison and the police were on foot all night."

"What!" replied another. "Don't you know? A plot of adventurers, foreign for the most part, who proposed to murder the French and change the government."

"In truth," said Monsieur de Marsan, "it is only necessary to let them carry on; their sagacity is proven and the nations cannot choose worthier legislators. Will this intoxication of peoples last much longer?"

"Fortunately," replied the second speaker, "It was so miserable that a handful of soldiers was sufficient to disperse them, and the rumor of their conspiracy probably won't reach as far as the Giudecca."

"But what do they want, the wretches? Their failed project can only serve as a pretext for a few new persecutions against the servants of the old French dynasty."

"Not at all! It's only a matter of Venice and her republic. Do you know that, if they had succeeded, we would be living today under the gracious government of Mario Cinci, Doge of Venice."

"Mario Cinci!" repeated Monsieur de Marsan, his fist closed on the hilt of his dagger.

"He's the god of the populace," added an old man. "It makes one tremble for the future."

"Don't worry, in the name of Heaven! The bandits were assured by precautions so prudent that not a single one could be arrested, but it's known by virtue of certain reports that Mario was not among them, for he rarely commits himself to the dangers that he makes those wretches run, whose lives are only a plaything of little value in his hands. He's enclosed, while others agitate for him, in the Torre Maladetta of the Tagliamente, to the great alarm of travelers, doubtless in order to devote himself to the manufacture of false money and poisons, like all his family of parricides."

"Malediction!" I cried, standing up. "All that is horribly false. Whoever told you that is an infamous calumniator, more culpable than the mercenary assassin who sells his soul and his stiletto to the hatred of cowards. It was Mario Cinci who thwarted the project of those horrible Venetian vespers of which you speak; it was his enemies who has conceived them. It did not cost the soldiers any great effort to dissipate the conspirators, for no one is unaware now that they were searching a deserted palace, and as they were French, I swear to you that the noise of their footfalls was repeated by an echo that was not capable of frightening them. The governor of Venice, whom I visited this morning in order to inform him of my departure, only sees in that pretended conspiracy what there really was, the base speculation of a few spies, who flattered themselves with attracting favors and recompenses, the fee of lies and the shameful alms of the police, by supposing crimes in order to make their services seem valuable.

"That is the truth, Messieurs! As for Mario Cinci, I do not know what errors of his youth have been able to attract such universal reprobation to him, but I confess that I do not believe the foolish hatreds of the multitude, and I scarcely believe any more in the blind wrath of fatality. All that I know of him has shown me the most generous of men. The injustice of the opinion that pursues him magnifies him further in my eyes, and I ought to warn you, Messieurs, at the moment of quitting you forever, that this conversation cannot be prolonged without imparting movements to my heart that I would rather avoid. Mario Cinci's cause is mine; and what ally can submit without transport and without vengeance to insults made to an absent friend, Venetians, I ask you?"

"Your friend?" said Monsieur de Marsan. "Do you know Mario Cinci?"

"I have only seen him once; his voice did not strike my ear for five minutes; but I am prompt to seize an affection, and my affections are never belied."

"I have never seen you in this excitement," he said, approaching me, for the general conversation had finished and the guests had distributed two by two in the grand hall, without testifying the desire to converse any further. "And yet I cannot hold against you," Monsieur de Marsan added, "errors of a madly affectionate heart, which takes part without reflection in a quarrel about absentees. Experience should have taught you sooner that it is necessary not to trust imposing appearances in the judgment one brings to the first come, when he has, like Mario, the stature of Antaeus, who wrestled

Hercules, but who only recovered his strength by embracing the mud from which he had emerged. The imagination dupes the heart. I won't speak of it any more, although that passionate explosion had cruelly tormented mine. There is question of another matter between us, and the keen interest that Diana testified to you today seems to announce to me that the opportunity has never been more favorable and my anticipations more accurate. Accompany her to her apartment, and remember that I await my sentence in yours."

In fact, and I confess it, I had scarcely perceived it, so disinterested did I believe myself to be in that hope, Diana, who had quit her place immediately after me, came to link her hand with mine, and, as far as I could judge without having seen her again, her head leaned over my shoulder, almost in a manner to touch it. I turned toward her and saw that she was quite pale. I pressed that hand, which was trembling; I escorted Diana to her apartment, and made her sit down; more disposed to quit her than to trouble her with a futile emotion. I was about to leave when she retained me.

I sat down. We remained silent for some time, but her fingers, which I would have liked to squeeze so many times, at the price of my life, were narrowly united with mine; they were warm and moist. She was palpitating with an emotion that I could not comprehend; I did not know whether it was a subject of joy or despair, and that lasted for several minutes, those long minutes with which you are familiar, expanded by the troubles and anxieties of amour.

"Maxime," she said, "how I love you!"

"Be careful!" I cried. "The words that you have pronounced here are frightful for me, if you cannot foresee their consequences. Perhaps you don't know, Diana, that I have come to ask for your hand, because your father has promised it to me!"

She stood up, paced back and forth, passed in front of me with her arms folded, her forehead inclined and her bosom heaving. She stopped; she placed her hands on my shoulders, joined them behind my neck, and said to me in a voice that died on my cheek: "Poor Maxime! Mario Cinci's friend did not know his secret, then, when he defended him just now?"

I did not reply; a veil ripped before my eyes, but I did not divine everything.

"Why, without that," she continued, "would I have insulted the tenderness of a good and worthy young man? Oh, that would have been odious if I had not loved him. But I loved him, you see! He was my soul and my life! He disposed of it forever, and your amour filled me with dolor in straying toward me, who could not repay it. The character and the aspect that I adopted in order to put you off ought to have rendered me hateful. I flattered myself with that bitterly, because it was necessary for your happiness that I make you hate me; and understand what it cost me, Maxime, who loved you from the first day like a brother, and would gladly have given you a whole heart if I had had two. Can you forgive me?"

For some time I was speechless and devoid of sight; then I looked at her.

She was weeping.

I kissed her palpitating arms, and then her cheeks, her eyes moist with tears, and I mingled my tears with hers.

"You love Mario, Diana. It's a worthy choice. May Heaven favor you."

"I love him, you say!" she said, forcefully. "My existence is more complete than you believe. I am his wife."

"His wife! And your father, Mademoiselle, have you thought about him?"

She lowered her eyelids, as if she were afraid of having allowed me to read her soul.

"My father . . . ! My excellent father . . . ! Oh, might nature prolong his days at the expense of mine! May it embellish them, at the expense of my happiness! But when Mario, prostrate before him, sought to vanquish his heart, my father said: 'Your wife! I'd rather she were dead!' He said that. My father would have killed me, as he wished, but Mario will take me away alive."

"Is your reason troubled, Diana? What are you saying?"

"What I am saying the future will explain; but don't criticize my will; it no longer belongs to me. Conserve a memory of me, a rigorous memory if you wish, provided that a little amity, dear Maxime, softens its severity . . . and if my life still interests you, have no fear that I will dispose of it without your consent.

"The hour is approaching now when it is necessary . . . are you ready, Anna?"

Her chambermaid had come in, and came to sit down beside her.

"My father is waiting for you, Maxime; go tell him that you're accompanying me to my gondola."

There was only one door to open. He was waiting for me with fixed eyes, ardent with impatience; I fell at his feet.

"In the name of Diana's happiness and yours, my friend, amend your unjust prejudices against the noble Mario Cinci! He is the spouse that you owe to Diana in order to save her life . . ."

"Mario Cinci!" cried the old man, pushing me away harshly. "Let her marry him and let her die! One parricide more in the family of the Cinci! Beatrice and Diana!

He was marching precipitately, and he dragged me after him, for my hands were clutching his knees.

He stopped, saying to me: "Get away traitor!" Then he looked at me with pity. "Go away," he said, more softly, putting his hands under my arms to aid me to get up. "Go away, poor child, and may I no longer hear any mention of all that I love, for the repose of my old age needs solitude and repose."

I returned to Diana. I offered her my hand without saying a word and she did not interrogate me, for I had left the door open in the disturbance of my action, and it was impossible that she had not heard.

When I quit her at her gondola, I approached her fingers to my lips; she withdrew them, and threw herself into my arms.

A moment later, I was alone.

I followed Diana's gondola with my gaze, among all the others, for a long time, and I recognized it from afar because that day, contrary to custom, it was marked by a floating knot of crimson ribbons.

I presented myself in vain that same evening at Monsieur de Marsan's house; it was prohibited to everyone.

At sunrise, on a sad and cold day in January 1809, the small boat that was taking me to Trieste emerged from the lagoons into the open sea, which was high and rough for the night had been very bad. Our captain hailed a few mariners' boats, which seemed to be occupied in removing a wrecked gondola from the point on an islet.

"Has someone perished?" someone shouted from our deck.

"Apparently," replied the master, "but it's probable that the cadavers have been carried away by the waves, since they weren't fond in the wreckages. The gondola, devoid of a number and a name, was only distinguished from others by this sheaf of ribbons,"

I seized it; I attached it to my shirt, and I fainted. It took a long time for me to come round.

The next day I was in Trieste.

Episode Two
The Tungen-Bund

The sole particularity of my first story that it is necessary to remember now is that I had reason to believe, on arriving at Trieste, that Diana de Marsan had died, the victim of a shipwreck or a suicide. A note knotted with a crimson ribbon, like that of the gondola, which the captain handed me on disembarkation, extracted me from that cruel anguish. It was not signed, and I was not familiar with Diana's handwriting, but it could only have come from her. I can report its own expressions without difficulty, for, as you can imagine, I have not lost it.

Don't be alarmed, Maxime, by the rumors that might reach you; a heart that you have penetrated with gratitude and amity is still palpitating for you. A heart! It is necessary to say two. You are engaged not to forget the rendezvous, nor the church, nor the signal, and I feel that I am interested too in the accomplishment of your promise, by a sincere desire to see you again.

All was thus explained. The rendezvous of which it spoke to me was certainly the one that would reunite me with Mario Cinci, in the church of Codroipo, at the chapel of Saint Honorine. My anxieties vanished, and I was no longer thinking of anything but reposing from past agitations in the mild emotions of study, which was already becoming the first of my pleasures.

The dining table at which I sat down every evening offered few resources for conversation, and I was glad of that. The guests were ordinarily very worthy people, very occupied with their affairs, who let me enjoy in peace the good fortune of having none, and who also had the goodness, to put me entirely at my ease, to talk to one another in one of the fifty Slavic dialects or one of the fifty patois even more impenetrable to my intelligence, of the Frioul islands, the Tyrol and Bavaria. However, the daily renewal of those meetings ended up establishing a sort of intimacy between a few of my fellow lodgers and me. There were two among them who spoke excellent French with a great elegance, and who were more versed than me in the technology of the physical sciences, my principal object of study and affection. We were soon acquainted.

The first was known in Trieste as Doctor Fabricius, and it is thus that I shall designate him in future, although I have heard it said that he had another name. In his exterior life he had made a high medical reputation founded on singular theories, extremely contested by people who claimed to understand that hypothetical art, to which he attached little importance.

The second was a young Pole named Joseph Solbioski—not Solbieski, as the biographers say. Joseph had all the intelligence and heart necessary to draw a soul less tractable than mine, which only asked to like someone. I liked him immediately. He was almost the same age as me; what I liked he liked too; what I knew, he knew better. I was taller and stronger; he was gentler, wiser and better looking.

One forms indissoluble sympathies with that. I did not believe him to be far from my opinions, but an opinion is so little compared with an affection. We both held ourselves, for fear of offending one another reciprocally, in such a narrow reserve with regard to the political questions with which everyone as occupied, and I attached, for my part, so little importance to making sure to making sure of one harmony more in our sentiments given that others were sufficient to unite us for ever, that I did not seek to know more. As he has obtained since, in Germany, a historic reputation of which the rumor has probably reached you, you will forgive me for introducing him with more detail at the beginning of a story in which we were hardly apart; but we shall commence with the other.

Doctor Fabricius was nearly seventy years old, but he was one of those septuagenarians adolescent in soul and imagination, who impose their verve and vivacity on the young. What was most striking in his singular physiognomy was a very pronounced type that was not at all German, the thin, tapering, projecting contour of which was more reminiscent of Andalusian or Moorish. His brown and bony thinness, which almost laid bare the active and passionate play of his muscles; the penetrating acuity of his ardent and mobile eyes, the disks of which were embers and the gaze a dart; and the strange neatness of his still-black hair, which bristled as if spontaneously at the slightest crease of his forehead, formed an extraordinary ensemble that gave him something of the aspect of an eagle. I have heard few men more abundant in speech; but his full, sustained, eloquent loquacity, even where it was diffuse only expanded in episodes and figures by virtue of an excess of riches, and took pleasure therein without losing itself.

A man thus organized could not be entirely a stranger to the great thoughts that were then moving Europe, but he abstained with a sort of affectation from all conversations in which the natural movement of minds caused those ideas to enter involuntarily. The preoccupations that dominated him seemed to be an exalted spiritualism and a speculative theory combining the principles of Swedenborg, Saint-Martin and perhaps Weishaupt;[1] but his expansive enthusiasm for the books of Arndt[2] and a few other tungenbundist philosophers revealed in him a profound sentiment of liberty.

The doctor had only stopped in Trieste in order to regulate a few affairs of interest with the stewards charged with the administration of his wealth, in a rather extensive spectrum, for he was said to be very rich—which could not have been divined by the modesty of his expenditure or the simplicity of his habits. There was, in consequence, nothing surprising in often seeing him in conference with visitors who came to see him and who did not stay long. If I had divined them then, however, I would have had enough time to observe them and to conserve a memory of them present enough to

---

1 The philosopher Adam Weishaupt (1748-1830) was the founder in the 1780s of the Bavarian Order of Illuminati, which became notorious as a quasi-Masonic secret society, the objectives of which remain somewhat unclear, although they appear to have been broadly libertarian and antireligious.

2 The German nationalist Ernst Moritz Arndt (1769-1860) published the first volume of his anti-Napoleonic *Geist der Zeit* in 1806 and had to flee to Switzerland.

depict them, but I have already said that no species of political contact existed between my new friends and me.

Those strangers succeeded one another every day; there was Kolb and there was Marberg, the Pelopidas and the Thrasybulus of the Tyrol; and there were the worthy Woodel brothers, executed by firing squad at Wesel on the eighteenth of September the same year. There was the innkeeper Andreas Hofer,[1] whom I noticed more because I had often heard him named in the home of the Marquis de Chasteler with regard to the events of 1808; and that one is so well-known that the impressions he left me would teach no one anything if they did not differ slightly from those that my readers have been able to obtain from history. The celebrity of all of them, however, only attained its apogee a month after the passage of Andreas Hofer through Trieste—which is to say, with the memorable victory of the peasants, of which the Tyrol marks the glorious anniversary on the twenty-ninth of February.

I had formed several conjectures regarding the appearance of the Samson of Passeyer in our paltry hostelry of the Bear, but without drawing any consequences therefrom. It was quite natural that Andreas Hofer—who, by virtue of his profession, had a very extensive network of business dealings, as is commonplace in the Tyrol—might have interests to settle with an opulent property-owner like Doctor Fabricius. As for the very active part that Joseph Solbioski played in their secret negotiations, it was no more difficult to explain, Joseph being destined to become the son-in-law of the doctor fairly imminently, for they were "anticipating the future." I have un-

---

1 In 1809 Andreas Hofer (1767-1810) became the leader of the Tyrolean rebellion against the Napoleonic invasion during the War of the Fifth Coalition, in which the Austrian Empire and England were allied against Napoleon's Empire and Bavaria; subsequent history made him something of a legendary folk hero. His entry in the 1823 edition of *Biographie nouvelle des contemporains* cites Kolb and Marberg as fellow insurgents but the Woodel brothers remain obscure.

derstood since that the expression in question, which covered a mystical meaning in the jargon of secret societies, might well have hidden a double meaning from me, but I am not very curious and I was already so inclined to let go of those mysteries that it did not occur to me once to seize any other meaning than the literal one.

There were few men of those recent times with whom the Germans were more passionately occupied than Andreas Hofer, and there was certainly no one who justified their enthusiasm more worthily. The virtue and piety of Andreas Hofer had earned him the nickname the Saint of the Tyrol, as Cathelineau had been nicknamed the Saint of Anjou fifteen years before, and no man among all those I have seen responded better than Andreas Hofer to the idea I had formed of Cathelineau.[1] It is necessary, however, that I grant immediately one important point of criticism, which is that that opinion has only been composed since based on slight and fleeting impressions. I only saw Andreas Hofer during two days and never addressed a word to him, for the excellent reason that he knew very little Italian and no French at all. The recent impression of his first historical role interested me in seeing him, however, and the one he played some time later in the events in Germany forced my mind to remake the physical and mental type, perhaps with as much vivacity as if I had not lost sight temporarily of the model, with the result that I believed I knew him as well as those who have depicted him.

What distinguished him in war as in administration was a profound moral sentiment extended, so statesmen said, to the

---

1 Jacques Cathelineau (1759-1793) was a leader of the Vendean insurrection during the Revolution; a former peddler, he raised a peasant army loyal to the Monarchy and the Church before being appointed generalissimo of the Catholic and Royal Army; when he was killed in action by a sniper the rebels split into factions and were soon defeated. His descendants were ennobled during the Bourbon restoration and he was venerated locally, although never officially beatified.

point of puerility. He had a philanthropy so mild that he did not have to reproach himself for a single drop of blood shed in battle, in which he always took the lead. No one had seen him employ an offensive weapon. In society, he was a simple creature, benevolent, cheerful and as affectionate as a giant caressing dwarfs can be, an old man who made himself a child with children. For the multitude, Andreas Hofer was really only a good man, and he would be nothing more than that for me if he had not been Andreas Hofer.

I arrive at Joseph Solbioski, whose name recalls, as I have said, more personal sentiments, and whom a month of affectionate relationship had almost given to me as a brother. The son of one of the noble and unfortunate warriors who fell in the wars for Polish liberty in 1794 under the flag of Kosciusko, he had been adopted at ten years of age by Doctor Fabricius, and that alliance, probably founded on some political sympathy between the fathers, was sufficient to explain the strong direction that had been imprinted on his studies under the eyes of one of the most enlightened men in Germany. Solbioski expressed himself with an often eloquent facility in the majority of the languages of Europe, and possessed, to a degree rare even among professional scholars, the doctrine and nomenclature of the physical and philosophical sciences., the analysis and method of which had just made such great conquests in the sole land of invention and improvement that still has a right to believe in the progressive march of human intelligence. He certainly owed that rich education to the fortunate tutelage in which hazard had placed him, and he reported the results of it religiously to his adoptive father, for the tenderness of his soul ceded nothing to the elevation of his mind.

That grateful and pious devotion doubtless contained the principal secret of his life. His amour for one of the doctor's daughters, of which he had three, must have done the rest; but you know already that I had only entered into his confidence by chance. I only learned later that Joseph Solbioski had been, during the campaign of 1808, the soul of the generous enterprises of Andreas Hofer, whose narrow and sound, but scantly developed, intelligence, could not have suffered the complication of the affairs in which his new fortune engaged him when he became, by the force of events, the military and political leader, the commandant and legislator of the Tyrol. It was an epoch almost unique among all epochs, in which a man of the people, unlettered and without ambition, found himself the depositary of authority without having wanted it, and used it without abusing it. No one is unaware that the administration of Andreas Hofer was compared then to that of Sancho Panza in the isle of Barataria, and I doubt that one could make an eulogy more magnificent and more complete, for peoples cannot have a better arbiter than the common sense of a natural and moral man.

Thought doubtless smiled in some of those circumstantial laws, improvised by a poor village innkeeper who had been invested by war. surrounded by enemy battalions, with the rights of supreme power; but emotional tears are mingled with smiles when one reads, like us, the text of his paternal proclamations, inspired by a profound love of humanity. What he recommended to his brothers and his children, hunted in the mountains like wild beasts; what he begged them to grant to his amour, for he only ever ordered in the name of affection, was to spare the effusion of foreign blood except for cases of legitimate self-defense; and then, to sanctify their weapons by prayer, good deeds and good morals. One of them, issued from Innsbruck, which he had just entered as the vanquisher of the Bavarians at the head of twenty thousand peasants, in which that giant of forty years, whom nature had organized like any other for he passions, addressed himself to the piety of women, recalling the to antique modesty and imploring them to hide their breasts and arms, following the chaste custom of their mothers. Perhaps that is quite ridiculous, but it is sublime in Plutarch, in the life of Scipio, Aratus or Philopoemon.

I have not lost sight of Solbioski in that digression, since he was, in the epoch that I am recalling, Andreas Hofer's secretary. Between those two noble creatures there was a sort of identity. They were one body and one soul. Judge Joseph by that! At first sight his fresh and pure complexion, his mild gaze, his ever-affable but often bitter and melancholy laughter, his long and curly blond hair, did not announce the hero of difficult times; and yet, the singular effect of his lashes, his eyebrows and his brown moustache permitted him sometimes to animate his physiognomy in an imposing manner. Then he acquired the air of resolution and pride that a great character reveals, but it would have required more experience and perspicacity than I have ever prided myself on having to divine the conspirator in that blue-eyed angel.

We only talked between us, therefore about friendship, love, poetry, the beauty of reawakened nature, the charms of the spring countryside, and everything that enchants a young heart that misfortune has not yet desiccated. That did not last long. The doctor's affairs, which seemed to become more complicated by the day, forced him to absent himself frequently. The acquisition of an old manor in the vicinity of the Tagliamente kept him away for a week, and it only required as much for the term of my rendezvous to fall due when he arrived in order to depart again with Joseph, for he was accompanied this time by his daughter, who was staying with him in the home of a friend.

Our adieux were sad, and yet I tried to prolong them. I remember that Joseph and I had difficulty quitting one another, although he smiled with a kind of malice at the idea of our eternal separation, and we were walking rather late our arms enlaced, by the light of the torches that illuminated the square and the peristyle of the theater, because it was a day of joyful intoxication and noisy gaiety for the people, the day of the carnival, which has conserved its attraction for a long time in the Venetian states.

I scarcely noticed the spectacle—me, a poor young man whom ten bolts kept in reclusion during the dazzling fêtes of the rich and the fortunate of the imperial court, which Madame la Duchesse d'Abrantès[1] has described with so much style and grace—but it must have had an aspect particular to Trieste, where it caused to swarm under the colonnades and through the illuminations the home-loving part of the population, which is also a spectacle: the Greeks, the Albanians, the Turks, in their varied and picturesque garments; the pretty Jewish girls who pierced with such sharp and ardent gazes the elegant ringlets of their black hair; those of Istria, almost entirely enveloped in their long white veils; the peasants of the littoral with their floating ribbons and opera outfits, which the season permitted that day, for it was as warm as one of the most beautiful in May. I have no need to tell those who remember the Trieste carnival in 1809, if anyone does remember it, that it was magical.

A woman in a domino had taken possession of my hand, and it was a woman, for I had touched hers. I dare say that she must have been very pretty; one knows that so well! Joseph, who had been conversing with us momentarily, had taken advantage of that moment of preoccupation to draw away, and I was veritably not sorry, for the last word of that last

---

1 Laure Junot, Duchesse d'Abrantes (1784-1838) was the wife of a French general, to whose mother Napoléon had once made an offer of marriage; the latter referred to her as *petite peste*, but treated her generously when he became First Consul—which did not take the edge off the sarcastic slanders she issued against him in her memoirs, nor did it dissuade her from conspiring against him to bring back the Bourbons after the catastrophe of 1812. The eighteen-volume memoirs in question, composed in the 1820s with the aid of Honoré de Balzac, her reputed lover, and published in the early 1830s, made her briefly notorious. She was a member of the cénacle.

conversation had cost me dearly to say to him. In any case, the conversation of the unknown woman soon absorbed all my thoughts. An incomprehensible mystery had allowed her to read my life. The person that she knew could only be known to her in that locale, where I was a stranger to almost everyone, and my heart palpitated more with astonishment than fear when she bid me adieu, calling me by my name, which could only have happened, even in Venice, by virtue of the correspondence of my most secret friends. I was sure that Diana had never heard it pronounced, unless by . . . but Diana was taller.

She tried to escape; I retained her. The fascination of the mask, the attire and the voice had been augmented in a moment with all that is gripping and extraordinary in an apparition or a dream.

"I'll follow you anywhere," I exclaimed, "or I'll find you again if you try to flee me."

She stopped. "Why not?" she said, laughing, "but it will be a little far, perhaps, and it wouldn't be for only a single day. Are you determined to join me anywhere I might be . . . on Saint Honorine's day?"

"Wait, wait, Madame! Saint Honorine's day? Oh, that's not possible; my honor is engaged."

"Adieu, then," she said, disengaging her fingers from mine. "Go where your honor summons you."

"I'll go. But may I know, at least, where I might see you again on that day, if it is permissible for me to search for you?"

"Where you will see me again? I'd like that. In the chapel placed under the invocation of my patron saint, in the church of Codroipo, when the priest has given the benediction of the first mass."

When I came round, she was hidden in the crowd. That rendezvous was the one I had received from Mario Cinci.

A few days went by in new and solitary walks, but on Saint Honorine's day I had already been waiting for a long time before the façade of the church of Codroipo when the doors opened.

The sun had scarcely risen; the nave was still damp and dark; only a few lamps that had been lit all night indicated the saint's chapel; the sacristan was finishing illuminating it.

I was not devout, but I was pious, and no adventure of gallantry or caprice of sensuality had ever distracted me in a temple from the profound emotion inspired in me by the house of God, especially when it is empty and the soul finds itself meditative in the presence of its creator and master. I had, in any case, interpreted that second adjournment in another manner than one is borne to do in Italy. I was placed under the empire of an immense association, which might include women in the number of its most active and most intelligent affiliates, and the most apt to regain a lukewarm discouraged adherent by means of the illusions most appropriate to his age and his character. I ought to say to my honor that I had not doubted for a moment.

I went into the chapel, therefore, without any other design than to pray and to offer to Heaven the sacrifice of my blind devotion, for I know not what word that had linked me with generous sentiments to the cause of the old faith and the old liberties.

My eyes had soon scanned the narrow enclosure. I was alone; the sacristan had left and the priest had not arrived, but the tableau of the altar was already resplendent with its festival decoration; it was an imposing moment, a solemn moment, a fine spectacle for a Christian; and every time that misfortune had weighed upon me, or solitude had returned me to myself, I had found myself as sincerely Christian as in my mother's arms when she dressed me proudly a long vest of silver fabric with compartments of red and blue glass in order to receive the benefit of the eucharist for the first time in the parish of Saint-Marcelin.

When that effusion had finished I looked at the tableau: Saint Honorine, condemned to die of hunger in a dungeon, pale, disheveled and palpitating, offering in her features a mixture of human dolor and divine resignation but reaching suppliant arms toward me, as if imploring succor. Her eyes had a gaze, her lips movements. How touching and sublime she was!

What struck me most, however, was one of the resemblances that one is liable to find when one is in love, a poignant and mortal resemblance in the situation in which she had been seized: the portrait of Diana! Fortunately, that marvelous image was only Il Pordenone's masterpiece.[1]

I was cold; I was suffering from that emotion, as vivid as reality. I stood up; I walked aimlessly around the chapel, around the church, where the radiance of daylight was beginning to pierce the stained glass windows and tremble on the walls. No one was moving, inside or outside. The only sound that troubled the silence of the vaults was that of my footsteps resonating on the paving stones. I tried to reach the door; I leaned, shivering, on a baptismal font placed at the entrance.

I listened, and thought I could hear moans, without knowing whether they were coming from the chapel or the parvis; but I thought for a moment that it was the saint again, who was weeping with anguish and hunger. Impatient to free myself from that illusion, which was troubling my reason, I ran down the steps. The tears and the moans pursued me into the street, already entirely illuminated by sunlight; I turned round toward the portal, where I had been preceded by my faithful Puck, who was summoned by a sentiment of more than human compassion, caressant and consoling, wherever he heard laments. I have mentioned Puck to you.[2]

---

1 "Il Pordenone" was the nickname of Giovanni Antonio de' Sacchis (c1484-1539). The painting is fictitious, as is the church.

2 This remark is curious in the context of the present story, where no mention has been made of the dog in question, although he had featured in a story recounted within the text of the visionary fantasy *Histoire du*

Then I saw a little girl, thirteen or fourteen years old, as fresh and as pretty as a rose, whose eyes must have had an incomparable charm when they were not drowned by tears. She was sitting on top of the staircase, near the door that I had just passed through, her chin supported on her hand, her elbow on her knee, her blonde hair abandoned to the air; the poor girl was sobbing bitterly while looking at a little tray deposited in front of her, covered by a cloth whiter than snow.

"Poor Onorina!" she said.

At the sound my dog made in launching himself to her side, she changed attitude, and, her sight pausing on me, she suddenly cried: "Buy, Monsieur, buy my beautiful lasagna! Be the first, be the first, for the little merchant."

I went up two or three steps and sat down a little above her.

"Why are you weeping, dear child, since your basket is full, and no accident appears to have befallen you?"

"Buy, Monsieur, buy my beautiful lasagna! There's no better lasagna in Venice!"

She wiped her eyes with the tips of her pretty fingers in order to appear more engaging.

"I asked you, my child, the cause of your chagrin, and what might soothe it. Reply to me with confidence."

"Oh, of chagrin, Monsieur, I have a great deal. Buy, Monsieur, buy my beautiful lasagna! It's necessary to tell you that today is the feast of Saint Honorine, my patronne, and all the young women of Codroipo, in their best clothes, will accompany her reliquary in the procession . . . a superb reliquary garnished with long ribbons, and each of them will

---

roi de Bohême et ses sept chateaux, where the narrator—presumably the dreamer "Théodore"—makes a present of him to Gervais, the blind man of Chamouny. That story and parts of this one might have belonged to the same narrative before being readapted to new contexts; if so, it is possible that *Jean Sbogar* was derived from the same source-narrative and that he and Mario Cinci evolved from a common stock.

hold one, matched by its color to the ribbons of her adornment. Oh, it's very beautiful to see. Buy, Monsieur, buy my beautiful lasagna! Then four of them will carry, two by two, large baskets full to the brim with violets, primroses and all the flowers of the season, stopping at intervals to throw handfuls over Saint Honorine's reliquary. And they are the best behaved and the prettiest, and the ones that people look at the most. I was one of the four last year, and I only put on that day my beautiful dress of floral Persian cloth. Buy, Monsieur, buy my good lasagna!"

"But the ceremony is about to begin, Onorina. Why haven't you put on your beautiful dress of floral Persian cloth today?"

"Why, Monsieur, why? That's why I'm weeping. My father has remarried and my stepmother told me this morning, when I asked for my dress: 'It's a fine thing, brazen child, to want to deck yourself out like Saint Honorine's reliquary before having started your day's work. You'll be given the dress you want if you've sold your lasagna before the time of the procession.' Buy, Monsieur, buy my good lasagna.'"

And she recommenced weeping.

"Calm down, my child. There are remedies for everything, and you still have time to go any take last year's place next to one of the big baskets full to the brim with violets, primroses and all the flowers of the season. I swear to you that you'll be there."

"Oh! Truly, I wouldn't have been in difficulty," she said, "in the time of Signor Mario Cinci. For a long time he came every month to Codroipo for provisions for his house and for the poor, and two months ago he came twice a week; he took away all my lasagna and never went away without leaving me some ring, some pin or some little trinket and without saying to me, while putting me on the cheek: 'Be good, Nina, be good, my beauty, and one day you'll make a good marriage, for you're truly as nice as your poor mother.'"

"Well, dear Onorina, you now have two reasons to console yourself and rejoice, since Mario Cinci is going to arrive."

"How can he arrive," she cried, "since he's dead?"

"Mario is dead!"

"You know him and you don't know that? A fortnight ago he was where you are, and, contrary to habit, he had spent the night in Codroipo in the home of his friend, the rich Doctor Fabricius, in order to make his devotions. I sold him my lasagna. Buy Monsieur, buy my good lasagna."

"It's bought. Go on, Nina, I beg you, and don't hold anything back."

Her eyes cleared; they were radiant. The contrast between the nature of her story and the innocent joy of the little girl, so glad to put on her floral dress of Persian cloth again, clutched my heart intensely. I placed a sequin on her tray and listened to her thereafter without looking at her.

"You're giving me too much, Monsieur, and I can't make change . . ."

"I'm giving you too little, Onorina, but go on, just go on!"

"The night had been very bad, but no matter; nothing could stop Signor Mario when he put his mind to something. 'It's necessary that I cross the torrent no matter what the weather,' he said to the doctor. 'I have reasons for that; at any rate, I'll be back soon, and if I'm delayed, the information I've given you will enable you to do without me.' Alas, he didn't come back, and he never will come back."

"Again, at least tell me how that happened . . ."

"I'll tell you what I've heard, Monsieur. Every day had been fine since the storm; it was so beautiful in the carnival! The snow had melted in the mountains; the streams were swollen, so that the Tagliamente, augmented by the previous day's rain, was as broad and as rough as an arm of the sea. The boatman didn't want to risk the crossing but Signor Mario started rowing with his Albanian—I don't know if you know him—and they rowed for a long time, a long time, very far, very far, without mishap; but they were no sooner in the middle of the current than a wave came that rose up as far as the eye could see, which passed over the boat, and the boat disappeared. Signor Mario, who can swim like a fish, was scarcely worried, but the Albanian, who was an old man, nearly forty, was struggling in vain against the wave, The people who were watching from the shore said that it was a terrible thing, for Signor Mario had scarcely cleaved the water with a few strokes than he had to turn back to grab his domestic and swim with him, because he was so good and courageous, the brave man, that he would have risked his life a hundred times for that of a poor peasant. That lasted for an hour, and all the boats had advanced as close as possible to the current without entering it, in order to bring them help. Then they saw distinctly the Albanian wrench himself away from his master's arm and plunge into the gulf, with the design of dying alone. Oh, the noble Mario was quite capable of reaching the bank if he had wanted to, but he kept diving after the Albanian, who was obstinate in drowning again, shouting things that no one understood. He brought him back to the surface, and went down with him again, came back up and went down again—and finally, neither one of them could be seen, and their cadavers haven't been recovered. The local people assure everyone that it had been predicted by the prophet of Ravenna, or another."

I let my head fall on to my knees, and I did not say anything, or think anything.

Onorina tugged me gently by the flap of my coat.

"The hour of the procession is about to sound. Buy, Monsieur, buy my beautiful lasagna; there's no better lasagna in Venice."

"Are you still there, child? Haven't I paid you? Go put on your dress of Persian cloth and your ribbon, before someone takes your place."

"Then take your lasagna, Signor," she said, "for if I reappear before my stepmother with the basket and the money, she'll suppose, wicked as she is, that I've earned my daily wage by some work of sin."

In the meantime, she introduced into the long pocket of my overcoat a copious bag of lasagna.

"What do you want me to do with your lasagna?" I said, laughing involuntarily. "I have no need of it."

"What about the poor," she replied, "and the hungry? Madame Saint Honorine died for want of a bag of lasagna."

That idea struck me; Pordenone's painting was presented before my eyes again as I had just seen it. I experienced an invincible desire to see it again. I got up. Ornorina was no longer there.

The first mass was quite advanced; I knelt down at the back of the chapel. After a few moments of recollection, I scanned the faithful with my gaze: a handful of poor people who had come to implore the intercession of the saint and the grace of God before resuming their daily labor; worthy and pious families of indigent who works, who believes, who prays and who loves and to whom the kingdom of Heaven is assured, according to my heart as well as the gospel. Only one woman, who was confounded with the crowd by her fervor and her humility, was distinguished by a sort of elegance of attire, a black silk cape with a fringe of silver lace. She passed before me when the service was over, negligently lifting a corner of her veil and stopped at the door, after dropping something into the collecting-box that she had hidden in her hand.

"Honorine?" I said in a low voice, approaching her in order to accompany her, as Italian politeness authorizes.

"Honorine Fabricius," she replied, gaily, when we had arrived on the parvis, "And to better recommend me to the touching interest that you take in all ladies, the fiancée of your friend Joseph Solbioski. I leave you to divine the occupations that retain him this morning in the vicinity of Codroipo, but he will wait for you tomorrow morning at the boats of the Tagliamente an hour before daybreak, and this singular sign that he had charged me with handing to you will not permit you any doubt, according to him, of the authority of my mission. Promise, then, and don't follow me."

The sign was the fragment of the mystical twig that Mario had broken at the vendita. It was tied, like Diana's letter, with a little crimson ribbon, like the livery of her gondola.

I protested my exactitude with a respectful nod of the head, and Honorine disappeared without difficulty into the multitude that covered the stairway and encumbered the street, for the procession was arriving with all its magnificence, in order to fetch the reliquary. I looked around the baskets of flowers for little Onorina. She was already there, superbly clad in her dress of floral Persian cloth, and so preoccupied, the fortunate girl, with her adornment and her beauty, that I was not at all astonished that she paid no heed to me; she had many other things to think about!

I had not yet arrived at the rendezvous the following night when I heard myself named in the darkness by a familiar voice. I stopped immediately and embraced Solbioski.

"You won't see anyone from the doctor's family this morning," he told me. "She left yesterday for Saint-Veit, on the shore we're about to reach, and Monsieur Fabricius will only join us tomorrow at the manor of our unfortunate friend Mario, of whose destiny you can't be unaware. He believed that he ought to make the acquisition of those ruins, the sojourn in which, it's said, would be too severe for women. Don't impute our separation, therefore, to any insulting precautions of jealousy, although you've given me reason to conceive a little. In a matter of days my Honorine has received from you a fraternal kiss, and the mobility of your heart promises me that you will easily forget an amour contracted under a mask."

I was about to justify myself. He embraced me again, laughing.

"Listen to more essential explanations," he said, "and begin by pardoning me for not having opened my soul to you entirely in our conversations, Delivered by the misfortune of my destiny to the ideas that have nearly doomed yours irreparably, I saw you with pleasure distracting yourself and distancing yourself by studies full of charm, to which you were summoned by all the memories of your education and all the penchants of your character. My father learned, however, that you belonged to Mario by virtue of an oath; he learned that on a solemn occasion. It was the eve of the tragic accident that has stolen from Liberty its Italian sword. That last misfortune might have deterred us more than ever from drawing you into our endeavors and our dangers, if a few words that escaped Mario had not led us to believe that the Torre Maladetta hides a few secrets that are only known to you. The signals that he sent you—the broken stick, the ribbon, the colors—are a mystery that remains sealed to us if you don't discover it, and might perhaps compromise the lives of a multitude of our brothers, if the search that we're about to carry out doesn't enlighten us. That's what decided Monsieur Fabricius to take possession of the old manse of the Cincis, where you'll only stay long enough to direct us, in the case that you don't refuse to go with me."

"I'll follow you to Hell, if necessary," I replied, "but this mystery is as impenetrable to my thought as it is to yours. Mario took it with him into the torrent. Like you, I can only guess it. I'll tell you everything I know."

And I told him everything I knew.

"I've heard mention of that event," said Solbioski, after a moment of reflection. "A woman abducted! No woman has ever been abducted to Venice in ten years that people haven't come to search for in the Torre Maladetta, but always without success. Mario owes that tribute to his romantic reputation, which I think a trifle fantastic. A search was mounted there for Diana, who wasn't there, and they took advantage of that opportunity to visit the most hidden corners of a retreat so justly suspect to our enemies. There are not two opinions today about that deplorable story. The commemoration of Diana's colors in Mario's last message proves nothing. It was only one appeal more to your memory. Mademoiselle de Marsan did indeed perish on the day of her departure from Venice, after having written the note that you received in Trieste, and I'm convinced that her father received the sad proof of it, since he only survived her by a few days."

"Her father too!" I cried. "Diana's father too! Monsieur de Marsan is dead!"

"Well, what can you expect?" said Solbioski, putting his arm around me. "Everything around us must die, the old men before us, stolen from us in time by a generous death. Return to Codroipo, my brother, or come with me to the Torre Maladetta, and I believe that we shall be very unfortunate if any secret still remains to us this evening. Perhaps there are some that interest the fate of our friends and that of the human race."

I responded by jumping into the boat; while we had been talking we had reached the wave-beaten strand, already blanched by the dawn.

"Courage," said the boatman. "The crossing will be bad this evening, but Signor Mario wouldn't be dead if he had made it, like these noble lords, before the hour when the sun warms and melts the ice. Oh, it's a dangerous season for the poor traveler. But he didn't care about that; he would have wrestled the demon if the demon had dared face him on land. So the demon was careful; he waited for trap in which he caught him, to the misfortune of the poor people of the country. Look! See how the current is flowing already. That seething is an evil presage for the evening. Forward, boatman, forward!"

And he sang. The waves were, in fact, beginning to roll around the oar in foaming swirls. The clouds were clearing gradually, and when we had emerged from the current to return to dead water the sun was already shining gaily on their surface, marbling them before us with large dark-green diamond shapes, framed with trembling threads of golden yellow. A few sea-birds, which come that far upriver at high water, skimmed it with their wings, and the place of disembarkation spread out, sad, severe and profound under the horizontal light that gradually reached the shore. Solbioski, exhausted by late nights, was leaning on me drowsily, and I was alone in enjoying that spectacle, when a new incident changed it.

The boat suddenly turned its prow around a point that I had not noticed. The horizon there was closed by an immense rock in the form of a cube, surmounted by a high keep, the ruinous summit of which was tilted like the head of a mortally wounded giant. The vast walls that had once supported it, degraded by time, lightning and cannon fire, were only linked by a few stones to its unequal shoulders, and extended from one side to the other like fatigued arms going to repose their broad hands on the corners of the mountain. What struck me most forcibly was a rounded balcony, the sole vestige of its platform, which remained suspended over the abyss, and which appeared to have been adapted to that abode of terror in years of peace and joy. I was close enough then to distinguish all those details, and to comprehend that those buildings and their base were isolated from the entire world and all the floods of the Tagliamente.

We disembarked then, and we no longer had more than twenty toises to cover before reaching the steps carved into the rock, which led to the castle. The boatman returned to open water abruptly after having quit us.

The ground was made up of enormous rounded boulders, oval or spherical, which had blackened there for centuries under the alternate action of air and water, but many of which were heightened by hideous patches of blood-colored lichens. The footing was scarcely secure there, for there was no traced route, and the fear of the sometimes-sudden invasion of the Tagliamente in the long defile between the river and the mountain kept away the river-dwelling peasants as well as ancient and formidable superstitions. Solbioski's domestic, laden with our meager baggage, only engaged upon it with a kind of terror. Puck did not precede me at his ordinary pace; he followed me, howling.

Solbioski's silence made me think that he had not entirely shaken off the morning slumber that had gripped him, doubtless after many days of fatigue and emotion.

"Where are we going, my friend?" I said taking him by the arm in order to assure our march mutually.

"Can you ask me that?" he said, turning a dejected gaze toward me, for he had not taken long to share my impression. "We're going to the Torre Maladetta, and the Torre Madadetta, this is it!"

Episode Three
The Torre Maladetta; or, Famine

Since the doctor had made acquisition of the Torre Maladetta it had been occupied by one of his stewards, whom I had seen in Trieste, a man short of stature and capacity, very lame in his right leg and in his judgment, singularly exaggerated in political doctrines—that is a prerogative of fools—extraordinarily meticulous in execution, but more cunning in affairs of interest than one could have expected of his intelligence. I did not have an opportunity to talk to him, and it will be sufficient to know that his name was Bartolotti.

When we arrived Monsieur Bartolotti was not in the castle. Fear had dislodged him three days before.

"Fear, Signora Barbarina," said Solbioski to the old and irremovable concierge, on learning that news from her mouth. "Fear, you say? And what fear can one experience in the Torre Maladetta, except for that of one day being crushed by its collapse? But it has lasted for such a long time, always threatening to fall, and so many generations have laid down at its foot, that it is necessary to hope that it will remain standing at last as long as us."

"It's not just that," replied the old woman, after having sat us down in the vast parlor on the ground floor. "There are many other things to say about this noble habitation, to which I've been accustomed since childhood, for my forebears have always lived here, the first having come from Rome with the first Cinci. Now I'm left here alone, as decrepit and inclined as the tower, without leaving anyone who'll take the trouble to throw a poor shroud over my bones. The Tagliamente will cover us, the tower and me, and everything will be finished. May Heaven grant peace to those who, like us, have a clear conscience! But I no longer recall what I was saying to you just now. Ah! I've seen many events in the Torre Maladetta, if not in these recent times, when I've become old and infirm, and I scarcely have the strength to walk from the parlor to the door and come back from the door to the parlor, so overladen am I by age and ennui.

"For some years I was no longer anything in the castle, Monsignor's Albanian always came in first and took the keys from me brutally, for he was imperious and reckless like his master. Sustaining me, to hasten my march, he locked me in here with a double turn, shouting at me in his coarse voice: 'Good night, Barbarina! Women of your age are good for nothing but sleeping!' I ask you, Signors, if that's how one should treat an old domestic, born of pure Roman blood, who watched over us in the cradle and carried us so often in her arms to the crenellations to see the stars at closer range.

"That was the idea that tormented the signor's sleep when he was little, and his mother, the poor signora, already ill in bed, shouted to me: 'What are you doing, then, Barbarina, that you aren't carrying Mario up to the crenellations to see the stars? Do you want to let him die of cramp and choler?' Then I wrapped him in his sheet and I covered him with my cape or his father's cloak and I climbed up all the way to the top of the keep; but no one has gone up there any longer for twenty years. And it was a contentment when he saw the stars! He couldn't talk yet, but he had cries to name them all. Alas, it's not from the earth that he sees them today, my poor child!"

"That's good, Barbarina, but it takes us a little far from our subject. We judge, to begin with, from the beginning of your story, that you've had cause to complain of Mario's procedures."

"Me, complain about Signor Mario! My God, did I say that? It's not his fault if he'd become sad and grim! But he no longer told me his chagrins, as in the time when he was young. He only had confidence in his Albanian. When I reproached him for that, he stopped in front of me and folded his arms, laughing, and it gave me pleasure to hear him laugh. 'Brava, brava, Barbarina! I won't act any longer without consulting you, but on condition that you never allow yourself to lack anything, that you live here like a chatelaine and go to bed early. As for locking you in, that's a precaution that concerns your safety and mine.' And with that he kissed me on the forehead, still laughing, and took me under the arms to sit me down in my armchair."

"Let's get to the subject of Signor Bartolotti's fear, Barbarina."

"Well," replied Barbarina, "don't you think there's reason for it, when one isn't used to it? Truly, for myself, I no longer pay any heed to it. But the muffled noises one hears in the vaults, as if someone wanted to overturn them, the plaintive cries that emerge from all parts of the ruins, sometimes here and sometimes there; and the two black ladies who deploy red and white scarves, as a sign of desolation, over the balcony of the old platform, with heart-breaking groans! You can't be unaware, Messieurs, of the names of Signora Lucrezia and Signora Beatrice Cinci?"

"Yes, yes, we know that story; but they've been dead for more than two centuries."

"Dead, indeed, and that's why they come back to where the living can't go, for no living being can ever reach the balcony of the platform now, either from inside or outside, if they don't have the wings of a bird. I'd already heard them twice in my overly long life, when Felippino Cinci, Mario's grandfather, was killed by thrusts of a stiletto in the Piazza San Marco, and then when his father Andreas had his head cut off by the sentence of the law, facing the arsenal, but their groans were never more dolorous, be sure, than since the death of my worthy signor, the noble Mario; and that's quite natural, as he was the last of the race. Finally, God be praised for having exhausted his wrath. Those poor souls no longer have anything to mourn!"

"That's sufficient," I said to Barbarina. "We know, my dear lady, everything that we wanted to know. One of these children who guided us will go to fetch Monsieur Bartolotti from the nearby village, where he has taken refuge. Your domestic," I added, turning to Solbioski, "will take care to make up beds for us, if possible, in the chamber that this good lady will indicate to him, and make sure in the vicinity of provisions sufficient for the total flood of the Tagliamente. Finally, we'll take advantage of the daylight, if you believe me, to explore everywhere and see everything. Either I'm strangely mistaken, or it will be worth the trouble."

The distribution of the interior did not offer us anything that might merit being recorded. Old partition walls, old woodwork, decrepit furniture, tapestries in tatters, the entire dilapidated appearance of an old house crumbling for lack of care or money; not a place to hide a crime or a good deed! Puck, who searched with more skill than me, went to lie down yawning.

When that futile search was concluded, we went back down on to the rock.

"Now let's make a tour of this enclosure," I said to Solbioski, "in order to identify the most accessible points, for it's from the exterior that the mysterious authors of these fears must come, if they're founded on anything real. In the meantime, I shall visit these walls carefully, and discover whether there's any means of penetrating them."

Their approach was very difficult at the base, because of the numerous degradations they had suffered and the enormous heaps of rubble that had accumulated there; but at the place where their ruinous declivity, augmented over the centuries, caused the two lateral surfaces to hang over the ground, they could be climbed almost as easily as an unequal ladder prolonged between two abysms. That was child's play for my habits of a naturalist, my footing of a mountaineer and my eyes accustomed to sounding the most frightful precipices without fear of vertigo.

Thus, I engaged in that extraordinary route without looking behind me, and without paying any heed to the crumbling, all the way to the place where the keep rose up on an entablature more comfortable and better conserved than the rest. I had not forgotten that that part of the castle leaned visibly above the Tagliamente, and I took advantage of that inclination to reach the summit, introducing my hands and feet successively into all the places where the fall of a stone had left an empty space. I was soon standing on the tottering top of that colossus, which I had measured fearfully in the morning.

The spectacle that one embraced from that height was so broad and so deep that, in spite of all my assurance, I felt that my head was about to spin. I had often found myself on higher summits, but solid underfoot, and perpendicular to the gaze at the most. This one was trembling almost beneath my feet, and it overhung in a horrible manner the valley of the Tagliamente. I sat down on a heap of stones formed by the debris of the parapet, which time had amassed there confusedly, and I turned over the blocks of stone one by one, with the intention of making my footholds firmer on a more uniform surface.

When I had piled up a rather large number beside me I tried to walk in order to discover from there in its entirety the scene that extended before me. I heard a kind of metallic sound resonating beneath my boots and bent down hastily in order to find out where it was coming from. With my hand I moved a few stones that were still in my way; there was a trap-door.

I sat down in order to continue clearing it and to expose the trap completely, two sides of which I could already see. It seemed important to make sure whether it was retained in the interior, or only held by its own weight in the stone frame in which the opening that it sealed had been fitted. I understood, however, that the progressive inclination of the tower, by over-loading it with an enormous burden on the side where its hinges must be fixed, had rendered its movement impossible, or very difficult, and the long time during which its simple mechanism had remained exercise, at least according to all appearances, must also have contributed to sealing it in place.

I had soon uncovered it completely, but I was not carrying any other implement than a mineralogist's chisel and hammer, which never quit my belt. I introduced my chisel into the crack that I judged to be opposite the catch and I produced without too much effort, to my great satisfaction, a displacement of a few lignes. No more was required to convince me that the trap-door was not fixed internally either by hinges or bolts, and that this means of introducing ourselves into the tower would be infallible if it ever became necessary.

Then I climbed back down slowly, making sure of my footholds carefully on each of the accidental steps of the ruin, in order to contemplate at intervals the modifications that the slightest change brought to the general picture as I worked my way around the face of the keep, sometimes following with my gaze the long ribbon of the Tagliamente, which was still seething, blue dappled with white waves, rapid and sonorous but still a long way from the base of the rock; sometimes reposing it on the brown, square and solitary tower of Saint-Veit, the plebeian sister of the noble tower of San Marco; sometimes straying into the distance over the lagoons and the channels, mat and vitreous green like those with which manufacturers of knick-knacks ornament landscapes in relief that are given to children, through the innumerable islets reddening like spring buds.

My absence was long enough to cause anxiety, for Solbioski had retraced the steps of his circular voyage, stopping at the place where it became impossible to continue, and Monsieur Bartolotti had returned to the castle. Puck, who had picked up my trail, was moaning lamentably on the last stone of the inferior walls, gazing at the tower and whining.

I arrived, and I exchanged a few details rapidly with Solbioski. The discovery of the trap-door of the keep preoccupied him seriously. We agreed to send his domestic to keep watch from the only accessible point he had remarked, in order to protect us from an unexpected incursion, and we went to the communal room where a very modest banquet had been prepared for us. Night was beginning to fall, but the moon was superb.

Monsieur Bartolotti seemed so anxious, so inhibited, and so painfully attentive on the chaise longue where we had placed him in honor that we sensed his sadness involuntarily at the commencement of the meal. After some time, however, Solbioski and I looked at one another, as if to enquire whether we sympathized with the melancholy dispositions of his mind, and we burst out laughing. That hilarity turned us away from the black ideas that the sad abode naturally inspired, which seemed in conformity with the decor of a large room where our three beds had been established at intervals like funeral couches, imperfectly illuminated by the two slender candles on the table where we were seated. Nevertheless, our conversation reverted of its own accord, as usual, to the ideas that we were most concerned to avoid, but sustaining the bantering tone that is the bravado of strong minds.

Solbioski finally stood up and held out his glass solemnly in order to clink it against mine. "I drink," he said, "to the eternal repose of the Cinci family, and all the dead who have ever inhabited these redoubtable walls! May Heaven open one day to their tragic manes, and may the earth be light upon their tombs in the meantime."

I was about to respond to his provocation, for it was time to go to bed, and the fatigues of the day were making us feel the need for it, when a violent shock shook the vaults under our feet.

For a moment, we did not speak.

"It's nothing," said Solbioski. "The Tagliamente is doubtless rising and coming to strike the foundations of the tower by means of a subterranean path that it has made."

"That's probable," I replied, heading toward the window; but it was visible that the Tagliamente had not grown on the slightest. I saw it whitening at the same distance as before against the same rocks.

In the meantime, the same noise was renewed several times, followed by groans similar to the plaints of someone dying.

Puck stopped, his eyes ablaze, his ears pricked, accompanying them every time with dolorous barking. Monsieur Bartolotti was as pale as a specter, his teeth chattering with fear.

"There is certainly something extraordinary here, not far away from us," I said then, "which it's important for us to identify. This room is surrounded on all sides by walls, but on what do they repose? If I'm not mistaken, the noise is coming from below."

At the same time I lifted up the old carpet that covered the floor, and discovered in the four corners nothing but a coating of firmly cemented pozzolana, of which I had difficulty chipping away a few fragments by striking redoubtable hammer-blows with my chisel. I finally penetrated its entire thickness, but I was stopped by solid rock.

"The rock!" I exclaimed. "Nothing except the rock! Oh, this mystery is horrible!"

Solbioski drew closer to me, seized my arm and dragged me into the embrasure of the window.

"This mystery," he said, "humanity gives us a duty to fathom; but we'll only find the explanation in the tower. I've remarked here everything that might be useful to us in making use of the discovery you made this morning, and I'll wait for you at midnight or that expedition, at the foot of the ruins from which you reached the keep. Only think that we can't bring that feeble man into the secret of our enterprise without breaking him completely with terror, and that it would be better to reassure him by means of an affected insouciance."

He went to sit down at the table again. "We're quite mad," he continued, to allow ourselves to be disturbed by false appearances that are clear enough. Doctor Fabrcius, who has frequented this castle for a long time, has thought it appropriate to test our resolution by a proof of a new kind, as is customary in the Tugendbund, probably because he is reserving for us tonight the honors of the advanced initiation that none of the three of us has yet attained. If Monsieur Bartolotti is in his confidence, I'm ready to believe, that he is one of the essential actors of this scene, and in the perfect talent with which he has just played the emotions of fear, so difficult to counterfeit for a brave man like him. Fortunately, hearts like ours don't allow themselves to be vanquished by the illusions of fiction, and we'll issue a challenge with this glass of Sebenico, prepared for a toast, to all the perils that might alarm a human soul.

Bartolotti, flattered and proud to be flattered, as people of scant courage and intelligence usually are, had indeed recovered sufficient assurance to present his glass without trembling to Solbioski's bottle and allowed it to be filled with a horizontal red border of which he did not lose a drop.

I will confess that the hypothesis encountered so appositely by Solbioski was not deprived of all plausibility for me, and that it enabled me to understand quite distinctly the extraordinary absence of the doctor at the moment when the flooding of the Tagliamente might render the Torre Maladetta inaccessible for several days. We thus arrived at competing in bravado, as if all the synods and all the venditas of Germany and Italy had heard us, to the point of covering all the noises that might rise up under our feet, and we went to bed more or less tranquilly, but with the difference that Solbioski and I, who did not destine the night for sleep, did not take off our clothes.

When silence was reestablished, I listened more attentively than I had done before. The resounding impact had ceased to make itself heard, but I seized from time to time a lamentable plaint like the knell of a distant bell, and Puck, half asleep, emitted over that murmur the dolorous murmur of a dream-ing dog.

Solbioski eventually went out first, as we had agreed, in order to equip himself with a lever and other instruments that he judged necessary to our nocturnal expedition. A short time later I slipped outside, pulling the door closed quietly behind me, in order that Puck would not risk following me in a route forbidden to his courage and his fidelity.

I reached the slope of the walls and waited momentarily. Joseph joined me with all the equipment necessary for such an adventure contained in a hunting-bag. Our belts were each furnished with two pistols, and mine with a good dagger as well as the customary hammer and chisel. I marched in the lead, a muted lantern in my fist. Joseph, less experienced in such routes, leaned behind me on the strong iron bar that was to serve us to raise the trap-door. The access to the keep, which was apparently the most perilous part of our voyage, offered few difficulties under the full and pure light of that resplendent night.

After some efforts, our march, emboldened by the first obstacles, slowed somewhat. I distinctly heard Joseph's footsteps following mine. I turned round and saw that he was catching his breath. I have said that we were already fatigued by the morning's explorations. I encouraged him with my voice; he climbed; but soon stopped in my turn. We had not gained three or four toises of height when the space apparently deepened to the right and the left in a proportion that no longer had any relation to our real progress. I was not accustomed to the vagueness of the light, which disrupted all the calculations of sight by changing the form, the color and the distance of objects of comparison. The ditches no longer had any bottom and the tower looming up over our heads no longer had a summit. The slightest cavities were redoubtable to see, the slightest inequalities perilous, and the debris that we left behind us here and there gave the impression of raising menacing heads in our pursuit. As the horizon became broader and brighter, the slope we were climbing seemed to become darker and narrower; the inferior region that we had just quit, inundated with lunar light, appeared as infinite and as empty as the sky; and of all the noises of the earth, only the furious voice of the Tagliamente, always increasing, which was biting its banks and crying out, reached our ears. It was as frightful as a vision.

We were fortunate, I confess, to sit down on a little projection of the keep, although it was no longer the ledge that was required for us to lean comfortably against the tower a hundred and fifty feet above the ground. It was just in time; the last stone on which Joseph had supported his foot shook, rolled, and dragged a hundred others with it in its fall. They arrived at the bottom with a thunderous din.

"That's our path destroyed," he said to me, suddenly pressing against me.

"That's it renewed, I said, "and much easier to travel when we return. You know better than I do, my friend, that all conical or pyramidal constructions that crumble under the action of time or human effort only reduce their slope and enlarge their base. It was similar accidents that allowed us to climb this far."

"You're right," said Solbioski, "but the tower, this horrible tower, do you have a means of getting up there?"

I was twenty feet above him before having replied to him, and he followed me attentively from void to void or step to step, according to whether the tower presented intervals or projections to my lantern, turned to the wall, sliding his hands into all the places that my feet abandoned, or supporting his feet on all the ridges where they had reposed. Having reached the summit I relieved him of his lever and the rest of his irons, and threw them into the interior of the keep, where he arrived almost immediately after me, although he had not tested the difficulties of that extravagant ascent in the morning, as I had.

The retreat would perhaps not be easy, but we scarcely thought of that. We were on top of the Torre Maladetta, and we embraced one another, laughing, on the keep, where it was permissible for us to believe that no one had ever laughed before. We found ourselves so comfortable in the environment of that fresh and elastic air, which played in our hair. The weather was so beautiful, the night so mild, the serenity so suave and caressant, and he, my Joseph, opened his heart to such a beautiful future. There was a brief but delightful conversation between the earth and the firmament, like that of two children of heavens, I dared I think, who had alighted on the Torre Maladetta while flying.

"Pardon me," he said, "if I have afflicted you with my joy. Honorine is there," he continued, showing me Saint-Veit, whose tower was outlined on the horizon under our feet like a frail column of black basalt, and I forgot that if Diana had remained among the number of the living, she would not have belonged to me.

"Come," I replied, embracing him again, "and let's leave my weaknesses and griefs there. Someone in this tower is suffering."

We introduced the lever easily under the trap-door with the aid of my chisel. Soon—and who could express our joy— we heard the hinges groan upon their rusty axis. The heavy door lifted and leaned almost vertically against the stones that I had cleared away in my first voyage to the keep. My lantern plunged into the crypt, by means of a string on which I hastened to suspend it, and stopped on a solid floor at a depth of six feet.

I went down; I paraded the light in all directions, over all inner sides of the entablature, and found myself placed at the top of a spiral staircase, much less degraded than the exterior.

"Wait, wait," I cried to Solbioski. "Either I'm much mistaken or we're about to know what we have so much interest in knowing."

He would have attempted to follow me in vain, for I must have disappeared as I finished speaking. The stem of the spiral was so tight in its well that one could not discover at the same time more than two rotations of the spiral. By dint of turning around it I felt my courage weakening and my eyes becoming troubled. I let myself fall, half-dazed, in the last step, on to a species of parvis that surmounted a broader and perfectly straight staircase, where three men could have passed abreast. I was struck then, in following it with my gaze to the bottom, by an unexpected gleam, which I mistook at first for a residue of dazzle. Having recovered somewhat, I passed the lantern behind the long column on the spiral, and looked again. It was not an illusion; it was the sky, the sky with the velvety blue of the moonlight, so magnificent and so soft in the midst of the darkness of that frightful edifice.

"The moon and the sky," I said, climbing up again hastily. "The moon and the sky! An issue! An issue! The tower is open!"

"An issue," Joseph responded. "Oh, may we get out of here without climbing down those walls!"

At the same instant he launched forward, but he was scarcely beside me when the iron trap fell back above us, shaking with the frightful commotion of its fall the tottering ruin of the keep, which resounded throughout its height.

"What have I done?" he said. "Now we're prisoners, and forever, in the Torre Maladetta, for I've left all the instruments that might serve for our salvation outside."

"But have I not announced, Joseph, that I've found an issue—a facile and sure issue that you didn't remark this morning?"

"I saw," said Solbioski, anxiously, "everything that a man can discover of the exterior of this tower, and if it has some ruinous and inaccessible entry over the banks of the Tagliamente, dare you hope that the Tagliamente hasn't flooded?"

"Come on, come on," I cried, "and don't abandon yourself to futile anxieties. In a few moments we'll be out. See, rather—look, look . . ."

"Ah!" said Solbioski. "It's the sky! It's the coast of Saint-Veit! And the beach is still exposed!"

We went down a dozen steps of the new staircase and embraced one another, breathless with hope, for there was no more dread. I wanted to arrive even more quickly; I ran.

"Stop!" cried Joseph, and he seized me with all his strength. "Can't you see, fool, that the staircase is broken?"

We sat down then. Cautiously, I let out two brasses of the string sustaining my lantern.

"Good, good," I said. "Broken? Say rather interrupted by design, for the wall of plaster that replaces the steps appears to be of much more recent construction than the rest of the building. Mario had doubtless decided to impede communications from outside with the interior of his castle. It's a stupid precaution, for a child could descend here without danger, and you can see that the steps don't cease to be prolonged beyond this short interval. They descend all the way to that door of light that will render us liberty.

"A child could descend from here," replied Solbioski, "but the wall is new, and a man couldn't climb up here. Come back, Maxime, come back. Four vigorous arms might be able to lift the trapdoor . . . we haven't tried. Tomorrow, we'll have Frédéric follow us, whom I sent away inappropriately, and who is enterprising and robust. We'll make better use of our precautions and our resources; we'll indicate our itinerary to a few courageous neighbors whom we'll attract to the castle with money, if the flood hasn't yet separated us, and we won't expose our lives to perils without remedy, and perhaps without utility."

Neither of us had calculated the effect of an action produced by the four vigorous arms of which Solbioski spoke, a toise above our point of common support. The trap stirred under our efforts, but it would have required other arms at the ends of ours to lift it and replace it vertically against the stones against which we had initially leaned it. My chisel only gave us assistance of little value, and we had only made two or three attempts before, broken near the hilt, it fell at our feet. I refrained from risking the point of my dagger in that impotent enterprise; it might be useful for something else.

We went back down without speaking, and a moment later we were at the base of the wall that cut the stairway so abruptly. I assured myself that it was impossible to reach that height with my hands if we were forced to return; but the moon was still shining, and its light, even brighter and more extended as it reached its setting, inundated all the lower steps to the extent that they could easily be counted. The exterior space was limitless.

There were twenty steps there, which we descended with an almost joyful insouciance. But there too the route was closed, and the height of the cutting would have been terrifying if the weight of the higher constructions had not given it a slight slope.

"Almost nothing, my friend, almost nothing, I swear to you! Fifteen or eighteen feet at the most, and we'll be free. And we have no other means of emerging alive from the Torre Maladetta, for the return is impossible. See the sky! See the daylight that is about to appear! One can hear the noise of the Tagliamente from here, and it's the coast of Saint-Veit!"

I had told him all that already. He fell beside me and ran toward the light.

"Oh my God!" he cried. "Doomed! Doomed forever! It's not an issue, it's the issue from life to death. It's the balcony of the destroyed platform, the balcony where Lucrezia and Beatrice appeared, and which Barbarina told us yesterday no living being can reach without wings! And it would, indeed, require wings to go back up that tower or to descend from it! Maxime, we're doomed!"

I advanced and leaned over the balcony; its elevation was immense, because it overlooked perpendicularly the most profound side of the shore. To complete the misfortune, the

Tagliamete had not paused in its flood; it was rising, still rising. I sat down on the flagstones and put my head in my hands.

After a moment of reflection, I returned to myself, for if I yield easily to discouragement, I did not take long to find good reasons for regaining confidence in my destiny. Solbioski had not emerged from his dejection.

"Our position is unfortunate," I said. "It's perilous, if you wish, but it requires a great deal to be desperate."

"And who can get us out of it, poor wretches that we are? Do you have wings?"

"Calm down and don't refuse me a moment of attention. Our almost fantastic disappearance from the room where we went to bed will doubtless take Bartolotti's fear to the ultimate degree, but that man's imagination is not one of those that accord a great empire to the marvelous. I've observed that the nature of his fears was more positive, and I'm sure that he'll attribute our absence to a natural cause. He won't act, it's true; I can no longer count on anyone but you, but he'll talk. The doors won't take long to open, for day is about to dawn, and they'll only emerge from the castle in order to look for us.

"Puck followed me yesterday, as far as he could follow me, all the way to the base of the keep. He'll indicate the route we took, and a recent collapse will easily be recognized, for more than one of those black and mossy stones that crumbled under our footsteps will present to the sunlight one of its faces that has never been struck by it. Monsieur Fabricius will probably have arrived; he has a keen interest in rejoining us, and the progress of the torrent, which is visibly rising will doubtless convince him to leave Saint-Veit early, before being separated from us for several days. You know his activity, his resolution and his courage.

"On the other hand, the good Frédéric, whom you placed on watch beyond the low-lying areas that the water in threatening to invade, won't wait for their irruption in order to rejoin us; he will have calculated with his usual penetration and won't have remained on unnecessary sentry duty at a post that has no need to be guarded when the Torre Maladetta is about to be closed off by the flood. He'll arrive at the summit of the keep as easily as us; the steps are marked so visibly that I found them again by night The discovery of our lever, our bag and our abandoned instruments next to a mobile trap-door with finish directing him.

"He won't fail to deliver us from here on his own, with two or three brasses of rope that he'll procure without difficulty in the castle, and we'll see the sun again, which is beginning to climb over the horizon, at midday from the main hall, for our expedition has taken longer than I thought. Don't worry, then, my friend, and have no fear that Providence has abandoned us."

"So you're counting on the arrival of Monsieur Fabricius," said Solbioski, shaking his head, "because the Tagliamente hasn't overflowed, and on the arrival of Frédéric because the Tagliamnte is overflowing!"

I felt the weight of that objection.

"I'm counting on one or the other, Joseph," I said, abruptly pricking up my lantern. "And nothing proves, as yet, that this fragment of an esplanade doesn't communicate with anything. It isn't from the top of the tower that the ladies were brought to this marvelous balcony, which the art of a Medieval architect had opened for the pleasure of the eyes facing one of the most beautiful pages of picturesque nature. I guarantee that with a little attention . . . and look! That embrasure is as narrow as a loophole, but it's open and practicable."

It was, in fact, open for the passage of a man in profile, and so narrow in its length that my heart was beating violently at the thought that the slightest disturbance of the ruins might close the entrance to the hole forever while we searched for an exit. We had already taken more than fifty paces when the succession of solitary paving stones that composed its entire width descended a slippery and sheer slope, where I could scarcely keep my footing.

The lantern extended by my right arm, I fixed an anxious oblique gaze on the narrow space that it illuminated in front of me. I stooped abruptly at a cylindrical opening where lateral walls of the mysterious passage closed in an impenetrable angle. It was a spiral of the same kind that we had already negotiated, but which was only just wide enough to receive the body of a man. There was no reason to hesitate, and I engaged one of my feet therein cautiously; it settled on a solid step, and we plunged into that abyss, fearful of encountering an obstacle, for the return movement would have been difficult to execute.

We finally reached a vast chamber, regularly constructed, the walls of which we hastened to touch. The inferior parts were carved in the living rock. We were undoubtedly in the subterrains of the castle, a few toises, so far as we could estimate, below the habitable constructions.

That room, of an imposing and somber aspect, offered nothing remarkable except for a well hollowed out in the center, which must have required incredible labor to be extended as far as the level of the waters of the plain. A bucket, empty but still wet, was placed on the edge. The rope that sustained it to its pulley was not entirely dried out at the place where it was knotted to its iron handle.

"What further proof is necessary," I said to Solbioski, "that this place is inhabited?"

"I had no doubt of it when I departed," he replied, sadly, "but it's not without anxiety that I'm waiting to encounter its inhabitants."

While we were speaking I had moved aside an old door-curtain that was suspended from the wall by means of a rod supported on crampons. It closed a room even more spacious than the one via which we had penetrated those horrible dungeons.

There, in fact, everything announced the dwelling of a family—or the lair of a gang—that had been neglected for some time. Its four sides were garnished with antique armchairs of large proportion; a deformed fireplace, the channel of which appeared to terminate above the strand of the Tagliamente, was surmounted by a Venetian looking-glass, the reflection of which frightened me, so redoubtable is the sight of a human being for an isolated man who lacks the support of institutions and society. A discovery more reassuring for me was that of double bronze candelabra fitted to the two pillars, which were still charged with intact candles, but blackened by damp and time.

That apparatus, so extraordinary in such a place, filled me with a childish joy, which augmented greatly when I had looked at the muted lantern. It only had a moment to shine, and the many different troubles that we had just experienced had caused us to forget the most serious of our dangers. Our torches and tinder-boxes were still in the bag abandoned on the keep. The wick, leaning over a coating of wax that had accumulated around the socket, was only throwing our a few white and blue plumes, which were dancing around it as if they were about to quit it, and were only flickering by virtue of a whim of sorts.

I took possession of the two candles, and with great care I rotated on its skewer the bulbous crystal that enclosed our treasure, for fear that the agitation of the air might steal it from us. With what tremulous anxiety I approached the cotton of that feeble residue of flame, ready to go out! With what delight I saw a broad light ignited, and communicated it from one candle to the other; for I lit them all, in order to make sure that at least we would have no lack of light.

Everything shone resplendently around me, but the distant corners of the room, where the light gradually decreased until it petered out entirely, appeared even more obscure and more formidable. I was plunging my gaze into them with horror, when a scream rang out behind me. I turned round, and Solbioski's head fell on to my breast as he wrapped his tremulous hands around my neck.

"There! There!" he said, pointing with his finger toward the part of the room that was opposite to us. "It's there."

"Eh? What, my friend? You haven't even told me what you think you've seen."

"A cadaver! A cadaver! The body of a murdered woman!"

I took one of the candles.

There was, indeed, a cadaver, a woman in a black dress, extended on a low couch, the arms of which were trailing on the floor. I lifted them up and replaced her on her bloody bed without observing any other wounds but those of her mutilated hands, which one might have thought half-chewed by the teeth of a ferocious beast. I expressed that conjecture aloud.[1]

"Look, Maxime, look," said Solbioski, moving aside one of the white curtains that hung over her and showing me the imprint of five bloodstained fingers. "The ferocious beasts of the Torre Maladetta have hands!"

"Joseph," I said, with as much calm as that scene of terror permitted, "pardon me if I'm forced to prolong the anguish further, but it isn't this unfortunate creature whose cries we heard yesterday evening, scarcely more than twelve hours ago. Every aspect of this cadaver announces that life did not withdraw from it less than three days ago. There were, in any case, two ladies in black on the platform, and there's only one here. According to all appearance, we have a victim to save."

"But where do you expect to discover her, since we've looked everywhere?"

---

1 The wounds in question are left to the conjectures of the reader to explain; that might imply that there was an earlier version of the story from which certain details have been diplomatically suppressed in the published version.

"Everywhere thus far. She's behind that other door-curtain next to the fireplace, which I remarked when I illuminated this room."

We armed our pistols, moved aside the curtain, and went into a third room.

This one was quite different from the previous ones in its decoration. The waist-high rock and the wall that surmounted it were carefully coated with fresh bright stucco, the application of which could not have antedated the best years of Mario's youth. At intervals, long sheets of velvet fabric or painted paper varied the monotony of the background in the Venetian manner. Five or six good paintings by masters, placed between agreeably sculpted bronze portmanteaux, further heightened the appearance of that sad abode, which someone had at least tried to render pleasant. A few musical instruments for the use of women and a complete dressing-table charged with books of imagination and poetry scattered amid ribbons, lace and perfumes, indicated its destination well enough The alcove was garnished with an elegant bed that someone had neglected to remake, the crumpling of which indicated that it had been occupied recently.

The fireplace was wide and high, in accordance with ancient custom, but artfully worked and richly ornamented. The pendulum and the hands of the clock were motionless. Already, doubtless for several days, the measurement of time had been neglected. The four candelabra that garnished the two extremities of the mantelpiece bore no light, but in half of them candles had finished dying and the remainder had not been lit. That precaution reminded me of the necessity of conserving those that remained in the subterrain, into which no ray of sunlight could ever penetrate, and where absolute darkness must be horrible.

I lit two of the candles in the candelabra, conserved one in my hand and hastened to extinguish all those that I had imprudently ignited while traversing the dead woman's room. Then I returned in order to take part in Solbioski's anxious explorations. No reassuring circumstance had relieved his funereal presentiments. He was plunged in silence, in an armchair in the corner of the fireplace, where the debris of a few firebrands, probably cold for a long time, had blackened amid the ashes.

"There's no longer anything here," he said. "Nothing but that exhausted cupboard one reaches via those steps, which I visited with a glance. That was probably where the unfortunate prisoner stored her provisions, but they're so completely exhausted that no indication remains that might show the place where she kept her bread. Only the woodpile is stocked."

"The woodpile!" I replied, running to the staircase. "Well, fire, fire! Cold, fatigue and lack of sleep have dulled my senses to the point that I can't recover my presence of mind and firmness without a moment's repose. Fire, Joseph, a big one, and we'll dream of some means of salvation, for night has always brought me counsel."

I had already passed into his hands I don't know how many logs of resinous pine, which only demanded to crackle, when, having abruptly lifted up one log more, I carelessly struck the ceiling of the shaft with its end; it rendered a metallic sound, the extraordinary resonance of which surprised me, and Solbioski and I exchanged glances, consulting one another mutually.

"Yes, yes," he said, responding to my thought. "You're not mistaken. We've heard that sound before; it's the one that was renewed several times yesterday under the great hall in the castle."

I hurled myself on to the woodpile and struck the same spot with my hammer; the sound was repeated, more intensely and easier to recognize.

"This is evident," I said. "Look, they haven't even taken the trouble to disguise the frame of the trap-door, and it's through this that the unfortunate woman was lowered, because there certainly isn't any other issue at the foot of the tower. The age she announced, in any case, so far as I could judge by the fearful glance that I cast over her, wouldn't have permitted her to climb the walls, and even if we didn't know that Barbarina hasn't climbed to the keep for twenty years, the state in which I found the ruins that I visited first wouldn't leave any possibility of doubting it. Only, it's no longer a matter here of a mobile trap like the one to which we owe the deadly consequence of these mysteries. This one is solidly sealed outside under the carpet that covers a layer of pozzolana, by means of which it's been cleverly dissimulated. It's on this point that it's necessary to act, for it's here that our deliverance ought to arrive, and I have no doubt that we can be heard."

"Who will hear us?" said Joseph, looking at me dolorously. "Bartolotti, who has fled? Frédéric, who hasn't returned? Monsieir Fabricius, whose passage has been closed by the Tagliamente? Barbarina, perhaps? You didn't take it into your head to lift the carpet in its full extent, and you expect her to do it?"

Meanwhile, we attacked the trap-door in a manner to shake the tower all the way to its summit, but there was no response.

We went back down and we lit a large and ardent fire. We disposed the mattresses of the bed on either side of the fireplace, without exchanging a word; but we went back up from time to time in order to renew our efforts against the sonorous but unbreakable vault, where our futile percussion rumbled over us like a threat and a sentence of death.

In the silence that we maintained after each attempt I thought I seized a murmur of complaint or an agonizing voice. I bent down, for it seemed to be coming from my feet; I saw something then that resembled a second cadaver. I touched it, shivering; it was a woman lying face down at the extremity of the wood-pile. I picked her up and I carried her away in my arms. I deposited her on one of the beds that we had prepared. I parted the long hair that covered her face in order to make sure that she was still alive, but her eyes were closed and the little life that remained in her convulsive lips was as frightful to behold as death . . .

And when Solbioski had brought the light closer to us, I felt my own life escaping; my senses were troubled, my legs buckled, my soul was on the brink of annihilation. The dying or dead woman was Diana.

"Diana! Diana!" I cried, falling to my knees beside her and bearing her cold hand to my mouth.

"Everything is explicable now," said Solbioski. "Mario, justly suspected of the abduction of Mademoiselle de Marsan, had found no other means of securing her from the searches than hiding her until further notice in these subterrains, with her chambermaid. As unusual provisioning would have given away his secret, he multiplied his brief voyages to Codroipo in order to substitute for it. He died on the return journey and these two unfortunates died of starvation in this prison, where we're going to die."

"Dead!" I said. "Diana isn't dead! She's alive! She won't die! The warmth of the fire is beginning to reanimate her."

"Too bad," replied Solbioski, bitterly. "Alas, it would be better if she were dead; we can only prolong her sad agony by cruel aid. With what are you going to nourish her?"

"A curse upon Heaven!" I said, standing up and striding around the room in a fit of frenzy and horror. "Providence is thus as deaf as the void! No salvation for Diana!"

"And no salvation for us," repeated Solbioski, whose lugubrious voice resonated over mine like the melancholy response of a Trappist: *Brother, it is necessary to die!*

My hands clenched, hanging over my coat; it was my traveling overcoat; one of the pockets rejected my hand.

"Ah!" I cried, with intoxication. "She won't die! I said that she wouldn't die! Thanks be rendered to you, Onorina! Poor Onorina, may heaven protect you! My God, forgive me! Saint Honorine, pray for us . . . !"

"What are you saying, my friend? Despair is troubling your reason. Your mind is wandering. Calm, down."

"Saint Honorine, pray for us! Diana won't die! There's water, fire, vases and lasagna."

What followed immediately has no need to be recounted. Our religious and grateful astonishment; our surges of amour for momentarily-misunderstood Providence, which had sent us that miraculous benefit; our haste to help Diana; our precautions in bringing her back to life with cleverly managed transitions that had nothing dangerous, are all more easily comprehensible than could ever be written.

After an hour, her pulse was beating, slowly but with regularity; the blood, reanimated in her veins, had risen again to her pale lips; her mouth was respiring, her heart palpitating beneath my hand; her eyes opened; she paraded them vaguely over the whole enclosure, paused them momentarily on me without showing any surprise, and closed them again with a sigh.

I guessed only too well for what she was searching, and trembled to divine what she had understood.

Our cares continued, as much as was required to reassure us as to her existence, and we forgot then how faint were the hopes that remained to us of maintaining the fugitive breath that we had just reanimated. The human soul allows itself to be uplifted in the most extreme circumstances by such deceptive joys! It has such a great need to believe in a tomorrow, to grasp an illusion, and that is what keeps it alive.

Since her resurrection, however, Diana had seemed to be incapable of articulating a word. Her fixed and bleak gaze, which had been partly detached from the darkness of death without losing that expression, had not even reflected a thought or an interior emotion. Once she squeezed my hand, as she turned her mouth away from the aliments of which she no longer felt the need, and closed her eyes again, but without giving evidence of any pain; then she went to sleep.

After having replenished the fire and renewed the candles, we also yielded to slumber; it lasted for a long time.

I woke up first, and it was necessary, for everything was about to be extinguished. Diana was reposing in a calm that seemed mild. I approached her as closely as was necessary to hear her breathing and feel the warmth of her breath. I placed within her reach, on a small table illuminated by two candles, what remained of the lasagna. Then, equipped with my lantern, I returned silently to the stairway to the balcony.

I could not imagine that no steps had been taken to find us, and I only feared that the searches might have stopped at the narrow tunnel, where it was seemingly not natural to seek a passage.

Nothing responded to my conjectures. There had not been any change; no one had come.

The sun had already passed the point in the sky that it occupies at midday. The previous day, of which we had only seen the dawn, must have been beautiful. The thaw was continuing. The Tagliamente had flooded its banks; it was rising in white waves and falling back in vapor against the foot of the rock. The country that separated us from Saint-Veit had entirely disappeared under an immense lake, in the middle of which its tower loomed up like a motionless mast. I thought that Monsieur Fabricius had not been able to set forth.

Solbioski did not ask about the reasons for my absence and I did not talk to him about it. He had time to learn that our best-founded hope had vanished

"Woe, woe!" he said sitting up on his bed. "Has the night brought counsel, as you hoped?"

"It has counseled me, my friend, only to count on our-selves. The trap-door in the cabinet can't be opened, and if it yielded to our efforts it would leave us a further difficulty to overcome, for the masonry work that weighs upon it hides some artifice in its construction that we can't penetrate. The shortest route is the longest. It's necessary to climb back up that stairway of despair, and for that, a ladder is imperative, which we can soon fabricate. In the backs of the armchairs that we remarked as we came in there are struts in their struc-ture that only need to be fitted solidly enough to carry us in turn. The instruments that Mario accumulated in disorder in the corners of the woodpile for the service of his hearth are sufficient for that work, along with the point and cutting edge of my dagger, the superfluity of the string that sustains our lantern, and perhaps our arms, our mere arms. As for the trap-door, we'll lift it without difficulty. I observed that one of the bars of the balcony only requires and effort to be detached from its molding, and a stroke of that little hand-saw hanging from the fireplace will reduce our ladder to the proportion necessary to raise us up as far as the rebellious point that only resisted our efforts because we were attacking it from too far below. Only have courage, for there's no time to lose."

"Indeed," he said, "that resource is the last, the unique resource that remains to us, if the Tagliamente has flooded."

Then he sat down on his bed, wiped his forehead, went pale, and said: "I'm hungry."

"The first irritations of need are not renewed for some time when one has vanquished them initially; that's a state of grace for prisoners and the actors in civil wars. Think that in a few hours we can be delivered."

And I hastened to distribute between us the various parts of our task.

Oh, that labor was long! We were equally inexperienced in the work, and the rigor of our apprenticeship was augmented by our ever-increasing weakness. Independently of the necessary distractions we gave one another from time to time, Diana's light meals, for which I had divided the almost-exhausted lasagna into three small portions, had taken us away alternately from the languor and weakness that caused the tools to fall from our hands. We finally came to the end of it, if it is permissible to regard as finished work the deformed and crude objects that we had sketched with scant solidity. We were happy, though.

After that, we disposed everything in the apartment for the time that our absence ought to last, in accordance with our estimate, and we returned to the balcony, with difficulties that the embarrassment of our equipment multiplied at every step.

Who would believe it? The hours that had appeared so long to my impatience were even more numerous than I had thought. The opening of the platform was illuminated by daylight—by a new day, by the sun of the third midday. I was astonished to have suffered so much and to have measured the length of my suffering so poorly. Dolor marches rapidly.

Solbioski hastened to run to the balcony. I had nothing to learn there, and remained behind him.

"The Tagliamente has overflowed," he said, letting his head fall over his breast.

"What does it matter that the Tagliamente has overflowed?" I replied. "We're going to the keep, not the shore."

Then I tried to shake the bar that I had felt vacillating, and which I could probably have detached the day before if I had tried. It resisted. My blood froze in my veins, because, without the aid of a lever, all the other preparations of our enterprise became futile.

As I searched for one that was looser, without finding one, and without making the subject of my anxiety known to Solbioski, a long, hard and rounded object rolled under my feet; it was a bar that had fallen of its own accord in response to the shocks of the storm or the consequences of the degradations of time. I picked it up dragged it after me, step by step, because it was heavy. We climbed slowly, with heavy paces, making multiple pauses, for we lacked courage, even to liberate ourselves.

We rested briefly at the bottom of the steps that ended at the spiral staircase, in order to saw our ladder at the height of the trap-door. We left the rest, which was the longer part, on the flat part of the last wall, and we arrived at the summit.

We sat down again; we embraced one another, and exchanged a few words of encouragement, of which we had need.

Finally, our backs turned to a sidewall where our lever could act in any direction with facility, we wedged ourselves on the rungs of our short ladder, of which we had taken care to choose the most robust and solid, among the most securely embedded in their sockets. We curbed our shoulders under the iron door that separated us from the sky and life, and gradually introduced the point of out sharp bar at the point where the edge of the trap-door was least hermetically fitted to its frame. We exerted on its opposite extremity the combined effort of our four hands with the scant vigor lent to us by hope—or desperation.

The hinges creaked as they had the first time; the trap yawned, and opened wide enough to let a man pass through; the bright morning light penetrated into the tower in dazzling beams, with the pure and keen air of that elevated region.

"We're saved!" I cried. "One moment more, and we're saved!"

At the same instant, all the stones surrounding the trap-door, shaken by its movement, fell upon it with a frightful din; it fell back like a thunderbolt and threw us violently on to the flagstones.

"We're not saved," replied Solbioski, putting his arms around me. "I told you—we're doomed!"

We remained silent for a while, to the noise of the debris that continued to pile up overhead, for the collapse had spread to the more unsteady parts of the parapet on the side that inclined over the tilted face of the keep, and the stones that crowned it were still falling and rolling.

I thought, without dreading it, that it was about to collapse entirely and annihilate us; but the noise finally ceased, although the depths of the building still repeated it with their echoes. The tower vibrated momentarily like a poplar whose crown has been struck by lightning, or a pendulum pushed by a finger, gradually reducing the arc of its oscillations. Then everything became mute and motionless.

Our lantern, fortunately closed, had not been extinguished by the commotion. I picked it up with an appearance of security, the illusion of which I was trying to make for myself, and I gripped Solbioski's hand.

"Come on," I said. "There's no cause for despair yet. That catastrophe will make itself felt all the way to the courtyard of the castle, where fragments of the wall will have fallen from the summit. Their natural direction is on that side. The accident that has overtaken us will enable our efforts, our position and our danger to be divined. Be assured that, as I speak, the inferior trap-door is open. Come, in the name of Heaven, which won't abandon us."

Solbioski rested his gaze upon me, in which a dolorous incredulity and a sad derision were mixed.

I turned my eyes away, and I drew him after me into the spiral staircase.

We descended without speaking. Our ladder adjusted easily to the first wall in spite of the diminution we had inflicted upon it in order to remove the section that we had just left at the summit. At the second breach in the direct stairway it was much too short. That was an inconvenience easy to anticipate if we had foreseen that we would be returning. I had not thought of it. We had difficulty attaining it by suspending it from our weak and trembling hands, after long and timid precautions.

Finally, we arrived, as at a place of refuge, at the inaccessible balcony over the Tagliamente.

It was dark. The moon, thickly veiled, was only casting a faint light over the torrent, but it was visibly retreating toward its bed; the north wind that was blowing had chilled the atmosphere again and dried up for a few days the source of the floodwater. The rapid and whistling clouds were whipping us with a piquant frost. I dared to rejoice with all the expansion that remained to me, in order to express a sentiment of hope.

"It's cold," I said. "The snows are no longer melting. The Tagliamente is retreating, the strand is free. If Doctor Fabricius hasn't arrived at the Torre Madadetta today, he'll certainly arrive tomorrow."

"And what will it matter to our salvation if he arrives tomorrow?" said Solbioski, fainting in my arms.

At first I made impotent efforts to recall him to the life that he appeared to have quit entirely. Finally, he was reanimated momentarily, only to weaken again an instant later. Gradually, the two states became alternate, measured by almost equal intervals. I understood that the same symptom was threatening to attain me in my turn, and that it was time to arrive at Diana's still-distant apartment.

I calculated the distance fearfully. The candle was about to go out, because I had not imagined in the morning that it would be necessary to take precautions for the return, the possibility of which I had not even considered. Strangely enough, physiological studies made with sufficient care under illustrious masters had not left me with any positive notion of the time during which a man can go without aliments. I was astonished still to be alive.

Alas, it is easy for me to spare you the details of that interminable journey, but I would try in vain to spare you the dolor of divining it. You will recall the strangled corridor that seemed to have been fashioned for snakes rather than humans. You will recall the narrow and profound well, the other spiral that only promised a tomb. It is there that you will follow in thought, with me, two dying men who are dragging themselves along in slow repetitions through spaces almost impenetrable to agility, strength and patience.

How long that lasted, who can say? How many times, overwhelmed by a fatigue without end and without hope, did we repeat: "That's enough; it's as well to die here!" How many times, reanimated by I know not what vigor of the soul, which provides the will to live, did we redouble our efforts to reach, pointlessly, the ground of another sepulcher?

We had reached the chamber of the dead woman, sometimes walking and sometimes crawling, when our candle suddenly threw off a more vivid light, and went out.

"Have we arrived?" Solbioski asked, lying down on the rock. "Why can't I see anything any longer?"

"We haven't arrived," I replied, "and we have no more fire. But the second door-curtain will be easy to find, if I'm not mistaken, by following the wall of the tower with a hand. Wait for me, my brother, wait for me."

I slid then, tottering, along the cold walls, resting from time to time on my knees in order to get my breath back.

A projecting item of furniture forced me to change course. Incapable of following it for its entire length without support, I put out my hand to find the wall again, which could not be far away, but I searched for it without reaching it. A horrible idea occurred to me; I lost my footing and I fell on the cadaver.

"Is it there?" shouted Solbioski. "Have you let the curtain fall back? Why can't I see?"

"It's not here yet," I replied, shivering with terror. "Wait for me, Joseph, wait for me."

I resumed my frightful route in that terrible darkness, of which no earthly night can give any idea. After a long time, the door-curtain ceded under my fingers. I pulled it abruptly. All the lights were extinct.

"Why have you closed the curtain on me?" said Solbioski. "You've arrived and I can't see you. Alas, have you abandoned me?"

I did not say a word. A minute's delay might finish dooming us. I headed for the hearth, sustaining myself to the right and the left on the beds where we had reposed on the second day; I searched it with my hands.

"O fortune!" I cried, with a sort of ecstasy. "Still, still there!"

"The trap-door is open?" said Solbioski. "The trap-door is open! Maxime, don't abandon me."

"A spark, my friend, a spark amid the embers!"

And the chamber was illuminated.

I thought I had returned to life. I led, or rather dragged, poor Joseph, whose agony was more advanced than mine, to my bed.

Then I went to Diana. Her eyes were open and fixed, as usual, but brighter, more ardent, more meteoric. Her complexion was inflamed; her pulse was beating precipitately, in a disorderly fashion.

"Has she eaten everything?" Solbioski said, raising himself up painfully on his hands.

"Yes," I replied. "Everything is eaten; but fever preserves from hunger; people say that it nourishes."

He let himself fall back.

I wanted to attempt one last means of attracting the attention of the inhabitants of the castle, if any still remained; but I feared that it might produce a mortal emotion in Diana, who had awakened unexpectedly, and I made her party to all the particularities of our situation, in a voice loud enough to be heard by Solbioski, allowing her to divine the names of the absent friends who were awaiting our deliverance, in order that she could at least console herself with the thought that Mario was still alive.

She stared at me, without moving as I spoke, as if she were listening to me with reflective attention. I thought so at first. When I had finished speaking, she did not respond to me with the slightest sign; she turned away and seemed to fall asleep.

I took from Solbioski's belt the two pistols with which he was armed. I went back up to the sonorous trap-door of the cabinet and I fired twice. After a moment's pause, I renewed the detonation of my two, and I lent an ear to the exterior sounds.

It seemed to me that I could hear a confused murmur, like the noise of footfalls and voices, but in two or three days, those sounds without a cause had obfuscated my hearing and my brain so frequently that I was no longer capable of distinguishing reality from the illusions of my sick senses.

I wanted, however, to take advantage of the chance of being heard; it was the last. I lifted up a pine log in order to strike the trap-door one more time; I hoisted it a few feet above the floor and let it fall back. I bent down in order to take hold of it and lift it again, but I could no longer lift it.

I descended then with uncertain steps toward the fireplace, in order to reanimate the fire and renew our funereal light. I employed all the wood and candles that remained within reach in doing so. I knew that we might not need any more. An hour, perhaps two, passed in that labor, and I spent another slipping into the shroud with which no hand would cover me.

It was finished forever.

Solbioski turned toward me and said, in an extinct voice: "What day is it?"

I thought that it must be the beginning of the fifth, but I did not reply.

The time thereafter was divided between incredible suffering and annihilating languor in which I thought life was about to escape me. There were moments of illusion in which all objects took on a fantastic and capricious aspect, like the decoration of a spectacle or the apparitions of slumber. The shadows on the distant walls moved, were detached, mingled with strange and gigantic forms, embraced one another, linked themselves with one another, swirling around me, urgent, confused and howling. The flames of the candles leapt so high over the holders that I had difficulty following them.

Familiar voices introduced themselves into my ears like a breath, or resonated above my head with mocking and insulting laughter. If I closed my eyes to hide from those fascinations, the last perception that an inexplicable liaison of ideas had brought to my mind was prolonged in an indefinite manner in my thought. It was a limited song, a monotonous refrain, a Greek or Latin verse, to a deafening rhythm, the chorus of a virelay or a redondille, whose importune obstinacy seemed to attach itself to me for an eternity, like the terrible horse-fly that always comes back with an infallible precision to the place from which one has chased it away.

Sometimes I passed from a delirious faint to slumber, and the scene changed then in a strange manner. In my dreams there were air, sunlight, women and flowers. I suddenly found myself in joyous assemblies, in which people were only occupied in pleasures and feasting. Splendid tables were laden with delicate dishes, which I tried to attain but which changed in my mouth to insipid or bitter sand. Onorina came back everywhere with her little tray heaped with appetizing lasagna. "Buy, Monsieur," she said, "but my good lasagna and my fine Paduan vermicelli? It can serve on the occasion, and there's no better in Codroipo." But when I tried to precipitate myself upon her lasagna my hands could not reach out to seize it, nor could my spongy teeth firm up in order to chew it . . .

Then I emerged from my dreams with a start, to the sound of a heart-rending plaint that dragged on for some time over my awakening.

"What's that?" I cried, once, with all the strength that remained to me.

"Nothing," Solbioski replied. "It's probably Mademoiselle de Marsan, who is dying."

"My God," I said, "have pity on me. Saint Honorine, pray for us."

That time cannot be calculated, for my slumber was sometimes bleak and long. I recall that a moment arrived when, on opening my eyes, I could no longer perceive light. It was the final darkness, the eternal night that I had anticipated with so much horror, and delayed with so much care the previous day, or the one before, or another day before that. It was my last darkness.

I tried to get up. I could not.

That's all right, I said to myself. *It's all over. This is death.*

And I shifted my position, in order to die; but in trying to extend my arm in order to set my head on it, I rested it on a cold arm.

"Who's there?" I murmured, shuddering, as if encountering a murderer could have frightened me. *A murderer, alas! A murderer! There's none so cruel that he wouldn't break his bread with me!*

"It's me," Solbioski replied. His strength, which had collapsed before mine, had been conserved longer. "Don't tremble! Don't be afraid. I don't mean you any harm. I only need your dagger."

"What can one do here with a dagger? Do you think there were men hiding in the subterrains of the tower?"

"No, there are only cadavers; but there's one whose obstinacy in living importunes me, and I have the right to get rid of him. Give me your dagger and drink my blood; it's said that it sustains life. Who knows? Perhaps the Tagliamente has descended between its banks again. Perhaps Monsieur Fabricius has come back."

I threw my dagger as far away as I could. I was quite sure that we wouldn't go to look for it there. That thought I had had.

"My brother," I said, weeping, "you're lying on the rock. Come, come as far as me, Joseph, don't leave me. My God, have pity on us."

I do not know whether I drew him toward me or whether I drew nearer to him, but we ended up touching one another.

"Honorine!" he cried. "Poor Honorine! The young fiancée who is preparing her ribbons and bouquets! And you, Maxime, whom I love and will never see again. Oh, if daylight would only illuminate us one more time! But it's too far away and the balcony is too high . . . Never, never!"

I was struck by an overwhelming vertigo. When Joseph said no more I tried to lean over him to ascertain whether he was still breathing. He turned away from me with a frightful groan. I heard vague noises: I lost them, as if they had never been. I tried to grasp them again. Finally, my thought escaped me entirely. I fell back into the vagueness of my dreams. Again I saw the feasts that I had quit, and little Onorina hawking her lasagna, and Saint Honorine extending her consoling arms to me from the depths of Il Pordenone's fantastic tableau.

However, the noises always came back. There was a pickax, there was a mattock, there was the Tagliamente that was passing under the tower, groaning; there was the mine that blew it up; there was Onorina all in tears on the threshold of the church, who never ceased repeating: "Buy, Monsieur, buy my good lasagna! There's none better in Codroipo!"

I went to sleep.

When I woke up I said to Solbioski: "Are you asleep?" and he did not reply.

My stupor became more and more profound. I lost the memory of time and places, and myself. I wondered vaguely: *Where am I?* but my memory was an abyss in which I could not rediscover myself.

I ended up no longer thinking. Only hearing still brought me incomplete and confused sensations, cries, lamentations, a din of cataracts and tempests. I tried to respond with lamentation and cries, in order to put myself in harmony with that suffering nature that was about to die, but my voice was lacking.

The clock of eternity would not be sufficient to measure such hours. When they had passed I found myself somewhere, in a place where daylight was coming from the sky. Perhaps it was morning. I closed my eyes as soon as I had opened them, because the sunlight wounded them. My mouth was less ardent, my organs less languid. Some flavorsome juices soothed my palate and I tasted them again. At least I could sense my suffering. I imagined that I was alive.

That's better, I said to myself. *It's necessary to remain and die like that.*

I looked again, because a new sweet and substantial beverage had reanimated my life. There was a very strange spectacle. A hall, so vast, where I had never woken up, which was not my father's house, which was not my inn, which was not my barracks, which was not my prison. The ground, especially, astonished me. It was profoundly stirred and covered in scattered lava. There was a large opening in the middle that seemed to communicate with a cellar.

"The Torre Maladetta!" I cried. "The Torre Maladetta! The trap-door is open! Diana! Joseph! Anna! Come to me, come! I've found a way! Oh, don't delay in coming, there are already so many dead!"

"No one is dead except Anna," Doctor Fabricius replied. He was leaning on the head of my bed. He was too late.

"Fabricius! My friend, my father," I said, seizing his hand. "And Diana! And Joseph!"

"They're alive. But you're better now," he continued, "and I can give you an explanation. It's necessary, for time is pressing. You'll know later the obstacles that delayed your deliverance. Today the story would make us lose precious moments. The hopes of the world will be annihilated in a few days. Brilliant successes have intoxicated Napoléon's partisans and armies. The cause of the independence of peoples isn't lost; doubtless it never will be, but perhaps it's reserved for my old age to enjoy its triumph. My head and Joseph's are menaced, with a price on them. At the first glimmer of salvation that I glimpsed for him, I hastened to have him transported to a safe place, from which he can regain our Germany. It doesn't yet belong entirely to the tyrant. The Torre Maladetta can't fail to be invested shortly. I couldn't quit you until you'd been returned to life. The moment for us to separate has also come. Do you have the strength to leave?"

"Joseph! My dear Joseph! He told me that we would never see one another again! Diana, my friend, where is she?"

"Diana will live. Time, more powerful than my aid, will probably bring her out of the state of mutism and alienation in which she has been plunged thus far. No word has escaped her lips, no emotion has been painted on her face, even when the new chambermaid I have given her presented her this morning with the mourning-dress that she ought to wear as a widow and an orphan. I'm counting on that help; I've confided myself to it in despair of all remedies. Only, on the proposition I made her to withdraw for the time being to the Annunziata in Venice, where she has compatriots and, I believe, relatives, she appeared to respond to me with a sign of consent; since then, her anxious and urgent agitation has often manifested the need she is experiencing to quit this tower, which must remind her of such frightful memories.

"I'll come to what concerns you personally. The desire that Mario testified to see you again here is easily explained by a story that Solbioski kept to himself, and which he communicated to me yesterday. The spectacle of what he called his happiness, the unfortunate young man, was the smallest price by which he could recognize your generous amity. Another motive has come to supplement that one, if I can judge by this letter from Chasteler, which charged him to let you know that the warrant for your arrest has been lifted in France, and the advice ought to have reached the Venetian authorities. No new evidence has been able to compromise you since then, and nothing opposes your return, finally, to your father's arms. Your security demands that, as does your happiness, for if you were surprised in the Torre Maladetta, in which such cruel circumstances have dissimulated your sojourn, you could not escape the proscription that has afflicted its last inhabitants.

"I know what you want to say to me, but that blind proof of a futile devotion would only embarrass our misfortune with one misfortune more. You have, in any case, a more sacred mission to fulfill today. Diana's condition does not permit that she be abandoned to herself in order to reach her last retreat, and where, in the midst of the sad concerns that my own family inspires in me, could I find a more faithful and more reliable friend than you? Try, then, to recover your strength in a more abundant and more solid meal, and get ready to leave with her this evening when the sun has set, for nothing indicates to the vigilance of our spies the place from which you will leave. You'll find a boat fully prepared at Porto Gruaro, and Diana is expected at the convent.

"Now go, my son," he continued, hugging me in his arms, "and suffer that I occupy myself with my pressing dispositions without tenderizing our separation with longer adieux. Old as I am, I shall not renounce yet seeing you again, but whatever happens, conserve your heart for your friends and your life for liberty."

As soon as night had entirely fallen and it was dark—for the moon was no longer shining—one of the doctor's domestics came to inform me that the carriage was ready, and conducted me to the place where I was to take it. I climbed into it and sat down facing two women that I could not see.

Two hours later we were in Porto Gruaro; a few more minutes and we were sailing over the lagoons. I had offered my hand to Diana in order to climb into the boat, and her hand, forcefully linked to mine, had not abandoned it. She did not speak, but she sighed, dreamed, and sometimes drew nearer to me, trembling, as if she had been seized by a sudden fear.

That scene is vague in my memory, and yet I never recall it without shivering. It had something of the journey of two shades on the boat of the Underworld, but two shades of a different anticipated sentence, condemned to two different destinies, who are about to be separated for eternity. I fell asleep nevertheless to the monotonous sound of the oar, which was beating the waves rhythmically, and the melancholy song of the boatmen.

I only woke up to the movement of the waves that announced the open sea. The sun was more beautiful than I had ever seen it, the sun that I had believed that I would never see again. The azure of the gulf unfurled beneath it like another sky, and Venice, with its high frontons, its towers, its domes and its steeples, was radiant in its aspect, as if it were its palace. The immense plain of the waters was like a great parvis of lapis before the miraculous city. I thought that I was still asleep, for I had almost forgotten how to live and how to enjoy my life.

Diana's hand still reposed in mine; I turned toward her in order to know whether she shared my enchantment, and whether she had been reborn, like me, to that brilliant resurrection of nature. Her motionless gaze only expressed the silent despair that I had read there in the Torre Maladetta. I remember that, among those pompous facades that were illuminated by turns in passing from the most tender pink to the most vivid vermilion, and that hue akin to that of fire, illuminated as if for a day of joy, she was able to recognize the dwelling of her father. I recalled that less than three months before, perhaps the same boat had furrowed the same waves, transporting her, dazed by love, on Cinci's heart. All that was represented vividly to my thought; I contained my foolish expansion; I ceased to be happy and delighted; I fell back with an inexpressible anguish into the sorrows of the real world.

My hand had relaxed, for I did not understand how it had been interlaced with her fingers for such a long time. I don't know whether Diana understood me. Why not? There are so many things in that language. But she retained me. I looked at her, and I thought I saw a dolorous smile pass over her lips, like a flash of lightning over clouds.

We disembarked in the midst of an active and tumultuous population of seamen.

"Alas," said a nicollotto who was standing on the shore awaiting a burden, "that's the boat of the brave Cinci, who gave his deniers to the poor mariners of Gruaro, but the brave Cinci is no longer there!"

"Shut up," I said to him, in a manner to cover his voice, while slipping a sequin into his hand. "Take the packages that will be given to you and carry them to the Annunziat; but don't speak, on your head."

Fortunately, Diana's vague attention was distracted then by the hasty cares of two lay sisters who had been waiting for her since daybreak; the worthy young women had only ceased glorifying the piety and sanctity of their convent when they had understood that Diana was mad and that she was mute. They walked ahead of us, rolling the polished beads of the rosary in their agile fingers all the way to the threshold of the holy house. The door opened and we were introduced ceremoniously into the reception room.

The abbess was French. She had been beautiful, among the young and beautiful women of the emigration, and her name, which is no longer written anywhere but her tomb, poor Claire, would have been sufficient for her worldly glory, if such virtues still had anything in common with the world.

She took me by the hands with abandon, and with tenderness, although there were other sisters present, because we had known one another as children.

"I know, dear Maxime," she said, "everything for which our beloved sister is indebted to you. You will have your recompense one day, my son, if you seek it in Heaven. Adieu!"

In the meantime, Diana had looked at me with more attention, as if she were only learning to recognize me; then she plunged back into her thoughts. I drew away slowly.

"Maxime! Maxime!" she finally cried, in a clear and strong voice. "Adieu, Maxime! Adieu forever!"

At the same moment, two doors closed: the one that cloistered her in that house of refuge and peace, and the one that threw me back in order to perish in the midst of the troubles and anxieties of life.

I marched under the ardent sun, aimlessly and almost devoid of thought. My forehead was burning. Confused ideas were colliding in my mind; my unsteady legs were giving way beneath me. When I arrived at my usual hotel I collapsed, overwhelmed by dolor and, I lost consciousness.

I spent the next three months in alternations of delirium, the mental inertia of an ataxic fever. I only learned afterwards, by the comparison of dates, how long that had lasted. I recall nothing of it.

I finally found myself in a condition to leave Venice on the sixteenth of July. My strength was far from reestablished, but I was in haste to get away from the cruel impressions that all the objects by which I was surrounded renewed incessantly in my soul. I went out a ten o'clock, although the boat was not due to be ready until midday.

I sat down, in accordance with my former custom, outside the Café Florian, in the gallery of the tower, and asked for a chocolate.

There was a crowd to either side of me; people were reading newspapers hastily, and all the insouciance that the profound weakness of my faculties could inspire did not prevent me from lending a vague attention to what was happening. For more than a hundred days, in that memorable epoch when every day furnished a page to history, I had been as much a stranger to earthly events as if the trap-door of the Torre Maladetta had not reopened over me. I knew, at the most, by a few of the words of Doctor Fabricius, that the hopes of liberty had gradually been lost for Germany as for France, and I chanced to remember that. I therefore cast a glance over the newspaper. It was Abbé Coletti's *Courrier de Trieste*.

People gathered in order to hear the last lines of the *Bulletin*. I listened.

"The victory won on the sixth of this month at Wagram by the Emperor's arms," said the Italian reader, with his picturesque accent and his mimic declaration, "has destroyed forever the hope of the enemies of France and of the human race. Never has the magnanimity of his Imperial and Royal Highness been manifest with more splendor; it has covered with his indulgence the aberrations of peoples. The law will only strike the seditious.

"The castle where the conspirators assembled, which belonged to the so-called Marius Cinci, nicknamed the Doge of Venice, has been razed. A multitude of cadavers has been found in the subterrains. An infamous agent of intrigues named Fabricius, but in whom it is believed that the illuminate Hooschmann has been recognized, an accomplice of Arndt, Palm and Chasteler, has succeeded in escaping thus far, He is being pursued.

"A price has been put on the head of the coward and hypocrite André Hofer. That monster, covered with crimes, will not escape the punishment that is due to him. His secretary, Joseph Solbiesky, a Bohemian adventurer, supposedly Polish, has already been captured. Solbiesky is a cunning, ferocious bandit of uncommon strength; he will receive prompt justice."

Solbioski! I said to myself. *Solbioski ferocious and cunning—
and the wretches don't even know his name!*

I bit my fists with rage and despair. Oh, why had I not died
in the Torre Maladetta?

"Wait, wait, Messieurs," said the reader smiling. "There's a
postscript from the editor.

"This morning, the thirteenth of July, at ten thirty precisely, at the tip of the Point Saint-André, the traitor Joseph
Solbiesky was executed by firing squad in the presence of an
innumerable population. The wretch showed some courage."

How I Gave Myself to the Devil

Do not be frightened, debonair and pious friends, by the incendiary title of this story.

I attest to you that I do not believe myself to be damned, and that this is a matter, at the most, of a case of conscience that the slightest *absolvo* of your village curé would regulate amiably; but, in sum, I am growing old rapidly, and very rapidly, since the world no longer amuses me, and I would not be sorry to have a clear heart regarding the least of my scruples.

I confess, therefore, that I have had two great and puerile passions in my life, and that they have absorbed it entirely.

The first of the two great and puerile passions that I have had in my life was the desire to find myself the hero of a fantastic story, to put on the hat of Fortunatus or the Ogre's book, or to perch stupidly on the golden branch alongside the blue bird.

You might tell me that the desire in question is inexcusable in an intelligent creature who has made extensive studies, but it was my mania.

The second of the two great and puerile passions that I have had in my life was the ambition to write, before dying, a good fantastic story, very extravagant and very innocent, in the vein of Mademoiselle de Lubert[1] or Madame d'Aulnoy,

---

1 Mademoiselle de Lubert (1702-1785) was a leading contributor to the renaissance of unlicensed *contes de fées*, best-known for Princesse Camion (1743; tr. as "Princess Camion").

because Monsieur Perrault appeared to me to be too strong, and to amuse by that means, at least for a few generations, a small posterity of merry children with plump and rosy cheeks and alert gazes, who would remember my inventions during the most arduous hours of labor, and even in delightful hours when they are not doing anything.

As for the other posterity that you know, a pale, emaciated, insignificant, stupid figure that will be pointed out to you at the next salon, and which holds suspended at the end of two skinny arms, two meager crowns of plaster laurels, I swear to you on my honor that I have never thought about it.

At any rate, I cannot hide it from myself that those two frenzies have singularly discolored my real life and my sad métier of a frivolous storyteller.

It is necessarily so.

Far be it from me to recite a patent fact, an event that happened *coram populo, senatu et patribus*;[1] one of those stories on the sincerity of which one could go to the devil without anyone crying fantasy.

I am talking about three charming women that I loved very much, in all honor, and whom I have seen die in five years.[2]

"Three women dead in five years! But that's a fantastic, absurd fable!"

Wait, Monsieur, if you please. I loved seven hundred during that time, which renders the mortality rate a little less hyperbole.

In any case, I am talking to you deliberately and very exclusively about my posthumous amours, because another genre of confidences would have been in bad taste in my youth, and I suppose that nothing has changed in the matter of decency.

1 Before the people, the senate and the patricians.
2 This statement makes no sense unless one assumes that the present narration, which followed soon after "Mademoiselle de Marsan" in the pages of the *Revue de Paris*, was also supposed to follow "Célestine" and "Amélie" there.

The modesty of these mysteries will only be freed from its veils by taking on those of mourning and widowhood, and it is only then that the dolor of the survivor is permitted the respectful and delicate effusion of a long-hidden sentiment.

"Well, all the more reason, damn it! Fantastic! A fantastic story if there ever was one!"

Fantastic, if you wish; fantastic, since it is necessary.

Alas, I ask for nothing better; I would dearly like to find the fantastic in my memories. What would I not exchange for a little of the fantastic, especially when I have known the truth of this world, when experience has made me perceive it and absorb it through every pore?

The fantastic—my God! I would have given ten years of my life, and made a good bargain, to have encountered a sylph, a fay, a sorcerer, a somnambulist who knew what he was talking about, an ideologue who understood it; to meet a gnome with flamboyant hair, a ghost with a dressing-gown of mist, a will-o'-the-wisp as big as nothing, an imp more succinct in body and poorer in spirit than any that has ever blighted the parsley since the devil of Papefiguière.[1]

Impossible, Monsieur! If there had been anything fantastic for three thousand leagues around, it would have been for me; but there was none!

And I do not know, in truth, if anything poetic would ever have happened to me in the marvelous world if I had not yielded one day to the strange idea I had of giving myself to the devil.

That is, frankly speaking, a rather hard resolution, but it simplifies the question admirably.

In the epoch of which I am speaking I would have been very sorry not to be reputed as a bad lot, firstly because it was

---

1 "Le Diable de Papefiguière" is a fable in verse by Jean de La Fontaine, the name of the mythical land in question being derived from *papefigue*, a word coined by Rabelais to indicate someone who makes a rude gesture at the pope, i.e., a heretic.

fashionable, and then because it is agreeable to occupy women who are only ever occupied with bad lots.

I had, therefore, become a bad lot, and I had taken licenses, to the great regret of my excellent father, who paid my professors dearly for me to take the most honorable licenses; but I ought to say right away, in order to forearm the reader against the infallible disgust that attaches to the renown of Lovelace and Monsieur le Chevalier de Faublas,[1] that I was nothing similar; truly, I refrained carefully. You will not find in my entire history three pages that could make your valet de chambre envious of my good fortune, if you have one—and I hope you have not, for it is a great embarrassment.

I was a bad lot without prejudice to morality or sentiment, a timorous bad lot with regard to anything that might impose respect, or anything that might alarm decency: one of those amiable conquerors who only attempt their invasions in the land of good will.

However, everyone knew that I was a bad lot because I was an overt bad lot, an advertised libertine, a known seducer of anyone who wanted to be seduced, in order to do myself honor.

Save for that enormous fault, I dare say that no one had principles more settled regarding morals, and that I applied to them always and everywhere a degree of Judaic observance, the combination of which, incredible with my expansive disorder, was not typical of my time.

One could now call that eclectic debauchery, or doctrinaire libertinage, but it is not worth the trouble, because it is no longer encountered, the times having become too bad.

In order to make my philosophy comprehensible—for it was a philosophy, if you please—it is necessary to set an

---

1 Lovelace is the rake in Samuel Richardson's *Clarissa* (1748); *Les Amours du Chevalier de Faublas* (1787) is a libertine novel by Jean-Baptiste Loubet de Couvray (1780-1797), a radical Jacobin lucky to survive the Terror—but not for long.

example alongside the definition, and I am still afraid that I might not be understood.

The idea of troubling for a moment an innocent heart that society refused me, the idea of loosening in the slightest, by a criminal action, a bond that society had formed, would have been sufficient to make me suffer a very real anticipation of the woes of Hell.

I would have run away at Clarens at the first significant smile of Julie d'Étanges,[1] for fear of her bitter kisses. I would have left my cloak in the hands of Potiphar's pretty wife, even if it was worth as much as Elijah's, by means of which one became a prophet; but nothing stopped me from tasting a fruit that had lost its flower, and which had fallen from the nourishing branch without being plucked by the disdainful hand of the gardener.

"My word," I said, "it's agreeable and sweet, and I can savor it without doing anyone any harm."

With the consequence that if the master had chanced to be there I could have replied to his reproaches: "I beg your pardon, master; I'm not stealing, I'm gleaning."

And that conviction had procured me the inappreciable security of heart that is the first recompense of virtue.

That is precisely why I was a bad lot then, which had caused me to be called a bad lot *par excellence*, like a veritable prototype of the species.

I came to saying things to myself so flattering that I have some shame in adding further to them.

However, I owe it to myself, as they say, for the exactitude of this story, which is almost the only thing in the marvelous genre that I have written; the only marvelous thing is another matter, and that is a matter of taste.

The most extraordinary result of my theory was that I recruited pupils among the good and worthy young men of my

____

1 Rousseau's "nouvelle Héloïse."

age, born with a singular aptitude for perfectibility, and who I fortunately succeeded in turning away from crime by means of the facility of vice, while waiting for my lessons to bear the best fruit and convert them completely.

Twenty years later, they were model citizens.

Time has done them no harm, but it is perhaps to me that they owe having no remorse, a pleasant and precious lightness for their old age.

I do not know how it came about, but women of good company held us in execration.

The first of my acolytes was named Amandus. He was my lieutenant, my twin, my alter ego in all those affairs of the heart in which the heart had no involvement, which were multiplied solely by the act of will, uncomplicated by the slightest condescension to politeness, which would reduce a pacha without auxiliaries to becoming war-weary in a week.

Amandus was, in sum, a complete fine fellow.

With a costume to be painted, the gift of the gab and an overwhelming conceit, he played all games to perfection and never gambled without losing; mounted a horse like a centaur and broke a limb every month; handled a sword like Saint George and routinely emerged from duels with his arm in a sling.

Heir to a fairly considerable fortune, he had dissipated it in six months, which was evidence of great intelligence, and still found debts to pay, which is evidence of even more.

Finally, there was only one cry in his regard when he traversed a drawing room, which was that Amandus was charming.

Amandus had no common sense. Amandus' excellent education had been neglected on one point that certain pedestrian minds held to be capital. There are spots on the sun. Whether by virtue of incapacity or preoccupation, Amandus had never been able to learn to write.

I am inclined to believe that it was because he did not feel the necessity, and that disdain hid a very philosophical idea.

It was not that Amandus could not have written if he had wanted to, but that he was better off if he did not. It was not that he did not have his own orthography, when necessary, but it was so much his own that no one could understand it—which is not the same as being unable to find fault with it.

If I told you that it was the orthography of Monsieur Marle,[1] which will one day be that of the Académie, you would doubtless respond that there is no great harm in writing like the Académie, especially if you are in the Académie, as that can happen to anyone; but it was not the orthography of the Académie, it was the orthography of Amandus, a miraculous orthography!

Amandus had taken the view, contrary to Monsieur Marle, that genius in writing consisted of disguising the spoken word with all the figures that he had seen scattered in his spelling-book. He used all the articles, all the pronouns, all the particules, all the parasitic letters of the last portion of plurals; the accent on mute or atonic letters; the trema on diphthongs the apostrophe in the middle of a word; beautiful capitals and commas—my God, commas especially, never had so many commas been seen!

In the habits of vulgar amour that I mentioned, that was of no consequence; the majority of our heroines could not read; but if they had been able to read, they would have been in a cruel embarrassment.

There were, however, difficult occasions, chances of gallant notabilities, in which I became an immense help with my trivial orthography, which I had not judged it appropriate to enrich with all those magnificences.

---

1 Charles-Louis Marle was an enthusiastic promoter of phonetic spelling in the 1820s, but his suggestions never caught on; the Académie of which he was president was not *the* Académie but one of his own invention, which was retired to oblivion.

The only one of Amandus' friends who had remained faithful after he was ruined, I devoted myself bravely to the interpretation of those hieroglyphs, the impenetrable obscurity of which would have cause the savant shade of Champollion to shudder.

I had given up on Hebrew; I applied myself to Amandus. I succeeded in reading it fairly fluently after three or four months, and I finally risked substituting my own ideas when a scabrous and rebellious text defeated my erudition or fatigued my patience. Translators often make the same decision when they can no longer understand their author.

Amandus, despoiled of his grammatical luxury, then copied word for word and letter for letter, like Homer under the dictation of Apollo. The comparison is a trifle elevated, but not too disproportionate.

That time, I will admit, was not lost for my studies, for I learned in that way to turn out a love letter appropriately, and I had previously been obstinate in never writing any.

Writings remain.

We did not frequent what is known as bad company, but the nature of our occupations rarely took us to that called good. Nomadic voyagers in the midst of life, we pitched our venturesome tents every evening between two worlds in which we participated equally, retained in the first by the bonds of education and habitude, continually recalled to the second by convenient pleasures and conquests devoid of alarms.

If the topography of that double hemisphere is not exactly known to you, I shall have the advantage of informing you that the contingent point between them is occupied by the theater, and in order to characterize the locality more precisely, by the first gallery in good provincial towns.

Scarcely had the curtain lifted than a dozen brown or blue eyes—I am talking about ensemble scenes—came to seek us out on our divan, and to welcome us with delectable reproaches and seductive promises.

The furtive gaze of a beauty who was sighing from the wings before making her entrance, peeped at us mischievously from behind Harlequin's cloak, or sprang in flashes through the enormous gaps of an ill-fitting frame between two painted canvas rose-bushes. She finally entered, deploying the riches of the throat of a nightingale, or any other throat that it pleases you to substitute for that one. She entered to the flattering murmurs of an assembly that only seemed to be applauding for us, for we provided half of all the ovations.

It seems to me that we sometimes also had our part in the whistles, but it's necessary to know how to adapt to circumstances. I even feel sure that of the two of us, I was the more interested in the disgraces, because my impatient and fickle character rendered me luckier, but Amandus and I shared as brothers and did not keep score.

I remember, without going any further, that my evil destiny had imposed on me that months a five-foot-seven-inch Dugazon with an ample figure, but designed for the gold-braided coat of a drum-major rather than the corset of shepherdess. When she played Babet[1]—God, what a Babet!—and happened to favor me with an amiable wink while rummaging through a basket of wilted flowers with her stout hands and singing in a voice fortunately more delicate than her formidable person: "It's for you that I'm arranging them . . ."—oh, believe me, I would have blessed the beneficent blade that might have pierced my breast.

But what can one do?

It was one of the essential conditions of my happiness, because it was one of the indispensable safeguards of my innocence.

I have forgotten to say that she was very ugly, but she squinted horribly.

The other half of the world was in the boxes, and this is quite clear if you will be kind enough to follow my metaphor.

---

1 In *Blaise et Babet* (1783), the *opéra comique* by Nicolas Dezède.

Our morality forbade us to look at the boxes, but not to see them, and by virtue of having seen what it good to see, one looks at it. That is because there is always, in one of the boxes of the small theater of a small town—and I shall not tell you exactly which town it was, in order that you are perfectly free to seek it in the west—in the third box to the right, one of those angelic faces that damn men and make saints dream.

I cannot paint, but you can paint her marvelously if you have a palette. Posit sixteen years, the figure of a reed, white but animate skin, beneath which blood circulates like a spirit of life, coloring everything without blushing at anything, blonde hair that floats like a mist above shoulders over which the gaze runs as a hand might; heighten that with something pure and celestial that cannot be described, features that would have forced the sculptor of Venus to cut his throat with his chisel, and a wide blue gaze that enchants like the heavens and burns like the sun, and you will only have the idea of a thousandth part of Marguerite's perfections.

Marguerite had lost her father and mother while very young. The poor child had been left with an annual income of eighty thousand francs in the care of a maternal aunt, a widow still alluring, so little past forty that it is scarcely worth mentioning, and whom no one accused of being insensible to the sighs of a smitten heart.

I had found myself very keenly, and even very significantly, smitten with her—the aunt, that is—two or three years before, and that had cost me God knows how many hours of projects, anguish and hope, but with no other result, because that passion had overtaken me on the eve of the day to which the memorable era of my philosophical amours dates back.

Since then I had not thought about her once, even in ecstatic moments when the soul is cradled between two slumbers, and my imperturbable memory, so faithful to the names of flies and butterflies, might even have lost the name of the aunt if the aunt had not had a niece.

I have no need to say that the age and the innocence of that charming child—it's the niece that is in question now—cast an insurmountable interval between her and me. Eighty thousand francs of income was even worse. I scarcely had capital on loan.

"You're breaking our rules," Amandus said to me one day. "You're looking at the boxes."

"As children dead without baptism gaze at Heaven from Limbo," I replied, "and without summoning a gaze in response from so high. Besides which I have my reasons, and will not make you a mystery of them.

"Time marches pitilessly while we believe that we are eternalizing the present in a few hours of folly; and, handsome young fellows as we are, we risk growing old, just like as the seven sages of Greece.

"You still have in prospect a pleasant enough life passed between the amiable leisure pursuits of idleness and the gallant exercise of hunting foxes in the groves of La Vulpiniere if your uncle, disarmed by a more exact conduct, wished to leave to you at his death, which cannot be long delayed, his dilapidated manse, his dovecot and is brushwood.

"Personally, I have no uncle, no manse, no dovecot, no brushwood and no hopeful foxes, and will be very fortunate, when my creditors have shared out my sad spoils, to find a public kind enough to read my romances, and above all to buy them. I therefore need, in order to inspire me, some type that will live forever in my memory, some adorable figure of whom to dream, to caress and to nourish in my thought; and when I encounter her, I take her."

"Little Marguerite," said Amandus, deploying his opera-glasses and turning them brazenly toward the divine figure before which my eyelids were lowered by admiration and respect. "She's veritably angelic, divine, almost unimaginable . . . an apparition, a phenomenon. A ravishing privilege of innocence, a strange sympathy of beautiful souls! Alas, my virtuous friend, what a pearl, what a diamond she would be, at a milliner's counter or in a chorus line! Blind fortune has spoiled everything—but it never does otherwise. It's necessary to admit that destiny has been horribly stupid to perch that delectable face in a carriage instead of showing it to us between two Argand lamps in the corridor of sighs."

I quivered with indignation.

The corridor of sighs was the fourth to the left.

"Well, inspire yourself," said Amandus, leaning his head on my shoulder, and sprawling in his banquette, to my great scandal, for Marguerite could see us. "Inspire yourself with Marguerite, if it suits you, for I have more dealings than ever with your inspiration. Write romances, Maxime, write romances! Mine, if I'm not mistaken, is approaching a fortunate denouement. My uncle doesn't lack good will toward me, and I know that he's decided to assure me of a slender fortune on the day when I perform my first act of wisdom by marrying honorably."

"Marrying honorably!" I cried. "Do you think so, Amandus? You're thinking of marrying?"

"Why not?" he continued, with a burst of laughter. "Do you think me incapable of a serious idea and a firm resolution? My God, how ugly Aglaé is today, and how suitable the bad taste of her costume is to her elephantine simpering! It's necessary to put an end to it, Maxime, an honorable end, a serious and very serious end, when one no longer has any money. That's my uncle's opinion, and it is wisdom. You don't know what wisdom is, but it will come to you. Look, she's singing off key now.

"Inspire yourself, therefore, in order to turn me out a little declaration, very expressive, very passionate, very sincere; a confession without overlooking my weaknesses and my errors, anything you wish; I shan't look at it. Carve, slice, augment if

you wish, retrench if you dare. You're my conscience, you're
my heart, you know all that reposes of tenderness and good
sentiment in this fraternal bosom that is beating against yours.
Have you noticed that possessed by Laure, who has not taken
her eyes off me this evening? But she has to pinch her lips; she
has two teeth missing."

"It would be more appropriate," I said, without paying
attention to his digressions, "if I had some idea of the fortunate girl who has fixed your choice, in order to match my
correspondence to the suitability of your proposal. *Est modus
in rebus; sunt certi denique fines* . . . And then, I can't guess . . ."

"There's no finesse or rebus, Maxime; and if you guessed
you'd truly know more than I do about the future into which
I'm diving head first in order to save myself from the present.
If you guessed, I'd beg you to tell me what I think, and who
is the object to which the first of my reasonable amours is
attached.

"I'm not asking you to guess, by all the devils; I'm asking you for a gracious and formal circular, in good style, like
Télémaque or *La Pricesse de Clèves,* which could be addressed to
anyone, an epistolary passport, a document of your invention
that I can risk playing in the lottery of marriage. Talk about
candor, virtue, beauty; don't bother with hair color, because
that might make me fall into error. I'll copy everything with
exactitude; the post and my star will take charge of my hopes,
and my worthy uncle, who wants me absolutely to take a
wife, will have nothing for which to reproach me when I can
demonstrate to him that I've been refused by five. Or two,
three, or a dozen will come—I don't know how many—and
then you can choose immediately after me, better than me
perhaps. You have such a fortunate hand!"

The traitor! Aglaé was singing, though . . .

"Me!" I replied, bitterly. "Leave it out. I don't have the
domain of La Vulpinière!"

"What! Does the feeble hope grip your heart? I'll wager it against your horse, or Aglaé, at the first foray."

"I sold my horse yesterday; I'll give you Aglaé this evening, if you wish: as for the letter, I'll do it if I think about it . . ."

The correspondence took its course, for, to my great surprise and doubtless that of Amandus, it was not at the expense of his initiative. I only judged its progress, however, by its importunities, for he had become discreet and I have never been curious.

When we reached the stage of formal proposals I fell from my perch. The difficulties no longer proceeded from anything else, and I was astounded by the idea that Amandus had found someone sufficiently intrepid to believe his incredible promises.

We still went to the theater, but rarely—Amandus especially, who was beginning to maintain, in accordance with his promise, a certain respectability. Unfortunately, I was retained, as you know, by another bond; my colossal shepherdess had not yet staved in the boards, and no man bold enough to rid me of her had been found, although it was a good time of passage for the cavalry. I did not feel at ease at the arrival of a regiment of dragoons, brilliant with epaulettes, dust and glory, whose horses whinnied under her window.

Vain hope! The hussars followed them, but those butterflies of pleasure and war, who steal pollen everywhere, did not even deign to brush Aglaé with a wing-beat.

I counted in vain on the proven courage of the cuirassiers; Aglaé reserved in that long proof all the honors of a cloudless fidelity, and took advantage of all her rights. She was an impregnable woman, of mortal constancy. Of all the inconveniences that I have endured from amour, her virtue is the one that gave me the greatest desire to blow my brains out.

I was only looking for a pretext to exile myself forever from the world, and it was the purest of my moral sentiments that furnished it to me, at the moment when I least expected it.

I had already remarked that Marguerite was paying more attention to us than I would have wished. For some time, that preoccupation had even taken on a character that worried me, the expression of an affectionate interest, a dreamy sensibility, something vague, tender and ideal that announces in the modest face of a young woman the development of a secret penchant.

Misfortune and desolation, I said to myself. *Will you be condemned by your unlucky star, poor and gracious child, to love one of us two? Oh, at least I will not be accomplice to its rigor. The time of the examinations is coming, and I haven't opened a book in preparation. Well, I shall renounce in favor of hard work all those temporary deceptions that are called sensualities. I shall read, if necessary, the ten volumes of Jacobus Cujacius in the edition of Annibal Fabroti,*[1] cum promptuariis; *I shall read then,* horresco referens, *before occupying myself with a woman, and I take as my witness the shade of Justinian!*

With that, I left the auditorium and went home, in order to dispatch a definitive dismissal to Aglaé.

I have no need to tell you that the resolution in question liberated me from a great burden. There was probably a persuasive assurance in the communication of my new plan that I made the next day to my father, for he immediately made me a present, in recognition of my sacrifice, of his entire library and the pretty pavilion that contained it; they were the two things he loved the most, after me.

I spent the day arranging everything that might serve for my studies or to embellish my voluntary exile, and I perceived, at the satisfaction with which those agreeable cares gave me, that happiness had more than one aspect.

What am I saying! The pure happiness of soul content with itself prevails over our imaginary happiness in its duration as

---

1 Charles Annibal Fabrot (1580-1659), the publisher of hundreds of abstruse Latin texts, including the works of the humanist expert on Roman law Jacques Cujas (1522-1590).

well as its object. I was happy until the evening; never had so much arrived.

In the evening I yawned; I looked at my watch twenty times in ten minutes; the first stroke of the orchestra bow pursued me; the almost discordant noise of the boxes opening and closing resounded in my ears; my nostrils solicited in vain in an atmosphere that was, alas, too pure, the nasty aroma composed of the vapor of fuming lamps and the exhalation of perfumes.

I requested the delectable gaze of Marguerite from all the attics and all the wainscots; I asked for it from all the shelves of my library, but my eyes only encountered Annibal Fabroti's Jacobus Cujacius.

I would be curious to know, I finally said to myself, *whether her gazes were for him or for me, and, as he has hired a post chaise this morning, he must be traveling. A better opportunity to clarify my doubts will never be presented, I shall be all the more confirmed, whatever the result, in the reasonable plans that I have made. I'll work tomorrow!*

This time there was no mistake; I declare that to you with all the conceit that the most unexpected amorous windfall can inspire in a fool. Those gazes were for me, for me alone! You might tell me that I was alone, and that, like the marvelous fossil whose marvelous pores, amorous of the light, still contain a few pale atoms of it long after sunset, I was perhaps for Marguerite only the Bologna stone of Amandus. That idea did not occur to me; and anyway, if I knew what I was about—and what man does not believe that he knows what he is about—there was in the intelligent and significant expression of that physiognomy a thought that could only relate to me, and was only awaiting from me the exchange of a thought.

I tried, I shivered with comprehension, I armed myself with a heroic courage, and I fled the death in the heart by dint of believing myself to be fortunate!

No, no, Marguerite, I shall not violate the sanctuary of your innocent soul in order to ignite or maintain therein a passion that would doom both of us! No, I shall not transplant your stem, so fresh and so delicate, with its embalmed flowers, into the sterile desert of my life! And yet, who, apart from me, could love you as you ought to be loved?

I would have been the altar of your feet, the harp of your sighs, the vase of your perfumes; I would have burned before you like incense; I would have been annihilated in the radiance of your eyes like a drop of dew in the midday sun. Oh, do not believe that I would have untied the strings of your virginal dress with male hands! I would have purified myself in the crater of a volcano before approaching you, and my lips would only have been glued to your breast through a veil, for fear of profaning it . . .

But you are rich, Marguerite, and there is no possible event that can despoil you completely enough of all your futile wealth to reduce it to the equal of my fortune. You would still be too far above me, and worthy of kings.

No, Marguerite, no, I shall never see you again—unless the devil involves himself with it . . .

In finishing that poetic rhapsody, the trivial ending of which spoiled the beginning slightly, I collapsed in my armchair, which was fortunately supple, elastic and profound. Dine lit three candles on my desk, an unaccustomed luxury of my nights, which testified with one proof more yo my family's satisfaction, and I remained delivered to my studious solitude.

I leaned over my balcony momentarily.

The sky was as limpid as a lake, enameled like a meadow.

Scarcely a breath of air could be heard in the branches of my young trees, and it seemed only to be traversing them, playfully, to bring forth a suave emanation. A nightingale was singing in the distance; moths were fluttering quietly under the leaves.

It was a beautiful evening for an amour other than the one that was known to me, a magnificent empyrean in which I would have liked to travel the innumerable spheres with the rapidity of the fires that were cruising there in all parts, but whose depths my soul could no more fathom than my eyes.

I closed everything in order to free myself from those immense distractions, and I sat down, with the intention of getting down to work once and for all, after having let one last smile of satisfaction fall upon the admirable order of my study.

Its description is no less necessary here than a map of Latium to Virgil's *Aeneid*. My father had had that pavilion constructed in happier times, between his courtyard and his garden, above a large coaching path, which could easily have accommodated in its flanks the cabriolet that I never had. The entire building only contained one long room shaped like a parallelogram, illuminated to the west and the east by ogival windows, and which overlooked to the south a garden of small extent but well-designed in its distribution. That point was the only one by which my room could be reached, whether one came from the courtyard or via the garden—which was not difficult, its narrow enclosure communicating on all sides by ever-open doors to the large enclosure of our neighbors. That was the philosophical rendezvous of Academus and his friends, excellent old folk, accustomed to see one another since childhood. The double spiral staircase that led from the balcony only had six steps, because it was elevated over a terrace.

The second of the narrow sides of the long quadrilateral, which faced the entrance, was occupied by my bed, a modest student's couchette, around which, arranged in a bell, a white curtain with long pleats was passed over a gilded spire. The rest of the interior walls offered nothing to the eye except the spines of old books.

My black table, shaped in a smaller proportion in the same figure as the little monoecious edifice, the memory of which still charms me, formed the exact center of it, but left free all the room necessary to circulate around it, and to measure the four faces in twenty-four or twenty-five paces, in a time that hastened and slowed by turns, at the whim of the stroller's emotions.

I covered a lot of ground that day. Nevertheless, I sat down, and extending my hand behind me negligently to the shelf on which my armchair was leaning, I tried to take down the first volume of the fine *Traité de la procédure civile* by Robert-Joseph Pothier, but brought back in front of me Dom Calmet's *Histoire des apparitions*—which is, as everyone knows, one of the finest collections of infernal buffoonery that one can read.[1]

The page was curious. I turned the leaf over six times.

What a pity, I thought, finally, *that such a learned man was able to give himself wholeheartedly to such nonsense, like an old village woman who dreams about spirits and demons while picking up dead leaves and a few sticks on the edge of the woods! I would truly like the devil to appear to me, and it's only up to me to evoke him, since I have here the* Clavicle of King Solomon *and the* Enchiridion of Léon[2] *in an authentic manuscript, the precious heritage of a Dominican of the family, who made use of that grimoire a thousand times for the deliverance of the possessed. The conversation of the devil in person would be as amusing and as instructive, if I'm not mistaken, as that of Pothier and Cujas, and if it is difficult to obtain that favor, which cost Agrippa and*

---

1 The actual title of Antoine Augustin Calmet's famous volume was originally *Dissertations sur les apparitions des anges, des demons et des esprits, et sur les vampires ou les revenants de Hongrie, de Bohême, Moravie et de Silésie* (1746; expanded under a slightly abridged title in 1752). The section dealing with apparitions of evil spirits is brief.

2 In the same genre as the older and more notorious *Key of Solomon*, the *Enchiridion Leonis Papae*, is an eighteenth-century hoax, pretending to be a book whose original was given by Pope Leo III to Charlemagne.

Cardan so dearly, at least it merits being attempted by a resolute mind.

It depended, in fact, on a simple act of my will, for I had that very evil grimoire before my eyes, between my writing-pad and my blotter.

I do not know whether the devil had put it there.

I extended trembling fingers toward it, as if the mere contact of the frayed parchment might have passed into my senses some influence of malediction.

It was only cold, dirty and unhealthy.

I unfolded its eight pleats without it exhaling the slightest atom of sulfur or burning bitumen. The earth did not tremble; the flames of my candles remained calm and pale over their blue stubs; my unshakable volumes remained asleep under the learned webs of their bibliophilic spiders.

I became emboldened; I tried to read; I launched into the air in a loud voice the solemn formulae of the spirit of Python, by which I commenced to be animated, to the extent of making my innocent windows resonate, which had never vibrated under such words.

But it was quite another grimoire than I had imagined. I had not read a dozen lines of the fatal book when I found myself interrupted by unintelligible and truly diabolical signs, by impenetrable symbols and letters unnamed in the alphabets of the earth, which cut off my speech.

Another might have lost courage at the sight of those gnomic monograms, those otherworldly hieroglyphs, which might well have been, in the final analysis, merely the caprice of a charlatan copyist.

Imprudent, but determined, I planted myself proudly amid my candles, and cried oit in an energetic voice: "Come to me, holy and credulous Sperberus, savant Khunrath, immortal Knorr von Rosenroth, and you, good Gabriel de

Colange,[1] who once used such a worthy life to render yourself the translator of the indecipherable Trithemius! Come, and develop for me these mysteries, of which only ignorance can be frightened!"

The devil did not budge any more than before, for it is necessary that I inform my readers that it was not the names of demons that I had just pronounced but quite simply the names of cabalists. Perhaps for the first time, those worthy authors saw their yellowed bookmarks, the broken corners of which had aged over the dust, floating over pages exposed to the light of candles.

I did not feel any surprise in comprehending, through the long labyrinth of a mad science, all that was necessary of leisure, patience, and above all of good will, to recover so much of dead languages, not excepting that of the angels, which is the most reliable; but a task does not frighten me when it amuses me.

I completed that in twenty minutes, which are sufficient to know all that it is useful to know, if one employs them well.

I declaimed the grimoire clearly, and, I dare say, faultlessly.

Midnight chimed as I finished, but the devil, who is essentially rebellious, did not come.

The devil very rarely comes; he no longer comes in the form that you know, and yet he is not proud of that, for he has all the intelligence necessary to take the most seductive when he is sure of having something to gain by it.

"It's necessary to agree," I said plunging back into my cushions, "that I've gambled for high stakes in that experiment in stupidity. What an embarrassment for me if he had appeared, asking me, as is customary, in a hollow and terrible

---

1 The references are to the alchemist and cabalist Julius Sperber (1540-1616), the hermetic philosopher Heinrich Khunrath (1560-1605), the cabalist Christian Knorr von Rosenroth (1636-1689) and to an eighteenth-century French translator of the 1508 *Polygraphiae* of Johannes Trithemius who signed himself Gabriel de Colange.

voice, what I wanted of him! One does not summon him with impunity. His questions require responses, and he's an adverse party of which one does not rid oneself like an inept barrister with some surly refusal.

"What grace would I have tried to obtain from his evil power in exchange for my poor soul, which I had thrown on to the green baize of damnation like a chip of small value?

"Money? What would be the point? The cards have been so favorable to me this week that the price of my horse has almost been multiplied tenfold in my purse; one gold coin more could not be contained there, and I could pay my creditors three times over if I wished.

"Knowledge? I have more of it than I need, without vanity, for my particular usage, and the honest people who have the generosity of taking a little interest in my future success have no difficulty in predicting that a pedantic varnish of good enough taste will spread over my works, if I ever write any.

"Power? God preserve me from that! One only succeeds in obtaining it at the price of repose and wellbeing.

"The gift of foresight, perhaps? A fatal advantage, for which it is necessary to pay with all the sweetness of hope and all the delights of uncertainty! The vagueness of life is what makes its charm!

"Women and adventures? That would be to abuse his complaisance; the poor devil is only too well exercised in that chapter . . .

"And yet," I continued, half asleep, "if he had presented me with that young Marguerite, so fresh, so delicious, so blonde, so rosy . . .

"Damn! That's another pair of sleeves, as Monsieur Buffon said.

"If Marguerite, emotional, palpitating, her hair in slight disarray, with a wisp hanging over her breast, and the breast almost liberated by a poorly-attached thread . . .

"If Marguerite, the beautiful Marguerite had suddenly climbed my staircase with a furtive step; if, having arrived at my door, she had knocked three times on it with a timid hand, desiring and dreading to be heard, *tap, tap, tap* . . . !"

I was half asleep, as you know and I repeated, vaguely, "*tap, tap, tap* . . .*" as I went to sleep entirely.

Tap, tap, tap . . . That—O incomprehensible marvel!—was no longer happening in the tenebrous regions of my soporific thought. I believed so momentarily, however; I bit my fingers until they bled to assure myself that I was awake,.

Tap, tap, tap . . . "Someone's knocking!" I exclaimed, quivering in all my limbs.

My clock chimed one.

Tap, tap, tap . . . I got up; I marched precipitately; I recalled and recollected my fearful intelligence.

Tap, tap, tap . . . I armed myself with one of my candles; I advanced resolutely toward the balcony; I opened the shutter.

O terror! Never had nature showed itself more ravishing to amorous eyes; I thought that I would die of fear.

It was Marguerite, leaning on the glass of the door, a thousand times more beautiful than I had seen her, more beautiful than one can imagine; Marguerite, emotional, palpitating, her hair slightly undone, one wisp hanging down over her breast, and the breast almost liberated by a poorly-attached string.

I made the sign of the cross; I recommended myself to God, and I opened the door.

It was really her; it was her soft, velvety, delicate hand; it was her trembling hand that I touched without burning myself.

Utterly nonplussed, I led her to my armchair and waited for a sign from her eyes to sit down nearby on a folding chair.

She learned on one of the arms of the armchair, her head on her hand, and veiled her face with her pretty fingers.

I waited for her to speak. She did not speak; she sighed.

"Dare I ask you, Mademoiselle"—it was me who commenced—"to what inconceivable hazard I owe such an astonishing visit?"

"What, Monsieur!" she replied, sharply. "My visit astonishes you! Was it not something agreed?"

"Agreed, Mademoiselle, agreed, that's true, although the convention has not been stipulated in accordance with all the forms requisite in such cases, and it is far from being as positive and valid in good justice as you appear to believe. Such strange ideas arise in a sick mind that an imprudent amour has led astray . . . In sum, to tell you the truth, I did not count at all on the good fortune . . . that is overwhelming me . . ."

I no longer knew what I was saying.

"I understand you, Monsieur; the denouement has put you off the enterprise. Accustomed to brilliant but facile pleasures, you had never measured the range of the sacrifices of veritable amour . . ."

"Stop, Marguerite, and don't outrage my heart. The range of the sacrifices of true love I know . . . or so I flatter myself."

(I found that one a trifle excessive, however.)

"But still, why has he not come? Why has he not accompanied you? It required between us, at least, the exchange of words that is the first condition of the synallagmatic contract. I don't know whether you know it."

"After having abducted me he quit me at the bottom of the staircase, and he will only come to collect me at daybreak."

"Collect you, my dear child? But I beg you to believe that I only treated for myself . . . if I treated. I would tell him that if he were here."

"He did not dare to show himself to you, because he foresaw your scruples."

"He did not dare to show himself, you say? Impossible! I did not believe him to be so timid."

"I suppose that he might have been frightened of the irritability of your sentiments and the delicacy of your principles . . ."

"I'm very obliged to him; that always gives one pleasure; but it's necessary, in the end, that I see him . . ."

"At sunrise, in three or four hours from now."

"Three or four hours," I said, expansively, drawing nearer to her. "Three or four hours, Marguerite!"

"And in the meantime, Maxime," she said, softly, drawing closer to me, "I have no shelter and no protector but you, since it's necessary that the doors are open to let the post-chaise pass through."

"Ah! It's necessary that the doors are open to let the post-chaise pass," I replied, rubbing my eyes like a man waking up.

"He would have spared you the anxiety and the responsibility of the service you are rendering us both if his respectable mother had not died last year of a pulmonary fluxion."

"Wait, Mademoiselle," I cried, pushing my folding chair with my foot to the other extremity of my study. "His mother is dead of a pulmonary fluxion! But who are you talking about?"

"I'm talking about Amandus, good Maxime, Amandus, who is so attached to you and whom you love so much. Since you don't know the details, learn that he came to fetch me this evening at the hour indicated between us to abduct me from my aunt's house, because she was obstinate in refusing him my hand. It was the only means, you'll agree, of obtaining a more favorable resolution from her; but as there was a soirée, the courtyard was full of comings and goings, and of domestics who would have perceived our flight, and we escaped through the gardens. Scarcely had he seen your lighted window than he said to me joyfully: 'You see, Marguerite, the sage and studious Maxime is still working; Maxime, who is my brother, my confidant, my providence; Maxime, who is not unaware of any of my secrets, and who will be only too glad—I know his heart—to give you shelter until daybreak. Go up and knock with assurance, Marguerite, while I arrange everything for our departure.' With that, he quit me. I came up, I knocked several times without reproach . . . and you know everything."

"I know it all too well; but all things considered, I prefer that to the other thing. The main thing, Marguerite, is that you can be happy. You have a very decided passion for Amandus, then? It's for him, isn't it?"

"For who else? I have only spoken to him three times, but he wrote with such a penetrating warmth, with such a persuasive tenderness! He expressed with such a passionate energy the sentiments that he felt for me, Amandus, my dear Amandus!"

"Wait, wait! It's his letters that you're talking . . ."

At that moment I stopped dead, because I was about to say something enormously stupid, according to all appearance.

I meditated my thought; like a character is a melodrama, I took refuge in a mysterious "aside." *No, no, my friend,* I said to the demon, *you have not entered by the weak side of amour; you shall not enter, I tell you, by that of vanity.*

"You find, then, that Amandus writes well," I murmured, with an affected insouciance, nailing my tongue between my teeth.

That's because, I thought, silently, *she's as intelligent as she is pretty.*

"You were distracted by another idea, Maxime, and that is not the reply that you wanted to make to me."

"Your observation is just, Mademoiselle. I did what you ought to have done—suffer that I tell you that—before making a resolution as hazardous and as temeritous as yours!"

"And what is that?"

"I reflected. Amandus lost his head, with good reason, when he took it into his head to make you spend the night, beautiful and sage Marguerite, in the room of a brainless fellow of my species, a man devoid of principles, with neither faith nor law, who nearly gave himself to the devil half an hour ago—a bad lot, in sum."

"You speak too rigorously, perhaps ironically, of two or three follies of a young man which do not compromise the character, and which do not lose you anything in the esteem of honest men. Amandus, who has a few faults of the same kind for which to reproach himself, justified himself in his letters with an eloquence by which even my aunt was touched, although she is extraordinarily rigorous. A bad lot, Maxime! Oh, you don't have the semblance of it!"

"I thank you, Mademoiselle, for the good opinion that you deign to have of me. But this long, mysterious meeting, excessively embarrassing—let's be clear—for the virtue that you are kind enough to suppose in me, is at least of a nature to render your innocence suspect to the vulgar wretches who make a less favorable judgment of my juvenile purity, and I shudder for you on thinking about it. Permit me, in the name of your reputation and out of compassion for mine, to find you another refuge until morning. I'll return to you momentarily and I leave you sovereign mistress of all your actions, except going out alone or opening the door to anyone."

I waited for her consent; I obtained it, and I did better. I made sure of it, *ne varietur*, by locking the door with a double turn.

My resolution was made, for I had the sharp and sudden ideas of youth.

There was a soirée at the house of Marguerite's aunt, I had just learned, and provincial soirées are of enormous length in all regards.

When I approached, the last carriages were drawing away; I slipped in, as nimble and subtle as a bird, between two lackeys who were about to lock up.

"Where is Monsieur going?"

"To see Madame."

"Everyone has gone."

"I've just arrived."

"Madame is going to bed."

"That's all right."

To that decisive response there was no objection, and ten seconds later I was in Madame's bedroom, where I had never set foot, either so late or so early, although I had sometimes thought about it.

The noise that I made caused her to turn round as she was about to undo—God forgive me!—the penultimate fastener.

"What horror!" she cried. "You, Monsieur . . . in my house . . . at this hour! In my bedroom! Without being announced, without regard for the most common decency!"

"As you say, Madame, I know none when I am obeying the impulsion of my heart."

"Eh!! Have your returned to your old frenzies, Monsieur? I beg you to keep all that display of sentiments, which are expressed with so much vehemence and forgotten so quickly, for a more appropriate moment."

"It would be difficult, Madame, to choose a better one, if I had to talk to you about the subject to which you attribute my visit, but I have been summoned to your home by more serious motives, which will not suffer any delay." I seized her hand. "In the name of Heaven, Clarice, listen to me!"

"Serious motives, you say! Some desperate resolution of which you are only too capable! You're frightening me, Monsieur, you're frightening me terribly, I know your recklessness, I have violence to dread, Monsieur; I'm going to ring."

"Refrain carefully, Madame," I said, taking possession of the hand that was still free and constraining her rather abruptly to sit down on her sofa. "This must pass between us, Madame, in the most profound mystery, far from all ears and all eyes, and it is at your knees that I implore you to listen to me for a moment! We have no time to lose!"

"Woe is me!" she sobbed, in a stifled voice. "I had to send my women away!"

"They would be in excess, once again, and if they were here, I would demand that they leave; the slightest outburst would doom you."

"But this is a trap, an assassination, an unimaginable crime! Monster, what do you want, then?"

"Almost nothing, and if you had listened to me you would already know what it is. Only do me the kindness of telling me where Marguerite is."

"Marguerite? My niece? What a strange question. What has Marguerite to do with the outrageous scene you are making? Marguerite goes to bed early, especially when I have guests. It is one of the scrupulous practices of the tender but stern education I have given her. Marguerite is in her room, in her bed; Marguerite is asleep; I'm as sure of that as of my own existence."

"God, who is the master of everything, might have permitted it, like so many inexplicable things that it is impossible to deny, but it would be very curious. In any case, that is her door, if my memory serves me right; it is easy to convince yourself that she has not gone out, if she really has not gone out, and to get us both out of an afflicting doubt that interests the responsibility of an aunt more than that of a neighbor . . ."

"Wake that child, Maxime, and wake her when there is a man in my apartment!"

"Oh, you won't wake her," I replied, making sure that my key was not absent from my pocket. "She is well awake, I'll answer for that, awake if anyone ever was, and if you find her asleep in her bed, the devil knows more today than in the days of Dom Calmet."

She picked up a candle, went in, took a few steps, and returned just in time to faint on the sofa. As I had expected that event I had furnished myself with a bottle of smelling salts from her dressing-table. I unfastened the belated clasp, struck lightly the ten plump fingers that were clenched on mine, and kissed their extremity even more lightly, with all the modesty of which I am capable.

I wanted to avoid a fit of nerves, because a fit of nerves drags on.

"We don't have the time to yield to futile emotions, beautiful and adorable Clarice." Where the devil does one get these things? "The circumstances demand a prompt resolution."

"I know that full well, alas! But who can I address except you, who have penetrated this horrible mystery—you, Maxime, the accomplice of this crime, perhaps the guilty party!"

"In truth, no," I said, sighing.

"You know where she is, Maxime! You know, my friend! You can't deny it! Return her to me."

"That, Madame, is forbidden to my loyalty; I have her secret, but it will not emerge from my heart, and you would scorn me if I abused it. What I attest is that she is under the guard of a man of honor, who will only return her to your hands when you have consented to let her pass into those of a husband, as is your duty, Clarice. Yesterday, it was a question, today, it is a necessity; that is what I have to tell you."

"A husband! Amandus, no doubt! A madman, a debauchee, a dissipater! A fine marriage, in truth!"

"One does not marry as one wishes, Madame, when one has been abducted, and the man who passes lightly over that scruple, in consideration of an opulent dowry, is a thousand times worse than a madman; he is a wretch. Amandus is not a very exemplary person, I agree, but a noble amour might correct him. My heart has never understood better than today the facility of that metamorphosis. I don't believe his debts to be considerable; he is an orderly man, and since he no longer has anything, he has been very regular in his expenditure. I know reliably, since it is him who has told me, that his uncle's

324

fortune will be assured to him by a marriage contract. The domain is not very productive, but it is a fine hunting-ground. As for the dowry of a minor," I continued, "it is easy to protect it against the dilapidations of an extravagant husband by means of fifty precautions of which I shall make it my duty to inform you as soon as I have finished my immense labors on Cujas, and that will not be long; I am spending entire days and nights on it; I was working on it only a few minutes ago.

"The alliance is, in every other respect, as suitable as can be desired, and even Amandus' faults do not obscure brilliant and honorable qualities in him; he is honest, loyal, kind and brave . . ."

"And he writes marvelously; he turns a letter to perfection; that's a justice that it's necessary to render him."

"What, Madame, you deign to think . . . ? It's an effect of your indulgence."

"Don't you share that opinion? I fear, Maxime, that you're speaking out of envy."

"On the contrary, Madame; I respond blindly to your liking; I only hope that you don't find the style somewhat uneven in future. But his style has nothing to do with the matter, as I understand matrimonial decency; it's a matter here of precautions and proprieties other than oratory precautions and proprieties. You will judge by means of ten minutes of reflection—and the urgency of the present situation does not leave you any more—the nature of the means to adopt to deflect from your household the scandal that threatens it.

"First of all, this changes nothing of your fortune. Marguerite is formed, as you can see; she is very advanced, extremely advanced for her age. It would have been necessary sooner or later to marry her, when you saw that she was ready to marry herself.

"Oh, she's a lovable child; it's very fortunate that she has fallen in love with a scatterbrain whose past life submits in advance to all concessions, instead of throwing herself at the head of a man with money or a man of law. The legal process would have entered your home by the same door as the sacrament if she had had the whim to become passionate about an advocate; you would have been obliged to involve yourself in it. I'm not saying that one can be passionate for an advocate; that's a supposition. With Amandus, there's no complication; he's so casual in business that there are days when he'd acquit you of the entire succession for a stack of corroded louis; he'd also be the man to pay the notary and give the head clerk a good tip: a sublime character!

"On the other hand, the child is visibly growing up. Her infantile beauty, which is very remarkable, will end up having the impertinent pretention to rival yours, and I've already heard fools crying from one box to another: 'That lovely person must have married very young!' They mistake you for her mother!"

"Fie, Maxime! I wasn't yet in school when she came into the world."

"To whom are you talking? In sum, the event has been pronounced, and I know that she is of a mind to put an end to your irresolution."

"It's easy for you to talk. The event! The event! It will not be known if she returns, and I can count sufficiently on your discretion."

"My discretion, Madame, is proof against anything—but Marguerite won't come back and the event will be publicized tomorrow. And even if Marguerite did come back, and the event chanced not to be publicized tomorrow, it probably would be between now and . . . Permit me," I continued, pretending to calculate on my fingers, for it was only an imaginative effort, the captious argument of a speech, recommended by rhetors. I leaned toward her ear then, and whispered a few words.

"What a horrible idea!" she cried, almost allowing herself to faint on her cushions.

"It is as I have taken the liberty of telling you; the world moves at a frightful pace!"

"Monsieur," she said, standing up with dignity, "You know Marguerite's retreat; go there, find her, and promise her on my oath that she will be Amandus' wife within a fortnight, since she wishes it . . . Well? You haven't gone?"

"On your oath, Madame? Can one not count on that for her happiness, as for that of others?"

"Go, go, Maxime. Kiss my hand, and bring back my niece—but don't go without fastening my clasp again. I'd appear in a fine state in her eyes!"

I took Marguerite back, after having convinced her by means of a further speech of the sincerity of the promises that I had just received for her.

The aunt was austere but reasonable, the child respectful but resolute. Things passed perfectly on either side; Marguerite embraced me. I would gladly have dispensed with that.

"You have accommodated many difficulties in a short time," the aunt said to me as she showed me out; "you're an admirable man for terminating family disputes; I hope that we shall see you at the wedding?"

"Yes, Madame, and we shall resume last night's conversation there at the moment when it commenced."

"If you wish . . . but you would lose nothing by resuming it where it ended."

That was very nice, but there are delightful words that lose much of their charm in not being mimed.

It's necessary to agree, I said, on returning to my pavilion, *that I have, in fact, accomplished in a few hours enterprises of intelligence and works of heroism that do not have much to cede to the labors of Hercules. First of all, I have learned the Grimoire without missing a word or a letter, a spirit or a sephiroth; sec-*

ondly, I have married with her lover, against all expectation, a young woman with whom I was passionately smitten and who did not appear too ill-disposed on her part to wish me well, since she did me the favor of coming to spend the night casually in my bedroom; thirdly, I have paid court to a woman of forty-five, if not older; fourthly, I have given myself to the devil, which is almost the only means of explaining how I have got to the end of so many marvels.

The last idea vexed my mind so much at the moment when I finished turning my key in the lock that I did not have the strength to take two steps on the carpet; luckily, I found inside the door the folding chair that I had thrown there brutally as I received Marguerite's unexpected confidence, and I sat down on it with my legs crossed, my arms folded and my head inclined under the weight of a chagrined meditation, sighing from time to time, like a soul in pain awaiting its judgment.

My eyelids, fatigued by long wakefulness and worry, only lifted slowly. Two of my three candles were extinct; the last was dying, throwing here and there vacillating gleams that lent strange movements and colors or unaccustomed shadows to all the objects.

Suddenly, I felt my hair stand on end and my blood freeze with horror. My armchair was occupied, like Banquo's in the tragedy of *Macbeth*; there was no doubt about it.

My first thought was to run directly toward the apparition. But my limbs, enchained by fear, refused their office to my impotent will.

I was reduced to measuring with a fearful gaze the thin, fleshless, livid specter that had come to take Marguerite's place, as if to punish me for the sin by a hideous parody of the illusions that it had produced.

It had indeed to be a phantom of a woman, to judge by the long tresses of her black hair, under which something vague and terrible was confusedly designed, which almost took the place of a face.

From the place where the shoulders ought to have been found in a creature of normal conformation, two thin and disarticulates arms of a sort descended to the two arms of the armchair, clinging to them at their extremities by means of a pair of pale claws, the leathery sheen of which heightened their whiteness. The accoutrement of the funereal larva consisted, moreover, in the simple apparel "of a beauty just snatched from slumber."[1]

"Protection of the Lord," I cried, raising my arms to the heavens, "will you abandon me in this terrible extremity? Will you not deign to descend, for pity's sake, on the unfortunate Maxime, who has—without knowing it and without wanting to, my God!—summoned the Devil in person to his father's house!"

"That's precisely what I imagined," responded the phantom, in a shrill voice, ranging itself up to its full height and falling back, as if thunderstruck, on the back of the chair. "May Heaven have pity on us!"

"What! Dine, is that you who spoke? By what miracle are you here, at this hour?"

Dine, whom I have named elsewhere without making her known, had been my mother's nurse half a century before, and while my mother was alive had never quit her. Since her death she had remained in the family, as the titled housekeeper and absolute governess.

I loved Dine tenderly.

"I haven't entered by a miracle," Dine replied, muttering. "I entered with the duplicate key that enables me to watch over all the cares of the household, and to tidy Monsieur's apartment in his absence."

"That's just as well, my good friend; but one scarcely tidies apartments at two o'clock in the morning—and you'll permit me to say," I added, smiling, for that turn of events had

____

1 The quotation is from Jean Racine's *Britannicus* (1669).

rendered me a little confidence, "that with your still-youthful physiognomy and your residual air of impropriety, the moment is singularly chosen to introduce yourself into the room of a young man who has given proof of temerity."

"It was necessary, bad joker, since you haven't let me sleep tonight—and what a vigil, Holy Virgin! A sound of imprecations to make one shiver! More diabolical words and names than there are saints in the litanies! Wandering lights going back and forth, black and white spirits falling naked into the garden, black spirits that come from both sides and white spirits that open your windows as if to take the air, humming theatrical ballads, and the most terrible of all, which took you away before my eyes to some purgatory, from which my prayers have probably extracted you! What have you done, Maxime?"

"Everything is explained marvelously, my poor Dine, and Dom Calmet himself could not have represented those infernal hallucinations with more energy and naivety. But since you're awake, it's necessary that you hear my response, for you're a woman full of intelligence, judgment and experience, and there's only you who can liberate me from my scruples. Listen to me then with attention, if you don't fall asleep."

With that, I recounted to her everything that I have just recounted—and I suppose that you will not be curious to hear it recounted twice.

I recounted it with a compunction so penetrating and an anxiety so sincere regarding the consequences of my sin that the Devil himself would have been touched if he had heard me.

When I had finished, I waited tremulously for Dine's response, as my supreme sentence.

She took such a long time that I feared that she had gone to sleep while I was recounting. That might have happened.

Finally, she took off her spectacles solemnly, which she had probably put on in order to follow the play of my physiognomy by the light of the candles, renewed by her cares since my return.

She rubbed the lenses one by one with her sleeve, put them back into their case and put it back in her pouch—worthy housekeepers who pride themselves on precaution and exactitude are never separated from their pouches—and then she stood up, and marched in a straight line to the folding chair in which I was still sitting.

"Go to bed, naughty boy," she said, striking both my cheeks gently with the back of her hand. "Go to bed, Maxime, and sleep tranquilly, my child. No, truly, you aren't yet damned his time—but it isn't the Devil's fault!"

The Candlemas Novena

Intimate life in the provinces has a charm of which people in Paris have no idea, which is felt above all in the early years of life. One can like living in Paris in the age of activity, passions, the need for emotions and success, but it is in the provinces that it is necessary to be a child, that it is necessary to be an adolescent, that it is necessary to savor the sentiments of a soul that is commencing to awaken and to know itself.

It is not in Paris that one could ever experience the incomprehensible emotions that are awakened in the depths of the heart by the sound of a certain bell, the sight of a tree, a bush, or the play of sunlight on the tin of a little solitary roof. Those sweet mysteries of memory only belong to the village.

The other day I heard a very intelligent woman complain bitterly of having no fatherland. "Alas," she added, sighing, "I was born in the parish of Saint-Roch."

God preserve me from making a reproach to Paris for that slight imperfection. It is not so much a vice as a misfortune; the great metropolis of civilization has, in any case, to console it, all that it is possible to imagine of seductions and amusements: the Opéra, the Bal Musard, the Bourse, the Association des Gens de Lettres, homeopathy, phrenology and representative government. I only think that the lot of the provinces is worth more, but I think it with my customary spirit of tolerance. It is necessary not to dispute tastes.

The mere remembrance of those young and tender impressions, which can never be replaced, still conserves a part of its power, even when one has distanced oneself, by misfortune or by choice, from the places where one has received them, and that is easily remarked in writers who have a style and a color. The prose of Rousseau reeks of the majesty of the Alps and the freshness of their valleys. One would divine that Bernardin de Saint-Pierre has seen daylight on flowery river-banks, and rocked to the sound of Ocean breezes. Under the magnificent language of Chateaubriand there is often something calm and bucolic, like the murmur of his lake and the soft rustle of its shade. I have sometimes thought that Virgil would perhaps not be Virgil if he had not been born in a hamlet.

Only a province, a small town and fields, form the charming impressions that one day become the gracious consolation of the annoyances of old age, and the pure amours that have all the innocence of the first human amours in the natal paradise, and the warm friendships that are almost worth as much as amour. With a sensible heart and a mobile imagination, one dreams of all those good things in Paris, but one never savors them there. The God who spoke to Adam cries to you in vain: "Where are you?" and there is no longer a voice in the human heart that replies to him.

In the provinces, all the cradles touch one another, like nests placed on the same branch, like flowers blooming on the same stem when, at the first ray of sunlight, all twittering and all perfumes are confounded. People are born under the same gazes, they grow up under the same cares, they grow up together, they see one another every day, at every moment; they love one another, they tell one another so, and there is no reason ever to finish loving one another and telling one another so.

Even the difference between the sexes, which imposes here a prudent and necessary, but ever and serious, reserve, only excludes later the ingenuous intimacies and delightful sympathies that have not yet changed object. It is the passions that mark that difference, and the child has none. The familiar abandon of the first relationships of life are prolonged without danger beyond the age at which the slightest abandon becomes dangerous, when the slightest familiarity between girls and boys becomes suspect in great cities.

The most ardent affections continue to be felt with the tenderness of brother and sister, and that is mingled with too much regard and modesty for morality to have anything to fear from them. Furthermore, the adolescent who begins to divine the secret of his senses still exercises a kind of protection over the weak child that he loves, and whom nature and amour seem to have confided to his guard. The more he learns in the deadly science of the passions, the more he becomes attentive to protect the gentle and timid creature in whom he invests his happiness or his hopes. He is not content to defend her against foreign inspirations; he defends her against himself, in the interest of a future that will be common to them. He respects her and fears her.

And how many sensualities, impossible to describe, that delicate amour of a soul that has just begun to know itself leaves to be desired in the age that follows it!

Oh, the first sign of the preference of that angel of thought, the first expressive gaze that the girl addresses to her friend between the battens of a closing door, the first articulations of her penetrating voice, which is emotional and softened in passing between her lips, the first impression of a hand delivered to a hand that has seized it, the warm moisture of her touch, the fresh perfume of her breath . . . and far less than that; a flower fallen from her hair, a pin fallen from her corset, the sound, the mere rustle, of the dress that brushes you while running, that is what amour is, that is what happiness is! I know the rest, or very nearly, but that is what I would like to recommence, if one could recommence.

One cannot recommence; but remembrance is almost recommencement.

One savors in Paris the sweet leisure of childhood; one knows the value of its games there; one enjoys there the delightful evenings of doing nothing that follow the laborious days of study; but it is only in the provinces that a fortunate habitude prolongs those innocent pleasures under the attentive eye of mothers until the ardent season of adolescence. One is already a man in thought, but one is still a child in tastes; one begins to experience strange and turbulent emotions, to which one is always subject in certain hours of forgetfulness: sentiments full of grave and naivety.

One sometimes asks what is true between the past that one is quitting and the future that one is commencing; but one divines, in plunging and anxious gaze into it, that the future will not be worth as much as the past.

There are even simple and tender minds who would willingly be tempted not to go any further, and who would sacrifice without hesitation the uncertain sensualities of tomorrow to the pure enjoyments of yesterday.

At eighteen years of age, I would have made that bizarre bargain with the familiar angel that presides over changing human destinies, if he had communicated with my prayers; and we would both have gained by it, for I imagine that my insensate emancipation might well have given him some chagrin.

On the twenty-fourth of January 18**, I was not yet there. I loved the beautiful young women with whom I spent the sweetest hours of the day, with all the force of a heart accustomed to loving them, but without fever, without anxiety and almost without preference.

I was very comfortable among them; I was very comfortable on my own, because my imagination was beginning to form, in solitude, a type that did not resemble any woman, and which only one woman could resemble completely, although I thought I had found her a hundred times.

That was my cherished dream, and in the vague immensity in which it appeared to me, it gave me a more distinct idea of happiness than all the realities of life. However, I only glimpsed it through a thousand dubious forms; but I kept searching, and the delightful phantom was never lacking in my dreams. Sometimes it came to extract me from my melancholy by striking my ear with mischievous laughter and dangling the black ringlets of her hair over my forehead; sometimes it placed a foot on my schoolboy's bed while looking at me with a sad eye, hiding beneath a lock of blonde hair a tear ready to flow; and my swollen heart surged toward it, hammering as if to break my breast—for I knew that all my felicity consisted of the possession of that ungraspable image, which even refused me its name.

On the twenty-fourth of January, therefore, we had gathered, as usual, before supper time—for we still had supper—and we were chatting tumultuously around our mothers, who were chatting more gravely about matters that were no less frivolous. Our conversation fell upon the choice of a game, a question that was fundamentally indifferent, the interest of a game reposing entire in penitence, and who does not know that penitence is the accomplishment of the duty that redeems a pledge? It is the moment of confessions, reproaches, whispered secrets, and above all of kisses.

It is the moment of the evening for which one lives all day, and of all the moments of life the one that leaves the least bitterness after it, because the sentiments that one is beginning to exercise are not yet taken seriously; when one has emerged from it once with one of those stormy ideas that torment the heart one has emerged from it for the last time; the pleasure is no longer in it.

"We wouldn't be so embarrassed," said the brunette Thérèse, "if Claire had arrived. Claire knows all the games that have been invented, and when, by chance, she can't recall one, she invents one immediately."

"She certainly has enough imagination for that," remarked Émilie, biting her lips and lowering her eyes in order to give herself the air of circumspection with which she always accompanied a petty malice. "One even fears that she has too much, and I've heard it said that she shows signs of madness from time to time. That would be a great misfortune for her family and her friends."

"Claire won't come," cried Marianne, in a petulant tone of voice that announced that she was only responding to her own thought, and that she had not heard Émilie's disobliging observation. "She won't come, I'm sure of it. She's beginning the Candlemas novena today."

"The Candlemas novena!" I said, in my turn. "Why? I didn't know that she was so devout."

"It's not by virtue of devotion," said Émilie, with a scornful gravity. "It's by virtue of superstition or ostentation."

I have forgotten to say that Émilie was a philosopher. Everyone dabbled in philosophy then, including little girls.

"Of superstition," repeated Marianne, who never grasped more than one word of the most coherent conversation. "Superstition, indeed: the most capricious, the most bizarre, the most extraordinary, the most extravagant superstition . . ."

"But what?" I interrupted. "You're exciting our curiosity without satisfying it."

"Good," said Marianne, looking at me with a marked expression of irony. "It's too stupid for a scholar of your species.

As for these girls, they're not unaware, I imagine, that the Candlemas novena is a devotion particular to young women of the people which has for its object . . . how can I put it?"

"Which has for its object . . . ?" murmured a dozen little voices, while a dozen little heads leaned toward Marianne.

"Which has for its object," said Marianne, "knowing in advance the husband they will have."

"The husband they will have!" repeated the dozen voices, with the various modes of inflection that twelve different organizations furnished them. "What connection can there be between the husband one will have and an act of devotion like the Candlemas novena?"

That's the question, I thought, quietly, *and I'd like to know, but if Marianne knows, she'll say.*

"You understand that I don't believe it," she said, "and if I believed it, I wouldn't care about it. What does it matter to me, the husband that I'll have, provided that he's an honest man, an aristocrat and rich. My parents wouldn't give me another. Handsome or ugly, young or old, amiable or surly, he won't be able to dispense with taking me into society, to balls and spectacles, and furnishing, in accordance with my fortune, the expenses of my toilette. That's what marriage is, I imagine? Then again, I don't worry about something so distant."

"Me neither," said Thérèse, moving her chair nearer to Marianne's. "But the means?"

Impatience was at its peak, but Marianne's didn't yield to ours, for she obtained more pleasure in talking rapidly and at length than anyone in the world ever obtained in listening to her. So she paraded a gaze of satisfaction over the audience, which she tried to render modest, and resumed speaking in these terms:

"You know," she said, "that there is no devotion more agreeable to the Holy Virgin than the Candlemas novena, and it's for that reason that people are persuaded that she recompenses with a singular favor the young women who render her that tribute. Personally, I don't believe it, and I never will believe it, but Claire believes it firmly because she believes anything. She's so good! Only there are a lot of ceremonies and fashions to that experiment, and I'm afraid of getting confused, if Émilie doesn't help me a little. She was with us the day when Claire told me about it."

"Me?" retorted Émilie, disdainfully. "I don't mingle in your conversations."

"I don't say that you mingled with them," Marianne went on, "but you listen to them. It's necessary, therefore," she added, after having bitten her pretty fingernails slightly, "to commence the novena in the evening, at the eight o'clock prayer, in the chapel of the Holy Virgin. Then it's necessary to go to morning mass every day and return to the prayer every evening until the first of February, with a piety that doesn't relent, with a faith that doesn't weaken. It's terribly difficult. Then, on the first of February, it's truly something else. It's necessary to hear all the masses in the chapel, from the first to the last; it's necessary to hear all the prayers and all the evening lessons without missing a single one. Wait, wait! I nearly forgot that it's also necessary to be confessed that day, and if, unfortunately, one hasn't received absolution, all the rest would be wasted effort, for the essential condition of success is to go back to one's room in a state of grace. Then . . ."

"Then they find a husband there!" exclaimed Thérèse.

"You're in a great hurry," replied Marianne, coldly. "I'm not yet half way through my instructions. Then one recommences praying; one shuts oneself away in order to accomplish all the conditions of a severe retreat; one fasts, and meanwhile, one arranges everything for a banquet, but for a banquet, to tell the truth, in which greed plays no part. The table has to be set for two people and garnished with two complete services, except for the knives, which it's necessary to avoid with great care. That merits an extreme attention, for there are frightful misfortunes to which one exposes oneself by forgetting that rule. I'll tell you them, if you like, shortly. I have no need to tell you that the setting requires a perfectly white tablecloth, as clean, as fine and as new as one can procure, and that the tidiness and good taste of the little apartment has to match the good appearance of the feast, for those are things that custom observes when one receives someone with consideration."

"You're talking about banquets and feasts," put in one of the girls, "but I haven't yet seen the slightest preparation of cooking."

"I can't say everything at once," said Marianne. "I warned you that the meal would be very simple. It's composed of two pieces of blessed bread brought back from the last office, and two fingers of pure wine divided between the two place-settings, which occupy, as is reasonable, the two sides of the table. Only the middle of the service is garnished by a tray, of porcelain, or silver, if possible . . ."

"We're finally getting there!" said the little girl.

"Which contains," Mariane continued, "two carefully blessed sprigs of myrtle, rosemary, or any other green plant, except box, placed one beside the other, and not in a cross. That's another point that it's essential to observe."

"And then?" demanded Thérèse—and the entire circle repeated her question, like an echo.

"Then," Marianne replied, "one opens the door to give passage to an expected guest, one takes one's place at the table, one recommends oneself very devoutly to the Holy Virgin, and one goes to sleep awaiting the effects of her protection, which never fail to be manifest, in accordance with the person imploring them. Then strange and admirable visions commence. Those girls for whom the Lord has prepared some unknown sympathy on earth see the man who will love them appear, if he finds them, or would have loved them, at least, if he had found them; the husband that one will have, if favorable circumstances bring us together—and those who encounter him are fortunate!

"What is reassuring is that it's said that a particular privilege of the novena is to procure the same dream for the young man of whom one dreams, and to inspire in him the same impatience to join himself to the half of himself of which a dream has made him aware. That's the beautiful part of the experiment. But woe betide curious young women with whom Heaven is not occupied in the distribution of husbands, for they are tormented by frightful prognostications. Some, destined for the convent, see a long procession of nuns filing past singing hymns; others, whom death is going to strike before the time—and this chills the blood In the veins—witness while alive their own funerals. They wake up with a start to the light of funereal torches and the sound of the sobs of their mother and friends, who are weeping over a coffin draped in white."

"I take God as my witness," said Thérèse, withdrawing slightly, "that I shall never expose myself to such terrors. One trembles merely in thinking about it."

"You could, however, risk it without dread," Émiliie replied. "I fear that you'd sleep soundly until morning, and that it would be necessary to wake up, as usual, to take your Italian lesson."

"That's my opinion," said Marianne, "and I'd be quite astonished if it weren't also that of Maxime, who seems plunged in reflection, as if he were trying to explain a difficult passage of some Greek or Latin author."

"I don't know," I replied, coming round, "and you'll permit me not to pronounce so quickly on a belief supported by the testimony of the people, who found almost everything on experience. The question is well worth being studied, it seems to me, but forgive me, dear Marianne," I continued, addressing myself to her, "if the details you have just given us with your customary grace have left something for my mind to desire. You have only put on stage in your story a young woman anxious about her future; and you'll agree without difficulty that the same doubt might torment the imagination of a young man. Do you think that the Candlemas novena only produces its effect on women, and that the Holy Virgin doesn't grant the same favor to the prayers of boys?"

"Not at all," Marianne exclaimed, "and I beg pardon for my distraction. The Candlesmas novena, accomplished with that design, has the same efficacy for all unmarried people, and the sex is irrelevant. Would you have the strange desire to make sure of it?"

"Truly," said Émilie, raising the sides of her pinched lips, "it would be a fine thing to see a reasonable young man, who seeks the society of enlightened people, and whose father was a friend of Monsieur Voltaire, indulging, like Claire, an honest but uneducated child, in those shameful follies!"

I did not reply, and I would not have contested well against Émilie, who had not read Voltaire but who quoted him with all the more authority because none of us had read him. "I got up quietly, under the appearance of a sudden preoccupation; I slipped gradually behind the bench of mothers, I picked up my hat and I ran to the chapel of the Holy Virgin, in order to commence the Candlemas novena.

II

I was not very devout; I could not be, either by habitude of imitation or by the effect of a reasoned conviction; but I found religion beautiful, I believed it to be good, I respected its practices without following them and I admired its devotions without practicing them. I had the faith of sentiment, which is perhaps the surest, and I professed in consequence an instinctive hatred for the spirit of examination that destroys everything. or which will destroy everything that it has not yet destroyed. I did not have, in truth, any plausible objection to the Candlemas novena.

Why should it not be thus? I asked myself, when I had taken a few steps toward the church. *Nature has twenty mysteries more marvelous than that one, which it has never occurred to anyone to put in doubt. Gross bodies, insensible in appearance, have affinities between them that summon them toward one another across an incalculable space; a magnetized needle, consulted at the equator, is able to recognize the pole; a butterfly that has just hatched out, flies unerringly to its unknown female; the pollen of the palm tree delivers itself to the desert winds, and goes on their wings to fecundate the solitary flower that awaits it. To humans alone, so privileged among all created beings, it is forbidden to foresee their destiny, and to go to join the essential part of themselves that God had kept in reserve for them in the treasures of his Providence? It would be to calumniate the power and the generosity of the common Father to believe in that neglect.*

But what if humans have lost that advantage by virtue of a sin whose expiation is imposed on the entire species? I continued, anxiously... *Well, would not the intercession of Marie, implored with confidence, suffice to lift the condemnation? To whom would it belong more than to the pure and mild Marie to protect chase amours and virtuous penchants? Is that not her most beautiful mission in Heaven? Or, if the marvelous myth that is hidden beneath that popular belief is not true, as I believe it to be, it's necessary to agree that it ought to be!*

Cold minds, which do not understand the charm of practical devotion, have always astonished me; disdain for pious works appears to me to be even more incomprehensible in those vibrant and passionate souls for whom the positive life dies not have strong enough sensations, and who are obliged to demand news incessantly from the imagination and sentiment.

What are, great God, the hypotheses of philosophy and the sciences, the prestige of the arts and the inventions of poetry, compared with the poetry of the heart that awakens to the inspirations of religion, and which transports thought into a region of sublime ideas where all is prodigy, and where, however, everything is truth?

It is necessary to believe, no doubt, but what it is necessary to believe is a thousand times more probable, a thousand times easier to believe, if it is permitted to compare things so different, than everything that it is necessary to believe in the common relationships of social life, in order to support it without bitterness and without disgust.

If we examine, after a few years, the sensations that we have enjoyed with the greatest intoxication, we shall probably not find one that was not an error or a lie. The illusions that we have savored, while taking them for illusions, were no more false, alas, than those we have taken for realities.

And we disdain religion, so fecund in ineffable joys, consolations and hopes, the religion that would still be the purest and most complete happiness of humankind if it were only an illusion. At least it would not have the anguish of disillusionment and regret; one is not disabused of it on earth.

I had, therefore, fulfilled, with a joy that was new for me, all the obligations of the novena, and, as if the habitude of those exercises had elevated my reason itself to a height that it had never even able to attained before, I made myself some reproach for only having delivered myself to them with the sole object of satisfying a puerile curiosity.

It was, in fact, my blind confidence in wretched children's stories that had inspired many acts of submission and faith of which a more sincere and more disinterested piety would have made a duty, of which I dared to expect the recompense, as if I had not found it in the satisfaction of my own heart.

That remorse seized me, above all, at the moment when, my preparations made and my door open to the imminent apparition, I got ready to proffer my final prayer.

It is probable that I expressed more regrets than wishes, and I do not know whether that reparation was accepted, but I could at least flatter myself, by virtue of the mild serenity that reentered my senses, and calmed momentarily all the agitations of my mind. I had scarcely returned to my armchair than I was surprised by the most profound slumber.

I don't know how long it lasted, nor how the darkness into which I had plunged was illuminated, but it suddenly seemed to me that I was no longer asleep.

My bedroom took on its customary appearance, by the vacillating light of my candles. I discerned all the objects, I heard all the sounds, the faint, indeterminate sounds without a detectable origin that only seem to rise up momentarily in order to reassure the soul against the invasion of the eternal silence. The external parquet did not creak, but it rendered a little murmur, as if it had been caressed by a tuft of feathers or a bouquet of flowers. I turned my eyes toward my door and I saw a woman there. I wanted to launch myself forward in order to receive her, but an invincible power retained me in my place. I tried to speak, but the words were nailed to my tongue. My reason did not lose itself in the mystery; it understood that there was a mystery and that the prayers of my novena had been granted.

The unknown woman approached, perhaps without perceiving me, as if she were obeying a sort of instinct, an irresistible impulsion.

She arrived at the armchair that I had prepared for her, sat down, and remained thus exposed to my curiosity, of which nothing repressed the impatience, for her eyes were still lowered. I attached a gaze to her emboldened by her immobility and her silence. I had certainly never seen her before, and yet

I experienced, in the midst of the vague consciousness of a dream, the conviction that that existence, foreign to all my memories, was nevertheless real and vibrant.

Even the imagination of my soul, purified by meditation and by prayer, could not have produced anything approaching that dream. It belonged to an order of inspirations to which humans cannot elevate themselves, and that the delicate and choice science of sensations that is nowadays called esthetics is incapable of counterfeiting. My metaphysics of schoolboy philosophy was still alert in its slumber, but it was humiliated before the work of the power of God. I understood that a creation as pure and as perfect could not be my work.

I shall not talk about the beauty of that young woman; one cannot make portraits with words. I have sometimes doubted that one can make them with lines and colors. There is in the ensemble of all the forms of an animate being a certain play of passion and life that cannot be reproduced much better by the brush than by the pen, and what is no less sure is that the ensemble in question is not equally intelligible for everyone. Everyone reads it in accordance with his aptitude for disentangling its characteristics, penetrating its meanings and appropriating its spirit. When it strikes a note in perfect harmony with the intelligence and the sensibility of the person gazing, it is felt a thousand times more than it analyzes, and the effect is too gripping, too simultaneous, to leave the slightest room for the observation of details.

I imagine that it is necessary already to be a trifle blasé regarding the impressions of amour, in order to pause on the piquant effect of a crease of the lip or the eyebrow, a tooth that is raised imperceptibly in its enamel keyboard, a rebellious little curl escaped from the arrangement of the hair. The powerful sympathies that decide an entire life proceed in a more sudden manner, and it will be remembered that the apparition of the Candlemas novena is only accomplished by reason of a complete and absolute sympathy between the persons that it puts in communication. I did not ask myself why I loved that woman, I did not even ask myself whether I loved her; I *knew* that I loved her. I said to myself what Adam must have said when God completed the benefit of creation in giving him a wife: *I have finished being; I am.*

The stranger appeared to be dressed, like me, for a betrothal celebration; but her garments were not those familiar to the new brides of my province. They reminded me of those I had glimpsed several times in similar circumstances in a city not far away, which the invasion of our arms and our doctrines wanted to attach to the Republic. It was the brilliant and gracious costume of Montbéliard, which the highest society of the region still conserved in certain solemn ceremonies, and which has probably been abandoned today even by the people. She had deposited beside her, on the table, one of those small bags of polished steel mesh in which young women the enclosed the light fabrics of what they were pleased to call their needlework, and I had not taken long to notice that its plaque was decorated with nails forming two raised letters, which had to be the initials of the two names of my future wife, but I would rather have learned them in their entirety from her mouth.

Unfortunately, the charm that had forbidden me the power of speech had not been broken, and all the faculties and powers of my soul had passed into my eyes, for they had just encountered hers. The fascination of that celestial gaze would have been sufficient, in any case, to render me mute. I had difficulty conceiving the possibility of meeting it without dying, and I undoubtedly owed the strength to resist such a vivid emotion to the privilege of the novena, the mystery of which my mind had not forgotten. Never had the fire of an innocent tenderness animated softer eyes and revealed more fully the ineffable secrets of pure amour, for which no human voice could have found words.

However, a strange cloud suddenly obscured her eyelids. It seemed that a confused notion of the future that had just blossomed in her thought was gradually manifest there in a more sensible form, and had overwhelmed her with a horrible certainty. Her bosom palpitated, her eyelashes were moistened by a few tears, which she strove to retain. Gently, she pushed away with a hand the bread and wine that I had placed before her, seized with ardor one of the sprigs of blessed myrtle and passed it under one of the knots of her bouquet. Then she stood up and resumed the route by which she had come.

I triumphed then over the horrible constraint that enchained me in my place and I launched myself after her in order to obtain a word of consolation and hope.

"Oh, whoever you are," I cried, "don't abandon me to the horrible regret of having seen you and not being able to find you again. Think that my future depends on you, and don't make an eternal woe out of the sweetest moment of my life! Tell me at least whether I may press once more that hand which I shall cover with tears if I could see you once again!"

"Once again," she replied, "or never . . . Never!" she repeated, with a dolorous cry.

As she spoke, she escaped. I sensed my strength failing and my legs giving way. I searched for a point of support; I clung on to it, abandoning myself to it without resistance. The most obscure of the veils of sleep had replaced over my eyes the transparent veil of dreams.

I was only woken up in broad daylight, but the laughter of a domestic who was clearing away the preparations for my nocturnal collation, and who attributed that apparatus to the fantasies of somnambulism, to which I was, in fact, subject. I did not defend myself, but I neglected to make sure, in my trouble and confusion, whether the two sprigs of myrtle were still there; that was the only circumstance that could give or deny my dream a species of positive reality.

In doubt, a mind graver than mine would have abstained; it would have regarded the strange illusion of the previous night as the effect of a long preoccupation, of the imagination, and of fasting, and you are free to believe that it was nothing else. But an amorous young man of twenty, in love for the first time, is not capable of so much reasoning. And I loved with all the power of my heart, with frenzy, that unknown young woman who might not exist.

III

I did not have a character that easily let go of ideas by which it had once been forcefully occupied. That one became my obsession, the unique thought of my life, the sole goal of my destiny. I abandoned entirely the innocent and mild society in which my habits and pleasures had been contained thus far; I sought solitude, because solitude was the only manner of being in which I could entertain my wishes and hopes freely. To what docile amity or complaisant credulity would I have dared to confide them?

It seemed to me, in my delirium, that an imminent circumstance, almost as unforeseen as the one that had shown me my imaginary fiancée, would not take long to bring her back before my eyes; I expected it; I believed that I would encounter her in all the unknown women that hazard made me perceive from afar, but everywhere she escaped me, as in the dream in which I had seen her. That perpetual succession of illusions and disillusionments ended up acquiring a deadly ascendancy over my mind; it had become an assiduous, invincible, inexorable mania. My reason and my health gave way at the same time, and the physician summoned in vain to my sick-bed soon renounced the hope of curing me. The physician could not divine the cause of my illness, and a just modesty prevented me from confessing it.

I had not, however, neglected any means of discovering my mysterious friend. The initials of the bag of steel mesh had not vanished from my memory and I had made them known, under the reserve of a profound secrecy, to one of my young study companions who lived in Montbeliard, combining them with the most detailed portrait of the young woman whose name they must express.

The description could not lack resemblance; the features were, alas, too profoundly imprinted in my heart, where I sense that they are still alive. As for the danger of exaggeration, nothing was less to be feared. What expression, what language could exaggerate what I had seen?

The response was a long time coming. It suddenly arrived to animate my heart at one of those moments of extreme anguish in which my exhausted strength no longer seems capable of struggling with death,

The ideal being of whom I had dreamed on the night of Candemas really existed; the resemblance was perfect. The person that I had designated with so much care was faithful all the features of that description, including a little birthmark on the back of the neck, which she had allowed me to perceive as she fled.

Her name was Cécile Savrnier, and those names commenced with the two letters I remembered so clearly having seen on the steel mesh bag. She normally resided, alone with her father, in a house situated some distance from the town, and it was that particularity that had rendered the information more difficult and slow. They had returned to Montbéliard a short time ago, where the graces and beauty of Cécile were the object of all conversations.

My officious schoolfellow, who regarded that information as the preliminaries of a marriage request in which I had consented to act as an intermediary, felt obliged to insist on the incomparable qualities of Mademoiselle Savernier, but he finished by adding, not without expressing some regret, that she had little fortune.

That circumstance was no less agreeable to me than the others, for my fortune did not permit me to aspire to an opulent marriage, and there was, in any case, nothing more distant from my understanding of marriage.

It was no longer a dream. My illusion took on substance, my chimera became a reality. It was Cécile Savernier that I loved, and Cécile was no longer the capricious infant of my dreams. She existed a few leagues away; I could, I had to, find her, to spend close to her, with her, an entire life as sweet as the first thought of amour.

My languor disappeared with my anxieties; my health improved; nothing remained of my illness but a little trouble and weakness, and my father, consoled, happier from day to day, finally rejoiced in the assured hope of my cure.

One day he pressed my hand tenderly, leaned on the bed that I had not yet quit and said: "God be praised; you have triumphed over your dolor and returned my son to me. Thank you."

"My dolor?" I replied, drawing nearer in order to embrace him. "Do you think you have the secret of it?"

"Oh," he replied, smiling, "all the chagrins of your age come from amour; I have known them like you. Today I can see from a great enough distance those which tormented my youth only to think about them with disdain, but I know that they can be mortal. So I shall not hesitate to hasten toward your wishes if they can be fulfilled. I congratulate you on having made your stand against an inevitable woe that the future will not take long to repair, which you will count cheerfully one day among the foolish deceptions of an eighteen-year-old imagination. Only promise me to take me into your confidence first when a new sentiment surprises your heart. We'll talk about t seriously, like two friends, one of whom has the advantage over the other of experience, and I promise, if you persist, to spare no effort to render you happy. Tell me sincerely, dear child, whether that arrangement suits you."

I seized my father's hand and bore it to my lips. "You are the best of fathers," I replied, "and your son will not forget it for a moment; but are you very sure of not being mistaken regarding the cause of my malady? I cannot understand how you divined it!"

"It wasn't as difficult as you imagine," said my father, with a new smile. "It was amour, and your gaze and your silence confessed it to me ten times over. It was only a matter then of seeking the object among the young women who are part of our habitual society. It was not Thérèse; she is too light-minded and too superficial to occupy you. It was not Marianne, whose chatter amuses you, but has neither solidity of mind nor reflective tenderness of soul, and who is only good by virtue of instinct. It was not Émilie, who is cold, pinched and rational, and who has learned to read in Baron Holbach. It could only be your cousin Claire, who is pretty, simple and modest, and whose naïve exaltation accords so well with your turn of mind. Do you think that my understanding is too poor in divination?"

"Claire!" I cried, with sort of impulsiveness that was able to deceive my father, for he was far from knowing its subject. It was precisely that young woman who had made the Candlemas novena at the same time as me, and whose example had suggested the idea.

"In truth," I continued after a moment's reflection, "you were right to suppose that I would prefer Claire to all the others. I love Claire as a friend, as a relative, as an excellent person, who will, I hope, be a worthy wife and mother, but I have never thought of making her my wife and the mother of my children. Believe, I beg you, in the sincerity of my words."

My father looked at me with an astonished expression.

"I had no reason to doubt it," he said, "but your response has belied my conjectures. It isn't Claire's marriage, then, that has reduced you to the state of melancholy in which I saw you ready to succumb, and which has caused me such frightful anxieties?"

"Claire is getting married?" I retorted, raising myself up on my bed. "Claire is getting married, you say . . . Oh, don't worry, my friend, I haven't deceived you. This transport is only joy; may that marriage be in conformity with the wishes of Heaven and fill her with a perfect happiness!"

"I hope so," said my father. "And I like to hope so, although it has something very extraordinary about it. Claire had refused three very advantageous establishments this year, and her mother thought her disposed to embrace the religious life, the practices of which she was following with a singular ardor, when an unknown young man, arrived almost the day before, obtained her consent at the first interview. The information has been favorable and the two families reached agreement swiftly. Claire is happy with the union, for which, she says, the Holy Virgin had prepared her since Candlemas. You will recognize in that the mystical and romantic imagination that made me believe in some sympathy between you."

"I protest, Father, that I understand Claire's marriage marvelously, and I don't think that she could ever have made a better one."

"Good!" he replied, bursting into laughter, "and that depends on the manner of seeing of both of you. But aren't we going to talk about yours?"

"Do you think that it's already time to occupy ourselves with it? I'm only twenty."

"Between us, it's your own affair, but why not? I married too late, or the years have gone by too rapidly; I will have missed savoring the sweetest joys of life if I die without having loved a daughter that you might have given me, without having played with children, without confiding the memory of my features and that of my tenderness to the memory of a new generation emerged from me. That, my friend, is immortality, the material immortality of a man, the only one that the weakness of our organs and that our intelligence permits us to foresee clearly. The other is a great mystery that religion and philosophy abstain prudently from explaining. Your marriage has become the principal object of my thoughts and my hopes, and I will say frankly that I have been much occupied with it since Candlemas . . ."

"Since Candlemas, Father!"

"Since Candlemas," he replied, testifying slight surprise and staring at me. "That's the time when ideas of marriage begin to ferment, with the young season, in the hearts of young people, and come to awaken the solicitude of fathers, for there are secret harmonies of instinct and foresight between them; but I remember that that date might have reminded you of the foolish preoccupation of our poor Claire. What is certain is that I conceived the same project for you at the same time, and, according to all appearances, without the knowledge of the Holy Virgin. If I neglected to mention it to you, you know the reasons. The long illness commenced at that time from which you have only just recovered, and which made me fear for your life. If amour has nothing to do with your suffering, we still have time today to talk about my views, but without being able to take the slightest consequence therefrom, in case they have the misfortune of conflicting with yours; for I intend expressly that your choice and your establishment should remain free, and I will not depart from that promise."

"You fill me with gratitude and joy," I cried, sitting up on my bed and adjusting my clothing, for a sensed my strength returning with the hope of finding and obtaining Cécile. "I expect of your tenderness that you will not impose an engagement upon me to which I cannot subscribe, and which

I cannot contract without violating the holiest obligations. I swear to you for my part, my unique and perfect friend, that I will never have a secret from your heart and will not bring into your house a daughter that you have not adopted in advance."

"As you wish," said my father. "And yet that idea, of which it is necessary that I make the sacrifice to you, was the most pleasant of the dreams of my old age. Let me at least talk to you about it for the last time. Perhaps I have never pronounced before you the name of one of those childhood friends the memory of whom recalls one day the only real amity that one has savored in life, the sincere and disinterested amities of college. That one, however, had not been lost to my memory, but a great difference in vocation, habitudes and domicile seemed to have separated us forever.

"He had become a colonel in the artillery; he emigrated, and that last circumstance rendered our separation more irrevocable, for I had followed, like so many others, the movement of the Revolution when I was far from having foreseen its end and its results. Fortunately, that temporary direction of a mind deceived by appearances earned me a political credit that I have sometimes found useful. My friend, disabused in his turn of another genre of errors, regretted his fatherland, always so dear to well-born hearts. I succeeded in obtaining the erasure of his proscription and rendering him his hearth, his paternal field and his natal air.

"We have not seen one another since, but his letters never cease to testify a tender gratitude that recompenses my efforts very nicely. Reciprocal confidences have made us aware of the smallest details of our interior and our fortune. My old friend Gilbert knows that I have a son on whom my future hopes repose, and whom multiple reports have enabled him to see him, he says, from the most advantageous point of view. He has a daughter sixteen years old, the eulogy of whom is in all mouths and who will certainly make the happiness of her husband, as she has made that of her father.

"I will not hide it from you that we have seen in that projected union an agreeable means of uniting us for the rest of our days, each of us being firmly decided not to quit his only child. It was a life of election that we had prepared in our foolish confidence, so true is it that one can deceive oneself at any age, and that old age, ripened by experience, nevertheless brings its illusions, like adolescence. That perspective was delightful, but it is necessary to renounce it!"

"I beg your pardon, Father, a thousand pardons! Why has Heaven condemned me to recompense your tenderness so poorly?"

"Don't worry," he said to me. "I shall easily forget the joy that I promised myself in seeing my hopes realized, in order no longer to think of any but yours. But it's truly a pity, for Cécile Savernier is said to be the prettiest girl in a land where one has the right to be difficult."

"Cécile Savernier!" I cried, leaping out of bed. "Cécile Savernier! Oh, my Father, did I hear you rightly?"

"Marvelously," he replied. "Cécile Savernier, daughter of Gilbert Savernier, former colonel of artillery, resident in Montbéliard, département of Mont-Terrible. She is the person I'm talking about."

I fell at my father's feet in a state of agitation impossible to describe; I took possession of his hands; I covered them with my kisses and my tears. I stayed there for a long time without being able to find words, or even a voice. My father lifted me up anxiously, pressed me against his heart, and interrogated me ten times before I had the strength to make myself heard.

"Cécile Savernier! It's her, it's her, Father!" I cried finally, in a shocked voice. "It's her that I asked you for on my knees!"

"In truth?" he replied. "Then your wishes will be easily granted, since the affair is almost made; but do you believe yourself to be certain of that resolution? On what is it founded? Where can you have seen Cécile? Montbéliard is the only town in France in which she has appeared since her return from abroad, and when you traversed the region two years ago I'm positive that she was not yet there."

I blushed. That question touched too closely a secret that I had not the strength to reveal, and in which my father could not see anything but an illusion or a lie.

"Believe," I said, "that I have seen Cécile and that I am authorized to think that she will not reject my amour. Regarding the circumstances or the event that brought us together momentarily, I beg you not to ask me anything more."

"God preserve me," he said, embracing me. "I respect that genre of mystery too much to rob you of the merit of discretion. There are secret knots, there are sympathies that are known to lovers, which cannot be divined at my age. This one responds so well to my desires that I have no interest I enquiring as to its origin. Why, in any case," he added, laughing, "should the saintly influence that has been felt for some time in my family not have contrived two marriages instead of one? Let us occupy ourselves solely with yours, which will be accomplished without delay as soon as you have graduated . . .

"That delay seems to alarm you but it is not as long as you imagine. Your success in the schools has been my happiness and my glory for some years, and that time that your malady has caused you to lose will be rapidly regained. You can conceive that it would not be appropriate to present yourself for the most solemn act in life without bringing an honorable and serious dowry to it. Don't be alarmed, moreover, by the rigors of a separation of which I am extending the term slightly, and which will render you the most perfect felicity, for the happiness for which one hopes is the surest happiness in life. It is, in any case, entirely in conformity with decency that you see your future father-in-law before taking things any further, and that you obtain an admission even more positive than the one with which we are both flattering ourselves. Since your convalescence is well under way, I hope that a month's sojourn in Montbéliard can only confirm it, and you can witness Claire's wedding in passing, for it will be held half way, in her pretty house in the Bois d'Arcey. What do you say? Does that arrangement suit you?"

I threw myself into his arms; he kissed my forehead, returned to his study and soon came out again with a letter addressed to Colonel Savernier.

I left the next day for Montbéliard, happier than one can say.

What, my God, are the joys of men?

IV

I have said that the strange illusion that filled all my life and absorbed all my life after the night of Candlemas had become equivalent for me to the most positive verities. The result of my research had given it an extreme resemblance. The unexpected concurrence of my father's projects with the epoch and circumstances of my dream caused it to emerge from the class of ordinary dreams. It was no longer a dream but a revelation. God himself, touched by the submission of my prayers, had chosen the wife that I was about to seek. That idea augmented my happiness with all the security of which the fleeting happiness of humans has need in order really to be something.

Disposed by character easily to see again the impression of the marvelous, I abandoned myself to that one without resistance. Hearts that resemble mine will have no difficulty in comprehending me.

I embraced for the first time the thought of a happiness the serenity of which nothing appeared to trouble. I flew toward Cécile in complete confidence, in the total abandonment of my heart; and by a singular coincidence that seemed to be expressly made for me, the end of that mild winter had suddenly taken on all the graces and adornments of spring. The frosts had disappeared from the base to the summit of the mountains; a warm and embalmed air circulated through the evergreen groves of pines; the precocious shoots of the other trees were beginning to be colored by the bright red hues that painted the buds ready to expand; and little flowers, unknown in the season, were enameling the moss like a sprinkling of pearls.

It was, however, only the end of January, and I was struck by a strange frisson when I realized that the day of Claire's wedding was that of Candlemas. I arrived in time to witness the celebration: a modest and religious joy, unalloyed with any anxiety, filled all minds; the physiognomy of the newly-weds expressed a perfect but celestial contentment, calm and meditative.

The young man was handsome, full of tenderness and attentions, but nevertheless serious, with the consequence that he was less reminiscent of the fortunate fiancé of the day before than an angel sent as a witness by the Lord to the marriage of a Christian.

When the ceremony was over I approached my cousin and I said to her quietly, while I raised her hand to my lips: "I'd like to believe, little friend, that this husband is the one that was announced to you last Candlemas."

Claire looked up at me, blushing, with a gaze that seemed to say: *How do you know that?* Then she responded, while squeezing my hand: "I would not have married another."

No, undoubtedly, for she knew full well that it was God who had made that destiny of her life. I felt agitated by a delightful emotion impossible to describe, thinking that such a felicity was promised to me.

While the celebrations of Claire's marriage retained me in the Bois d'Arcey a little longer than I would have liked, my excellent father had alerted Colonel Savernier regarding my visit, of which the latter, curious to know me first, had not judged it appropriate to inform Claire.

When I had presented my letter to the colonel, he contented himself with casting a glance over it, and came to me with open arms.

"I have no need," he said, with an affectionate cordiality, to inform myself of your name; you resemble the friend of my youth so closely that I seem to see him again as when every morning brought us together. You are simply a little taller. Be welcome, my boy, as a friend, as a son, if your heart can make itself heard, as I hope, by my Cécile's. Now, sit down and rest while I read your father's letter and consider you more at my ease."

The warmth of that welcome caused a few gentle tears to come to my eyelids, which I tried to repress as I cast my gaze over the interior of the apartment.

A straw hat garnished with a bright sky-blue ribbon was hanging from a nail; it was Cécile's. A harp was placed in one of the corners of the drawing room. It was Cécile's harp. A steel mesh bag had been abandoned negligently on an armchair near mine, and I distinguished easily thereon the raised monogram that had struck me on the night of my vision; it was Cécile's monogram.

And yet, what if it were not Cécile's? That idea, which had not yet occurred to me, suddenly surprised my mind and chilled me with terror.

I found myself engaged in the most sacred and irrevocable manner, by the desires I had expressed to my father, by the step I had taken with regard to Monsieur Savernier, and my blind precipitation might perhaps only result in separating me forever from the spouse that was promised to me.

A mortal frisson ran through my limbs when I perceived, some distance away, a portrait of a young woman coiffed with a straw hat; I gathered all my strength in order to run to it, convinced that even the awkwardness of a village painter could not succeed in dissimulating entirely features so deeply engraved in my heart.

I arrived, and I was petrified by despair. A thunderbolt falling on my head could not have struck me a crueler blow. It was the portrait of a charming woman, whose physiognomy had some similarity to that of my imaginary Cécile.

But it was not her.

My legs were buckling beneath me when Monsieur Savernier's arm, passed around my body, sustained me.

"Alas," he said to me, wiping away a tear, "you'll no longer see that one. That's Lidy, my beautiful and sweet Lidy; she's the mother of our Cécile. May you never experience like me the horrible dolor of surviving the person you love!"

I turned toward him, leaned on his breast, and bathed his cheek with my tears, but without discerning, in my emotion, whether they were produced by tenderness or joy. There was no longer anything that belied my hopes; nor was there anything that appeared to confirm them, but my fear vanished.

"Yes, you will be my son," Monsieur Savernier went on, in a tone of solemn resolution. "You will be my son, for you have a soul. You will be Cécile's husband if she consents to it. And why should she not consent?" he added, looking at me complaisantly and embracing me again. "I had really not yet noticed that you were so good-looking.

"Let's chat now," he continued, making me sit down and taking my hand in his. "Decency does not permit you to lodge in my home, but we'll see you here every day during the time that you spend in Montbéliard before going to resume your studies. The sweet intimacy that ought to precede a serious and inviolable engagement will be established of its own accord. It's necessary not to proceed lightly in the affairs of an entire life and eternity. That epoch of proofs has, in any case, a charm that even happiness sometimes regrets, and I imagine that your father has told you that, as I have. Then again, it will neither be long nor rigorous, for old men have better reasons than young ones for hastening to be happy.

"I am speaking to you about all this as if I had no doubt to form regarding a reciprocal consent between the young woman and you, and God preserve me from being mistaken! But I am authorized to do it by the communications your father has made to me, from which it results, to my great astonishment, that you already love my Cécile. What is even stranger, if it is possible, is that her naïve heart, which has never hidden anything, feels drawn toward you by the same penchant, although you have never seen one another, unless my vigilance has been deceived by one of those artifices that youth practices instinctively, and which old age forgets. Oh, I declare to you that that is a point on which I desire clarifications ardently and my good and frank amity for you gives me some right to obtain them!"

The colonel looked at me intently, and the trouble into which his question plunged me could not have escaped him. I lowered my eyes, I hesitated as I searched for a response and did not find one.

"I swear on my honor, Monsieur," I finally replied, "that I have never seen Cécile, that I have never seen her portrait, that I have never had the audacity to write to her, and that her name had only been known to me for two days when my father pronounced it before me. However, I have loved her for nearly a year and I shall love her all my life. I have loved her even more than I had ever believed myself capable of loving since the moment when you deigned to tell me that our souls had understood one another. That is the truth, Monsieur. The rest is an incomprehensible mystery for me."

"Incomprehensible indeed," said Monsieur Savernier, with an anxious expression. "Quite incomprehensible, for I don't suppose that you can be lying. And yet . . ."

"And yet I have not disguised anything from you; I take as my witness the unknown power that had stored so many felicities for me, and which has cast into my bosom the amour of which I have just requested the price. Are there no examples of these sympathies that take possession of us unknown to ourselves, and which draw us with all the vehemence of a passion? Does the Providence that watches over the future happiness of families never prepare similar rapprochements in the treasure of its favors? What it has done for all created beings, has it never done for humans? Of that I am profoundly ignorant. And yet it is necessary that I believe it, for I have no other explanation to give you."

"Good, good," said the colonel. "One would swear that they were concerted; is it not necessary to believe now that they have seen and loved one another in a dream? If the secret of that kind of rendezvous becomes widespread, it will put an end forever to paternal surveillance. I defy it to go as far as that. What does it matter, anyhow," he added, "provided that you love one another, since I do not want anything else? That is what we shall all know before long, in a more positive manner, for you shall dine with Cécile . . . tomorrow."

"Tomorrow!" I cried.

I did not take long to regret that indiscreet expansion, but I had flattered myself with the hope of seeing her sooner.

"Tomorrow," he said, smiling. "It's later than you would like, but the delay is not long enough to cause you a veritable affliction. Tomorrow, so redoubtable for lovers, is only eternity for the dead. I had not wanted to inform Cécile of your arrival; I had reserved myself the pleasure of discovering, at your first encounter, when I knew you a little better, what was genuine in your sympathy, and I seized the opportunity willingly to keep my daughter at a distance at the moment when I expected you. A numerous Catholic family in the neighborhood, which counts no less than six friends, all sisters, is celebrating the birthday of a grandmother, who is my old friend. As the long retreats of Candlemas are over, the time that remains to us between now and Lent is consecrated, by immemorial custom, to more or less innocent diversions, which piety does not forbid; people dance, they rejoice, I even think that they will be masked. Have no fear, my boy; the program of the fête only admits women, and no man will be received there—husband, father or brother—before the hour when it is agreed that the meek ewes return to the fold. In the meantime, we shall dine together, for Dorothée is summoning us . . .”

Our petty repast was as agreeable and as cheerful as it could be without Cécile, for Monsieur Savernier had a cordial and jovial character, like the majority of men of a certain age whose life has been good and honest.

When we were ready to quit the table he suddenly said to me: “Do you know that an idea has occurred to me for which you will probably be grateful, for your impatience was betrayed jut now by a movement that I could not mistake. We shall try, at least, to deceive it until tomorrow, since tomorrow seems so far away to you, and this is the means. I have reassured you regarding the composition of the little society of which my daughter is a part today, affirming to you that only parents are received there, and that is exactly true, but the rule is not so rigorous that I cannot bend it in your favor. I will go in alone at first, and in a few minutes of conversation I will doubtless have smoothed out all the difficulties. A domestic, posted in advance, will await the agreed signal to introduce you, and you will be welcomed, without any clarification, as a friend of the house. It’s agreed that we will play our role with all the skill of which we are capable, and we shall take care to appear to be complete strangers to one another. In that manner, I can appreciate what is real in the marvelous sympathies of which you spoke a little while ago; for nothing will prevent you, except seeing Cécile, from conversing with her freely, and

I hope that you will have no difficulty in recognizing beneath her disguise as a bride of Montbéliard."

"She's disguised as a bride of Montbéliard, you say? A bride of Montbéliard! Is it possible?"

"Well, yes, as a bride of Montbéliard," he continued, without paying any heed to my agitation, the motive of which he did not suspect. "That's a good augury, is it not? But the costume is so gracious, it has so much attraction for young women, that more than one of her companions might have chosen it, as she has. In that case, you will distinguish her from the others by a little sprig of myrtle detached from her bouquet, which she has had the whim of attaching to her bosom, and by which I will recognize her myself."

That second circumstance, which reminded me so vividly of one of the circumstances of my dream, caused me a further emotion, but I succeeded in mastering it, and I only responded to Monsieur Savernier's proposal by testimonies of the most tender gratitude.

An hour later, he had executed his project in all its points and I was in the company of Cécile. I distinguished her easily by means of the indications that her father had given me. It even seemed to me that I would have recognized her without them. For her part, she had manifested some emotion at my approach, and when I had obtained permission to take a place that remained vacant beside her, I thought I perceived that she was trembling.

"Excuse," I said to her, "a temerity that the mask and the disguise explain at least partly. Unknown to everyone here, I am probably importuning you with the proximity of a stranger, and I suspect strongly that my features remind you of one of those memories that provide material for malicious conversations at masked balls."

"I don't understand that kind of pleasure," she replied, "and I cannot imagine any circumstance that might inspire me with the whim to indulge in them. In any case, you do not have to fear in me those petty annoyances that occupy everyone here, and which people seem to find amusing, for I do not believe, in fact, that I have ever had the honor of seeing you before."

"Never?" I said to her. "In truth?"

"Never," she interjected, with a forced laugh, "unless it was in a dream; and you can take my word for it, for I am incapable of pretence. I have not even attempted to disguise my voice."

It was, in fact, her voice, the voice I had heard more than a year before but had never ceased since to retain in my heart.

"Permit me then," I replied, warmly, "to seek between us some motive for rapprochement that might substitute for the habitude of an acquaintance already made. My name, or rather that of my father, must have been pronounced more than once before you by yours, and I'm not unaware that it is to the daughter of Monsieur Savernier that I'm speaking. That name would be rather unfortunate not to awaken in your soul any species of sympathy. My name is Maxime . . ."

I had scarcely pronounced two syllables more when Cécile shuddered, turning toward me a gaze that seemed to express a mixture of affection and fear.

"Yes, yes," she cried, in an altered voice, "your name is well known to me; it is dear to my father, and to me also, because it reminds us of memories that are never effaced in an honest heart, those of gratitude . . . It's true, then," Cécile continued, talking to herself as if she had suddenly forgotten my presence, but in such a manner as not to allow me to miss a single one of her words. "It wasn't an illusion! Everything has been accomplished thus far; everything will doubtless be accomplished. Let the will of God be done!"

And she fell into a somber dejection in which all her ideas appeared to be annihilated.

One of her hands was almost touching mine. I took possession of it without her making the slightest effort to remove it. She only gazed at me with a more attentive eye.

"It's him!" she said.

"Oh, the sight of me ought not to cause you any alarm," I said, pressing her hand in mine. "The sentiment that has brought me to you is as pure as your heart, and it has the admission of a father whose only thought is your happiness. You are free, Cécile, and our future destiny only depends on you."

"Our future destiny only depends on God," she replied, inclining her head over her breast with a profound sigh. "But you've spoken to my father; you've doubtless seen him. He knows that at this hour of the night I've been experiencing for some time an inexpressible malady that is stifling me and is killing me. I wanted so desperately to prevent the fit! Why has my father not come?"

Although the colonel had said something to me about that accident, which had not inspired any dread, the expression of suffering that accompanied her words chilled my blood. Cécile's father had, in fact, stopped before us at the moment when she appeared to be searching the room for him with an anxious gaze. I was astonished that she had not seen him.

"I'm beside you," he said, enveloping her with an arm, which sustained her, for she was about to faint.

She leaned on his breast and spent there one of those instants of anguish that are so long for dolor. One of her hands, which I had not abandoned, had immediately clenched over my fingers, and had then relaxed and gone cold, as if gained by death. I uttered a cry of terror.

Cécile's friends had hastened around her, and during the cares that they lavished upon her, they had displaced her mask. Alas, all my doubts were dissipated; but a frightful pallor covered those features, so dear to my memory. I sensed the life beside me escaping, when Cécile breathed in, raised her head and fixed her gaze on the young women surrounding her.

"Ah!" she said. "That's good; I'm better; I'm no longer suffering. I beg your pardon and I thank you all. The crisis never lasts long, but I would have liked to spare you the concern of it. I should not have come, or should have left sooner. And yet," she added, half-turning toward me, "I would have regretted not having come or having left too soon. I won't interrupt your pleasures any longer; fresh air and walking will complete my cure."

We left a short time later, and Monsieur Savernier, reassured, confided his daughter's arm to me. She was beside me, next to my heart. I communicated freely with her thought; I respired her breath; I possessed the ten minutes of full and happy life that God had reserved for me on earth and I enjoyed them with delight, for no care altered their purity. Cécile was no longer suffering; she had said so, and she repeated it at every step. She walked with a light and assured stride; she seemed to be happy; she laughed as she talked about the capricious malady that only seized her to frighten her with the uncertainty and rapidity of our pleasures.

Her father, with one arm around her, was glad to find her so well and to be able to attribute the temporary malaise she had just experienced to the fatigues of the dance, or to the sudden emotion of which he refused cheerfully to penetrate the mystery. The distance we had to travel was very short, and I did not know whether I ought to desire that it be prolonged endlessly in order to eternalize the pure felicity that I was savoring, or that the terminus should be attained more rapidly in order to render to Cécile the repose of which she had need.

We had arrived; Cécile's hand was disengaged from mine, and something told me that the night would be too long. I grasped the hand that had escaped me again, and although I did not dare raise it to my lips, perhaps I pressed it more amorously, and I believe that Cécile's hand responded to me . . .

The door was open.

"Until tomorrow," said the colonel. "Until tomorrow! Tomorrow, the most beautiful day of all our lives, if my hopes are not deceived . . . But the night is half over; that beautiful tomorrow must already be approaching its second hour, and Cécile needs to sleep for a long time, for her health has already caused us a little anxiety today. Until four o'clock in the afternoon," he continued, embracing me, "and this time we shall all three be at table, awaiting better. Many occupations will be able to abridge for you the time that remains for us not to be together: slumber, toilette and hope."

They went in; the door swung slowly on its hinges, and Cécile bid me an adieu in an emotional voice that I can still hear.

V

The slumber that my old friend had promised me did not grant me its sweetness, and I waited for it in vain until sunrise, in a restless and feverish insomnia the alarms of which I could not explain. It only surprised me later in order to change my torture.

I saw Cécile, however, but I saw her as she had appeared to me momentarily, pale, faint, her forehead covered by the shadow of death; or she leaned her head veiled with scattered hair over my ear, and repeated the sinister adieu that she had addressed to me a few hours before I turned toward her then in order to retain her, but my hands only grasped a vain phantom.

Sometimes, I felt as if my face had been brushed by the flight of a nocturnal bird, and when I tried to follow with my gaze the unknown object of my dread I perceived Cécile again, fleeing on wings of fire, summoning me to follow her.

"Will you not come?" she cried to me, with a long groan. "Why have you let me go first? What will become of me in these deserts, if I am not accompanied by someone who loves me and can protect me?"

"Here I am!" I replied, finally; and the sound of my voice woke me up.

The day was well advanced. That endless night had been prolonged through all the hours of the morning. It was Sunday; the bell of the last office was being rung in the Catholic chapel.

I had already reproached myself vaguely for not having recognized by a single testimony of piety the benefit of my divine protectress. I hastened to the church and to mingle with the small number of the faithful. I arrived at the moment when the priest was going to the pulpit.

He was a man with white hair, whose noble face bore the imprint of a profound chagrin, tempered by resignation and by faith. He paused momentarily in front of me and stared at me, as if he were surprised by the sight of a Christian stranger in his usual audience, or as if he had been preoccupied, at the moment of seeing me, by an impression that I had just retraced in his mind.

He sighed, passed on, mounted his pulpit, devoted himself for a few minutes to an act of worship, with which I associated myself by means of fervent prayers, collected himself, and spoke.

His sermon had for its object the vain hopes of humans who have invested their future in the things of the earth, and who have reckoned, in order to regulate their life, without the decrees of Providence. He deplored the blind presumption of the creature, whose feeble intelligence cannot comprehend either the causes or the motives of the simplest events; who knows nothing of the past and nothing of the future, who knows nothing that touches his only veritable interests, the interests of his immortal soul, and who revolts to the extent of despair against the wretched disappointments of this fugitive life, because he is incapable of penetrating the secret views of God.

"And yet," he added, "what is this life that occupies all your thoughts, for one to attach the slightest importance to its most serious vicissitudes? What are poverty, misfortune and death but imperceptible accidents of position and form in the immensity of the centuries that belong to you? Necessary proofs of an ill-affirmed soul, or irrevocable conditions of the universal order, those accidents that make your pride indignant and break your constancy must concur in the sublime plan of creation, with the ensemble of its marvelous harmony. That which is, is that which must be, since God has permitted it. You do not know why he has permitted it and you cannot know; but what you do not know, God knows!"

The language of the venerable priest was new to my mind. The meditations into which he had plunged me absorbed my faculties to such an extent that I scarcely perceived my solitude in the middle of the church when the last candles were extinguished in the sanctuary.

It was the hour that the colonel had indicated to me, the hour so impatiently awaited, the hour so slow to come in which I was finally to see Cécile—Cécile, by whom I could believe myself to be loved. I named her aloud, as if she were already able to hear me, and all my ideas, all the inexplicable anxieties by which I had been tormented since the previous day, were annihilated in the sentiment of my good fortune. It seemed so good to know that she was mine, and that she was mine forever.

The street along which I went, which I had seen almost deserted the day before, was full of people. At first I attributed that difference to the solemnity of Sunday, but I could not explain why the crowd, which ought to have been summoned in different directions by the leisure of a feast day, were, on the contrary, motionless, limited to forming into silent groups here and there. As I was in haste to arrive, I frayed a passage rapidly through those little gatherings, and only grasped a few confused words at hazard, the majority of which made no coherent sense.

"An aneurism" someone said. "One doesn't die of an aneurism at that age!"

"One does when the hour of death has come," replied the interlocutor.

A little further on there was a young man who seemed to envy me. "Why am I not in the place of that stranger," he said. "At least he didn't know her."

Further on, a little girl, dressed up and veiled, to whom one of her companions was listening, weeping, said: "At half past two, after leaving the ball. She had said that she would never be betrothed!"

A horrible light dawned in my thought. I was no more than twenty paces from the house. I ran . . .

My God! So many years gone by have not been able to weaken the impression of that frightful moment.

The door was draped in white; in the driveway there was a coffin draped in white. A few candles surrounded it.

"Who is dead? Who is dead in that house?" I cried, seizing a man violently by the arm who seemed to be keeping vigil over that apparatus.

"Mademoiselle Cécile Savernier."

I fell unconscious on to the pavement, and when I came round, at rare intervals, my reason had abandoned me. I don't know how many days that lasted.

Meanwhile, my eyes reopened entirely to the light, but I remained devoid of thought, reflection and memory for a long time, I had acquired the sentiment that I was, but without yet knowing what I was; it was necessary to remain like that.

Some movement that was made nearby, the sound of a sigh, perhaps a sob, finally attracted my attention. Standing beside me, I recognized the old priest whose powerful and severe words I had heard one day. He was looking at me with the impossible air of a judge who was only waiting for a word from my mouth in order to absolve or condemn me. Further away, toward the foot of my bed, another old man had just risen from his place, and precipitated toward me, holding out his tremulous arms.

"Father!" I cried, seeing his hands in order to bear them to my lips. "Father, is that you?"

"He has recognized me!" he said. "You can see that he has recognized me! I still have a son! My son is saved!"

My ideas began to clear; the past was slowly disengaged from the night of my dreams,

"Monsieur Savernier," I said to my father. "Monsieur Savernier—where is he?"

"Departed," my father replied. "He has returned to the extremities of Europe, but time might perhaps weaken his resolution, and I hope to see him again."

"And Cécile, Cécile!" I said, excitedly. "Has Cécile departed too? What have they done with Cécile?" I continued, retaining my father by the hand. "Oh my friend, reply to me without disguise, for I sense that I am calm and strong. Don't deceive my heart, which you have never deceived; there was a young woman here who was named Cécile; I saw her yesterday at the ball. I spoke to her; I pressed her hand as I am pressing yours. Is it true that she is dead?"

My father turned away, dissolving in tears, and went to throw himself into an armchair on the other side of the room.

"She is dead," said the priest. "The Lord has not permitted the union to which you aspired to be accomplished on earth. He wanted to render it purer, sweeter, more durable, as immortal as himself, by delaying it for a few fugitive minutes that do not merit being counted in eternity. Your fiancée is waiting for you in Heaven."

"What!" I retorted, staring at him. "You believe that Heaven is not closed to the tenderness of lovers and spouses?

You believe that amour is also resuscitated for a future without end, that two souls separated by death can fly toward one another before the God who had formed them, without offending his power, and that I shall find Cécile again?"

"I believe firmly," he replied, "that in human life, death only puts a term to the errors and miseries of life; I believe that the soul is benevolence, charity and amour; I believe that all the tender sentiments that God has placed in our hearts will participate in our immortality will compose its immutable and unalloyed happiness, and that they will be confounded, without being lost, in the love of God, which embraces everything,"

"Oh, the love of God that you make me understand," I said, moistening his hands with my tears, "is the most natural of the creature's sentiments, and the first of its duties. But why has he taken Cécile away from me?"

"By what right, young man," he cried, "Do you demand that God account for his will? Do you know whether, in the blow that has struck you, it was not in view of your felicity, and whether his infallible prescience has not preserved for you a happiness that will never cease, at the price of a happiness soon elapsed? Do you know all the reefs that might have broken your hopes, all the poisons that might have corrupted your honey, all the events that might have relaxed or dissolved your bonds, if he had not placed them in protection from the perils of this temporary life? Counting only today, the possession of Cécile is acquired to you without anxiety and without trouble, for it is God who is keeping her for you! Would you dare to criticize him for having watched over your interests more attentively than you, and for having reserved your entire future, in order to render it to you in exchange for a feeble and uncertain portion of that infinite future, which might perhaps have lost you the rest?

"When your father demanded from you that a year be accomplished between the moment when he granted your wishes and the one when Cécile's hand seemed bound to ful-fill them, did you not yield without effort to the counsel of his prudence? And yet a year is a long time in the life of a man, a delay more frightful still when it is compared to the brevity of youth, to the almost ungraspable course of that age which time bears away so quickly.

"Now, here is another father, who is the common father of all, imposing on you a delay of a few years more, a few months, or perhaps a few days, for the measure of our existence is known only to him, and it is not years, months and days that will pay for that feeble sacrifice; more prodigal toward you because he is more powerful, he is giving you all the time that will never end. If he is adjourning momentarily your temporal happiness, it is to perpetuate it through the myriads of centuries that are scarcely the minutes of eternity. Such is the bargain that you have just contracted, without knowing it, with Providence, and of which a pious submission to his decrees will one day enable you to collect the fruit. Submit to the judgments of God, my son, and do not criticize him."

"I shall be able to conform to his will," I replied, in a firm voice, "and I shall hasten its accomplishment by all the means that he has left in my power. Yes, Father, I like to think that God had blessed this marriage, and I believe that I have learned that from God himself. I believe that he has only separated me from Cécile in order to return her to me, and that he has not permitted us to be happy on earth because he is reserving us for himself. I will go toward him, Father, I will go soon. I will ask him for Cécile and he will return her to me!"

"What are you saying, wretch!" cried my father running to me. "Do you not also have your father, and do you want to quit him?"

I had, alas, forgotten in my aberration that my father was there.

"Calm yourself," said the priest, taking away his hand. "Have no fear that his thought will stop at those frantic resolutions of atheism and crime. Suicide, which despairs of the bounty of God, calumniates God. It is to do more than deny him. It is protesting against his soul and seeking annihilation as a refuge, but it will not find annihilation, for the soul cannot die. Everything that God has created will live forever, and if God could render to nothing a being that he has animated with his breath, it is annihilation that would be the punishment of the suicide, but the suicide will have another; he will know what he is losing; he will understand the wealth that patience and resignation would have acquired for him, and for which he can no longer hope. Perhaps the wicked can await some remission in eternity, but there will be no remission for the suicide; he will live forever—forever—in a closed world that will no longer have a future; he has broken with the future and his pact will never be resolved. Between Cécile and the spouse that her father had given her there are only a small number of moments that succeed one another and erase one another. There is infinity between Cécile and a suicide . . ."

"Stop, stop, my father!" I cried, leaning on his bosom. "I shall live, since it is necessary."

And that is why I have lived.